GOODBYE SECRETS

The Lost & Found Series

Book Two

JACQUELYN AYRES

Dedication

To all of the readers who fell in love with my characters, thank you so much for boarding this crazy train and wanting to stay on.

Your love, support, and excitement fills my heart to capacity.

Chapter One

I miss my business. I wish I could see Hazel—obviously, I miss her most and I haven't talked to her in so long. God, she's the only mom I have. Though Susanna *has* been very nurturing. She and Grayson had a long heart-to-heart before we left. They made up and he's been transformed into gentle and patient Grayson. This is just who I need holding my hand as I wait to be by my best friend's side.

"When do you get your new plane, Gray?" I try to break him out of his deep thought. We are waiting for clearance to take off, and it feels like it's been forever. But that may be because I'm anxious to get to Stacey.

"Next month. Sorry, love, I'm not all here."

"Me neither." I close my eyes and allow the flashbacks of our twenty-plus years of friendship.

Stacey and I were polar opposites, yet kindred spirits. We raised ourselves in every sense but on paper, and each brought our own special kind of crazy to the table. We were the dynamic duo going through life back to back, fighting one battle at a time. We thought we were awesome. Hell, we *were* awesome!

She was always the flirtatious one, never without a boyfriend and a backup just in case. I was always the smart-mouthed one, because I wasn't comfortable in my skin enough to flirt and, well, why bother? I was waiting for Joe McIntyre. Ugh! Mental head slap! When I did date, I kept my boyfriends at arm's length and they never lasted longer than a month with me. Of course, this somehow created in them some sort of obsession with me. That whole "wanting what you can't have" sort of thing, I guess. It took the guy I lost my virginity to eight years of playing cat and mouse before he finally got into my pants. *Eight years!*

Grayson suddenly bursts into a fit of laugher, pulling me out of my memories.

"What?" I ask him.

"Nothing, sweetheart." He bites his lower lip to stop. "I was just thinking about an article I read earlier. It wouldn't be funny to you." He shakes his head, indicating I should dismiss any idea of further inquiry. I shrug indifferently and go back to my thoughts.

Humph ... it only took Grayson three days, I think. Or was it two? I'll go with three; it makes me feel less whorish. It was, however, the longest three days ever!

George was obsessed. And Ray, Will ... Grayson. I think I've formed a solid pattern here. Only trouble is, I really don't know how or why. What is it about me?

"Sweetheart? What the hell are you thinking about?" Grayson stretches his neck to peer where I am staring. "What are you looking at?"

"I'm pondering." I lay my head back and close my eyes again.

"What are you pondering?" I sense him shifting in his seat.

"Well, I've been sitting here thinking about Stacey and me through the years, how flirty she always was. She was never without a boyfriend. While mostly, by my choice, I was. However, I was never without someone obsessed with me. It's the first time I'm realizing the quite solid pattern. I have no clue why ... it's a bit annoying." I hear Grayson laughing again, but mostly to himself. I open my eyes and catch him shaking his head. "What's so funny now?"

"I just realized I've joined the ranks of those other poor bastards! I've never been obsessed with any woman in my life ... well, besides my mother," he adds thoughtfully. I cringe.

"Eww ... is it a weird mom thing?"

"Oh God, Becca, no! That's absurd; I've never had an indecent thought about my mother! You, on the other hand, sweetheart—my thoughts are very naughty when it comes to you." He flashes me a wicked grin.

"Yeah, I don't get it ... really." I try to shake off the thought because, well, why bother?

"And therein lies part of the allure that is Becca Campbell," he murmurs, mostly to himself.

My thoughts refocus on Stacey. All of the stupid shit we did as kids. Our first apartment together. Our first grown-up jobs. Our trips. Our talks. Grayson just sits back, watching me laugh, then cry, then laugh again. I share with him some of the silly shit we did.

"Becca, that's absurd! Why would you pull up to a complete stranger's house and honk the horn as if you were picking someone up?" I'm pretty sure he's laughing at me because I'm in stitches with tears rolling down my face. Almost twenty years later and that prank still cracks me up.

"As Kellie Pickler says, 'I'm just a small town girl'! You either do silly stupid shit or you do real stupid, stupid shit. Silly was more fun." I shrug. My throat tightens up and my nose flares. "Grayson, I can't lose my best friend. Who would I do silly, stupid shit with?

She's my sister. She's the only person on this planet who knows everything about me. I can tell her anything. I can't do this, Gray!" I give in and allow my emotions and tears to storm over me. "What the hell is taking so fucking long?!" I yell as I unbuckle and head toward the cockpit. I bang on the door. It opens. "Smitty! We were supposed to be up in the air half an hour ago!"

"I'm sorry, ma'am. We were waiting for a new flight plan because of bad weather. We're all set and are about to be cleared for takeoff in a few minutes." He looks from me to Grayson, as if the Brit would be able to divert my fury.

"Very good then. Sorry. I just need to get to my friend." I try to calm down, aware that Smitty has no control over the weather. However, he could've let us know what was going on.

Within ten minutes, we are heading down the runway. I close my eyes and I'm seven again, taking off in a less luxurious airplane. The same exhilarating feeling comes over me. *Oh, how I love to fly!* Smitty's voice comes over the intercom, letting us know that we will be stopping in Louisiana for fuel and our six-hour flight will now take eight. I struggle to not lash out from this information—I just want to get there!

"I could think of something to get your mind off of things, but you'll probably throw me off the plane for mentioning it," Grayson whispers in my ear. I know he's trying to get a smile out of me.

"I just want to get there." I push away my tears and pull out the book I write all my lists in.

"What are you doing, sweetheart?" He leans over and holds the book down.

"My Christmas gift list." I continue writing down the names of all the staff.

"Don't worry about them, love. I'll give them bonus checks." He waves over my book.

"Oh my God, Gray! Charlie! I have to give him his check!" I feel my heart go up into my throat.

"Already taken care of, sweetheart." He pats my leg and grabs the book, which is precisely why I wrote his name and "Nosy Bastard" next to it. Apparently he finds it, because he starts laughing.

"How did you take care of it?" I refocus.

"I took last year's and increased by ten percent like you always do. Stop worrying." He kisses my head.

"I'm not looking to start an argument, Grayson, but that is my business and while I appreciate all of the things you've done and are doing, I don't appreciate you taking its control away from me! It doesn't even feel like it's mine anymore!" Well, that didn't end as calmly as it started. Okay, here we go, I'm waiting for it. There are two things that Grayson and I do extremely well together: arguing and uh ... um ... an edited flashback reel of Gray's and my sexcapades plays in my mind to the tune of "E.T." by Katy Perry.

"Sweetheart? Becca?" He gently takes my chin. I refocus. "E.T." is blasting in my head. Grayson bites his bottom lip and his eyebrows pop up. He must know what I'm thinking about. He knows my body language better than I do. I grab my phone and pull my face free to find the song, then unbuckle and head toward the bathroom. I look back before I enter to make sure he's following me. "Right here, doll." He leans down and kisses my ear. He wraps his left arm around my waist, resting his hand on my stomach, and pushes the door open with his right. I wonder what the staff is saying about us, or thinks of us. It's a quick thought though, and I dismiss it, not really giving the shit one ought to give.

Grayson locks the door behind us. I put my phone in the dock on the sink at the other end of the bathroom. I'm not one for knowing my measurements ... ahem ... but I'd say the bathroom is about seven by nine. The walls are steel blue with bronze accents—very masculine, very Grayson.

I strip down to my panties and bra. He pulls off his shirt and leans up against the door, taking me in. He's beautifully ripped. He's been working more on his shoulders. And—oh—that gorgeous long neck. *Mmm* ... I have a strong desire to run my tongue up it. I bite my lip and let my eyes scan his six-pack. His jeans hang loose around his waist, and the band of his boxer briefs hugs the final chapter of his torso. And I know there's a whole notha beautiful story waiting to be explored below that band. I press play and begin my seductive prowl toward him.

His eyelids go mad. I keep my eyes on his as I reach him, then search his chest softly with my hands. My tongue tastes every inch my hands uncover. His breath becomes erratic, and I push back the satisfied smile that wants to cross my face. I'll smile about it later. My tongue outlines every part of his six-pack as I slowly unbuckle his belt, and I tease his navel with it while I undo his button and his zipper. I'm thoroughly enjoying every moment of this. His sounds, his breathing ... the twitching of every muscle I touch. *God, this is making me so hot*. I guide his jeans and underwear to the floor and help him out of them. His enthusiasm is staring me in the face. I nip and slide my tongue up the V-line of his right side, then repeat the pattern on his left. Grayson groans like he's suffering from a slight torture. He takes in a deep breath and plants his hands on top of his head. It must be terribly difficult for him to relinquish this much control over to me—I'm impressed. I slide my panties off before I continue my teasing. I feel his eyes on me. I lick the tip of his penis and blow on it before I cup his balls gently and pull them back and away from his shaft. Another groan releases from his throat. I continue to do this as I wrap my left hand around his length, playfully biting and licking it from base to tip. I take him in my mouth fully and suck purposefully as I pull back, then tease him with biting and licking. Back up to the tip and deep into my mouth again.

"Oh God, Becca ... please, sweetheart."

I can hear the sweet torture in his plea. As I slowly pull back again, I slip my finger quickly in and out of myself. I slide up his body, his breath hot in my face.

"Open your mouth." I grasp his chin as his hands find and caress my bum. He does so, and I slide my finger in. "See what you do to me, baby? Can you taste it?" I ask seductively. His eyes widen with shock before softening into a smile as he sucks my finger eagerly. I lean in near his ear. "I'm so ready for you to fuck the hell out of me, baby." I lick the shell of it. With that, he pulls my hair to bring my face to his. There's a slight hesitation as his eyes scan mine, then my lips, before he attacks them. He lifts me off the floor, slams me up against the wall, and enters me with such fierce urgency it knocks the wind out of me. My efforts to match his thrusts are fruitless. I just hold on for the ride as he fucks me into next week, or another atmosphere—I haven't figured it out quite yet. What I am sure of is that I won't be riding Rocco anytime soon.

Grayson sucks in his breath and grits his teeth, slowing his pace as he unravels inside of me. I tighten around him and muffle his sounds with my mouth. He exhales harshly and gasps for more air. I kiss his forehead and push his sweaty hair to the side, then move my lips to the beauty mark under his left eye. His eyes are still closed as he tries to catch his breath.

"Becca ... sweet ... heart ... I'm sorry."

"For what?" I play with the stubble along his jawline.

"I didn't wait for you to come." He opens his eyes and stares into mine. It sounds like he finally has his breath under control.

"Oh, baby, I got off—believe me." I allow that satisfied smile I stifled before to grace my face. Slowly, he lets me slide down his body. We pull away from the wall, our lips greeting each other fondly. I let him deepen the kiss and am enjoying the feeling of our tongues exploring and playing together nicely when—bam! I feel fire in my right bum cheek from the sting of his palm. I release a surprised sob and kiss him with more passion. How can something hurt so bad and feel so good at the same time? Just then the seatbelt sign comes on and I hear Smitty over the intercom, telling everyone to sit down and buckle in. We're getting ready to hit a lot of turbulence.

"Should we tell him that was us?" I bite back my smile. Grayson is staring at me with such great desire, and I know what he's thinking about. I know from the way he just slapped my bottom.

"Grayson, c'mon, baby. Let's get dressed." I quickly kiss him. He refocuses and pulls on his underwear along with his jeans. His hair is still damp with sweat. This reminds me to check my own hair. I know they all know what we were doing in here, but I certainly don't have to walk out there showing evidence of it! I pull my hair up in a tie. I notice Grayson staring at me from the mirror.

"Theme song?" I ask, trying to pull him back from wherever he is.

"Huh? Oh, no, sorry. So what happened to me not getting any for a while?" He gives me that gorgeous smile as he holds my hips from behind. There he is ... my beautiful British bastard.

"Guess you were right, my BBB—I can't last twelve hours without you inside me." I match his grin, partly because I know I just sent him back to that "mad" place where he is trying to figure out what "BBB" stands for. He almost got it one day. I was feeling disappointed at the prospect, but alas, the last word was wrong again!

"Ugh, Becca!"

I start laughing. He hugs me from behind and we stare at ourselves in the mirror. Grayson pulls out his phone and takes a picture of us. I look up at him. God, I'm so in love with him. I don't ever want to be without him. I was so scared today. Now I feel like I should be the one walking on eggshells.

"Becca?" He looks down at me, his face full of concern.

"Mr. and Mrs. James, please return to your seats," Smitty says with urgency. I've gotten very used to being referred to as "Mrs. James." I don't bother correcting anyone anymore; what's the point? Grayson wants to make sure everyone knows I'm his, and pretty soon, he'll have the paperwork to back up the claim. Uh, yeah, I suddenly feel like a piece of property. I'll let it go, though—I know that's not his intention.

"C'mon, Gray." I tap the side of his face with my hand. Just as he opens the door, we hit a good pocket of turbulence and I lose my balance. Gray grabs me, preventing my fall, and we get to our seats quickly. For the next half an hour, I hold Grayson's hand—not because I'm scared, but because his color has drained at least three times. It's awfully cute how mad he gets at himself for acting this way. I just play dumb, pretending I have no idea the turbulence is affecting him. I close my eyes and try to rest as much as I can. Maybe I'll fall asleep—that would make this go so much quicker.

Chapter Two

GRAYSON

Becca's fallen asleep. I get up and get her a blanket. "C'mere, love." I gently pull her onto my lap.

"Huh?" She looks up at me.

"Lay your head on my shoulder, sweetheart. You were going to get a stiff neck." I kiss her forehead and cover us with the blanket.

"Something might get stiff on you now." She smiles sheepishly.

"That's okay." I hold her to me and lay my head on hers. Wish my new plane was ready. We'll have a bedroom on that one.

Derek hits the cabin lights for us, making it nice and dark. Good thing Becca's wearing jeans, or I'd be doing something very naughty to her right now. God, that was so bloody fucking hot before! I don't even know where the hell that came from! One minute she was yelling at me for taking over her business, and the next I could see she was thinking about sex! She can't even hide it: her eyes flicker back and forth as if she's watching what's playing out in her mind, then she bites her lip and her breathing becomes erratic. She's been doing that since the moment we first met. I don't think she realizes she does it, because she's always shocked that I know what she's thinking.

"What's so funny?" Becca whispers.

"Sorry, sweetheart, nothing." I kiss her. I close my eyes and lay my head back down on hers.

I squint and look at my watch as the cabin lights come back on. We're in Louisiana, getting ready to land and refuel. Derek informs me that Stacey was airlifted to Mass General Hospital in Boston, so now we're flying to Logan Airport instead.

"Why was she airlifted?" Becca lifts her head and reseats herself back into the chair next to me. She buckles up.

"Um, she was very critical. The hospital she was at thought it be best if she was somewhere more equipped to deal with her injuries."

I shoot Derek a nasty look for his lack of filter. I told them not to tell her anything that would upset her. It's pointless, though—I know as soon as she's with Stacey, I won't be able to protect her from the grief of seeing her friend like that.

We have a smooth landing. As soon as we arrive at the gate, we all stand up to stretch and move about the cabin. Melissa pats Becca's back softly, trying to comfort her, I'm sure.

"Grayson, does Ray know about Stacey?"

"How the fuck should I know?" I snap. *Christ ... ugh!* "Becca, I'm sorry, sweetheart. I'm not mad at you for asking." I pull her into my arms. "I'm mad because I can't protect you from anything you're going through right now. I have no control over any of this and it's driving me mad, darling!" She really doesn't need this shit from me.

"I know, baby." She leans up to kiss me.

"You hungry?" I wipe her tears away.

"No."

"Becca, you need to eat. Do you want to stay on the plane or come with me?" Those are the only choices she is getting.

"Uh, sir?" Derek speaks up.

"Yes."

"I'm going to advise that you and Mrs. James stay on the plane, sir. We would like to keep your whereabouts a secret for as long as we can."

Derek's right. Shit.

"Okay. Please call me and let me know which restaurants are out there, and I'll give you our order." I turn back to Becca. "Well, sweetheart, looks like we're both prisoners." I try to make her to laugh, but I get barely a smile. "Ugh, Becca, baby, c'mere." I pull her back to me. Most of our staff gets off the plane to grab dinner. "Becca, sweetheart, it's been almost six hours. How are you holding up?" I try again to lighten her mood.

"Six hours since what?" She looks up at me quizzically. I raise my eyebrows. "Oh, Grayson! Shut up!" She laughs and hits my chest playfully. Ah, there we have it!

Becca grabs the keys to the rental out of my hand and walks briskly toward the car.

"Becca!" I call after her.

"Grayson, I know Boston. I need to get to my friend," she says, and unlocks the car.

"Okay." This is not the time to argue with her, and she's actually right. Becca has us at Mass General before I can mutter a *holy shit!* at her driving. *Bite your tongue, Grayson, bite your tongue!* I, along with Derek and Melissa, run after her. We head up to ICU.

"Are you family?" The nurse asks. *Crotchety old bag, she is.*

"Yes, I'm her sister and this is my husband," Becca says frantically. All I can focus on is that she called me her husband. I think it's the most wonderful sound in the world. Of course, it does not replace *Oh God, baby!* Never get tired of hearing that out of her lovely mouth. Lucille, the crotchety old bag, points us in the direction of Stacey's room.

"What is it with old women dying their hair flaming fucking red? It's a nightmare to look at!" I'm disgruntled by her goddamn attitude. We rush into Stacey's room. Becca takes in a huge gasp and almost falls to the ground at the sight of her best friend. Her face is swollen and bruised beyond recognition, and there are bandages around her head. Her right leg is in a cast. Her arms are lined with bruises, and some of her fingernails are missing. She's on life support. It's quiet in the room besides the sounds of the machines and Becca's sobs. Becca wipes away her tears and walks over to her comatose friend.

"Oh, no. No. No! This won't do at all, Stace!" Becca pulls it together and takes her friend's hand. "Really, sweetie, do you know how many good-looking unmarried doctors there are here? You need to open your eyes so you can win them over with your charm!" Her voice is adamant, but there's a hitch in it as she despairingly adds, "Oh, Stacey, I'm so sorry!" Becca sits in the chair I have pushed behind her.

A nurse comes in. Thankfully, without nasty nightmare hair!

"Hi, I'm Jen. I'm Stacey's nurse until seven in the morning. You're Stacey's sister?"

"Becca. This is my husband, Grayson." After a brief pause, she continues. "Jen, can you tell me exactly what her injuries are?"

Instead of focusing on Becca's question, Jen stares at me and licks her lips. "Yes, Jen, he's very handsome and amazing in bed. Now, can you please tell me about my sister's injuries?" Jen and I both look at Becca in disbelief. "Sorry," she says, then adds, "but, my sister?"

"They performed a hemicraniectomy today to help with the brain swelling. That's why she was brought here. We have the best neurologists and neurosurgeons in New England; third in the country. Um, she has four broken ribs, and her right leg had a compound fracture. She was, um, raped, and—" Becca puts her hand up to stop her.

"What is a hemicraniectomy?" I pipe up.

"They have removed and frozen part of her skull until her brain swelling goes down. This has already helped immensely." She offers an encouraging smile. "Any known drug allergies?" Jen looks to Becca.

"No, but she does have the factor V gene. She has no history of blood-clotting issues, but our parents do, so she got tested for it. I don't know if that will affect her treatment in any way, but I thought it would be important to let you know." Becca continues to go over Stacey's entire medical history. I'm in awe. She really is like a sister to her. Jen leaves and Becca takes her place at Stacey's side. "Oh, Stacey, why did you drop the security? Grayson, why did he do this to her?"

"Who did this to her, Mrs. James?" I look up to find two detectives in the doorway. A middle-aged black man in a suit and tie, and a female—brunette, roughly around thirty. They both seem bone-tired. Becca stands up.

"You are?" she asks.

"Sorry. Detectives Williams and Cahill." Detective Williams stretches out his hand first. We all walk to the opposite side of the room, out of Stacey's earshot—just in case. "Mrs. James, who do you think it is that attacked Mrs. Bergman?" he asks Becca again.

"We're going to need these." I start pulling up chairs.

BECCA

"Okay, so, first of all, just so all records are correct—my name is Becca Campbell. I am Stacey's best friend, not her sister. Please don't tell them, because in our minds and hearts, we are sisters. Grayson and I will be married after my divorce. Now that we have all that out of the way, the man you are most likely looking for is George Campbell."

"Your current husband?" Detective Cahill questions for clarity.

"Uh, yes. He was a military man. He was recently discharged. He was extremely abusive to me. Seven years ago, he went on another tour to Iraq and was declared dead from an explosion that took out several guys from his unit. According to all documentation, George was at that location at that time, although a body was never found. So, actually, he was not declared officially dead until one year later given the documentation.

"About six or seven weeks ago, I looked out the window of my store, which is adjacent to my bed-and-breakfast in New Hampshire. I could've sworn I saw him. Grayson had a security team put into place immediately. Within two days, he kidnapped me. My detail followed behind me. He took me up to an abandoned cabin and planned on keeping me there until my 'rich' boyfriends paid him eight million dollars. Melissa, my bodyguard, was able to catch him off guard and get me free. By the time the rest of the team arrived at the cabin, he had already escaped. The Ashland police can give you a full report, as can our security team. Grayson knows more about what they've been doing to track him down." I glance over at Grayson, who nods his head in agreement.

"Since then, Grayson's beefed up security for us and everyone we're close to. Stacey, for some reason, told her security team she didn't want their services. She moved out of the B&B without telling me, and I haven't heard from her since a few days after we headed out to California. George always hated Stacey. Then again, George hated anyone I gave any of 'his' attention to. Unless this was random, I don't see how it could be anyone else." I rub my face.

"Where was George all that time he was MIA?" Williams flips the page in his notebook.

"My team can give you a full report on that. They have the files on everything you may need ready and available to you. I can write down the contacts for you," Grayson says. Cahill hands him her notebook and he jots something down. "Gregory Thomas is the head of the team for our New Hampshire and California residences."

"I can tell you also what George said to me about being MIA." I search my purse for a mint.

"Anyone?" I offer. Cahill takes one.

"Go ahead." Williams nods to me.

"Oh ... sorry. So, while he had me in the cabin, I asked him what happened to try to calm him down. He told me that he was held captive until about five months before the day he took me. Then his captors up and left, leaving him to die. A local family found him and nursed him back to health. He was shipped to a hospital here in the states two months later. I don't know anything else after that except he went AWOL." I look over at Stacey as one of her machines beeps like crazy. *Oh, it's her IV; time for a new bag of saline.* "Um, can I please go sit with her now? It's taken me all day to get here." My eyes fill up again.

"Sure, Ms. Campbell. Mr. James, we have a few more questions for you." Detective Cahill glances at Grayson. He nods and kisses my forehead. I go back over to Stacey.

"Look at them over there. They are totally talking about you! I think you should wake up and tell them all to fuck off!" I bait her.

Nothing. "Well, I brought you a *People* magazine to catch you up on La-La Land. Oh, sorry ... it's two weeks old. Oh well." I open it up, and there I am with Grayson and Morgan at Disneyland. Thank God it's a good shot! "Stacey, you have to open your eyes and look at this! I am now a resident of La-La Land! Morgan too! Yeah, some guy is with us, I have no idea who that is." I laugh. "Oh well, I'll hold onto this for you and, of course, for me, too." I continue to read her all the articles that would interest her. Grayson's hands slide onto my shoulders as the detectives wish me a good night and head out.

"Sweetheart, it's after midnight. Let's go to the hotel. We'll get here real early tomorrow morning, and Aunt Hazel will be with us." He kisses the top of my head.

"Grayson, go ahead, honey. I can't leave her. Besides, I'm still on West Coast time. It's only nine o'clock." I pat his hand.

"Becca, I'm not leaving you here by yourself!" He hates when I tap his hands to dismiss him. Grayson pulls a chair up next to me. We sit and talk for hours.

"Sweetheart, it's three. You may be on Cali time, but the doctors here aren't. Let's go." He rubs my back, hoping I give in this time.

"Stacey, you and I both know why he wants to get me to the hotel. If you'd wake up for a minute, I'd tell you all about how I became the newest member of the Mile High Club yesterday."

"Newest member—she's the fucking president of the Mile High Club! You would've been proud of her, Stace! Wake up, love; it's worth getting jealous over! Maybe tomorrow then, doll. Becca, if Stacey were awake, she'd be telling you to get into bed with my hot British arse right now." I giggle a bit and take his hand. I bring it up to my face and kiss his palm.

"Thank you." I sigh, looking toward him.

"For what, love?"

"For being so very, very patient, kind, loving, and ... for making me president." I flash him a huge smile. What a trooper to do all this with me. It's moments like these where there are no questions, no doubts, no insecurities—you just know everything you need to know. I love him more now than twelve hours ago, when we were looking in the mirror together.

"Becca, what's that look for? What are you thinking in there, sweetheart?" He taps gently on my temple.

"How in love with you I am. Come on, baby, let's go. You're right. Stacey would kick my ass for staying here all night." I get up and kiss Stacey on the cheek. "I love you, Stace. Don't give up, give them hell! See you in a few hours."

"All right then, love, I'm gonna go shag your best friend now and I'll throw in an extra arse slap just for you! You better open those gorgeous eyes tomorrow. I'm not going to sit here and fucking explain how hot I look! You need to check me out for yourself! I'll even make sure you get a great view of my fantastic arse!" Grayson teases her before he kisses her cheek. They do have a funny relationship. Of course, that was before the whole weird Ray/Stacey shit. Hmm, I wonder if Ray knows what's happened. I won't dare ask Grayson again. I wonder if Steve knows. I will call him tomorrow, if he still has the same number. I take Grayson's hand and we head to the nurse's station to let Jen know we're leaving and to please call with any changes. A very tired Derek and Melissa follow us to our rental.

"Where are we staying?" I put the key in the ignition and start up the car. Grayson looks down at the key cards Ryan dropped off earlier.

"Taj Boston," he says. I put the car in gear and head out. We're there in like three minutes—because it's three-thirty in the morning, not because of my lead foot that Grayson yells about all the time.

We head up to the Presidential Suite. "Nice touch," I say, and tap the key. He looks down and offers a slight chuckle.

"Well, you are the president, Madame." We step into the foyer of our suite. I inhale deeply as we walk into the comforting golds and blues of the living-and-dining-room area. There's a bar on the left side, which I'm sure I will put to great use given the circumstances of our stay. It's spacious and beautiful; only a small step up from the luxurious inn I run ... ahem.

"Where is everybody else staying?" I glance up as I run my hand along the fabric of the armchair.

"With the exception of the two outside our door, they are in the room connected to this one." He grabs my hand to lead me to the bedroom.

"Well, shouldn't they stay in the living room so they are comfortable?" I mean, sitting out in the hall? That sucks.

"I pay them very well. They are quite comfortable." He smirks as we are greeted by a four-poster, king-sized bed. There is a balcony on the right, outside the double French doors. The blue carpet continues in here and is met by soft, golden-yellow walls. The duvet matches the walls and complements the golden pattern in the blue plush armchair in the right corner.

"Money doesn't turn an uncomfortable table chair in the hallway into a plush couch." I roll my eyes at him.

"It's their job, Becca. They work for us. They are not our guests, so stop acting as if they are."

He's right to a point, I guess. At least we're nice to all of them. It could be worse. They could be protecting two people who treat them like shit.

"Ugh, what, Becca?!" He takes our coats and tosses them onto the armchair.

"Nothing." I smile. "You're right. I was thinking that we treat them well in general, whereas another employer might not."

"Speaking of treatment, sweetheart—"

Oh no, he's getting *that* look.

"—your treatment of me in the airplane bathroom was completely shocking!" He pulls me to him aggressively. "I was very turned on by the whole finger incident. You are becoming quite the naughty girl, aren't you?"

"Yes, Mr. James, thanks to you, I have become very naughty indeed." I wrap my arms around his neck. "Take, for instance, a situation such as this, where my best friend is fighting for her life not three minutes down the road. Normally, the thought of sex wouldn't cross my mind. But, alas, my best friend lives to hear about our kinky fuckery." I pause for the smile he gives me at this reference. "How could I possibly go in there and tell her we went to sleep? She'd know if I lied. Therefore, I have no other choice than to be a very naughty girl with you. It just might be the thing to pull her out!" I smile at him through my tears and grab the hem of his shirt so I can pull it over his head.

"Becca, sweetheart, we don't have to do this. I was just teasing you, love." He cups my face and thumbs my tears away.

"I know, Grayson. I actually really just need to get lost in you. Please. Help me escape the horror of what I've seen tonight." I lean up on my tippy toes and gently caress his lips with mine. He complies with my wishes and I am completely and utterly lost in him and our lovemaking for the next hour, I guess. I don't even know what time it is anymore.

We fall asleep wrapped up in each other, in preparation for another long, hard day of waiting and praying.

GRAYSON

"Becca, sweetheart, wake up." My fingers trace over the new welts on her bum. God, why can't I stop doing this to her? It makes me feel so ...

"Good morning, baby," she murmurs. "Mmm ... that feels

good." I can sense her smile as I kiss the marks.

"Becca ... I ..."

"Grayson, don't apologize. It's okay ... really. I'm not upset. It was delicious." She turns to me and loses her hands in my hair. She brings her face to mine and I catch her lips.

"I'd love to stay here and revisit our earlier actions, but we should get to the hospital, love." I hate myself for pushing my self-ish tendencies away. I want her so bad, as always.

"Hmm, where is my selfish man?" She runs her hands down to my face and pulls me in for another kiss.

"Right here," I muster, and grab her legs. I pull her body down harshly, lifting her right leg so I can situate myself and enter her. I bring her to church as quickly as I possibly can.

"Grayson, are you okay?"

I lift my head to look up at her. My breathing mirrors that of someone who's just run the last leg of a marathon at top speed. I have a feeling her concern is not my breathing, though, so why is she asking?

"Besides the situations we've been finding ourselves in, I'm fine. As long as I have you, doll, everything is right with the world!" My lips play with hers as I slowly pull out. "Why do you ask?"

She just shrugs.

We get up and hit the shower. I successfully fight the urge to slap her bottom and take her again. It is quite the accomplishment on my part!

"Becca, please don't wear those jeans anymore, darling." I close my eyes to shake my thoughts away. Her arse looks delicious in them.

"Why?" She looks in the mirror to see what's wrong.

"They fill my head with naughty thoughts." This confession produces a satisfied smirk across her face.

It's rush hour, but we arrive at Mass General in three minutes flat with Becca as our stunt driver.

"Honestly, sweetheart, you should try out for NASCAR." I am half serious. While having her behind the wheel puts my heart in my throat, she is a very skilled, very confident, erratic driver.

"Stop it. Let's go!" We get out and Becca instinctively puts her hand in mine. We head over to the Ellison Building and hit the number four for the Blake Twelve ICU. I bring Becca's hand up to my lips to place several kisses as we await our destination. She leans into me for added comfort. In our relationship, we seem to always focus best when there is a crisis at hand. Sometimes, it's "For better" I worry about. The elevator dings and we head to Stacey's room at a quick pace. As soon as we enter, Ray jumps up. *Oh, Christ!*

"Becca! Oh God, are you okay?" He grabs Becca away from me, hugs her, and kisses her face. My team is on him like a fly on shit. "What the hell? Get off of me! I'm not going to hurt her! He's the one hurting her!" Ray yells.

"Ray, what the hell are you talking about?" Becca asks angrily through her teeth and raises her hand for Derek and Ryan to let him go.

"Baby, I got all of your messages. I've been trying to get to you. I had just made it to California when I found out you flew back and that Stacey was in the hospital." I knock his hand away from Becca's face and pull her closer to me.

"What messages, Ray? I haven't called you, texted you, or emailed you!"

Becca is looking at him as if he has five heads. I'm also finding this story very interesting. My team tracked him all the way to California. Who is the person on the untraceable line he's always talking to? I keep my mouth shut about what I know. I've got a terrible feeling, but I hope I'm wrong.

"Becca, I have all of the messages on my phone." He pulls it out and retrieves them. We hear a woman barely saying Ray's name and then some arsehole trying to imitate me yelling and hitting her.

"Ray, that is not me, and it's certainly not Grayson." Becca shakes her head.

"Abso-bloody-lutely not!" I yell. What a fucking idiot!

"It's not?" He seems miffed. "Who would do this? Becs, I don't understand. Who would do this to Stace?" Tears are pooling in his eyes.

"Well, we think George is behind it, and—"

I squeeze her hand, hoping she knows that means *shut the hell up!*

"Well, we still haven't found him." She looks up at me and winks. Smart girl.

"Becs, can I talk to you for a minute?" He grabs her hand and nods toward the hallway.

"Um ..." She looks to me. I reluctantly nod. She starts to walk out with him.

"Mrs. James, your purse." Derek pulls her bag higher on her shoulder and slips a small device into it. *A bug?* Oh man, he's good. Big bonus check for him! They walk out after she thanks him. He gives me a Bluetooth earpiece and asks via a small speaker on his sleeve for somebody else to begin recording.

"Brilliant!" I say to him. He places his finger over his lips. Right!

"Oh, Becs, I've missed you, baby."

He's fucking kissing her! My blood boils.

"Ray, stop!" *Good girl.*

"Please, just one kiss. You owe me that much after the way you treated me!" he snaps.

"Ray, I said no!" Her refusal becomes sterner. "I was going to email you back, Ray, but what I wanted to say, I felt you deserved for me to say in person. I am truly sorry for the way I acted. I led you on and I regret that. In my defense, I didn't know I was leading you on at that time. I was very confused and scared about my feelings for Grayson. You were my known, he was my unknown. I love you, Ray. I always will. But I'm so in love with Grayson. I want to spend the rest of my life with him. I want to have his children. I'm really sorry for the way I handled this. You are my best friend and I never meant to hurt you. I was selfish and irresponsible and I hope that someday you can forgive me and we can be friends again. I want nothing but happiness for you."

"Becca, do you regret making love to me?" He's barely audible.

"Ray, don't touch me like that. I regret the timing only."

My blood pulses powerfully throughout my body. I can hear it throbbing in my head. I want to go out there and choke him. Derek keeps his hand on me.

"Becs, we were so amazing together. There's not a day that goes by that I don't think of how we made love. Your sounds. Your taste. Becs, it was more than what you are saying. You know it. I know it. Your body knows it."

He's trying to fucking seduce her!

"Ray, stop it. I'm marrying Grayson. I love Grayson. Get out of my face!"

I see Becca pushing him away, but he grabs her hands and pins her up against the wall. I surge forward again to get to her. Derek nods toward Ryan and releases me at the same time.

"Grayson! Ryan!" she yells as we come charging. As we pull him off of her, my fist "accidentally" flies in the air and hits his face. Becca rushes into my arms. "Goddamn it, Ray!" she yells at him. Just then, Stacey's day nurse swings by.

"This is an ICU! We can't have this kind of behavior!" She's stern, but you can sense her nervousness.

"I'm sorry ... Sharon." I read her badge. "Mr. McNeil was just leaving."

Ryan escorts him down the hall. He keeps glancing back at

Becca. I've never seen Ray look so ... dark.

"Am I in the fucking Twilight Zone?" Becca turns back to me and asks.

"You know, sweetheart, I've been asking myself that a lot lately." I hug her again and we head into Stacey's room.

No change, with the exception of a decrease in her brain swelling. Sharon walks in to take vitals. "Sharon, I'm Becca. This is my husband, Grayson. I forgot to ask Jen this morning—is the coma from the trauma, or is it medically induced to help her body recoup?"

"No, this one is natural. We're not sure how long it will last." She frowns. Becca looks down and plays with her engagement ring. "That's a gorgeous ring." Sharon takes her hand to have a better look. Becca smiles and thanks her. "Lucky girl." Sharon winks at her as she looks from the ring up to me and back. Becca just grins, nods, and looks at her ring again. I feel my heart bathe in warmth.

"Oh, Gracie," Aunt Hazel gasps as she walks in and sees Stacey for the first time.

"Hazel!" Becca cries and runs to her. Aunt Hazel hugs her and kisses her head while Becca sobs into her neck. I feel a pang of guilt for keeping them apart. They go into the hallway to talk, and I sit next to Stacey.

"Stacey, c'mon now, sweetheart. Oops! I'm not allowed to call you *sweetheart*. I made Becca jealous doing that. It was the most fantastic moment!" I smile with satisfaction at the memory. "You must wake up and tell us who did this to you. It will help us put him behind bars. I'll give you anything you want! We need you—Becca needs you!" I kiss her hand.

Chapter Three

BECCA

After a little over two weeks with no change in Stacey, Grayson and I decide to finally take the drive up to my B&B. I can't wait to see Claudia and Rocco. I can't wait to have my divorce finalized.

"Excited to head home, sweetheart?" Grayson grabs my hand and glances over at me.

"Yes." I try to smile, but I do have very mixed emotions.

"Why don't we do our Christmas shopping while we're here?" He's been trying to get me out of the funky mood I've been in for at least three days now. I miss my daughter, my best friend is healing but still comatose, and I haven't been home in over a month. To make matters worse, Christmas is two weeks away, and I have nothing done and no Christmas spirit. "Becca, sweetheart, please, honey, I need you to snap out of this. You feel so distant." He's worried, worried he's losing me. But he's not losing me—I'm losing me. On top of all this stuff, the stress has done a number on me. I haven't felt a hundred percent for the past week. I scheduled an appointment with my doctor for a physical. That's tomorrow.

"When would you like to get married, sweetheart?" *Oh, Gracie, baby!*

"I'm hoping that Stacey wakes up soon. As soon as she's able to stand by my side, I'd like to get married."

"Bec ..." he starts. I can see the concern on his face.

"Gray, I know, obviously we will only wait an acceptable amount of time. I realize no one knows when she'll be out of the coma." I turn the stereo on. I don't want to talk anymore.

"Okay, love," is all he says.

We head straight to the courthouse and arrive fifteen minutes early. Attorney Brown greets us and pulls us into a room just to go over everything again. We then head into the courtroom and take a seat to wait to be called. After twenty minutes or so, I finally hear my name. Judge Sear goes over my file and asks me a few questions.

"State your full name, please."

"Becca Kirsten Campbell."

"Where do you live?" I give him the address to the B&B. "Where and when were you married?"

"July 15, 2001. Fort Dix, New Jersey."

"I see your husband was declared dead for seven years and it has come to your attention that he is alive, went AWOL, kidnapped you, and is still wanted for his crimes." He looks up at me over the top of his half-moon frames.

"Yes, sir."

"Names and ages of your children with your spouse."

"Morgan Alexa Campbell. Ten years old, sir."

"With whom does your child live with?"

"Me, sir."

"How long have you lived in the state of New Hampshire, Mrs. Campbell?"

"Six years, sir."

"Please state what you want."

"A divorce, Your Honor." The questions continue about possible reconciliation ... *No.* Child support and joint custody ... *No* and *no.* Documents are clarified. After ten minutes or so, my divorce is granted. I hug Grayson fiercely.

"Oh, I can't wait to marry you, sweetheart!" He kisses me over and over as we walk out of the courthouse. I suddenly don't feel so well. The room spins. "Oh, shit!" Gray yells. That's all I remember.

"There you go, sweetheart, that's it." I hear Gray and flutter my eyes.

"What happened?" I sit up slowly in a strange office.

"You passed out, Becca." The woman next to me smiles and throws out the smelling salt.

"Oh ... sorry." I offer a slight one back. Grayson is deep in thought. He holds out his hand and thanks her. We head out to the car. Grayson grabs my phone, looks up my doctor, and calls. He asks to get me seen today. Luckily, she can see me now if we head right over. "Sorry that happened." I squeeze his hand before I get into the car. He's silent the whole way there.

I place my hand in his as we walk into the doctor's office and up to the receptionist. Grayson gets on his phone.

"Susanna, can you fax Becca's insurance card to this number?" He reads the number off the business card at the desk. "Yes, both sides."

"Grayson, I have my insurance card." I pull it out.

"No, sweetheart, I canceled that one. You and your staff are under my company's plan," he says, then turns to the receptionist. "Ma'am, Becca's card is being faxed right now. Thanks, Susanna." He hangs up. She gives me a new form for updated info, and Grayson watches me fill it out. He squeezes my knee when I put his name down twice—as my emergency contact, and as the person to release medical information to. The littlest things mean so much to him. I hand in my form, sit, and wait. Julia, the nurse, comes out and calls me back. Grayson follows me in. She takes my vitals.

"Becca, your blood pressure is really low for you."

My eyes widen at this information. I always have excellent blood pressure. The only time I've ever had low blood pressure was during my pregnancy with Morgan.

"What is it, sweetheart?" Grayson looks down at me. I just bite my bottom lip to hold back my smile. "Becca?"

"Shh, the doctor's coming."

Dr. Peto walks in.

"Hi, Becca. What happened?" she asks. I tell her I passed out and haven't been feeling well, and that I've been under a lot of stress. She asks Grayson to leave the room so she can give me a full exam. He's not thrilled, but I nod him out. I have a few questions for her that I don't want him to hear.

"I think I might be pregnant," I whisper.

"I think you might be right." She smiles. She hands me a cup and I go into the adjacent bathroom to do my business. When I bring out exhibit A, she dips it and proceeds to give me an exam. I ask her the question I was going to ask tomorrow. We're both embarrassed, but she gives me the answer to the best of her knowledge. "Becca, you are definitely swollen." She smiles, then does my pap smear then pulls out the alien shoehorn. I hate that thing! She pulls her gloves off and walks over to the counter to check my results.

"Congratulations, Mama!" She laughs. I start sobbing—happily. "I'll set you up for an ultrasound right away, since you had a strange period last month," she says before heading out of the room to have her nurse call down. I start to get dressed.

"Becca?" Grayson's voice is gentle. I wipe my tears and turn to him. "What is it? What's the matter?" He pulls me to him.

"Hi." I find myself giggling now.

"Yes, hi, sweetheart. What did she say?"

"Um, well, I have to go downstairs for an ultrasound." I try to be serious.

"Why? What's the matter?" His eyes widen wildly as he cups my face—complete panic mode for Grayson.

"Apparently, there's a growth in my stomach. Well, my uterus, really."

"What kind of growth, Becca?" His brow furrows and the intensity of his stare softens.

I laugh. "The kind that's going to wake us every few hours at night for a feeding." Oh, there's the lightbulb.

"Bloody hell, Becca! We're having a baby?" he yells excitedly. I nod and hug him. "Oh, Becca! You had me so worried—why couldn't you just say you were pregnant?" He's happy and irritated. He lets me finish getting dressed. We grab my prenatal prescription and head downstairs for the ultrasound.

Tina globs goop on my belly and moves the wand around.

"Nope, we'll have to do the internal." Ugh! Off to the bathroom I go to pull everything off. When I come back out and lay down, Tina puts a condom-like covering on the wand. Grayson gasps.

"Where the hell is that going?"

I look at him as if he has five heads, and he laughs.

"Oh, Becca, that's awful. You women really get the raw end of the deal, aye?"

I shake my head and hold his hand as she inserts the wand, which actually looks like a boring BOB.

"There he is!" Tina smiles and points out the little bean.

"He?" Grayson asks.

"Oh, I say that for all of them until we know the sex. It's better than saying 'it.'"

"The heart's beating, so I guess I am about six weeks?"

I point the heart out to Grayson. A tear falls down his cheek.

"Becca, I love you so much. Thank you." He kisses my face over and over again.

"You are measuring at six weeks and two days, so you're on target. That puts your due date at August sixteenth." She prints out a picture and hands it to us.

We head out to the rental car in our new bliss.

"I can't believe we have to wait until August," Grayson complains.

"Oh, it will be here before you know it." I laugh and pat my belly. Funny thing about women: as soon as we find out we're pregnant, our hands instantly become obsessed with our bellies.

We arrive at the B&B and I take in a sharp breath. I'm afraid to face all the changes that have occurred without my knowledge or clearance. I look at Grayson. Shit! His eyelids are blinking faster than I drive.

"Fuck ..." I breathe.

"Fuckity fuck ..." Grayson adds. We both sense the calm before the storm. "Sweetheart, remember you are pregnant now. Try not to overreact." I hear the faint sound of a bell dinging. *All Sybeccas have their gloves up. Of course, Horny Sybecca and Porn Sybecca are facing the wrong way, wearing thongs.* TRAITORS!

"Grayson, you and I have different ideas about what is a normal reaction and what is an overreaction." I clench my teeth because he's already pissing me off.

"Becca, please remember that everything I do, I do it for you."

I laugh. "Channeling a little Bryan Adams, baby?"

"Huh? Oh. Stop it. You know what I mean, Becca. Please, I'm so happy today, I don't want to fight. Promise me you won't lose it." He palms my face.

"I'll try, but you know how I've been feeling." Tears plummet down my face. He thumbs them away and leans in slowly. His tongue beckons for my mouth to open up, and as I do, my theme song changes. I hear the beginning chords to "Let's Get It On" by Marvin Gaye. I laugh as I kiss him.

"What?" He pulls away, a bit annoyed. I imitate the chords and then sing the first line to the song. This blows his irritation with me right out the window. For the next fifteen minutes, we sit in the car like a pair of teenagers making out. Claudia bangs on the hood of the car, and we both jump.

"Jesus Christ! Some things never change!" she yells as I open the door and get out.

"Come here, you!" I grab her and hug her like I haven't seen her in twenty years instead of a month.

"Claudia, I barely recognized you! Just blue hair these days, huh?" Grayson teases her.

"Why, yes. I need to appear more managerial now!" She laughs, but I know it irritates Grayson that I don't ask her to look more professional.

"I see you have a new piercing!" he says with excitement, pointing to her eyebrow. I shoot him a "knock it off" look.

"Um, it's a redo." She fidgets a little, clearly uncomfortable now. I roll my eyes and she relaxes. "I can't wait for you to see all the changes we've made! So much has happened since we last talked." She grabs my hand and drags me. I look back at Grayson and shoot daggers out of my eyes. That fucking bastard did exactly the opposite of what I asked!

I take a deep breath and walk in the store entrance. Not much has changed in here except the color of the walls—they're now a light grayish-lavender. There are messages about being creative and capturing memories all done in white vinyl on the Cricut. It's very pretty. We head into the inn's main foyer and lounge area.

All the dark wood I loved is ... gone, replaced by an airy English Cottage aesthetic. It's bright and clean, with blues, yellows, and greens involved in a mixture of plaid and flowery patterns on sofas, chairs, and drapery. All of the wood has been painted over in a bright white. *I did not authorize this!* We talked about redoing the rooms, not the main common areas! There's also a bar and small stage in the dining room.

"For karaoke night." Claudia smiles.

"Humph," is all I can manage and, quite frankly, it's probably better than the scream I want to bellow out.

"Isn't it beautiful?" Claudia claps. "Come look at the kitchen." She pulls me along. All new maple-walnut cabinetry, stainless steel appliances, and a restaurant-quality stove. The dishes, silverware—it's all brand new, and I didn't pick out one fucking thing!

"I'm sorry, Claudia. I need to go to my room." I bite my lip.

"Becca, are you okay?"

"No, I'm really not." I head back to the dining room, into the lounge, to the foyer, and up the stairs.

"Becca, sweetheart, your room is being renovated. All your stuff is in the room we shared."

I stop and take in a deep breath.

"Do you have the key?"

"Yes." He charges past me and opens the door. I walk in and stop dead in my tracks.

"Wait, why is all the stuff from my upstairs craft room in here?" Oh God, I'm going to explode. I can feel the venom rising before he utters a word.

"We turned it into an employee room for overnights." He stands back.

"You did what?!" One-way ticket for the crazy train, first class, coming up!

"It's temporary. Besides ... never mind. Becca, please, you're hyperventilating, sweetheart. Please calm down." He kneels down next to me. I didn't even realize I was down here.

"You've taken everything from me. Everything that was me is gone. I feel like I have lost my identity. This doesn't feel like mine anymore." I can't control my sobs.

"Becca, now this is a clear case of overreaction! Do you not like anything that was done?" He's trying to be patient.

"Oh, it's gorgeous, but I had no say! I didn't even pick out the new fucking forks! Nothing had my stamp of approval—nothing. This is my baby, and you took it completely out of my hands. How do you not get this?" I stare at him, bewildered. "Grayson, what if I waltzed into your record company and made all kinds of changes without your knowledge and approval, just because I thought I knew better?" I'm trying my hardest to calm down. I really need him to understand what his control issues are doing—or are going to do—to our relationship.

"I wouldn't be very happy. I'd probably react the way you are." He exhales harshly and shakes his head, mainly at himself. "Becca, what can I do to fix this? I don't want you to resent me, sweetheart." He grabs my hands, his thumbs caressing the tops.

"Let's go see Rocco. Unless, of course, Rocco is no longer my horse and has been replaced as well." I bait him.

"Uh ... sweetheart, Rocco's at the animal hospital. They're not sure what's wrong with him." His eyes zone in on my flaring nostrils.

"How long, Gray?" I can barely contain myself.

"One week."

I'm on him like Ralphie on Scut Farkus, my arms flailing and complete gibberish flying from my mouth. Of course, it's not long before Grayson has me pinned down.

"*Enough!*"

Damn ... that was extra British. Why does he have to be so hot? Cue erratic breathing, please. His face softens and his brows dart up. *Shit.* He lets go of my arms and works quickly at my jeans.

They fly off, taking my panties hostage. His mouth is on mine. "E.T." plays in my mind again. Before I can blink, he's inside. *Honestly, is there not a single ounce of willpower in my body?* Wham bam, thank you ma'am! Grayson sits back on his heels and pulls his pants up as he stares at me. He grabs my panties, then slides each foot in and draws them up my legs. I raise my bottom for him. I do my jeans myself and head to the bathroom to clean up the spill in aisle ahem.

I open the door to find Grayson looking through some of my pictures.

"I want to go visit Rocco. Are you coming with me?"

He glances over. "No, sweetheart, go with Melissa. I have some things to tend to here. My stuff, not yours," he says quickly before meeting me in the middle of the room for a kiss. "Call or text when you're on your way back, love." He pats my bottom as I head out.

"Melissa, c'mon, we have to go see Rocco at the animal hospital." I grab her arm and drag her along with me.

GRAYSON

Christmas is two weeks away. I know what I'm buying Becca, but I have something special in mind that I want to make for her—even though I'm quite clueless when it comes to her craft. I thought of hiring somebody to do it for me, but it's very personal and she'd know. Maybe Claudia can teach me while Becca's out.

I run downstairs to find Claudia helping a customer. I wave at her to come into Becca's office when she's done. I look around. Claudia has pretty much taken over Morgan's side. It's only fair—she is the general manager and, despite her blue hair and multiple piercings, she's doing an excellent job.

"Yes, Grayson?" She comes in and closes the door.

"Claudia! Good—I need your help!" I clasp my hands in a plea.

"Sure, what do you need help with?"

"A Scrapbooking 101 class. From you. I have something special in mind for Becca for Christmas, but I don't know what to do or how to do it." I start chewing on a hangnail and abruptly stop when I realize what I'm doing.

"Um, Gray, Christmas is in—"

"Yes, two weeks, I know," I interrupt. "I have everything I want to do, I just need help with embellishments. Paper and stuff."

"Um, okay ... well, why don't you start by picking out paper you think you would like to use? I'll get the other supplies you will need, and we'll put everything in a box so Becca won't know." She opens the door for me.

I head out into the store and look around like a deer in headlights. Why do we need so many shades of each color? Is this really necessary? Well, I'm not going to pretend to know what I'm talking about when it comes to this stuff. I find a paper here, a paper there ... and then all of a sudden, my hands are full. It's like a drug! I have fifty sheets of paper that make me think of Becca, and only twenty-four pages to do! I walk into the crop room, arms loaded. Claudia has everything assembled. She goes over the paper trimmer, the punches, the Cricut, brads, tags ... *wah, wah, wah, wah, wah* ... I'm in full-blown Charlie Brown mode. Wait, what? Shit, she just left the room. Let me see where Becca is at and maybe I can get started here.

December 12, 2012   1:00 p.m.
Me: How's Rocco?
Becca: He perked up once he saw me. They think it may just be depression.
Me: Horses get depressed?
Becca: Um, yeah. I went away. Charlie went away. He doesn't

understand.

Me: I'd be depressed if you went away :(

Becca: Yeah, you're lucky I have no willpower when it comes to you!

Me: Yeah ... I am. How long are u going to stay?

Becca: Probably another hour or so. All right?

Me: Yes, of course! No riding though! Only me!

Becca: Yes, baby. By the way, love the way you buck!

Me: ;p Love you!

Becca: LY2 BBB

Me: Damn it!

What the fuck does that stand for? Ugh! I push it out of my mind and pull out my envelope of pictures. Before I know it, my cell pings. Wow, an hour and a half has passed!

December 12, 2012   2:38 p.m.

Becca: On my way. Do you want anything?

Me: Just your sweet arse, in every way ...

Me: Sorry ...

Becca: B home soon.

I clean up my mess and put the box Claudia gave me away where she told me to, then head to the lounge to look at the paper. I actually did three pages! Wow, never thought I would get excited over something like this. It's for Becca—that's why I'm so excited. Claudia sits down across from me, yawns, and grabs a magazine.

"Hey, loved the picture of you guys at Disneyland." She turns the issue of *People* toward me.

"That's from a month ago, Claudia! Why is it still out here?"

"Uh, because the owner has never been in *People* before, and we like to brag!" She laughs. Just then, Becca walks in.

"Hey, you two." She gives me a quick kiss and sits next to me.

I rub her back; she looks so tired.

"*Sind sie wütend auf mich dafür, daß alle Änderungen hier in der Nahe?*"

I look up at Claudia like she has five heads.

"*Nein, ich bin wütend auf ihn! Ich habe keine Sache hier wahlen oder einmal wissen! Ich wusste nicht entweder uber Rocco!*"

I turn my gaze to Becca. Fluent in fucking German, too?!

"*Warum erzählen nicht er sie über Rocco? Das ist schrecklich!*" Claudia seems pissed.

"*Ich weiss nicht! Er denkt, dass er mich geschützt werden, indem man mich im Dunkeln! Es ist dumm und reizend!*" Becca flips her hand. Her mouth may be speaking German, but her hands still say Jersey!

"*Geben sie ihm eine was fur?!*" Claudia shoots me a dirty look. I'm sitting here completely mesmerized by these two, and they're ripping me apart in another fucking language!

"*Ja! Und dann gab er mir ... auf Boden! Ich habe kein wille zur macht!*" Becca shakes her head in defeat.

"*Nun ist er verdammt hei!*" Claudia offers her a sympathetic smile.

Becca starts laughing. "You know curse words? You have to teach me!"

"There's an app!" Claudia offers.

"Number one: completely fucking rude to talk in another language in front of someone who doesn't speak it! And number two: are you two secret agents or something? I mean, who the fuck is fluent in German?!" I'm annoyed and turned on all at the same time. Just then, my email alert goes off on my phone. I take a look.

> **To:** Grayson James
> **From:** Ryan Paul
> **Date:** December 12, 2012
> **Subject:** I am! Translated conversation!

Claudia: Are you mad at me for allowing all of the changes around here?

Becca: No, I'm mad at him! I didn't pick a thing out here or even know about it! I didn't know about Rocco either!

Claudia: Why didn't he tell you about Rocco? That's terrible!

Becca: I don't know! He thinks he's protecting me by keeping me in the dark! It's stupid and irritating!

Claudia: Did you give him a what for?

Becca: Yes! And then he gave me one ... on the floor! I have no willpower.

Claudia: Well, he is fucking hot.

To: Ryan Paul
From: Grayson James
Date: December 12, 2012
Subject: Big Bonus! Big!
Don't tell Becca or Melissa you speak German!

Ryan walks by and nods.

"What was so funny in your email?" Becca leans over. I delete it.

"Sorry, sweetheart, I can't allow you to see this for your own good. I know it seems stupid and irritating, but there are some things I must keep you in the dark about. By the way, Claudia, you're pretty cute yourself. If I was into blue hair and piercings, I might be giving you a what for!" And with that, I get up and walk away to let them wonder how I knew what they said. It's great having "people"! I love it!

BECCA

"Becca, does he speak German, too?" Claudia's mouth is on the floor.

"No! Fucking Ryan emailed him with the translation." I laugh because Grayson thinks he really pulled one over on us.

"How do you know?"

"Because Melissa told me he speaks fluently. I didn't realize he was in earshot, or I would've switched to Danish or Russian. I saw him nod after Gray sent his reply." I shake my head.

"Men! Speaking of ... I have a new man!" Claudia pats her knees excitedly.

"What? Who?" I sit forward.

"He's actually one of my security guys. His name is Joshua. Can't call him Josh." She furrows her brow, mocking a serious face.

"How long?"

"Since he first started guarding me. It was an instant flirt-fest between us! He's so fucking hot!"

"Well?" *Please tell me I'm not the only damn whore around here!*

"Yeah, I have no willpower either. He considered my body thoroughly guarded by the end of the first week," she says quietly. I literally laugh out loud.

"Claudia! You ready, baby?" A man comes up behind her—Joshua, I'm guessing. Damn, he is cute! He's about five foot nine, very fit, dark brown hair gelled into a small Mohawk. Brown eyes that have a smokiness about them, and very full lips with a little button nose.

"By the way," Claudia whispers in my ear, "my eyebrow's not my only new piercing ..." She looks at me with wide eyes and glances down to her—ahem. I'm fucking rolling now!

"Get out of here, you crazy lady!"

"Good night!" She winks and heads out with him. I suddenly

feel exhausted.

I head upstairs to our room. I strip down to my panties and bra and look through the drawers to find some PJs. I suddenly feel a very painful slap on my ass.

"Ow—goddamn it, Gray—stop it!" I turn and push him.

He bites his smirk back and grabs my arms quickly. "You want to give me another 'what for,' sweetheart?" He tries to kiss me.

"Please, baby, stop. I'm tired. I need to lay down." I turn my head.

"Oh, okay." He lets go and I turn to find my PJs. "This drawer, sweetheart." He pulls out a comfy pair for me. I undress and put the PJs on. I grab a tissue and blow my nose. "Becca?" He chucks my chin.

"You've got to stop hitting me so hard. You're really starting to hurt me." I cry—not by my choice.

"I ... uh ... Bec ... um." His eyelids are going haywire. I just shake my head and climb into our bed. "Can I rub it for you?" He pushes my hair away from my face.

"No. I just want to go to sleep."

"Okay, sweetheart. I'll wake you for dinner." He kisses my hair. I drift off almost immediately.

Grayson's smiling down at me as we make love. I don't know where we are. I can only see his face. I close my eyes, then open them again. Ray is looking down at me with the same dark expression he had at the hospital. I try to fight him off, but he has my arms pinned down.

"Becca, you know it. Your body knows it. It's the least you can do. Becs ... baby ... Becs ... you want it."

I wake up with a panicked jump. I feel completely disoriented. Grayson is sitting on the side edge of the bed.

"Gray, is this real? Are you really here?" I grab him. He turns to face me. He seems upset. "What? What is it? Oh God! Stacey!" I almost yell.

"No. Everything's fine." He seems melancholy.

"Jesus, I just had the worst nightmare!" I put my head in my hands.

"Nightmare?" He looks at me again, confused.

"Yes, Gray! What the hell is wrong with you?" This is irritating.

"I came to wake you up, and you were calling out Ray's name." He looks straight ahead.

"Really?! Really, Gray? You're fucking jealous over a goddamn dream? He was fucking raping me in my dream, are you still fucking jealous? Move!" I climb out of bed, then head into the bathroom and run the bath with my dream—and the unhealthy levels of Gray's jealousy—still haunting me. As I wait for the tub to fill, I decide to grab my phone. I need to call the hospital and Morgan.

"Hey, what are we doing about Christmas? Because Morgan's going to ask." I smack his arm lightly. He doesn't reply. "Grayson!" I yell. He turns to look at me and takes the phone out of my hand gently, yet purposefully. "What is the matter with you?" I snap, but soften my face.

"Becca ... George is dead." There's a strange calmness in what he says.

"Grayson, how? When? Are you sure?" I pull up a chair.

"I got the call right before I came in here. That's why I'm a little off." He sits in front of me.

"Where was he found? How long has he been dead?" I'm in complete shock.

"In a ditch. Cross-country skiers found him. The police are at the scene right now. We'll have to wait for the autopsy, but Becca ... it looks like murder." He grabs my hands.

"Grayson, what ... what does this mean for us?" I should feel relieved, but this may only prove my theory—and, I'm sure, Grayson's—that George had a partner.

"It means nothing changes security-wise. Becca, his partner, if he had one, could be anyone. Do not do anything or see anyone without security, especially anyone who has had a romantic interest in you!" He's very stern.

"Grayson, you don't have to tell me," I start.

"Yes I do!" he yells.

"I've been very good about following the rules, Gray. Ever since Stacey." I touch his arm lightly to calm him.

"That could've been you!"

"Come. Take a bath with me." I lean forward and kiss him.

"Becca, I'd die if anything ever happened to you. And now we have a baby on the way. I'm sorry; you will now have two people with you at all times." His right hand palms my cheek. He's waiting for an argument. Normally, I would tell him to go to hell, but not today.

"Okay, baby." I kiss his palm.

"Really, sweetheart, you're going to listen?" He searches my eyes.

"Yes, baby, I promise." I seal it with a kiss. "Shit! The bath!" I yell, and pull away to run into the bathroom. I catch it just in time and hit the drain to lower the water level. I feel Grayson behind me, grinding into my bottom as I bend over the tub. I stand up quickly. He chuckles. The butterflies in my stomach seem to be performing a fancy flight show.

"Sweetheart, you're breathing quite erratically. Are you all right?"

Arrogant bastard!

"No. I feel I'm about to suffer a British invasion." I lean my head back on his chest.

"I would hardly call it suffering, darling." He slides his hands under my shirt to rest on my stomach as his lips caress my neck. Mazzy Star's "Fade Into You" is on Pandora. I'm hypnotized by the music, his smell, his touch. I love getting lost in him.

"Let's shower instead." I pull him over and turn the water on.

"Why, love?" He looks back to the bath.

"I'm pregnant, Grayson. We shouldn't have sex in the tub because ... well, just listen to me." I don't feel like explaining the issues that could arise. He shrugs and pulls off his shirt.

My focus reinstated, I tug my shirt off over my head and attack him. *Damn, I want him ... he's so fucking hot! Horny Sybecca is shaking her ass; she's sporting the British flag on her underwear.* We are both eagerly awaiting the British invasion. Grayson and I get *very* dirty before we get clean. The Lord has heard my prayers several more times ... in English, German, and French! I keep my other languages to myself.

"I'm starving, sweetheart. Let's go downstairs and eat." He wraps his towel around his waist and steps out of the shower.

"Sounds good to me." I follow in my towel.

I throw on a long-sleeve blue V-neck cotton shirt and the jeans Grayson asked me not to wear anymore.

"Seriously, sweetheart," Grayson rubs my bottom, "you love to drive me crazy." He slaps me there. My jeans protect me from the sting. We head downstairs.

"No, Becca. Just sit." Grayson pulls a chair out for me at a corner table.

"I thought you were hungry?" I squint a little. What is he playing at?

"I am. Somebody will be over to take our order." He scoots me in. His eyelids are going fucking mad again.

"Grayson, it's not a crop weekend. It's not even a weekend.

There is no dinner service any other time." I close my eyes to contain the temperature that is making my blood boil.

"Well, Adam is here full-time now, so we offer our guests dinner every night. Thank you, Karen." I open my eyes to see an employee whom I've never met before.

"Hi, Karen. I'm Becca Campbell." I smile.

"Hi, Becca. Is this your first time staying with us?"

She's very pleasant—unlike me at the moment. I shoot eye daggers at Grayson.

"No, Karen, I'm the owner here."

She looks at me with a bit of confusion.

"Well, it's nice to meet you. Here are our specials for tonight." She hands each of us a menu. Grayson gives her our drink orders. He almost ordered my red wine. I wish I found out I was pregnant tomorrow instead of today, because right now, I could really use that glass of wine ... maybe two!

"That's nice. I have all these new employees who don't even recognize my name as their boss's! I mean, their checks have my name on them!"

Grayson's eyes look everywhere but my way.

"Grayson, whose name is on their checks?" He says nothing. "Fix it, Grayson! You better fucking fix it!" I throw my napkin down and get up to leave.

"Becca, sit your arse down right now!" he says through his teeth. "Sit," he repeats, softer this time. I sit. I am infuriated with him. "We will go over all the changes and whatever you want fixed, we will fix. Okay? It's not worth you getting pissed at me every minute!" He runs his hand through his hair.

"Fine!" I say sharply. I pull my phone out and call the hospital to check on Stacey. Her nurse informs me of her status and the tests they did today. I thank her and look up at Grayson. "No change." He nods as I get off the phone.

"Becca will have the bacon-wrapped meatloaf, garlic mashed,

and sugar snap peas. I'll have the bacon-wrapped filet mignon, garlic mashed, and glazed carrots. Medium on the filet. Thanks, Karen." He hands her the menus. I don't even bother to look at them anymore when I'm with him. "Becca, I'm going to stay here for a few days while you're with Stacey so I can concentrate on work." I feel a bit shocked. He usually doesn't like to be away from me unless he absolutely has to be.

"Um, okay. Where am I staying?"

"Same place, sweetheart, same room. Don't bring Melissa and Ryan though; those two might be too busy shagging to protect you." He smiles.

"Okay. I'll take Melissa and—" I try to think of his name. "Jim?"

"No. Paul," he says, probably because Paul is not good-looking like Jim is.

"Okay. How many days will we be apart?" I sip my ginger ale.

"You're so bloody mad at me. You sure you'll miss me, Becca?" He rests his head on his fisted hand.

"Of course. You know I can barely last longer than twelve hours," I tease.

"Oh, don't worry, sweetheart. I'll hook you up tonight. Tomorrow morning, too, before you leave, for that matter." He flashes me that gorgeous grin.

"Hook me up, huh?" I laugh and shake my head. Some things just sound strange coming from him. "Grayson, you will call me with any new developments, right?" My right eyebrow darts up.

"Yes, sweetheart, of course."

"Grayson, I'm not kidding!"

"I know. Now stop and put your focus into eating. You are feeding two, my dear." He points an authoritative finger at me. Karen makes her way to our table and places our food in front of us. I dive in. *Mmm ... so delicious.* I glance up and notice Grayson just staring at me, a blanket of warmth on his face. I wish I could take a picture of him. He only gets this look when he's thinking of absolutely nothing but the thing that is making him truly happy. I'm amazed that it's me after the hell I've given him today. He really is a wonderful man, and he has done a wonderful job here. His approach was all wrong, but his heart was in the right place.

"Thank you, baby. For everything you've done." I grab his hand and squeeze it. I want to make sure he knows his efforts weren't fruitless. He winks and gives me a warm smile. I look back down at my plate and try to concentrate on my dinner.

"Gray, why can't you come with me and work at the hotel?" I really don't want to be apart from him. *Crap!* Why am I tearing up? What is it with us women? As soon as we find out we're pregnant, our hormones go crazy. It's like they're running around in there screaming, *She knows! She knows! Full speed ahead!* Are we irrational before we know and then more comfortable with the fact that we have something to blame it on? I don't get it!

"Becca? Sweetheart, why are you crying?" Grayson puts his fork down and sits in the chair closer to me. He touches my face softly and wipes away my tears, and I progress to full hiccupping sobs. *Really? What the hell is the matter with me?!* "Becca, calm down, love." Why do people say that to you when you are crying like this? As if it didn't occur to you that just calming down would stop all of this nonsense? It's fucking irritating! If I could calm down, I would! I close my eyes and try to focus. Grayson just holds my hand and waits patiently, probably scared shitless that he's going to have to deal with these mood swings for the next nine months.

"Sorry," I try to say calmly, but a gasp comes out at the end. I feel the worst is over, so I open my eyes to look at him. He's biting back a smile. "You're laughing at me?"

"No, sweetheart, I love you. You're so beautiful." He cups my face before kissing me. "Give me three days max, sweetheart, and I'll be down by you. I've got something up my sleeve for you for

Christmas, and I can't have you around while I'm getting it all sorted out. Okay, love?"

"Okay. But I still don't want to be without you." *Wow, that's pathetic! Surely I can last three whole days!*

"Theme song, love?"

"Huh? Oh ... no. Internal battle, sorry." I offer a half smile. "Don't ask." I put my hand up and wave when I see him trying to figure me out. "Finish your dinner, Gracie. I'm okay now." I start back at my plate. Grayson just pulls his over. We finish our meals in silence.

"Dessert, Becca?"

I take in a deep breath and shake my head.

"We should call Morgan." I sigh, remembering that I never got around to doing that earlier. So many distractions. When should I tell her that her father is dead—again? Very bizarre situation this is. Honestly, I don't think she'll care. It's not like he came back a changed man. Will this affect her when she's older? Here she is, ten years old and the chance to tell George how she feels has been taken away from her a second time. I'll have to ask my therapist what she thinks. Oh, I need to schedule with her while I'm here as well!

"Becca, love, here. It's Morgan." He smacks my thigh to gain my attention and passes me his phone when he succeeds.

"Hey, honey! What are you doing?" My smile is huge, although she can't see it.

"Susanna and I were just doing some last-minute gardening. We're having our first cooking class tonight!" She sounds excited. I feel a pang in my heart for two reasons. First, I miss her terribly. Second, I feel a little jealous that Susanna has her so excited about cooking. I lost her interest with it two years ago.

"Well, that's fun!" I'm overenthusiastic to conceal the fact that I'm upset, and it makes Grayson wince. He grabs my hand and thumbs the top. I offer him a grateful smile.

"How are Butterscotch and Rocco, Mommy?"

I debate for a moment over what to tell her, only because I think Grayson is starting to rub off on me. I push the idea away. With the exception of George, I have always been very honest with Morgan and careful not to sugarcoat things.

"Well, sweetie, Butterscotch is doing well, but poor Rocco has been very sad and had to make a visit to the animal hospital."

"Is he sick, Mommy?" I can hear the depth of her concern—she's ten going on thirty.

"No. At first they didn't know what was wrong, but when I went to visit him today he perked right up! That's when they realized he was just sad and missed us. He'll be back home in a few days." I nod at Karen to thank her for the tea and slice of cheesecake that apparently Grayson ordered for me.

"Well, that's good, Mommy! I miss them, especially Butterscotch. Mommy, what if she gets really sad like Rocco?" Her voice shifts to complete and utter panic. "Mommy! Tomorrow, take Daddy's iPad out to Butterscotch and I'll Skype with her!"

Grayson scrunches up his nose and mouths *what?* to me. Clearly he heard her excitement, how could he not? I had to pull the phone away from my ear, she was so loud.

"You know what, Morgan? I have to go visit Aunt Stacey in Boston tomorrow, so I'm sure Daddy will be more than happy to help you Skype with Butterscotch!" I can't help the stupid grin that comes over my face or the shaking of my shoulders when I giggle silently. Grayson's rolled his eyeballs so far they may just get stuck! He then points to me and makes circles at his temples with his index finger to indicate I'm crazy.

"Oh, good! How's Aunt Stacey, Mommy?"

"She's the same, sweetheart, keep praying for her! I miss you, Morgan." I get choked up again. Grayson's mouth pulls into a slight frown.

"Can I come home for Christmas, Mommy, or are you guys coming back here?"

"What are we doing about Christmas, babe?" I tap his hand. Grayson grabs the phone from me.

"Hey, Morgy girl! Shall you come home for Christmas, little sweetheart? Good then! You'll fly home next weekend, love. Okay. Here's Mummy. I love you too, more than you know. And you are my stars. G'nite, love." He hands the phone back.

"Okay, sweetie, so it looks like a white Christmas for us!" I'm very excited and squeeze Grayson's hand.

"I can't wait to see everybody, Mumsy!" Oh geez, back to an English accent.

"I love you, Morgy, talk to you tomorrow!"

"Love you, Mumsy, mwah!"

"Mwah!" I kiss her back, "Good night, baby."

"Good night, Mama." I hang up and quickly grasp Grayson's face to kiss him.

"Thank you, baby!" I smile against his lips.

"Of course, sweetheart, anything for my girls! Now eat your cheesecake!" He flicks his eyes over at it.

"Just a little, I am very full." I play with stubble on his chin.

"Don't worry, darling, you'll be working it all off." He kisses me again.

"I can't wait to work it all off. I want you so bad, baby," I murmur against his lips. This provokes a sharp intake of breath from him. His phone pings and the distraction pulls him away from me all too easily. I'm certain it's because we're in the dining hall and not our room. I'm also certain it's because it could be about a number of important things that we happen to be in the middle of. All of the sudden my theme song changes to "Yesterday" by the Beatles. It's not a completely accurate representation of what we are going through, but just the sentiment of yesterday, before all of this craziness, is fitting. Ping. Text. Ping. Text. He sets the phone down.

"What was that about?" I sip my tea and play with the tag, smirking at him. He chuckles and scratches his palms. I can't help but laugh. God, I love him! "Gray? What was that about?" I ask again.

"Nothing."

"That was a lot of texting over nothing. Your fingers must want to fall off when it's about something ... vs. nothing." I hold my hand out and wave my fingers for him to hand me his phone.

"Sorry, sweetheart, that's my thing, not your thing." He pushes my fingers to my palm to close my hand into a fist.

"I thought your *thing* was sorta my *thing,* as well." I bait him.

"My *thing* is most definitely more than sorta your *thing*. Incidentally, when did it become *The Thing*? He rather liked the original name you gave him, and so do I." Third thing we're really good at is baiting each other and turning anything from normal and usual into something sexual and provocative.

"Well, I can't help but wonder, is he *really* that incredible? It seems to me that I'm having a really difficult time recollecting how incredible he is. Hmm." I tilt my head as if to ponder.

"Oh, sweetheart, he and I would love nothing more than to refresh your memory!" He pulls my hand up to his lips. Keeping my gaze, he playfully bites at the top, then kisses it.

"Shall we go then, Mr. James?" I stand up abruptly.

"After you, Mrs. James." He matches my haste and we practically run through the lounge and up the stairs to our room. Grayson can't get the door open quickly enough for us.

"Damn it! I hate this!" he mutters impatiently before he finally manages to unlock it. He grabs my hand and drags me in.

"Gray!" I laugh as I almost fall forward.

"Sorry, love!" He braces me with both hands and slams the door with his foot. I kick my shoes off as he pulls my shirt up and over my head. I pull at his shirt and strip him of it. He works at my bra, me at his belt. Our mouths devour each other's. He pulls away abruptly and stares down into my eyes. His thumb traces over my bottom lip. He does this every once in a while, and it leaves me to wonder. Wonder what he is searching for? What is he thinking? Is he just holding on to a moment? His lips caress mine softly, his hands following suit over my body. What happened to the sense of urgency from not two minutes ago? His mouth travels down my neck, my sternum, and to my stomach. I lose my hands in his hair as he spends a generous amount of time kissing my stomach.

I hear him whispering *I love you* to my belly as he pulls my jeans down.

"You know, I believe if you say it right in here," I point to my belly button, "it works as an intercom system and the baby will hear it loud and clear. Well, once he or she grows ears," I tease.

"Is that so?" He grins up at me. "Hello in there, my little heartbeat. I'm your daddy and I love you! You'll be my moon and I'll be your stars!" He tests the theory out. I just stand there and fall more in love with him. It's amazing how he does that. "Where are you, sweetheart?" I open my eyes and look at him. His eyes are glued to mine as he slides my panties down.

"I'm lost in my thoughts of you." I step out of them. "Didn't you have something incredible to show me?" I give him my most mischievous grin.

"Patience, my love." He stands in front of me again, allowing his jeans to drop. I glance down at him and bite my lip. God, the site of him never loses its effect on me. He removes my bottom lip from my teeth before leaning down to bite it for himself. "God, I want you, Becca," he murmurs against my lips.

"I'm all yours, baby—forever."

"Becca, you promise?" He leans his forehead against mine.

"Yes. No question about it. I promise." I grasp his face in my hands and make him look at me. "No question. No doubt. One-hundred-fifty percent yours."

"No matter how angry you get with me? No matter how controlling I try to be? You know where my heart is? You won't run anymore?" His hands squeeze over mine.

"Never. I promise, no matter what. You are my heart. You are my soul. I love you with every fiber of my being. You ... you only." I shake his head a little for emphasis before I attack his lips. He lifts me up and carries me over to the bed. He lays me down gently. I try to focus on the task at hand here, but I can't help but wonder where the hell all of that just came from. Is it because we're here? Is it stirring up memories and insecurities for him? Is it the "Ray incident" at the hospital two weeks ago? No. No, why would all of this come up now? *Damn it!* It's because I won't be with him the next few days! He still doesn't trust me!

"Oh, Becca, c'mon, love. Where is your head at, sweetheart? It's surely not here with me in this bed." He sighs with slight an-noyance, but mostly disappointment.

"Sorry, baby. Just thinking about how much I'm going to miss you. I don't like being apart from you." I choose the road less trav-eled by us today—the non-argumentative one.

"Well, miss me later. Love me now." His lips collect mine. My hand dives into his hair to deepen the kiss. He climbs on top of me and pulls his mouth away from mine to stare down into my eyes again. My fingers play with his lip as I nudge him with my knee.

"Please, Grayson," I whisper, and nudge him again. He shifts a little and slowly I feel myself expanding around him. "Oh ... Gray." I close my eyes to fully absorb the sensation.

"Look at me, sweetheart," he beckons breathlessly. I open my eyes and he pulls out quickly, then fills me slowly again. He does this several times—enough to drive me mad.

"Please, baby, please ..." I think I shall truly lose my mind if he keeps this up. He bites my lip again and quickens his pace. *And deliver us from evil, for thine is the kingdom and the power and ... the glory ... forever ... and ... ever ...* "Oh God, baby ... oh God and Baby Jesus!" *All Sybeccas are in their robes having a revival. I think Cautionary Sybecca is there playing the tambourine.*

"Bec?" Grayson starts.

I raise my finger.

"Shh ..." I just need a moment to return to this planet. Whew. Okay. "Yes, sweetie?" I open my eyes, and once again I'm staring into his gorgeous ones.

"Did you pray to Baby Jesus?" He chuckles.

"I may have done that ..." I bite back my smile and push his sweaty bangs away. "Now, Mr. James, care to enlighten me on your pre-coital thoughts?" There was definitely something interesting going on there. I'm pretty confident he won't share, though. Probably to avoid the wrath of Becca Campbell for the third or fourth time today. Wow! I was really on a roll! In my defense, he's done a lot of things to piss me off! It's not like he was oblivious either as to how I may react. *Control freak!*

"I plead the fifth on most of it, Becca." He sighs as if he'll get the wrath just for that.

"Um, are you even a U.S. citizen? Because if you aren't, I don't think you can plead the fifth, babe." I poke at his chest with my finger.

"Well, sweetheart, since this isn't a real court of law, I don't really have to worry about technicalities." He sounds so melancholy. He squeezes me to him and kisses my forehead.

"Ugh, Grayson! What is the matter with you?" I lift my head off of his chest to encourage an answer.

"Sweetheart!" he says, with a bit of annoyance in his voice. "We're in the middle of a huge shitstorm! I think I'm entitled to be a bit all over the place, am I not? I mean, I'm trying to keep everyone safe and happy, trying to salvage my career and all of my businesses. I've been handling your business and your ungrateful attitude about everything I do for you! Christ, Becca! Do you think for once, just once, sweetheart, you could thank me for my efforts before you fucking chew me out?" He finally takes a breath of air as he plants his hands on top of his head and closes his eyes to either regain his cool or ... prepare for my wrath. God, I have been a bitch!

"Well, Mr. James, I have to say that you sound even more British than usual. Something must be done about that!" I opt for teasing instead of more attitude. I play with the stubble on his chin and trail kisses down his jawline. "What shall I do with you, Mr. James?"

"How about you fucking marry me?!" Annoyance. Again.

"Grayson." I lift my face. "I *am* marrying you! What are you talking about?" Christ, my divorce was only finalized today! Is the ink even dry?

"I want a date, Becca! I want you to pick a fucking date! I know you want Stacey there, love, but it could be days. It could be *years*! We're having a baby! The rumors that will fly around about me only marrying you because of that will be bad enough!"

"Wait, Gray! We've been engaged for a while and the world has known for almost as long. If people can't do the math, they're idiots!" *Years?!* How can he be so negative about Stacey's recovery?

"Becca, you say you're mine. I know it sounds stupid, but I need it in writing. I have to have everything ... well, under control. I can only do so much 'flying by the seat of my pants' crap! If this didn't happen to Stacey, we would've been married by Christmas!"

I sit up and pull my knees to my chest. This is because we're in New Hampshire, because Ray is ten minutes down the road. He wasn't carrying on about a date before we came back. He feels threatened. Apparently, he thinks a piece of paper will resolve these feelings. I, however, don't think five of these papers will change how he feels. Moving to another country might help, but that's a bit drastic.

Grayson sits up after a beat and leans over to retrieve his phone from his jeans.

"C'mere, love, let's have a look." I'm guessing he's pulling the calendar up.

"Your birthday, is it at the beginning of January?" I try to shake my smile.

"Yes—the third—why?" He flips to the New Year.

"Because you're a typical Capricorn—one duck out of the row and the whole pond will go missing!" I push back to sit next to him. I lean into him and look at the calendar as well. "You're a very bossy man, Mr. James." I sigh and feel his lips on my cheek.

"Thank you," he whispers near my ear, and I know it's because I'm choosing a date and not because I called him bossy.

"How about March?" I offer. "I'll be in my second trimester ... ugh, I'll be in my second trimester. Maybe we can have Billy Idol perform. He can sing 'Shotgun Wedding' instead of 'White Wedding.' Oh, but we might be taking the thunder away from the tabloids if we do that." *My sarcasm knows no limits or bounds.*

"How about Christmas?"

Please tell me his sarcasm knows no limits or bounds!

"Grayson, that's two weeks from now." I give him the "hell to the no" face.

"Sweetheart, it's perfect! I'm sure you've been wondering ... 'Ugh, what do I give the man who has everything?' Well, you can give me you! No hopeless search through the mall. Countless hours on the internet ... just searching ... wracking your brain ... 'What am I going to get Grayson?!'" I'm in hysterics.

"That has to be *the* worst imitation of a Jersey accent! Terrible, Grayson, terrible."

"Oh, I'm sure it's better than your imitation of me! I'm being serious, though, sweetheart. That would be the best gift ever and everybody would be here!" He raises his brows, thinking he's sunk my ship.

"What about Susanna and Sam? My Aunt Tess and Uncle Bill? Yeah, you didn't think about them, or your mates from university." I imitate him.

"Ugh! You're impossible!" He groans.

"Um, how about March?" I revisit. "I'll be in my second trimester. I should be done with nausea and vomiting, if that happens to me. I won't be tired and cranky."

"March, huh? What a great idea. Why didn't you say that in the first place?" He smirks and pulls March up. "Do you want a Saturday?"

"Yes. Fridays can be a pain in the ass for people, and any other day is simply annoying." How's that for not sugarcoating?

"Blunt, sweetheart, and to the point—liberating, isn't it?" He turns for a kiss.

"Yeah, babe, doesn't work with everything! Um ... how about the ninth?" I point.

"I was thinking the same thing." He taps on it and types *Our Wedding Day*. "There! Was that so hard?" He takes in a deep breath after he hits "save" and closes everything out.

"Look at that, baby! The pond has miraculously reappeared!" I hold my hands out in front of me.

"Shut up and kiss me, sweetheart." He pulls my face to his to celebrate our joint efforts in mitigating the problem at hand: his insecurity. I mean, our wedding date.

GRAYSON

Ugh—can't sleep! Becca, however, is in a sex-induced coma. She looks lovely. I love how long her hair is getting. She's been itching to cut it, but so far my pleas for her to keep it long have prevailed. I kiss her lightly freckled shoulder. Mmm ... she smells so good. My fingers gently trace her spine. *Look at that fantastic bum.* I fight the urge to slap it. Oh, I'd definitely love another go! This is one of those nights where I can't keep my bloody hands off of her! I know not seeing her for the next few days is probably the fuel behind my fire tonight. I need to finish her gift. If I work really hard on it, I may be able to get it done in two days!

I need to call the wedding planner—Francois, apparently the best in the area—and see if he can come on Monday. Unless, hmm ... I didn't ask Becca where she wants to get married. Maybe she would prefer the gardens on our ranch, or a destination wedding. I don't care, as long as she's there and all of our close family and friends can attend. I don't want to invite everyone from "La-La Land," as Becca likes to call it. Just something small and intimate. I hope Stacey pulls through before then. My luck, we'll marry on the ninth of March and Stacey will wake up on the tenth! If she doesn't pull through in time for our wedding, I fear it will linger over us like a dark cloud. It will be kept in that damn file women have for when they need fuel during an argument. Completely-out-of-left-field shit that has nothing to do with the conversation at hand. Women are impossible.

This woman—this beautiful, sweet, lovely woman—is so bloody impossible. God, she makes me fucking crazy! She's just lying there asleep, so peaceful, so beautiful ... with that bum I'm obsessed with. I want her there so badly. It's the forbidden fruit, and I'm drawn to it more and more every day. It's because I can't have it. It's her one no-fly zone, and it's driving me mad.

"Sorry, Becca," I whisper, and pull the covers off of her. She's on her belly with her left leg bent up. I move it over more so I can fit better and give her an incredibly rude awakening. I enter her— maybe a little too harshly.

"Ugh, Grayson! Jesus, baby," she complains, but moves her right leg and gets on her knees to allow me full access to her. She's half asleep, but still willing to please me. God, that's so hot! And yet, it's because she's just as bad as I am. We have an insatiable need for each other. It's never enough. We're addicted. I've never wanted someone this much or this often in my life. She is my drug of choice, and I am hers. "Better?" she asks as she scrunches her pillow under her.

"Yes, sweetheart." I grab her hair gently, like a makeshift ponytail, and wrap it around my right hand. My left hand finds her left hip and I grasp tightly. I move inside of her slowly at first—I don't want to be completely rude. I quicken my pace and harshen the power behind my thrusts. Becca yelps lightly as I yank her head back by her hair. I squeeze her hip harder to help her keep my pace. All I can do is stare at her arse. Oh, how I want her there. I let her hair go when she comes and grasp her shoulder as I slow my pace to welcome my climax. My hands palm her arse cheeks and squeeze hard as I have my last quake. I pull out and slap her bum hard; she yelps. Mmm ... so hot. I rub her bottom to take the sting out.

Becca doesn't turn into me like she normally would. Instead, she pulls the covers over herself and continues to face the opposite direction. "Too rough, sweetheart?" I rub her back softly.

"Yes," she whispers.

"Sorry, Becca. I got myself all worked up thinking about you—that lovely arse of yours. I'm quite obsessed with it, love." I kiss her shoulder.

"Grayson, I just want to go to sleep now, please." Her voice is shaky.

"Becca, I truly am sorry."

"Yes, Grayson, I know. Please, I want to go to sleep." She moves away from me. I move closer to her, wrap my arm around her, and pull her to me. She doesn't fight. *Good girl.* I close my eyes and sleep finally comes over me.

Chapter Four

"I'll be there as soon as possible, sweetheart." I give her one final kiss. She's been a little "off," and I wish I had controlled myself last night. I tried to make up for it this morning. I was very gentle and very into pleasing her.

"Okay." Half smile.

"Please, Becca, don't leave here mad at me. I love you, sweetheart. I'm sorry I got carried away." Probably about the tenth time I've apologized today.

"I'll be okay. I'm not mad," she lies. I think I can see her slipping this event into that damn file!

"I won't do it again." I can lie, too.

"Grayson, you are getting beyond aggressive. It's making me feel very uncomfortable in more ways than one. I need you to think about that while we're apart. Is it worth our relationship to be that rough and ... and ... *cold?*" She looks like she's fighting back tears.

"I didn't think I was being cold. I felt very, very hot," I try to joke. Nothing. "Becca, are you threatening our relationship?"

"No, Grayson—you are," she says calmly, and looks down.

"Really?!" I try to stifle my sudden anger with my teeth. "Go to Boston, Becca! I'm not dealing with your shit right now! I had enough of it yesterday!" I walk away. *Impossible woman!*

Just as I reach the stairs, my phone rings. I don't recognize the number.

"Grayson here."

"Mr. James, this is Maxine Caldwell. I'm pulling up right now." She seems a bit nervous, probably because she's fifteen minutes late. I'd be irritated, but I completely forgot she was coming.

"Yes, Ms. Caldwell, I'll meet you outside." I hang up. *Shit!* I was hoping Becca would be gone by now. My fault; I forgot Maxine was coming, and I needed to have Becca one more time this morning. *God, she felt so good.* I grab my keys and head outside as Paul loads the last bag into the car.

When Maxine pulls up, I wave to her. I can feel Becca's eyes on me as I greet Maxine and get into her car. I steal a glance at Becca. She looks like she doesn't know what to think. Maxine and I head down the long driveway.

"So, it's nice to finally meet you, Mr. James." She flashes me a very toothy smile. Maxine looks to be in her early fifties, at the very least. Her hair is blonde, thick, and frizzy—poor woman. She needs a new stylist. Her navy-blue pantsuit and well-manicured nails look very professional, and she seems pleasant and motherly.

"It's nice to meet you too, Ms. Caldwell. So, how many do we have today?" I glance down at her manila folder.

"Seven total, is that okay?" She seems unsure.

"Sure, but can we look from the most favorable to least?" Shit, I have a lot to do today! I don't want to be wasting my time on this. Seven is a lot to look at.

"Oh, yes, of course. First place is right down the street here." She makes a right and we travel about a mile down the road. She takes another right and we head up a long, winding driveway.

So far, so good. We pull up to a huge plantation like home. Hmm, everything is well taken care of, well at least for winter. My cell pings. A text from Becca.

December 16, 2012   10:00 a.m.
Becca: Mr. James ... I'm sore gonna miss you :)

I can't help but laugh wholeheartedly at her comment.
"Sorry, excuse me," I say to Maxine, then text back.

Me: Are you sore ... about that?
Becca: Very SORE ... just the way you like me.
Me: Good, sweetheart.
Becca: You've stamped my ass pretty well this time too :|
Me: I'd like to do more than put my stamp on it.
Becca: You want to make that sore too, baby?
Me: Oh, Ms. Campbell, what are you playing at?????
Becca: Just a simple question. Why? Feel the need to wear purple pants?
Me: If I were u, I would stop baiting me on this matter! I have to go. This isn't the END of this conversation!
Becca: Butt ...
Me: Becca, stop! I love u. Give Stacey my love.
Becca: Love you, BBB!
Me: Ugh!
Becca: Ohhh ... God, baby ... sorry, pothole.
Me: You're impossible!
Becca: Possibly!
Me: :)

"Ready, Mr. James?" Maxine smiles as I finally put my phone away.

"I'm so sorry. That was terribly rude of me. It was my fiancée," I add, as if that may help.

"It's okay. Let's go in, shall we?" She opens the door. This place already screams *Becca*. Suddenly, I feel guilty for doing this without her. Well, I'm just narrowing it down. We'll revisit again to make our final decision together.

After hours have passed, I determine only three out of the seven are possibilities. The best one being the first, of course!

"So, we'll keep the huge colonial down the street, the farmhouse, and the colonial with the ten acres of land and the stable." She goes through the paperwork.

"Yes, sounds good." I'm itching to leave.

"When will Becca come with us to look at them again?" She pulls out her calendar.

"Well, I want to see some others before we show Becca."

"Well, Mr. James, there isn't much more that fits your criteria in this area. We'd have to look further away, and you said your fiancée wants to stay in this town." She sighs as if her hands are tied.

"Okay, I'll talk to Becca. Thanks, Maxine. I will call you and let you know when we'll be available to look again. Right now, Becca's down in Boston visiting her friend in the hospital. She'll be gone for a few days." I step out of her car.

"Okay, I'll wait for your call then and keep looking. Thanks, Mr. James. Have a great day!" She waves. I nod and close the door. I text Becca, because she left four hours ago.

December 16, 2012   2:15 p.m.
Me: Where r u?
Becca: Boston. Why?
Me: Um ... haven't heard from u.
Becca: Doesn't your staff report 2 U?

Me: Yes. But I like to hear from u!

Becca: Oh, sorry. Stacey's in surgery.

This is stupid! I call Becca.

"Hey, baby."

"Hey, surgery for what?" I grab my hidden box to start working on Becca's gift.

"They are sewing her skull back on. There's no more brain swelling." Becca yawns.

"That's good, right, sweetheart? You tired?" I smile at the family picture of us with Mickey Mouse.

"Yeah, it's really good. I just feel terrible that all this has happened. Steve hasn't returned any of my phone calls. It's so weird. I can't believe he would be like this. He loved her so much. I understand that people fall out of love, but to not even return a phone call to see how she is? That's just strange. It's not sitting well with me at all. And yes, I'm very tired. I haven't the slightest idea why." She makes a humming sound as if she's pondering.

"I'm exhausted, too. There was a beautiful woman in my bed who I needed to conquer over and over again." I chuckle.

"What do you think about the Steve thing?" She ignores my comment.

"I don't know, Becca. Maybe Stacey hasn't been very honest with you. Look, I've got to go, I'm busy." I'm very irritated. Maybe we should just stick with texts.

"Well, you called me!" *Is she for real?* "Are you still looking at houses?" she asks quickly.

"How did you know?"

"Grayson, it's a small town. I know Maxine. So, did you find anything?" Boy, she's persistent!

"Only a few. We'll look at them when you get back. Okay, love?" Love this picture of Becca and I nose to nose with our lips puckered at each other.

"Yes. Gray?"

"Yes, Becca."

"I'm sorry I got upset with you this morning. I know why you've been this way." She seems almost hesitant.

"Yeah, you going to do something about it, then?" I say, then slap myself upside the head for being a jerk.

"You know ... you are such an asshole!" she snaps, and hangs up. I call her back and get sent straight to her voicemail.

"Sweetheart, I got carried away. You're right, I'm an arsehole. I love you and I miss you. Bye. Please call me when you're done being mad." I hang up.

Back to work, Gray! I start laying everything out on the tables, trying to piece together what I want to go with what.

Claudia pokes her head in.

"Grayson, do you want anything to eat?" She seems a bit concerned.

"Oh, is it dinnertime already?" I look up.

"No, Grayson, it's ten o'clock. You haven't even taken a pee break."

"What? It can't be!" I look at my watch. "Holy shit! I honestly did not think I've been in here that long!" I'm mystified. "Yes, whatever Adam has left over, Claudia! Thank you." I smile with great appreciation.

"How is it coming along?" She bends her head to the side.

"Actually, pretty well! I have half the book done!" I'm very excited.

"Wow, that's incredible!" she says in disbelief.

"Oh, well, there's a lot of pages that don't have pictures." I let her glance. "I hope she'll like it." I'm a bit nervous. She hasn't called or texted me again all day.

"I'm sure she'll love it. You know she's crazy about you, Gray. I've never seen her like this. I know it was rocky in the beginning, but you were definitely the right choice even though you are a controlling bastard!" She laughs.

"That's it! Bastard! Ugh, Claudia, I could kiss you!" I blow her a kiss and grab my phone.

December 16, 2012   10:15 p.m.
Me: Big British Bastard?

I wait for twenty minutes. My dinner comes. Nothing.
I eat.
Still nothing.
I call Paul. He answers quickly.
"Yes, Mr. James?"
"Where is Becca?" I rub my face.
"In her suite with Melissa, sir. Do you need me to get her for you?"
"No, Paul. Thank you. What time did she leave the hospital?"
"Two hours ago, sir. Mrs. Bergman made it out of surgery just fine," he adds. He must have guessed my next question.
"Good, thank you. And Becca, how has she been today?" I can't believe I have to ask a complete stranger how my fiancée is!
"Very weepy, sir ... the whole day. I understand Mrs. Bergman is like a sister to her, and this must be very hard for her." I have a hunch Stacey's not the only cause of her weepiness.
"Thanks, Paul. Yes, she's very upset. I'm driving her crazy with my concern, which is why I thought I'd ask you instead of annoying her." I chuckle, acting as if it's the real reason.
"Oh, my wife is the same way. Well, now that you got your answers from me, you can call Mrs. James and just say good night."
That would be a great suggestion if I wasn't at the top of her shit list!
"Yes, Paul! Thanks, mate. Have a good night!"
"You too, sir." We hang up. I text Becca again.

Me: G'nite, love. Glad Stace did well today. I miss u terribly. Can you at least text me and tell me to fuck auff?

Melissa: She's asleep, sir. Thought you should know.

Me: How is she?

Melissa: Very upset, won't tell me why. Sorry. :(

Me: Thanks. G'nite.

Melissa: G'nite, sir.

I push my plate to the side and continue to work. I want to get this done and get to her ASAP. Maybe I shouldn't rush to her side. Maybe she needs this break from me. *Well, that's depressing!* I'll just do one more page, then I'll only have *one, two, three, four, and five.* Five ... that's it! Wow! I'll have this done tomorrow! I finish the page I've started and add it to the book. I pack everything up and put it away.

"Good night, Gray!" Claudia calls from the office.

"'Night." I wave to her and head up the stairs. Not looking forward to being here without Becca. I enter our room. Seems so quiet and empty. I strip down and climb into bed. Tomorrow she'll call. Tomorrow ...

December 17, 2012   8:00 p.m.

Me: Becca ... I miss you ... please.

December 18, 2012   9:00 a.m.

Me: Becca, do you not want me to come?

"Are we going, sir?" Derek pops his head into the office.

"One moment." I call Becca again. Straight to voicemail. I call Melissa.

"Sir?" She sounds nervous.

"Put her on, please."

"Sir, she's in the shower."

"Melissa, don't lie to me. Put her on." I hear her talking to

Becca.

"What, Grayson?" Becca snaps.

"Becca, I ... forget it. Morgan will be here Saturday. Will you be home by then?" I can't believe she's still this angry with me.

"I'll be home tomorrow. Will my room be done by then?" What in the hell is she talking about? "I don't want to share your room with you," she almost whispers.

"Oh! We're back to this again? Confused, Becca? Maybe you need to fuck Ray to figure things out, huh?" She hangs up. "Derek, let's go!" I'm not putting up with this shit!

BECCA

"Becca, don't cry." Melissa hugs me.

"Let's go see Stacey." I wipe my eyes and grab my purse.

"Is he coming?"

"No. Please, let's go." We leave for the hospital.

"Becca, maybe you're overreacting a bit. I don't mean to pry, but that seems to be the biggest problem with you two. You guys are so intense, in every way. When you argue, it's almost ridiculous." Okay, Melissa has become a little too comfortable.

"Geez Meliss, tell me how you really feel!" I roll my eyes. She's right, though. I pull out my cell, take a deep breath, and text.

December 18, 2012   9:22 a.m.

Me: Baby ...

Gray: On my way, sweetheart.

Me: Can't wait to see you!

Gray: Me too! I miss you so much. Any chance we can forget our behavior?

Me: It's been brought to my attention that we can be ridiculous!

Gray: Whoever said that is right! We need to stop acting like this! I love you!

Me: I agree! Love you too! BTW ... not Big British Bastard! So close, one word off!

Gray: Ugh!

"Okay, all fixed!" I smile over at Melissa.

"That quick?" She raises her eyebrows in disbelief.

"Yes, I guess we're both tired of our behavior. By the way, he said you were right, so you may want to mark that down!" I laugh as we walk into Stacey's room and find Ray. *Oh, Christ!*

"Oh ... um, I'll come back in an hour?" I ask Ray.

"Becca, we're adults. I think we can both visit Stacey at the same time." He stands up and points to the chair to the other side of her.

"This is pretty early in the day for you to be down here." I sit. "Hey, Stace, brought you some magazines and the new Jennifer Weiner book." I grab her hand and squeeze.

"I had to meet a client down here this morning," he explains when I settle in next to Stacey.

"Oh, well, that's good! Business is growing for you!" I find it hard to look at him.

"Yeah. So, I see the Brit finally put a ring on your finger."

I look down at it and over to him.

"Yes, he was designing it, that's why it took so long." And I'm explaining this to him why? *Ugh! Shut up, Becca!*

"Saw you guys in *People* magazine a month ago, as well as all the others."

I look over at him again. His hair is getting that wild look I've always loved on him.

"You need a haircut, McNeil." I smile. I miss my friend. Why does it have to be this way?

"Funny, you always loved it at this length." He smirks.

"You always say it's unprofessional."

"It is, but maybe more to me than others."

"How's Annie?" Common ground.

"Well, she's healed up nicely. She's just a bit depressed." He frowns slightly.

"Why?" I miss her so much.

"Um, let's see. The woman who was like a mom to her up and left, taking her best friend with her. You know, you could at least call or drop her a note." He's a bit upset, rightfully so. I should've kept in contact with her. That wasn't very fair of me.

"You're right, Ray. I'm sorry. I will call her tonight. I do miss her terribly. Morgan's coming home this weekend. Maybe Annie can spend a few days with us." I think Grayson may strangle me for this.

"I don't know if that's such a great idea. Maybe one day, not a few." He runs his hand through his hair and shakes his head at me.

I'm tempted to ask what the headshake is all about, but the song playing on the iPod I left in here distracts me. The Smiths are singing "Girlfriend in a Coma." I burst into a fit of giggles.

"What's so funny?"

"Listen to this song. How ironic and awful!" I continue to giggle and turn it up.

Ray chuckles a little.

"That is awful, who sings that? Bec ... oh, baby!" He gets up to comfort me when my giggles turn into sobs. Paul and Melissa jump in front of me.

"Sorry, sir. You may not approach Mrs. James," Paul states sternly.

"Her name is *Ms. Campbell*! She's not married to that asshole yet!" he says through gritted teeth, then takes in a deep breath while clenching his fists. "She has two best friends in this world. One is in that hospital bed, and the other is right here. I am approaching her as a friend who cares deeply for her!" When Paul's expression remains unchanged, he turns to Melissa. "You know I won't hurt her!"

"Sorry, Mr. McNeil. Nobody is allowed to approach her." With a stolid face, Melissa is the most professional I have ever seen her. I feel proud, like an older sister would!

"Becca, this is what you want, baby? To be treated like a prisoner?" Ray sits back down.

"I'm not a prisoner, Ray. They are just protecting me." I wipe my eyes.

"From *me*?! I would never hurt you, baby! Becs, c'mon ... this is ridiculous!" How can I possibly tell him that I do need protection from him? It wouldn't just be a hug. He would try to kiss me. They know it, especially Melissa.

"Ray?" I look up at him.

"Yeah, babe?" He sighs, defeated.

"Why did you and Stacey ... why did you have her text me those questions and behave the way she did?" My chin is quivering because, honestly, I'm still very upset about it.

"What questions?" He closes his eyes.

"McNeil!" I bite.

"Because you do stupid things when you're in love, I don't know. I'm not proud of it! Stop biting your lip, baby." He gives me a half smile. "I love it when you do that," he murmurs.

"I thought you always hated it." I shoot him a look of confusion. He flashes me his boyish grin and shakes his head.

"Becca, you are so oblivious, babe! Before we had our first kiss, think about all of the times I would thumb your lip free. You blushed and looked away every time. Damn it! I wish I would've just kissed you then instead of waiting for you to be 'ready.'" His stare is intense. "You're blushing now, baby."

"I am not!" *Yes I am, damn it!* I can feel the fucking heat rise to my face! "Now you're biting your lip, McNeil," I point out.

"Jealous?" He smiles.

"No! Stop flirting." *Yes ... maybe a little.* Christ, I need my head examined.

"Is that what I'm doing, Becs, baby?" Boyish grin again. I laugh and bite my lower lip. Ray tilts his head, his eyes making a beeline for my lips. Realizing he's caught my habit again, I bite with a bit more exaggeration and widen my eyes at him—smartass that I am. He wiggles his eyebrows at me in response.

"You are impossible! What am I going to do with you?" I shake my fists.

"Oh, baby, I can think of a few things." He licks his lips, then shoots me an air kiss and a wink. I just roll my eyes.

"So, Stacey's husband hasn't even returned a phone call to me. Isn't that strange, Ray?" *Must. Change. Subject!*

"Uh yeah, that is, Becs," he agrees, then laughs.

"What?"

"Nice left-field action there, babe!"

My cell pings.

"Excuse me." I look down at it.

December 18, 2012   10:17 a.m.

Gray: If he calls you babe or baby one more time, I'm going to lose my shit!

Me: Mr. James, your stalkerish capabilities never cease to amaze me! I'm a bit turned on by it!

Gray: Really? Very interesting! I thought you would be mad. Will definitely take turned on over pissed off any day!

Me: :)

"Let me guess. Grayson?" Ray sighs.

"Yep. He's almost here," I lie.

"Is he being good to you, Becca?" He's very sincere.

"Yes, very good, Ray. I promise. I am sorry that I hurt you," I add.

"Well, it is what it is." He gets up. "I'm going to head back up now. You'll call for Annie?" He heads over to me. Paul and Melissa step up again. "Ugh! Becs, can I just hug you goodbye?"

"Yes, it's okay," I say to them as I stand. My phone pings. I ignore it. "Bye, Ray."

"Bye, Becs." He hugs me tightly to him. "I love you. I always will," he whispers, then kisses my ear.

"Drive safe." I try to pull away. Ray stares into my eyes. He leans in to kiss me. I turn my head so his kiss lands on my cheek.

"Later, babe." And with that, he's out the door. I look at my cell and barely get to read Gray's message telling me "it wasn't okay to hug him" before it's ringing.

"Please don't yell at me." Not the usual greeting I give when I answer a phone.

"Are you okay?" He's calm, thankfully.

"It was just a hug." I nestle the phone in the crook of my shoulder as I grab a nail file out of my purse.

"First of all, I know he tried to kiss you. You were upset and crying before; that's what I'm actually asking you about."

Oh.

"I'm okay. That was not a good song to hear. I also feel bad about Annie." My heart breaks at the thought of how disappointed she must be in me right now.

"He's using her to get to you." Grayson's tone miraculously remains calm. I'm impressed!

"I don't think so. I asked about her." I start filing Stacey's nails.

"He didn't ask about Morgan."

I can feel the power behind his arched eyebrow. I see it, though it is not in front of me.

"Uh, I did notice that."

"Okay, Becs, baby, I'll be there soon, babe ... to bite your lip."

Now I sense his teasing smile.

"You're awful!" I laugh. "When will you be here?"

"I don't know, an hour maybe. I gotta go, doll—my email alert is going off like crazy." He sighs.

"Okay, I'll see you soon then, baby. Love you." I pull the nail file away from Stacey's hand to hang up.

"Love you too." The line goes silent. I throw my phone back into my purse and continue on with her nails.

"So, I need you to wake up now, lazy bones! I'm getting married March ninth and I need my best friend there! C'mon, Stace! We have so much to do!" I lean into her ear. "Stace, I'm having a baby. I need you awake!" Staring at her, I'm just filled with so much sorrow. She's thirty-five, in the middle of a divorce, and hasn't had a child yet. An uncomfortable blanket of guilt comes over me. I shouldn't have told her about the baby. "What will it be? Magazines or a book? Okay, a book it is!" I grab the book and start reading it.

I get as far as chapter six when I feel familiar hands on my shoulders. I lean my head against his arm. He bends down and kisses me.

"Hey, sweetheart. How are you, love?" Another kiss.

"Better now." I tap his hand and get up to greet him properly. He palms my face and caresses my lips sweetly. His tongue softly runs across the line between my lips, beckoning to deepen the kiss. My lips comply and he pulls me closer. We're lost in each other, and the hypnotic theatrics of our tongues lovingly greet one another. I'm sure Melissa, Derek, and Paul are a little uncomfortable, but we don't care enough to stop. Three days without each other seemed like an eternity.

"Come up for air." Barely a whisper, but loud enough to grab my attention and pull me away from Grayson.

"Stacey!" I yell, practically pushing Grayson over to get to her. She blinks and smiles.

"Drink," she whispers. I press the nurse's light.

"Oh my God, Stacey! I'm so happy you're awake!" I kiss her face. She squints, looking at me. Jen, the nurse, walks in. "Jen, she's awake!" Jen smiles and greets Stacey. I go and get her water and ask the other nurse to call the doctor.

"Hey, sweetheart." Grayson comes up behind me.

"Hey." I turn to him.

"Sweetheart, Stacey doesn't know who we are." What the hell is he talking about? "Honestly. She just asked me who we all are." He grabs the pitcher of water from me.

"Oh, this is not good on so many levels." We slowly head back to her room. This must be temporary. *It has to be!* Yes, Becca, it has to be. I'm just going to do everything I can to help her. Stay positive. Stay positive.

We walk into Stacey's room. She opens her eyes.

"So, you're my sister? Did we have different fathers, mothers, or both?"

I burst into a fit of giggles. She may not remember me, but she is still herself! I wait for Jen to leave the room.

"Both." I laugh again and pour her some water.

"What?" She takes the glass from me.

"Stacey, I am Becca Campbell and I have been your best friend since the seventh grade. We've been through it all. You are more my sister ... my family ... than anyone besides Morgan. I told them I was your sister so they would let me stay with you and assist with the medical decisions." I help her move her hair out of her face.

"Who's Morgan?" She closes her eyes again.

"My daughter, and your goddaughter. She's ten going on thirty." I show her my cell. I have several pictures on there, including one of her and Morgan.

"She's beautiful." She smiles. "Becca?"

"Yeah, Stace?" I grab her hand.

"What happened to me?" Her eyes fill and her chin quivers.

"Stace, you were attacked and brutally beaten. That's all we really know. We were waiting for you to wake up and fill in the blanks." No tears are shed alone amongst best friends. Melissa passes us the tissues. "Thanks, Meliss." I smile and take them.

"I feel like I'm in a crazy dream. I don't know who anybody is here, including me." She cries.

"That's only temporary, Mrs. Bergman." Dr. Peterson walks in, rubbing sanitizer into his hands before he shakes Stacey's.

"Mrs.? I'm married? Oh God, please tell me we're the type of best friends who marry twin brothers!" She points to Grayson. I burst into another fit of giggles.

"Oh, Stace, you are not far away at all!" I kiss her forehead and stand back so Dr. Peterson can give her a full exam.

When he checks her pupils for sensitivity to light, she grabs his wrist.

"Please, why can't I remember anything?"

"You will, Stacey. You are suffering from retrograde—or temporary—amnesia. Things will start coming back to you as soon as today, maybe. Probably long-term memories first. You may not recollect what happened to you for a while, so don't push yourself too hard trying to remember. You will when you will. You are looking great. We'll keep an eye on you for another few days here in the ICU, and then we can move you to a regular floor." He pats her hand. "If you are in pain, let Jen, your nurse, know, and she will give you something. I'll be back to check on you tomorrow. Do you have any questions?" I like this doctor. He's very relaxed and sincere. I'd try to hook them up if he was single, but he's short and furry—not really her type. I mean, *damn* he's furry! There's brown hair pouring out of every part of his scrubs! He has a kind face, though, and dark blue eyes.

"No, I'm good for now." She tries to smile. Dr. Peterson heads out the door after reminding us to have list of questions for tomorrow. *Holy shit!* Somebody call Chewbacca; I think we found his little brother!" Stacey exclaims in her usual Stacey way when she's kidding ... but not really. I'm in stitches again and not alone— everyone, except for Grayson and Melissa, is trying to compose themselves.

"Oh, Stacey, love, you'll be back to yourself in no time!" Grayson barks.

"Stace, how is it that you don't know who the hell any of us are, including yourself, and yet you know who Chewbacca is?" I shake my head.

"He's an iconic character!" she says, defending herself. "Speaking of iconic characters," she looks to Grayson, her eyes wide in amazement, "are you Australian?"

"British, sweetheart." He grabs her hand and looks at me, his eyebrow raised. I roll my eyes at him. Like I'm really going to be jealous right now!

"Oh, please tell me you're my husband, and in your deep grief you kissed my best friend. Because I will forgive you." She smiles at him.

"Oh, Stacey, a man could only dream!" He teases her ... baiting me. "Alas, I belong to your best friend. Sorry, love." He kisses her forehead.

"Oh, you missed! Right here." She taps her lips. "Sorry, Becca, I don't know you yet, therefore—no loyalty!" I roll my eyes and shake my head at her now. These two! "Ugh ... well, a girl can dream, too! So, is my husband also a nice piece of eye candy?" She seems hopeful.

"You are in the process of finding new eye candy," I offer.

"Becca!" Grayson snaps.

"What? Oh, we can only be blunt when Grayson says it's okay?" What a double standard he has!

"Becca, you told me once not to be stupid about being blunt, and I not only took that to heart, but I agree with it. And this would be a stupid time to be blunt." He sighs.

"So now I'm stupid?" I gasp.

"Oh, bloody hell, Becca! I didn't say you were stupid! I said the timing was! Open your fucking ears, sweetheart!" he yells.

"Christ! Some things never change! Would you two knock it off? You always fight over the stupidest shit!" Stacey complains. "Oh shit! I remember you guys!" She throws her open hands out in front of her excitedly.

"Great! Our arguing has jogged her memory, Gray! Wonderful! That's the 'thing' that people think about when they think of us!" I snap and walk out of the room. Melissa and Paul follow me. My cell pings. I look at it.

December 18, 2012   12:35 p.m.
Gray: Good news, sweetheart! She also remembers that I spank and you swallow! Silver lining or what? Come back please! We're having a good laugh in here! :)
Me: Fuck auff! I need to think ...

I put my phone away. Paul's cell pings. I roll my eyes as he moves to stand in front of me.

"Mrs. James, please wait."

"Ms. Campbell or Becca, please." I allow myself to extend my irritation to Paul, but he says nothing. I feel Grayson's hand at my waist.

"Come; let us have a walk together, shall we?"

Paul moves and hits the button for the elevator. Grayson's hand comes off my waist and finds my hand. We get on the elevator. He glances at me, then away, then back at me. He's holding back a smile. What is he playing at? Oh ... I know. I give him a half smile. The door opens, and we head into the lobby, then outside.

"Where shall we go, sweetheart?" Gray squeezes my hand and looks around.

"Let's just walk, baby." We head toward the pedestrian bridge and cross Storrow Drive to walk along the Charles River. It's bitterly cold, gray, and cloudy—the kind of day that makes you want to lounge around in pajamas and take a nap.

"What made you two move here?" Gray breaks the ice with something easy.

"We fell in love with Boston on our trips here. I always felt like a New Englander, though."

A Great Dane greets me out of the blue.

"Sorry, this is my first day with Sasha," the man holding her leash says. I'm guessing he's the dog walker.

"Oh, that's okay," I say to him, then turn my focus to Sasha. "Aren't you beautiful? Oh yes, you can give me kisses! You are so sweet!" I scratch her ears and offer my chin.

"Wow. You're the first person she's been like this with today!" he says in disbelief.

"Oh, well, Miss Sasha, I am very honored." I pat her bottom, and we continue on our walk after bidding the walker a good day.

"That big dog didn't intimidate you at all, sweetheart?" Grayson looks back at Sasha.

"No ... I like big animals." I give him a crooked smile.

"Yes you do, don't you?" He laughs as he walks behind me and wraps me in his arms. He leans down into my neck and kisses me. I hold his arms to me and savor this carefree moment.

"We need to have more moments like this, Gray. Everything is so serious all the time. No wonder we're at each other's throats for stupid shit." I turn to him and hug his chest. I close my eyes and take in the lovely scent that is Grayson James as I listen to the tempo of his breathing. Grayson squeezes me tight and pulls his phone out. Really—he's making a phone call?

"Ten o'clock ... number two." He hangs up. His laconic conversation makes the hairs at the back of my neck stand up. I look up at him, then follow the invisible line that leads to the area he's concentrating on. There's a guy walking away quickly. He turns his head to look back.

"Will? What the hell is he doing here?"

"That's what I'd like to know." Grayson's jawline is twitching like crazy. I can see he's running on pure adrenaline.

"Wait ... did you call him 'number two'? What does that mean, Gray?" He ignores me, still staring intently. Will is running now. "Gray, what does that mean?" I ask again with more force.

"Becca—enough! Stop asking." He's terse, but softens his tone with his next words. "Please, sweetheart, there are things I need to keep you in the dark about right now. I know it's irritating, but I'm trying to keep you safe. It's necessary, love. Trust me. Please ... don't be mad." I welcome his kisses.

"Baby ..."

"Hmm?"

"Who's number one?" I continue to kiss him.

"Oh, you naughty, naughty girl." He smiles against my lips. I think he may be onto me and my approach for information. "Let's get back to Stacey." He grabs my hand and leads the way we came.

"Gray, who's number one? What does this even mean? Gray! Grayson! Ugh—you're impossible!" I quicken my pace in an attempt to keep up with his long strides, but I have to yank his hand. "Slow down!"

He stops and waits for me to catch up, then pulls my arm around his waist as he wraps his free arm around my shoulders. He kisses my head and we begin to walk again.

"Besides all this, how are you feeling ... Mama?" He whispers the last word.

"Okay. Just tired." I lean my head into him.

"Well, we'll have a short visit and then back to the hotel for a nap, Bec. You need to rest." The elevator pings open. Maybe I suffer from amnesia—I don't even remember walking in!

Chapter Five

"What time will you be here by?" I ask Hazel as I go around our room, picking up the clothes from last night.

"By lunchtime, hopefully. We just got on the road a little while ago. Becca, how's Stacey doing?"

"She's doing great! They moved her out of the ICU and she'll be discharged in a few days. I'm in the process of setting up therapists and nursing staff." I look over the list of people I have to call on Monday.

"What time is Morgan due in?" she asks. I catch a glimpse of Grayson out of the corner of my eye. He's been extremely attentive, sweet, patient, unselfish, gentle, and unaggressive—no hint of his usual self at all. I think with Christmas being only several days away, he's minding his p's and q's.

"Um, she should be here by three. She'll be so excited to see you two! I can't wait either! Wait until you see all of the changes Gray and Claudia have made!" I try to put some enthusiasm behind my statement.

"Oh yes, I heard how thrilled you have been." She giggles.

"Oh yes, I can't wait for one of our chats!" I laugh. Grayson frowns. He can sense that I'm going to unload on Hazel, which means she will unload on him.

"Okay, dear. I'll see you in a few hours."

"Okay. Bye, Hazel." I hang up and give Grayson my full attention.

"Rocco's back, love. Shall we go see him?" He holds out his hand.

"Yes!" There's a skip in my step as I grab his hand. "Why don't we go for a ride?"

"A ride where, sweetheart?" He looks at his watch as we get to the bottom of the stairs.

"Well, we'll take the trail that has no jumps," I say thoughtfully. *Yes ... that would be the safest route.* Grayson yanks me back.

"Are you mad?" He's angry, but I can see he's trying to control himself. "You are seven weeks pregnant," he reminds me quietly.

"I know, Grayson. I did research. As long as I take it easy and don't do any jumps, I'm fine to ride up 'til twelve weeks."

"No, Becca! Not even up for discussion!" He grabs my coat and helps me into it.

"You are not the boss of me!" I lash out.

"That is my child, too." He keeps his voice low. "I don't care what the Internet says—I say no. That's final, Becca! Not another word about it!" His teeth are clenched.

"Fine." I shrug away from him and head out the door. He follows at my heels.

It smells like snow. I'm so excited! Of course, I'd like it to wait until after Hazel, Charlie, and Morgan arrive. Grayson's hand grasps mine as he walks silently beside me. We get up to the stables and I practically run to greet Rocco. He licks my arm and nudges me.

"Yes, Rocco, of course I have an apple for you!" I laugh and hug him. I grab an apple from the bin where I keep the goods. "So, is there anyone you'd like here for Christmas, baby?" I ask Grayson. I can't believe this thought just occurred to me. I know Hazel has spent the last few Christmases with us. What did he do? Are we messing up his yearly tradition?

"No." He's flat. That's it?

"Well, what do you normally do for Christmas?" I am very curious now.

"Just go away."

"Where? With who?" He leaves me no choice but to dig.

"Home to London ... by myself." He's quiet.

"What? Why? You were welcome to come here." I'm miffed. Why would anyone want to be alone for Christmas?

"I know that. Aunt Hazel invited me every year. If only I had known then what I know now." He gives me a huge, boyish, un-Grayson-like grin.

"You chose to be by yourself?" The thought makes me feel sad.

"Yes. But no more, sweetheart, so let's please move on from that subject." He sighs and looks away, almost as if he's uncomfortable. Hmm ... what's that about?

"Well, I need to get some shopping done. I haven't been able to do much at all." My brain is suddenly inundated with the list of people and no ideas. Great! No problem! I still have eight whole shopping days left and nothing else to do! Suddenly my theme song becomes "The Twelve Pains of Christmas," and my sadness returns. I never feel this way about Christmas.

"What's the matter, love? You're frowning." Grayson's fingertips graze my cheek.

"I don't like my new theme song." I tell him the title and frown some more.

"Why is that your theme song?"

"Because I have nothing done. It's so unlike me." I pat Rocco one more time. "Bye, Rocs. See you later." I start walking away.

"Well, let's get your book and go do some shopping," Grayson offers.

"Um, okay." I sigh. I've got to get started at some point! I grab Grayson's hand and we head off down the slight hill to the inn.

A blanket of panic comes over me. Not only do I have to arrange my thoughts around Christmas presents for him, but then his birthday is a week and a half later! What the fuck? I already have one gift all set. Something I know he really wants. But oh, why does he have to have everything? *Think, Becca, think!* Okay, what does he like? Oh, crap! What *does* he like? He skis, he likes cars ... yeah, I think he's good with the nine he has! This is terrible! It's because I'm panicking. *All Sybeccas are now on deck, reviewing clips of all our memories.* Music ... he's laughing at some of my theme songs. Yes, I can make him a playlist of all our songs and put them on his iPod. Hmm ... what else? I begin to laugh as a few funny gift ideas finally push their way into my head. One will have him in stitches for sure!

"What? What's so funny?" he asks as we head in.

"Oh, nothing." I try to compose myself. "Be right back." I squeeze his hand before releasing it to run upstairs. Once in our room, I grab the notebook Morgan gave me a few months ago. She saw it when she was out with Hazel and thought of me because the horse on the cover looks just like Rocco. Ha! A horse! He doesn't have one! Yay! I'll give Jerry a call later and see what he has or where I should go. I prefer a rescue, and I think Grayson would, too. Then, for his birthday, I will get all the gear for the horse. Actually, I think I'll just take him away somewhere. The skip in my step is renewed as I head back downstairs to a patiently waiting Grayson. He offers a warm smile and extends his hand out to me.

GRAYSON

"Sweetheart, it's two-thirty. Morgan will be home soon." Christ, I'm bored out of my mind! I'm never doing this again! Who are all these fucking people she's buying for?!

"I think I'm done, baby." *Oh, halle-fucking-lujah!* We make our way out of the card store and back into the mall.

"Becca!" a little blonde-haired girl screams and runs up to her.

"Annie!" Becca sounds very excited and stretches her arms wide for a hug. Oh shit ... this must be Ray's kid. Oh yes ... there he is! Like somebody went and poured sprinkles on my ice cream sundae! *I hate sprinkles ...*

"Raymond! What a pleasant surprise!" My exaggerated and enthusiastic greeting with matching smile is my special way of telling Ray to go fuck himself.

"And I was just thinking to myself, I don't think this day could get any better!" Ray smiles back. And so our pissing contest continues.

"Daddy, Morgan's coming home today!" Annie breaks our testosterone-heated glares.

"That's right! I forgot to tell you!" Ray slaps himself upside the head. Boy, would I love to do that. Except I'd be a tad bit harsher.

"Becca says I can stay overnight! Can I, Daddy, can I?" She jumps up and down.

"Uh ... um, what day were you thinking?" He finally looks at Becca, and I can see the love for her pour over him like a blanket.

"How about Friday?" Becca's gaze shifts up from Annie.

"Sounds good to me, Becs."

I know he wanted to say *baby* after that. I'd grab Becca's hand or put my arm around her to stake my claim, but I have fifty million bags in my hands.

"Okay. Why don't I pick her up from school?"

"I can drop her off. Besides, she'll need her clothes," he adds.

Becca looks at me. For what? For approval? I shrug.

"Okay." She smiles. Annie dances all around.

"How's Stacey?" Ray asks just as we're about to leave.

"She's doing well, Ray," I answer for Becca. "She'll be home with us in a few days. Too bad you haven't had the chance to visit her since she's come out of the coma." And, of course, add in a hint of my suspicion.

"Well, some of us can't take months off at a time." He sneers at me.

"Oh, Mr. McNeil, I'm always working."

He ignores me and looks at Becca again.

"Any word on George?"

"Ray ... he's dead." She says the last word quietly.

"What? When?"

I'm taken aback. He actually seems genuinely shocked. Humph.

"A week ago." She slides her hands down Annie's hair and covers her ears. "Somebody murdered him," she whispers.

"What? Why didn't you tell me? Why all the security then?"

Becca looks to me, unsure of how to answer.

"Well, Mr. McNeil, this act raises a lot of questions, and therefore we are not lowering our guard until we have all of the answers." I think that should suffice, and from the look on Ray's face, it does.

"Well, Ray, it's time for us to go get Morgan. Annie, sweetie, I can't wait until Friday." Becca hugs her again.

"Keep me posted, Becs." He mouths *baby* to her. He did that to piss me off. Obviously, I don't give him the satisfaction.

"Bye, guys!" Becca half smiles and turns.

"At some point, you two really need to quit this pissing contest."

Becca helps me pile our bags into the trunk.

"But it's so much fun, sweetheart!" I chuckle. She rolls her eyes and gets into the car.

Fifteen minutes into our commute to the airport, Becca's reticent behavior begins to unnerve me.

"What's going on in that lovely head of yours, sweetheart?" I glance over. "Becca?"

She jumps slightly and shakes her head to pull away from her thoughts.

"Sorry, baby, what did you say?"

"What are you thinking about?"

"I find it odd that Ray didn't know about George. He has friends on the force, and he knows everyone else there as well. It was a crime that had to do with my ex-husband, who kidnapped me only two months ago. I just find it very odd. Why wouldn't anybody tell him? It's public record, not a secret. What are your thoughts about that?" She looks to me, unsure.

"I was taken aback by his surprised reaction. I didn't even know he had friends on the force." I give her enough truth without divulging the complete investigation my team has going on him.

"Gray, is he number one?" Sometimes, I really wish she wasn't this bright.

"Yes, love." It's not safe to lie to her anymore.

"Do me a favor." She plays with her fingers, seemingly nervous about her impending request.

"Yes, love?" I take her hand.

"Have your team look into his ex-wife. Liz Beth ... Connors, I believe was her maiden name." She glances out the window and takes in a shaky breath.

"I'll get right on it, sweetheart, but why?" I'm intrigued. What significance would his ex-wife have to do with all of this? We have the basic info on their union, but nothing was investigated too deeply.

"I don't know if it's paranoia setting in, but I have a really, really bad feeling."

She looks at me again, and the internal battle she's fighting is all over her face. She wipes her tears, closes her eyes, and exhales her grief away as we drive through the gate of the Newfound Valley Airport.

"Are you okay, sweetheart?" I palm her face and look into her very green eyes.

"Yes. Let's go get our daughter." She nods and kisses me. I get out and head around to open her door. We walk hand in hand to where my plane is taxied.

"What the hell is the matter with Smitty?" I ask aloud as he runs out of the plane, yelling and waving to us.

"What's he saying?" Becca looks up at me.

And then we're blasted by a wave of heat.

"*Morgan!*" Becca screams as my plane sits—still taxied—on fire. She starts running toward it, shouting Morgan's name. I and my team grab her in time for the second blast, which sends more debris flying everywhere and knocks us all on our arses. "*Morgan! Morgan!*"

I can't even breathe. *Oh God ... oh God ... not Morgan ... no ... no ... no!*

Becca fights as I hold her to me. My chest is so tight. My lungs burn, yearning for a proper amount of oxygen. *I failed. I have failed the two people I love most in my life.*

"Why?! Why?" Becca screams. "Not my baby ... not my baby!" Her fist pounds my chest as she hides her face in my neck. I hold her tightly, trying to take the pain away for her. How can I, though? I was supposed to protect them. *Oh God. Oh, my Morgy girl. How did this happen? How could this happen?!*

"Sir! Sir!"

Derek is yelling to me. I look up at him, Becca crumpled in my arms on the ground.

"Morgan ... she's safe! She's in the hanger, sir! She's safe!" he yells. It takes a moment for this information to register.

"Becca! Becca—she's safe! She's safe, sweetheart!" I shake her, forcing her to focus on what I'm saying.

"Let's go! Let's go! Let's go!" Derek yells. He, Melissa, Paul, and Ryan help us up and run us to the hanger.

"Mommy! Daddy!" Morgan cries. Becca and I both bolt for her. I grab her and lift her off the ground to look at her.

"Oh, Morgy girl, we were so scared!" I hug her.

"Gray, put her down!" Becca grabs her from me. I bring her back down to the ground and Becca grabs her fiercely. She kisses her face, hugs her, checks her over, and kisses her again.

"Oh, my baby! Thank you, God! Morgan ... oh, Morgan!" She crushes her daughter to her chest, and my emotions shift in an instant from relief to complete crazy anger!

"What the *fuck* just happened?" I scream at my team. "How the hell did my plane explode? My daughter could've been killed!" I am officially a madman.

"Sir, we don't know. I'm sorry. The plane was swept before takeoff." Derek looks nervous and mad at the same time.

"I want to know who exactly did the sweep. Conduct a massive investigation on that person, as well as anyone else who set foot in my plane!" I yell. "What's the status on Smitty?" I bark, glancing over to the window for any indication of what may be going on.

"EMTs have him. He's alive. They're taking him to the hospital now." Derek feeds me the information as he gets it in his earpiece.

"Tanya, how did you and Morgan end up in the hanger?" Becca asks, taking her hand now that she's finally got herself under control.

"Divine intervention, Becca. Thank you, sweet Jesus!" She does the sign of the cross.

"What do you mean?" I ask her gently, though I'm a bit annoyed at her explanation to Becca.

"To be blunt, sir, I got my period. I had nothing on me, and you had nothing on the plane. I couldn't wait any longer, so I broke protocol and took Morgan and myself off the plane before your arrival to see if there was something in the bathrooms here."

"Holy shit, Tanya!" Becca stares at her, the disbelief on her face probably matching my own look.

"Good day to be a woman, aye, love?" I ask her.

"It's a great day to be a woman, sir!" She offers the hugest smile I've ever seen in my life!

"Was there anyone else on the plane?" I feel terrible that I didn't think to ask this before now.

"No, sir." Tanya shakes her head.

For the next hour or so, we are inundated with questions from the police while reporters have a field day outside the gates of the airport. We're finally given the okay to head home. My phone rings as we get into the back of the Range Rover.

"Thanks for driving, Derek." Becca pats his shoulder.

"No problem, Mrs. James," he says as I answer the phone.

"Hallo?"

"Grayson, are you guys okay? What the fuck happened, man?" I can't believe my ears. *Ray*, I mouth to Becca.

"We're fine, Ray. A little shaken up, that's all." Hmm ... this is interesting.

"Is Morgan all right?"

"Yes, Ray. Luckily, she was off the plane when it happened."

"Becca?"

"Shaken up, but okay. Thanks for calling, Ray." I'm flat.

"Grayson, despite everything that's happened, you know I care about Becca and Morgan very much, right? Please, if I can help in any way, let me know." He actually sounds very sincere. I find myself debating whether this is an act or not.

"Will do! Again, thanks for calling." I hang up.

"Well, I haven't heard you two act that pleasant toward each other since the day you first met." Becca seems shocked.

"He was concerned. Wanted to make sure you two were okay, and ask if he can help in any way." I'm anxious to see what she makes of this phone call.

"Interesting, huh?" Her eyebrow darts up

"My sentiments exactly." I grab her hand and squeeze, then lay my head back and close my eyes. I feel wiped out from the massive adrenaline rush ... this is not the kind one looks for—it wasn't exhilarating at all! I think I can honestly claim that my life was boring before I met Becca Campbell. There were only red carpets, awards, traveling around the world, mindless women, and more money than I knew what to do with! Now my life is surrounded by impossible, intelligent women, kidnappings, explosions, murder, assaults, jealousy, rage, and ... love.

"Gray? Baby?" I open my eyes to find her beautiful green ones looking at me.

"Yes, love?"

"Thank you." I feel her lips on the back of my hand. How can she be thanking me? I've barely protected them! By the skin of my teeth and sheer luck, I have been able to keep them safe. I don't know what to say. There are no words. I just give her hand another squeeze and close my eyes again.

BECCA

It's been three days since the explosion. We've all been on edge—Grayson most of all. I've seen him ultra-focused before, but there is no pulling him out of "The Zone" this time. I'm really worried about him. We all are. I've even locked my smart mouth up and put it on a shelf (not an easy feat for me). He has security beefed up so much, I can barely breathe. We can't go anywhere. I have a team of seven surrounding me just to walk up to my stable to visit Rocco.

He has a security team on the horses as well! I feel the need to apologize to them every time I go out there. This is all very stifling. I just keep telling myself that it's temporary. Only problem is, I don't have any idea how long "temporary" actually is. Grayson is still keeping me in the dark. I thought that would've changed, given our conversation before the explosion, but alas, any hope of disclosure went up in flames with his plane!

The sun slowly brings us out of darkness. Seven sharp and Grayson, surprisingly, is still asleep. This is the only time he looks fully at peace. All of his worries are erased from his face at night, only to be repainted the next day. He is quite the sight. Straight nose, long lashes, a strong but not overpowering chin. He hasn't shaved in a few days. He looks very rugged—and still beautiful. I love his lips. I love how they frown during dictation of some words. I kiss the beauty mark under his left eye. That usually has such a calming effect on him. Not lately, though. Now, nothing seems to fully calm him down.

"How long are you going to stare at me, sweetheart?" He offers a slight smile, his eyes still closed.

"Forever." I nudge his lips with mine gently. "I miss you," I whisper against them.

"What do you mean, Becca? I'm here, love." He opens his eyes.

"Yes, I know. I miss hearing you laughing and joking around. I just want this nightmare to be over. I would like to go on with our un-normal normal lives." I let my smile hit my eyes, hoping it will provoke one from him.

"I'm trying, sweetheart." He rubs his face.

"Oh, Grayson, I know you are! You're working very hard! You're amazing!"

"Amazing? I thought I was incredible." His eyebrow shoots up and his lips twist into a smirk.

"Oh, no, you're amazing." I trail my fingers down and under

the blankets and wrap them around his already growing member. "And he's incredible." I offer a mischievous grin and slowly follow the path my fingers took with my lips. I listen to Grayson take in a sharp breath as I fill my mouth with him.

"Oh God, Becca! Oh ... sweet ... heart." His pelvis goes wild under my touch. Within ten minutes or so, I have him spilling his last drop. Grayson's breathing is erratic as I climb up his body.

"I love you, baby, and I appreciate everything you are doing to keep us safe," I whisper in his ear.

"Well, I do love how you show your appreciation, Ms. Campbell." I can feel his smile up against my hair. "Would you like to shower with me, Becca?" He pats my bottom.

"I'd love to," I say, and we climb out of bed and head into the bathroom.

"Gray ..." I sigh as he turns the shower on. I've decided to be brave and risk having an argument.

"Hmm?" He stands under the hot water first. I think he's trying to wash away some of his worry.

"Any chance you are willing to update me on any of the information you've received on anything?" At this point, I will take any bit of information, no matter how small. Grayson exhales a rather large breath. I'm not quite sure if it's laced with annoyance, reluctance, or resolve. I decide patience is my best chance at pushing him toward resolve.

"Becca ... unfortunately, most of the information we do have is all circumstantial. There are no new leads, baby. I'm telling you the truth. I wish I was closer to an answer. This is all driving me mad." Of course, my ADD and I just focus on the fact that he called me *baby*. It still sounds foreign from him ... pun not intended. It's not his usual endearment, but it's sacred to me, so he does tend to use it every so often to make sure I get his sincerity. I do. Such a funny little common word to hold such significance to me. I'm sure it would seem very silly to others. But to each his own.

"What about Liz?" I change tactics slightly instead of mentioning that he has not briefed me on any of the circumstantial information.

"Oh yes, sweetheart, I meant to tell you that we did get a trail on her and I will actually be updated on that today. I promise to tell you about the info I receive on that, love. Okay?" He pulls me to him and searches my eyes. I nod, knowing his look is to make sure I trust him. How could I not? I hate that he keeps me in the dark, but he's probably the only person in the world I'd allow to lead me blind through anything. That's how much faith and trust I have in him. I love him. I reach up and play with the stubble of his light beard. "I'll shave it today, sweetheart." He grabs my hand.

"It's okay. I like it if you want to keep it." I smile and get on my tippy toes to kiss him. He bends down to help me out with that. I open my mouth at the beckoning of his tongue and, within moments, we are lost in each other—our favorite place to be lost.

Grayson is in the crop room—or the "crap room," as I like to call it, since it is the official headquarters of our shitstorm—getting his morning debriefing. Well, his second, more professional one. A mental chuckle as I give a high five to Horny Sybecca.

"Hey, Becca, would you like some help with breakfast?" Hazel rubs my back as I watch Grayson. I turn and smile at her. I think we are both desperate for the old days of her and I doing all of the hustle and bustle around here.

"Yes. What shall we make this morning, Mum?" I turn and put my arm around her shoulders as we head into the kitchen.

"Hmm ... what shall we make? A little bit of this and a little bit of that?" She winks as she pulls leftovers out of the fridge.

"Sounds like a plan!" I get the bowls and cutting boards. "Let's work our magic!" We dive into chopping, mixing, baking, frying, and reheating to create a smorgasbord of delectable breakfast items.

"Becca?" Hazel stops whipping the eggs.

"Yes?" I ask as I wipe down the section of counter that I'm working on.

"You are aware ... no, how could you be?" She shakes her head.

"What?"

"Gracie has been out of sorts, but it's not just because of everything that's going on right now," she leads.

"Hmm ... his parents?" I look up.

"Yes. Well, especially my sister."

I note the blanket of sadness that covers her face.

"Hazel, is that why Grayson's gone home to London the past few years by himself for Christmas?"

"Yes, I think. He always tells me he's spending it with friends, but, well, he's not the only one with *people*." She taps her finger on the counter and widens her eyes. "He forgets I raised him there in that house from when he was fifteen 'til he went to university! I'm still friendly with the neighbors. Well, the ones that who haven't moved away or died," she adds.

"Well, what did he do?" A mixture of curiosity and sadness overcomes me. Hazel shrugs.

"He had a tree lit. My friends could see that. Other than that, who knows?"

"He did mention last week that he went home by himself, but he didn't really want to discuss it. Do you think he wishes we were in London?" I never even thought of that. I thought the other option was California, and I was pretty adamant about having Christmas here in New Hampshire. I feel guilty and selfish—not a good combo at all.

"Oh, I don't know, Becca. He's kind of hard to read these days." She sighs and starts the omelets.

"Well, should I ask him? What should I do?" I follow her over to the stove.

"I don't know. Even if he wanted to, I don't think he'd move us all to London right now. It's just too much. There's a lot going on, sweetie." Well, she's no help! Usually she thinks she has the answers to everything!

I prep the coffeemaker and hit the brew button.

"I'll be right back." I sigh and head out of the kitchen. I need to find him. I need to know.

The meeting is over. He's not in the office, lounge, or dining room. Huh ... maybe he's upstairs. I turn to head up.

"Becca," Melissa says quietly. I turn to her. "If you're looking for Grayson, he's in the stockroom. He's been in there for about fifteen minutes." I can tell from her face that she's worried about him, even though he fires her like every other week.

"Oh, thanks, Meliss." I can't help but furrow my brow. I head over to the stockroom and quietly walk in. I find Grayson in a corner with his back turned, his shoulders shaking. His left hand is on the wall, bracing him, and he has his right hand up by his face. I'm not sure what I should do. It looks like a very private moment, and he may be embarrassed by my intrusion. On the other hand, I am his fiancée, and he may find my presence comforting and much needed. I decide to go with the other hand.

"Baby?" I slide my arms around his waist from behind and kiss his back. I feel him freeze at my touch. *Oh ... maybe I was wrong.* I look to my right and notice two boxes on top of each other that haven't been unpacked yet. They're small and may just give me the leverage I need.

"What are you doing, sweetheart?" He glances quickly as I step up on them. "Jesus, Becca!"

He gasps when I lose but regain my balance. I pull him to me. He keeps his gaze down. I palm his face and bring it up to look into mine.

"You're not alone, Grayson. I am here to carry these burdens with you. I want to, because I love you. I cherish you. You're not alone, baby. I'm right here." I capture his lips with mine, and he pulls me into a fierce hug. We stand there for at least ten minutes, just holding each other in the safety of my stockroom. I can't help but allow a few giggles to release.

"What's with the giggles, sweetheart?" Grayson looks up at me.

"I was just getting a flashback of our many interesting moments in this very stockroom, Mr. James." I smile down at him. This brings a matching one to his lips.

"Yes, how is it that we've managed to leave this room shag-free when our sexual tension was always the highest in here at the beginning?"

"I don't know. That is interesting, though. Shall we christen it now?" I raise my eyebrows for emphasis.

"No. I don't think we should, sweetheart, at least not yet. There's something sacred and humbling, if you will, about it."

"Hmm ... I think you're right." I let him help me down. "Hungry, baby?" I lean toward the kitchen.

"For?" He pulls me back.

"Breakfast ... in bed." I add the last bit when I find his eyes searching mine. Cue erratic breathing.

"Sounds delicious, love." He thumbs my lip away from my teeth.

"Okay. Come!" I lead him again.

"Oh ... I will, sweetheart," he states, and follows up with a smack on my ass. *Mmm ...*

As Grayson and I lay in our post-coital afterglow, I find my mind racing at the speed of light. My bet is that the raging HGH levels are causing the increased tempo of my thoughts. I allow them to race instead of pushing them away, but do try to maintain some order in the process.

I know Grayson loves me, but man, I can't believe he hasn't gone screaming for the hills yet. I mean, what a guy! *People* magazine has no idea just how right they were in calling him the "Sexiest Man Alive"! If they only knew the depth to his sexiness, he would surely be the number-one pick for the next decade. Still, my life is a lot for anyone to take in, and I can't help but wonder if there is some resentment under there, waiting to boil over.

Then there's the matter of George's partner being somebody that has an unhealthy crush on me. I'll allow the mental eye roll. It just doesn't seem possible anymore. Maybe it was at one point, but to go as far as blowing up Grayson's plane trying to kill my daughter? That no longer screams *obsessive crush* to me. I can't help wonder if maybe it was coincidental. Maybe Grayson and his team are so focused on who is trying to get to me, they haven't even thought of who may be trying to get to him. He does travel in a way more affluent circle than me. Certainly a silent enemy of his would be more able to afford these tactics than a local guy who has a crush on me. Maybe there is a connection between the two!

And where the hell is Steve? Has Gray even looked into his whereabouts? I do wish he would fill me in on what they know and which roads they've gone down. I'm tired of playing the damsel in distress. It's not a part that sits very well with me. I might actually be of some help here! I have mentioned things on various topics that he has admitted to not even considering. So why won't he let me try to help?

"Tell me, Nancy Drew ... have you solved the case yet?" Grayson teases as he props himself up on his elbow. I can't help but giggle a bit. God, he knows me so well! "I can see you are trying to figure something out. It's all over your face. It looks like a real humdinger!" He grabs my nose gently and lightly shakes my head before he plants a kiss on my lips.

"Humdinger, huh? That does sound serious!" I prop myself up

as well.

"So, what were you working on in that beautiful little mind of yours?" His fingers caress my cheek.

"First, I'd like to bring to your attention that if I didn't know you any better, I could easily assume you mean that I have a small, schizophrenic mind," I tease. He offers me the eye roll I probably deserve.

"Well, come out with it already!" he nudges. I fear his playful tone will dissipate shortly.

"Okay!" I say, and take in a deep breath. Here goes nothing! "I was just wondering if you guys have looked at every possible angle." I so do not deserve the second eye roll! I slap his arm.

"Ugh, Becca! Congratulations, sweetheart, for lasting three whole magnificent days before nagging me about any of this! Okay. Come now, let me have it! Enlighten me please, Ms. Nancy Drew!"

"Mr. Holmes! Please refrain from talking to me in that belittling manner! I am quite the erudite woman, and you should feel honored that I am willing to allow such an arrogant audience!" I offer him my best English accent.

"That was very good, love! Have you been practicing?"

"Yes. I am English-fluent now." I smile.

"English-fluent? Not fluent in English?" He laughs.

"Yes, that's right." I smirk. "Oh, Mr. Holmes, please stop sidetracking me!" I add.

"Okay, love, what are the angles you believe we haven't looked at?" I sense the humor in him humoring me. I'll take what I can get ... I guess.

"Well, have you guys looked into Steve's whereabouts? It seems very odd that I haven't been able to get ahold of him."

"Uh ... um."

Hmm ... that's what I thought.

"Have you made a list of people who may have it in for you?" I ask. His lips part as if he wants to say something. "It may be coincidental that your plane exploded while we are investigating my ex-husband, his murder, and Stacey's assault. Maybe one has nothing to do with the other. Maybe there is a link between the two. I just don't think the guys around here have enough financial backing or know-how to pull off a stunt like that." I may have said that all in one breath.

"Done?" He arches his eyebrow just to be sure.

"Yeah ... I think so." I double-check mentally.

"Yes. We have considered the possibility that the plane's explosion was caused by someone who is out to get me. We are looking into several people. We have not looked into Steve, at least not in depth. That is a good point, sweetheart, and I will mention it to Greg Thomas today." He's courteous enough to finish his last sentence before he distracts me with his index finger. My skin prickles at the slight graze of it traveling down my neck and across my right clavicle.

I close my eyes at his touch. *Damn it!*

"I can't keep you in the dark for long, can I?" he asks, and I open my eyes again to look into his. "You are truly quite the intelligent woman ... and. I. Find. It. Rather ... sexy," he musters between kisses.

"Mr. James, are you trying to use your favorite method of distraction again?" I bait him.

"Yes. For me, love, you are far more interesting and mysterious then all of this other business."

"Oh, Mr. James, surely you don't find me mysterious anymore?" I giggle and bite the finger he traces my lips with.

"Always, sweetheart, and I love that about you—there's always a surprise up your sleeve for me." He pulls his finger away and bites my lip playfully.

"Anotha go, aye, Gov'na?" I do my best chimney-sweeper-from-*Mary-Poppins* accent. Grayson gives my imitation a good laugh. It's quite the glimpse of my usual company.

"Oh, sweetheart, I could have a go at you all day!"

"Please, sir ... can I have s'more?" I give him a little Oliver Twist as he slowly hovers over me, parting my legs with his.

"S'more of this, Becca?" His face turns serious as he enters me with one powerful thrust.

"Oh ... Gray!" I practically cry. *Sybecca, the class clown, returns to her seat. Country Sybecca raises her hand to take over—no sign of her Daisy Dukes anywhere!*

"Focus, Becca!"

I gasp as Grayson grabs a fistful of my hair and tilts my mouth up to his. Aggressive Grayson is back, and he's absolutely devouring me. He pulls my left leg up to get more leverage and sinks deeper inside me. His thrusts are slow and powerful all at once—I can barely catch my breath. With his mouth still locked to mine, his tongue explores urgently. I realize in this moment that he's most definitely trying to get lost in me again.

I thread my hands into his hair and tug, encouraging him to escape his reality. I feel myself climb and climb, and finally I have to pull away from his lips to pray. His mouth finds mine again right away, muffling my sounds. I squeeze around him tightly, beckoning him to follow my lead.

"No, Bec ... argh! Damn it!" He grits his teeth and comes undone—angrily, I think.

"Gray?" I'm breathless and worried.

"Yes, Becca?" It sounds like he's trying to catch his breath as well.

"Are you okay?" I kiss his sweaty head.

"Yes, sweetheart." He lifts his head and offers me a playful smirk.

"You seemed angry." I lay my head back, relieved.

"What time is the visiting nurse coming to meet Stacey?" He climbs off and lies on his back.

"Um, Stacy will be here by two, and Melanie is due at three."

He knows this. He's trying to avoid my comment. I wish I could say he's been all over the place the past few days, but he hasn't. Maybe a little withdrawn, which, of course, makes me very nervous. I can't help but feel that maybe he wants to be done with all of this ... with me. Every time that thought comes up, I feel a pang in my heart and I can barely catch my breath.

"Well, we should get up and at 'em. I'm going to head into the shower, unless you want to go first."

What?

"Um, can I go?" I feel tears sting my eyes, feel my nostrils flare. I don't know if it works, but Ray was right—I definitely do it to try to keep from crying. I turn away so Grayson won't see my face, then climb out of bed. I grab my robe and hurry to the bathroom. I can feel his eyes on me the whole way.

Between the iPod and the shower, I feel confident enough to release my sobs. I know being almost eight weeks pregnant is a big reason behind my emotional roller coaster, but the knowledge doesn't lessen the blow of my insecurities at all. He was ready to walk away from me a few weeks ago because he'd had enough. Maybe he's only staying now because of the baby. Maybe if I wasn't pregnant, he'd be running for the hills. *Cautionary Sybecca holds up an electronic ticker board. She looks away, pretending to whistle as the words "I TOLD YOU SO ..." run across it.* Shut up, bitch! Didn't you resign like two months ago?!

I make the water hotter now that I've gotten acclimated to the temperature. This is what I always do to wash away the difficult thoughts and frustrations of life. I sterilize them—or, at least, I like to think I do. One might see it as me trying to drown standing up, or boil myself to death.

"Becca!" Grayson pulls me back. When the hell did he come in here? "That's not good for the baby!" He turns the cold water up.

"Hot baths, not good for baby—hot showers, not a problem," I correct him.

"Your face is red." He lifts my chin and inspects me.

"Hot water." I point to the showerhead.

"Washing your eyes out with hot water as well, sweetheart?" He raises an eyebrow quizzically.

"Allergies," I offer.

"In December?"

"Dust." I look down.

"In the shower?"

"Soap in my eyes?"

"You're a terrible liar." He pecks my lips. "Let's wash. We'll talk after."

He grabs my facecloth and lathers it up. He gently starts with my left arm and works up to my shoulder, over my clavicle, around my neck, and over to the other side. Next he washes my breasts, ribs, and down to my belly, which is already beginning to swell a little. *Goodbye, size eight! It was nice to visit with you for a minute!* Down my left leg and up my right. He coerces me to turn, then washes my back. I lean against the shower wall for support.

"Shit, sweetheart, there is something incredible happening in here," he whispers against my neck. My backside feels the evidence. "I may have to take you like this." He follows the words with a nip to my earlobe. I gasp. Pretty sure it's a result of the nip and the feeling of him washing me between my legs. He drops the facecloth and brings the showerhead down to rinse me there. I'm almost waiting, no I am waiting for him to do something wicked and naughty like he did the last time he brought the showerhead down to rinse me. I brace myself, unable to contain my smirk—until I hear him place it back in its home.

Oh. Mental disappointed sigh. Grayson's right arm hooks around my waist from behind. His left hand reaches to the inside of my left thigh, pulling my leg up so that my foot sits on the soap shelf.

"Ugh!" I gasp again as he enters me harshly.

"Becca, sweetheart, I'm going to fuck you senseless now ... ready, baby?" *Baby ... it's sacred.*

"Yes." Before the "s" comes out of my mouth, he's off like someone shot the gun at the races. All I can do is try to concentrate on keeping my head from smashing into the tile. I'm sure rendering me unconscious is not what he meant by "fucking me senseless." In the midst of his fun, I draw up plans to install "fuck me" bars on the wall. I am all about standards in safety and the prevention of accidents caused by intense sexual acts!

"Jesus ... Becca ... God!" He bites my shoulder and slams into me one last time. *Um ... yeah ... thanks for coming in!* Would've joined you, but I was busy at a safety meeting.

He pulls out and releases me. *I'll just stand here for another minute, holding the wall up.* I suddenly feel the sting from him swatting my ass.

Grayson starts whistling as he washes himself. I half expect a faithful pup to roam into the bathroom with either his slippers or the paper. I suddenly feel crazy. Well ... it's more of a sudden acceptance of the probability that I am crazy.

"Take a Chance on Me" by Erasure comes on, and Grayson starts singing it. I open one eye mid–shampoo lather to catch a glimpse of him. He's dancing around. He smiles at me and grabs my hands, then starts dancing with me in the shower while sere-nading me. I find it hard to suppress my giggles. I'm not crazy ... he fucked himself senseless ... er, I mean I did ... oh, whatever! We both laugh as we dance and sing together in the shower—a well-de-served moment and a great memory in the making. The song comes to an end and we are in each other's embrace, staring into each other's eyes. His happiness is still evident in the corners of them.

"I love you, Grayson Michael James. You make me so happy. I feel so safe and so loved in your arms. You are my ever after."

"Geez ... it was just a dance, lady!" He rolls his eyes, then laughs. "Aww, Becca, you have to know I'm wild about you.

There's not a day that goes by where I don't feel grateful to have you in my life, to have your love, your faith ... your trust. I'm so afraid of losing you, sweetheart. If you ever left me, if anything ever happened to you," he inhales deeply, "you might as well cut my lungs out. I wouldn't be able to breathe anyway." His lips form an "O" as he looks up and exhales steadily. He's blinking in an "I'm passionate about what I'm saying" kind of way. I can see he's fighting back tears. I palm his face and pull his mouth to mine. My tongue encourages his lips to part enough for its entrance. I deepen the kiss with every bit of passion I can muster. It's my way of saying, *Everything is going to be okay, baby, I promise*. He crushes my body to his and we are lost in our kiss.

"Bloody hell, Becca! I think I got some of your shampoo in my eye!" He pushes me gently to the side to rinse his face. Who knew that shampoo not only washes away dirt, but also special moments?

"Sorry, an impromptu dance derailed me from rinsing." I nudge him with my hip.

"Well, let's see what we can do about that." He grabs the showerhead and begins to rinse my hair out.

"Do you want to talk about why you were upset?" Grayson looks up sheepishly as he buttons his jeans. I'm too busy biting my lip to prevent a drooling incident to answer him. He is fucking hot just standing there in his jeans and nothing else.

"Baby, you are quite the magnificent specimen. And no, let's just chuck it up to hormones." Honestly, what he said in the shower squashed my rising insecurities.

"You sure, sweetheart?" He reaches out and takes my hand.

"Yes." I look up at him. He completely towers over me. I love it, which is a bit odd for me. I never thought about height as a point of attraction. Then again, I'm not the same Becca from so long ago, the one who contemplated what she was interested in. For seven years, I turned those thoughts off or buried them. I'm not quite sure, but my preferences in the opposite sex were just not a thought that ever occurred to me. Obviously, I noted when a guy was good-looking, but it was just an observation. There was nothing behind it.

"So, I'm a magnificent specimen, huh?" He leans down and sweeps my lips with his.

"Yes, Mr. James. You are absolutely breathtaking. I could look at you all day." I hug him and fight off the urge to outline every muscle on his chest with my tongue.

"The feeling is mutual, Ms. Campbell, especially now with your slightly swollen belly." He places his hand there.

"Oh. You've noticed?" I can't hide my disappointment. I thought only I could see it.

"You're my favorite subject, Becca. I notice everything about you. Especially your body. I love seeing this." He kneels down and plants soft wet kisses all over it. "Becca!" he says sharply, and sits back on his heels. "You haven't told anyone, have you?" He almost seems panicked. Does he not want anyone to know? *My newest member, Insecure Sybecca, paces and bites her nails.*

"No, baby, why?" I thought he wanted this.

"No one at all?"

Whenever he says *at all* in an urgent matter, it sounds like *a tall*—it's so cute! God, I love his accent!

"Becca!" he snaps.

"Uh, sorry, no. Well ..." I wince.

"Well, what?" He stands and chucks my chin so I look up at him.

"I told Stacey."

"*Jesus H. Christ!*" he yells, then and runs his hand through his hair as he walks away from me.

"Grayson, I thought you wanted this. You're confusing me!" I meant to yell that last sentence, but instead, I'm crying. I feel like a blubbering idiot. *Fucking hormones!*

"Oh, sweetheart, no, don't cry. C'mere." He pulls me into his arms. "Of course I want this baby. I just ... Becca, with everything going on, it's best if no one knows about the little one." He palms my belly again. "Not until we're out of danger, sweetheart. Ugh, damn it." He lays his forehead on mine. "What did she say?"

"Nothing, baby. She was still in a coma. You didn't let me finish." I sigh, finding his sudden laughter peculiar.

"Oh, baby, you drive me mad! Honestly, Becca!" He shakes his head and captures my lips. He's calling me *baby* a lot. It's starting to sound more natural from him, and I like it. I wrap my arms around his neck and deepen the kiss.

Chapter Six

Hazel greets me at the bottom of the stairs like I'm her teenaged daughter coming in ten minutes past curfew. Her arched eyebrows ask, *What do you have to say for yourself, young lady?*

"I'm a devout Christian, Hazel. I like to pray every chance I get." I smirk playfully. She shakes her head at me, unable to hide her amusement. "Have you found Jesus yet, Hazel?" I ask in the most serious tone I can muster.

"Oh, Becca, what happened to my good girl? You're so naughty!" She swats my arm as we walk, but then releases a giggle against her will.

"Your nephew happened. You did have a hand in raising him. So, this must be all your fault!" I grab the piece of paper she's holding. "What's this?" I go to unfold it.

"Wait, let's go into the kitchen." She looks around nervously.

Apparently, she didn't receive the memo that we have a security team of twenty-five, give or take ... we are definitely being followed!

"Okay. Open it." She nods as we get into the kitchen. I walk over to the island as I do so. It's an itinerary of the few days before Christmas.

December 22nd Scottish Shortbread

   Fresh evergreens

   Ornaments

December 23rd Chocolate chip and peanut butter cookies

   Mincemeat pies

   Apple and Lancashire cheese pie

   Pumpkin bread

   Treacle tart

   Bakewell Tart

   Great British Pudding

December 24th Lasagna, sausage, and meatballs

December 25th Full British Breakfast

   Sausage, egg, bacon, and beans

   2:00 p.m. Dinner and Christmas crackers

   6:00 p.m. Christmas Tea

At least one hour of Christmas carols a night!

"What is this?" I look to Hazel.

"I was looking through a box of pictures to try and find a picture of Gracie with my sister to frame for him here. I came across this. I had him tell me everything they did for Christmas so I could keep it the same for him. When he went off to university, he didn't want to do it anymore." She shrugs.

"Well, I would like to incorporate as much of these into our traditions as possible. Let's just do it!" I smile. Hazel nods and she starts making a list of things we'll need while I get on the Internet to search for any British food stores. "Ugh, we have to get down to Nashua!" I show her the page for the British Aisles food store. "He's not going to let me go unless he knows exactly where I am." I lean my face on my fisted hand.

"We'll say we're going to the outlets down there. I'll ask him." She taps the counter with her finger ... she means business.

"What are you two hens up to?"

I jump at Grayson's voice and quickly click out of the website. I close the laptop as nonchalantly as I can.

"We were just discussing the Merrimack Premium Outlets. They opened this year. We haven't been yet." I slowly turn in his direction. *Shit!* He's looking from me to the laptop. I pretend not to notice and turn my gaze to Hazel.

"Yes. Gracie, Becca and I would like to go to finish up our Christmas shopping." Oh man, she totally hates this. Having to ask her nephew for permission? I'm right there with ya, sister!

"Becca's done with her shopping, Auntie." He looks back to me. Why is he so suspicious?

"Well, I have one more thing I need to get for you," I say quickly. Maybe too quickly.

"And I have several items I need to get, Gracie," Hazel pipes up.

"Becca, the only thing I want is you here safe. The answer is no. That goes for you too, Auntie." Why is it that when he looks at me and tells me no, he's abrupt and his jawline is twitching, but when he tells his aunt, he softens up? It's infuriating. Kinda hot ... but infuriating!

"Oh, Gracie, you're overreacting!" Hazel snaps. Uh-oh. *All Sybeccas put their earplugs in and hold on to anything nailed to the floor. Cautionary Sybecca locks herself in the panic room.*

"*Overreacting?!* Aunt Hazel, my fiancée was kidnapped by her abusive ex-husband, who was then *murdered!* Stacey was raped and practically beaten to death, and somebody placed a bomb on my plane that *blew* it to smithereens. They almost killed our *daughta!* I am not *overreacting!* If you disagree, well, then *tough shit!* The *ansa* is *no!* I'm not losing anybody else that I love!" He slams a cabinet shut—Hazel must've opened it to get tea earlier.

Man, he is so angry! That sounded *extra* British. I may need a panty change. I'm so focused on Hazel's reaction that I don't notice Grayson approaching me until I breathe him in and feel his chest against my shoulder.

"Now, Becca, why don't you show me what you were looking at?" he snaps. Cue erratic breathing ... *damn it!* "Feeling nervous, sweetheart?" he asks as he leans down and opens the laptop.

"No, Mr. Holmes." I whisper my new pet name for him. "I'm feeling like I want to fuck the shit out of you." I nip at his earlobe as he takes in a sharp breath. A slow smile starts to form at his lips, but he manages to control it.

"Let's see, what do we have here?" He works at retrieving the last thing I did.

I suck at his earlobe. "You sounded extra British, and you know what that does to me, baby."

"Email or website?" He's terse. I grasp his face with my hands to make him look at me.

"Stop, baby." I kiss him.

"*Ansa me!*" he yells, making me jump. I can't help my quizzical look. What is this about? "Email or website?" he demands, all up in my face this time. *I know what this is!* I no longer want in his pants. I want to *kick him* in his pants! "Email, I guess!" he says through his teeth and starts to investigate there. I get up and realize Hazel has already left. I follow her example.

I have two hours before Stacey gets here. Morgan's out riding with her team around her; that can't be much fun. It's been a roller-coaster morning. I decide to take a nap in Morgan's bed.

"Melissa, I'm going to go lay in Morgan's room. Tell her to please not come in." I grab the spare key to her room.

"Okay, Bec. Are you all right?"

"Just tired." I smile and head off to her room. I lock the door and pull off my jeans. I pass out as soon as my head hits the pillow, defeated. He'll never trust me.

GRAYSON

"Where's Becca?" Aunt Hazel asks from behind me. "What are you doing?"

"I'm checking her deleted emails. She left." I can't believe she's taking emails from him. Wait, maybe she sent him one!

"She wasn't looking at any emails, Grayson. She was looking at a website for a British food store so she could have all of your favorites here for Christmas! How did I help raise such an asshole?"

I believe my aunt just slapped me upside my head as if I were twelve. I deserve worse than that. I *am* an arsehole! Oh, Christ! Why do I keep doing this to her? She keeps proving to me that she loves only me, and I keep proving to her that her efforts are futile! I need to stop this. She's carrying my baby, for Christ's sake! I close the laptop.

"You've got issues, son!" Auntie points her finger at me. Her eyes become sad and her chin quivers.

"I'm sorry, Auntie. I love you." I hug her to me and kiss her hair. "I have to go find Becca. And grovel." I sigh and get up to leave the kitchen.

"Looking for Becca?" Melissa grabs my arm. I look back and nod. "She's napping in Morgan's room. She doesn't want to be disturbed." I nod again and head up to our room.

Well, Grayson, you really stepped in it now! I sit at the desk and try to come up with a brilliant plan to make up for my behavior. I hate Ray! I wish I could edit him out of our lives! I have to consider, though, where we may be had he not tried to come between us. Having Ray in the mix did indeed help her realize how she truly felt and get over the panic of her feelings. Still, I wish he didn't pounce on her like he did, though I would've done the same in his shoes. I'll just never truly be able to understand why she welcomed his advances so quickly. Because of their history? Because he waited so long, and she felt she had to reward him? She told him she regrets the timing. So she doesn't actually regret being with him? How am I not supposed to always wonder? They may have a history, but she doesn't really know anything about him, or at least his past. She has no idea of the amount of red flags he has raised. She's only now getting suspicious of him! She has no idea how much he has omitted and lied about!

I have to keep her in the dark a little bit longer, though. We have so much information, incriminating information, but no solid links yet. I want to tell Becca what we have, if only to keep her more cautious and safe. She's right—knowledge is power, and I am leaving her vulnerable.

I just don't know if I can trust her with this information. She tends to be impulsive, especially now with her raging hormones. I'm not sure if I should tell her about Liz, but I may have to. That's it! I'll tell her about Liz. That's the perfect way for me to apologize! Besides, Liz's predicament has nothing to do with anything going on here!

I spring up from my chair and, with a new sense of purpose,

head downstairs. I go to the front desk and look for the spare key to Morgan's room. It's gone. *Damn it!* I set out to look for Aunt Hazel—surely she has the master!

"Auntie, do you have a master key, love, for Morgy's room?" To sprinkle a bit of sugar on my request, I offer her my best boyish (*remember how much you love me?*) grin.

"Yes, I do." She walks past me.

"Erm ... can I have it, please?" This woman has a magical way of always making me feel like a twelve-year-old boy—and a spoiled one, at that!

"No. Leave her alone, Gracie. Give her a break." She sits in one of the new armchairs in the lounge and picks up her knitting.

"What are you making, Auntie?" I sit on the sofa near her.

"A baby blanket." She looks up briefly, then back down to her work. My mouth goes dry.

"Um ... uh, for who?" I stammer like an idiot, or a twelve-year-old boy who's trying to hide something. She looks at me quizzically. *Shit. Double shit!*

"Project Linus." She looks back down and continues.

"What's that?" I relax.

"It's a nonprofit organization that provides handmade blankets for children, mostly critically ill ones." She searches her knitting bag and retrieves a pamphlet, which she hands to me.

"Wow, Auntie, I didn't know you did this. What a fabulous thing to do! I've never even heard of it before." It's such a simple charity, but so meaningful. Maybe it's because I'm about to become a father for the first time, but I feel so deeply touched by the idea of this charity. I watch my aunt knit, smiling at my comment, and suddenly I'm transported back to London.

Every night, I'd practice piano and she would sit in the armchair near me, knitting and listening. I look over at the piano that's now in the lounge. *Hmm.* I make my way over to it and sit dutifully. I begin to play one of my aunt's all-time favorites.

"I see trees of green ... red roses, too ..." I glance over at her as I begin to sing. A blanket of warmth comes over her face. She's remembering. I continue on with the song—lose myself in it. I miss this great escape. It's been a while since I've just sat at a piano. I feel like myself again.

I finish the last chord and jump at the sudden applause. Turning, I find most of my security staff watching me. I'm a little embarrassed, but nod a little thanks toward them. Aunt Hazel holds up the key. I smile and go to retrieve it.

She pulls back.

"I always said you could charm the pants off a Royal Guard." Her smile hits her eyes and I give her big kiss on the cheek.

"Oh, I don't know about that, Auntie. I've tried!" I grab the key and take off for Morgan's room. I unlock the door and breathe deeply before I head in.

The window shades darken the room, but I can still see. It smells of Morgan in here. Bubble gum and vanilla, her scent of choice for bodywash and shampoo. Becca is fast asleep, hugging Morgan's pillow. I sit on the side and watch her. She looks so peaceful ... so beautiful. She jumps a little when I push her hair out of her face.

"It's me, sweetheart," I say quietly, although I'm not quite sure she'd find comfort in that.

"How did you ... ?"

"Aunt Hazel gave me the key." I answer before she finishes her question.

"Oh." She sits up and starts to smooth out the sheet next to her, avoiding my eyes.

"Erm ... so, I wanted to tell you that I got the information on Liz." I grab her hand.

"Oh?" She looks up at me.

"Hi." I smile and touch her face.

"Liz?" She looks away. *Damn it!* Okay.

"Well, she's in Maine at a nursing and rehabilitation center."

"What? Why?" She jerks her head back to me to give her full attention.

"She was involved in a terrible car accident a month after Annie was born. She was resuscitated, but her brain went too long without oxygen. She's in a vegetative state." I can see her mind is running seventy miles a minute.

"Why wouldn't ... why would Ray tell Annie she just up and left as if she didn't want her? Why wouldn't he tell her what happened, or at least lie and say that she died? He has Annie thinking her own mother didn't want her! What the hell, Gray? Anything else? Who pays for her medical bills?"

"He does, Bec."

"Are they actually divorced?" Her eyes are wide. I can't help the twitch I feel in my jaw.

"What the hell does it matter if they are divorced or not?"

Becca rolls her eyes at me.

"I'm just trying to understand what happened." She's irritated, and rightfully so.

"Why does it matter? She's alive and not buried in his backyard or anything." I tread lightly. This apology is not working out quite like I thought it would. She's too quiet. "I'll set everything up for you and Aunt Hazel to go shopping tomorrow." *Oh, Christ! Why did I just play that card? I don't want her to go out! Shit!*

"Never mind." She pulls the covers back on the other side and climbs out.

"No, sweetheart, it's okay." *What am I saying? It most certainly is* not *okay!*

"Grayson, you have enough to worry about. Maybe I can send somebody to get what I need." Becca Campbell is compromising with me? Even though I've behaved like a complete arse? I should feel relieved, but I'm actually uneasy.

"Becca?" I place my hands on her shoulders. She tenses up. "Baby, please, I know I've slipped up, but haven't I been good lately? I am trying, Becca. It is harder for me here. With everything going on. I'm trying, baby. You've got to know that." I think if I actually say the words *I'm sorry*, her head might explode.

"I do, Grayson. It just hurts. Every time I think we've moved on from it, you do something to remind me that it still lingers in the back of our minds." I can feel her trying to keep her composure. I pull her back to my chest and circle my arms around her.

"You smell so good, Becca." I inhale deeply at her neck and follow up with a soft kiss. She leans her head back on my chest and holds my arms to her tighter, and I know I am forgiven.

"Jesus! I didn't think I'd ever get here!" Stacey shakes her head as the EMTs wheel her in on a stretcher.

"Hey, Stace!" Becca runs up and hugs her. She leads them to Morgan's room. We decided to move Morgan upstairs by us, because Stacey's leg is still broken and Aunt Hazel's knees aren't so good. I had to remind Becca to move Morgan a few doors down from us so she'd have less of a chance of hearing us pray.

"Morgy, as soon as I get this cast off, you can have your room back, honey! Thank you for letting me use it!" She gives Morgan a hug. Morgan heads back out of the room with the oddest expression on her face. I decide to follow and inquire about what is going on in that brilliant little mind of hers.

"Say, Morgy girl?" I grab her hand.

"Yes, Daddy?" She looks up at me. Still one of my favorite sounds.

"Let's have a chat!" We head to Becca's office.

"Am I in trouble?"

"Morgan, are you ever in trouble with me?" I tap her knee playfully as I sit in front of her. "No, I want to know about that look on your face when you were leaving your Aunt Stacey." She winces a little. "Go ahead, sweetheart, you won't get in trouble." Knee tap again.

"Well, I'm just not too sure about her anymore. Is she going to start acting weird again?"

"Um, I hope not. But if she does, please come and tell me, little sweetheart, not Mummy. Okay? I need to know what kind of weird things she's saying." I'm not quite sure how to explain the reason to a ten-year-old, so I just stop there.

"Okay, Daddy-o!" She slaps my knee. That's it? No questions? God, this kid is awesome ... just like her mother. I chuckle to myself.

"Go on, get outta here!" I kiss her hair. As I leave the office, Derek approaches me with a young, quite attractive woman in tow.

"Sir, this is Melanie Jacobs."

"Pleased to meet you, Melanie." I shake her hand. Oh my. Wow ... she's beautiful. Long, strawberry-blonde hair, huge blue eyes, and a lovely pale complexion.

"Nice to meet you, Mr. James." She smiles a gorgeous smile.

"Well, let me show you to Stacey's room." I finally let go of her hand.

"Sure." A flash of that smile again. I lead the way to the room to find Becca sitting on the bed, laughing with Stacey.

"Sweetheart, this is Melanie Jacobs," I say a little too loudly.

"Oh, hi, Melanie!" Becca jumps up to greet her. Melanie keeps smiling. Becca brings her over to Stacey and I can't help but stare at her fantastic bum. It's very bubbly, but a nice bubbly. I glance up to find Becca watching me purposefully. I feel like a deer in headlights as I try to figure out her expression. She walks up to me and gently pulls my lip from my teeth, pats the side of my face, and walks out of the room. I didn't even realize I was biting my lip. I'm pretty sure that did not look good at all.

I follow Becca out and quickly get hypnotized by the tempo of her bum as she walks ahead of me. Hmm ... yes. Becca's bum is definitely my type of bum! It's beautifully round, as if it were a sculpture. It's so soft and ... and ... *damn it!* I grab Becca's hand to turn her around, then lean down and throw her over my shoulder like I'm a Neanderthal.

"Grayson, put me down!"

"You're a wiggly thing, aren't you?" I tease and slap her bum as I head up the stairs with her.

"Grayson!" she yells.

"I'll put you down in two minutes, love." I finish the last few stairs and head to our room where I happily place her on our bed. I stand up and pull my shirt off. I watch her drink in the sight of me in. I love seeing the want in her eyes.

"You seriously think I'm going to have sex with you after you were just salivating over Stacey's nurse?" It still amazes me how Becca can flip her switch so quickly. Lust one minute can easily turn into disgust the next. I say nothing. I pull out my phone and take a picture of her. "What are you doing?" She throws her hands up. No matter how hard I try, I can't help the smile that forms at my mouth.

"I'm recording a very rare occurrence," I say as I label the picture *second time jealous.* I toss my phone onto the side table and thumb the button of my jeans open.

"Rare occurrence?" She's annoyed. Possibly mad. Could be both.

"Yes, Becca, your jealousy is a rare occurrence. I like to capture it the moment it happens." I smirk and allow my jeans to fall. I hook my thumbs under the band of my boxer briefs and pull them down.

Becca swallows hard and clears her throat. "I know what you're doing, Grayson."

"Good, sweetheart, that makes two of us." I graze her cheek with the back of my knuckles. She swats my hand away. Oh, she's angry, all right! I bite my lip and close my eyes—this going to be so bloody fucking hot!

BECCA

I hand Melissa and Ryan my list for the British Aisles store. I think they are very grateful to get away from here for the day. I don't blame them!

"Meliss, don't forget the other!" I nudge her.

"I won't." She starts giggling, and I can't help but join her.

"What are you two hens cackling on about?" Grayson comes up from behind and swats my ass.

"Girl stuff." I give Melissa a hug.

Grayson shrugs at Ryan and pulls him in for a hug.

"I'm going to miss you, mate!" he declares.

Leave it to Grayson—he's such an ass!

"See you guys later, and thanks again for doing this." I roll my eyes and pull Grayson off of poor Ryan. We watch them head out the door.

"I was thinking we could go out for lunch today." He wraps his arms around me.

"Yay!" I say sarcastically.

"I'm sorry, Becca, but at least it will get us out of the house." I know he's going stir-crazy as well.

"Grayson, this is all a little much. Why can't we go out in daylight and do something fun? It snowed eight inches last night! Let's go down to the McKinley Farm and go on a sleigh ride with Morgan. Come on, please?" I turn to him and place my hands on his upper arms. "We'll have security with us!" I add, like anyone around here needs a reminder about that.

"Oh, Ms. Campbell, I do love how you beg." He gives me a mischievous grin, and something tells me he's not talking about the sleigh ride.

"So, that's a yes?" I can barely contain my excitement.

"Yes, all right, love!" He kisses me.

"Sweetheart, this blanket smells awful! Do they ever wash it?" Grayson makes a foul face, and my only option is to giggle.

"What do you expect, baby? It's on a horse-drawn sleigh all day."

"Yes, I realize that, but how long do they wait to wash them? Yuck!" He pulls it off of us.

"We'll keep each other warm, baby." I snuggle into him as the sleigh takes off.

"Morgy, you warm enough, sweetheart? Do you want to snuggle with Mum and Dad?" He asks, although that would be tight.

"No, I'm okay, Daddy." She smiles and sips her hot cocoa. "Mommy, remember last year when you dropped the hot cocoa all over yourself? You should have seen her, Daddy! She was covered ... face, hair, hands, clothes! You got it all over Ray, too! You two were literally a hot mess!" She laughs. I was laughing until she mentioned Ray. I dropped my hot cocoa because of him.

The girls wanted to sit together, so Ray and I shared the bench-like seat across from them. It was awkward for me because it was the first thing we had done together since our kiss six months before. The girls were laughing and telling secrets and completely ignoring us.

"Warm, Bec?" He put his arm around my shoulder and his free hand on my right leg, pulling me closer to him (for warming purposes, of course). Mental eye roll. I nodded, gripping my hot chocolate for protection ... I think. Not quite sure how I thought hot chocolate was going to protect me. I expect so much from chocolate. In the end, it just makes me feel like shit.

"I miss you, Becs. I miss your laugh. I miss your advice on everything, especially with Annie. I miss our talks. I miss all of our outings. I miss your theme songs. Look at our girls, Becca—they're so happy, baby. They're like sisters." He took in a deep breath and rested his forehead up against my right temple. His hand suddenly felt higher on my leg, his thumb noticeably caressing the area it covered. I remember feeling trapped in a situation I asked him not to put me in.

"Becca, I love you. I will do whatever it takes. I will wait as long as you need me to. There's no one else for me. You're the only woman I want to spend the rest of my life with." He kissed my cheek. *"You look so beautiful today, by the way."* I remember thinking, *What was the point of throwing that comment in?*

I was rendered speechless. How could he say all of these things to me? And in front of the girls, no less? I mean, they didn't hear him, but what kind of response or reaction could I give him in front of them? He knew I didn't want him to do this to me, that I wasn't ready for a relationship or committing to the possibility of one.

As I stared at the red and green plaid wool blanket on our lap, I realized that was exactly why he did it in the presence of the girls. He knew I'd have no choice but to listen and not react poorly in front of them. His hand came out from the blanket and reached up for my face. He palmed my left cheek and brought my face to face his. I remember seeing Morgan's eyes notice and go wide before I brought my gaze to him. I could've sworn I heard my nine-year-old telepathically say, *Oh shit, Mom! How are you going to get out of this?*

"Hot chocolate?" I asked quickly as Ray began to lean in. It was all I had! His eyes opened wide. I could see him fighting back a smile.

"Ladies first." He gave me his boyish grin, then licked his lips. I took a very drawn-out sip, which made him chuckle a little. *"Done?"* He raised his eyebrows when I finally pulled the cup

away from my lips.

"Yes. Here you go." I offered the cup.

"No, I don't want any from there." He leaned in. "There's some right here that looks delicious." His thumb traced my bottom lip. He leaned in and kissed the corner of my mouth, then worked his way toward being fully on my lips. The death grip I bestowed upon my cup finally made it buckle. The hot chocolate prevailed at protecting me! We were covered in it, abruptly pulling him away from his intentions. The girls laughed their asses off, causing us to laugh.

"Death by chocolate. Who would've thought it could mean killing a moment. Huh, Ray?" I said it jokingly, but I knew my face showed Ray how I really felt, and he got the message loud and clear. His expression looked as if I had ripped the sunshine out of the sky and shoved it up his ass. He knew better than to corner me like that! And to use the girls to guarantee success ... well, that was just unacceptable! The rest of the sleigh ride took forever. Even the girls were asking if it was almost over.

We were supposed to go to lunch together that day, but given the many circumstances, we decided not to. Annie's disappointment was more evident than Morgan's. I felt bad and offered to keep Annie overnight, forgetting that the girls had school the next day. After Ray reminded me, I noticed he breathed a sigh of relief. We got into his truck and headed back to the inn. I stared straight ahead. Ray's gaze bounced back and forth between me and the road.

"Why don't you girls go in for a few minutes so Becca and I can talk?" he suggested as he pulled into a space. They bolted out of the truck before I could even object. Ray locked the doors. Kind of silly—I do know how to unlock a door. He leaned his head on the steering wheel on top of his clenched hands. "Okay, let me have it." He sighed heavily in defeat.

"What's there to say? You know what you did. You know how you did it. You know why you did it the way you did it! What is there

left to say, Raymond?" I yelled. He smiled and bit his lip. "What is so funny?"

"I'd tell you, but with the way you are feeling right now, you'd probably hit me." He laughed more to himself and shook his head.

"If you don't tell me, it will drive me crazy, and then I will hit you for sure!" I snapped.

"True dat ... true dat." He nodded thoughtfully, knowing I would laugh at one of our many inside jokes. I remember getting pissed at myself for caving so easily. I hit him for it. He caught my hand when I yanked it back, and I tried to pull away. "Stop." It's the way he said it that made me cave in again. It was low and sexy, and it ignited butterflies in my belly that sent a bolt of electricity to my groin.

"Why were you laughing?" I asked, hoping to pull his focus away from kissing the top of my hand over and over again.

"Whenever you call me by my full name, whether it's in shock, or you're appalled, or mad, it's like the effect has a direct line to my groin."

"Raymond!" I couldn't even help myself. I was shocked, not only by what he said, but that he basically just described what he had done to me.

"Wow, did that hurt?" He chuckled.

"What? Did what hurt?" I was annoyed.

"The mental head slap you just gave yourself." He laughed. Damn it, I was laughing with him. "Oh, Becca, baby, can't you see how good we are together?"

"Ray, don't call me that." I sighed.

"Becca, I have called you 'baby' since the day I met you!" It was his turn to be annoyed.

"It gives people ideas," I tried to reason.

"Oh wait, that gives people ideas?" he asked, and I nodded. "Hmm. Well, let me ask you this!" Ray had his "sit and spin" look on his face. "What kind of idea do you think people get when they

see us grocery shop together, go school-clothes shopping, attend town events, pick up each other's kids on a regular basis, or attend church together? Do I need to continue on with the list? Because I can keep going, baby!"

I just sat there, doe-eyed and watching his anger and irritation unfold.

"Yes, I think I will!" he said. "We pick up each other's pre-scriptions, we are each other's emergency contact, and we are list-ed as the other parent to call for our kids. Nobody gets any business from the inn for maintenance or repairs because I take care of it all! Eric the jeweler pulls out your client list when I walk through the door."

"What's that?" I asked. Damn ADD!

"A list of all the jewelry I've bought you to help he and I keep track. Becca, what idea do you think the townspeople have, baby?" I was speechless again. It doesn't happen often, but most bask in the glory of it when it does. "Don't bite your lip, baby." He thumbed it free from my teeth, and I turned away. His face was so close to mine. His fingers traced my jawline and trailed down my neck. "You know what idea they have, baby? They think you're in my bed at night ..." His lips followed the path of his fingers. "Oh, Bec, I want you in my bed. Please, I need you."

And that was the point where I pushed him off and tried to unlock the door.

"The child lock is on, babe!" he snapped, and hit the button. "Go ahead, fucking run again! I'll see you in six months, I guess!" He was pissed. I mean, really pissed! He had never been this mad at me.

"No, I'll see you for Christmas Eve." I didn't want to hurt Annie again, too.

"What about Christmas morning?" He pulled me away from the door.

"Yes, we'll go to church." I thought I was agreeing to our usu-

al plans.

"Drive yourself! I don't want anyone getting any ideas about us!"

I sat quietly, feeling guilty.

"Theme song?" I finally asked. Usually he likes to know.

"No, babe, I don't have one."

"No, I do. Do you want to know what it is?" I played with my fingers; his hands were still on my arms.

"What is it?" He chucked my chin so I'd look at him.

"'Under Pressure' by Queen and David Bowie."

"I have been nothing but patient with you, Becca ... for years!" he said through gritted teeth. "Pressure? I'll show you pressure!" he snapped as he hit the button to recline my seat and climbed on top of me all in the same move, I think. I remember begging him to stop and cursing his truck for having a passenger seat that reclines flat. He was between my legs, grinding into me. "See what you do to me, baby? Feel it?" He bit at my earlobe. My arms were pinned, his mouth all over my face and neck as he kept grinding. "Feel the pressure? Just wait until it's inside of you." At that point I had a flashback of George and began to cry.

"Please ... please don't hurt me," I begged him calmly, holding back my sobs. I remember feeling scared. Ray looked up at me quickly.

"God, baby. No ... no, I'm sorry. I would never hurt you. Oh God, Becca, I'm sorry." He climbed off of me and pulled me up. "I'm sorry. I'm sorry. Please forgive me." He was in tears now, too. I let him hug me. I cried in his neck for at least ten minutes. I cried because George damaged me so badly that I couldn't even allow myself to be fully loved by this wonderful, amazing man in front of me. I couldn't allow myself to love him in that way.

After that day, he never brought up his feelings or made any more advances on me. We acted as if it never happened. Really well, I guess, because this is the first time I've thought about it since. How do I just forget something like that? It makes me feel so nervous. Is there anything else I've blocked out? Christ!

I open my eyes and focus on the here and now as I hear Grayson and Morgan laughing.

"Hey there, sleepyhead." Grayson kisses my hair.

"Oh, sorry." I smile meekly because I know I wasn't really asleep.

"The ride is almost over, love. Are you still up for hot chocolate and cookies inside?" He grasps my chin with his thumb and forefinger to raise my face up to his. I squint from the sun.

"Yes, that's fine, handsome." I kiss his lips.

"Handsome, aye? Must've been a good dream." He kisses me again.

"No, actually, a bit of a nightmare. Glad to wake up to you." I hug him tightly.

"I love you, Becca." He squeezes.

Chapter Seven

I'm in the middle of the meadow with Rocco, who leans down to drink from the creek. It's a gorgeous spring day, and I run my hands over my very big belly. Two masculine hands join mine. I lay my head back on his shoulder, allowing him access to my neck.

"Oh, Becs, I'm so happy. I can't wait to meet our babies."

I turn my head to look at him.

"No. No, this isn't yours. They are not yours. No!" I try to tell Ray.

"We're going to be great together, baby. I'm so in love with you." He leans down to kiss me.

"No! No, stop! It's not true! Grayson, where's Grayson?" I ask, panicked.

"Dead, sweetheart. Sweetheart, it's okay. Wake up, love." Ray is talking, but it's Grayson's voice.

"No! No, you're lying! Where's Grayson?" I cry.

"I'm right here, Becca! Please, sweetheart!" Ray grabs my arms and shakes me.

I open my eyes to Grayson and grasp his face with both of my hands.

"Are you real? Are you here?" I cry.

"Yes, sweetheart, I am." He pulls me into his arms. "Jesus H. Christ, Becca! I couldn't wake you up! What were you dreaming about, sweetheart?" He brings my face up to look at his.

"I was on Rocco in the meadow ... " I start to tell him my nightmare as I try to control my crying.

"Oh, Becca, sweetheart, your dreams are crazy because you're pregnant, love. I'm here. I'm fine. It was just a dream!" He kisses me. "It's still so early. Why don't you try to go back to sleep? I bet part of this is from being exhausted by our excursion yesterday—and our activities last night." He nudges my nose playfully.

I climb on top, straddling him.

"I need you, baby. Grayson, I love you. You are my world," I cry out in between the kisses I run down his neck and shoulder. That dream freaked me out, and I just to need to be as close to him as possible.

"You have me, sweetheart. I'm here. I love you, baby," he declares, and swiftly enters me.

"Oh God, baby." I moan and attack his lips with mine.

"Can I sleep in a bit, love?" Grayson asks as I get up for a shower.

"Sure." I give him a quick kiss when I come around to his side of the bed.

"You okay now?" He holds my arms and stares into my eyes.

"Yes, much better now. I've just had a session with my sextherapist." I giggle.

"So he was he able to help you, then?" He gives me a half smile and tucks my hair behind my ears.

"Oh, yes, he's got a great way of showing me that things are always looking up." I kiss his nose and then his lips again.

"Hmm ... so what time will the man of your nightmares be dropping his daughter off today?" he asks.

"Oh shit, it's Friday?" Christ, I really don't want to see Ray today.

"Yes, dear."

"Probably after four, before dinner. Well, it'll be nice to have Annie. You'll love her, Gray!" I do miss Annie terribly.

"I absolutely *can't* wait, darling!" His overexaggeration tells me something different.

"Hey, Stace, how ya feeling today?" I plop down on Morgan's bed.

"Becca, please help me take a shower today." She's practically in tears. "Melanie is a sweet girl, but I just don't feel comfortable. She's so young and perky and I feel like crap. I feel even uglier when I'm around her and her gorgeous teeth and perfect hair. Look at me!"

My heart breaks for her. Out of everything, she's devastated that most of her hair was shaved off. We've just been keeping it in a ponytail to try to hide where they operated as much as possible. Stacey has always been vain about her appearance—she never leaves the house without makeup unless, of course, she's planning to apply it in the car while driving with her knee. *Ah-ha!* I'm going to send Grayson out with her when she's all better and have her drive! That ought to shut him up about my driving for the rest of ... my life!

"Stace, your hair is already starting to grow in!" *Encourage.*

Encourage. Encourage! "And yes, I'll help you shower." I know what she means about Melanie. Grayson's lost interest since the first day she arrived, but man, I thought his eyeballs were going to pop out of his head!

"Do you have time now?" she asks, sounding hopeful.

"All yours. Let's get to it, lady!" I pull her covers back and help her swing out of bed.

"They said this walking cast is waterproof." She stands up.

"Oh, shucks—no garbage-bag leg?" I tease. We head into the bathroom and I help her undress. "Hey, your skin is really clearing up!" I say enthusiastically.

"Just think, Becca, last time you said that to me, we were teenagers and I had been on Accutane for a month." She laughs.

"Well, at least I'm not talking about age spots," I joke. We both go quiet and I know we are silently pondering when we'll be having that conversation. Oh God, please not for another ten years, at least!

"So, tell me how you and Grayson are doing." She sighs as she steps under the hot water.

"We're doing really well. We have our moments, and that usually leads to other moments." I nudge her and giggle.

"Well, you guys have been together for three months now. You must be visiting church a little less nowadays." *Huh?*

"Um, Stace, have you seen my fiancé?" I look at her like she's crazy.

"Yes, well, I haven't seen him in all his magnificent glory, but you guys are still on each other every chance you get? Really? I saw the way he was looking at Melanie," she adds.

"Yeah, Stacey, we're still going strong. What are you playing at, anyway?" I scrub her back roughly.

"Sorry, Becs. I didn't mean to upset you." She tries to turn to me.

"Stacey, are you still pining after Gray?" *Enough with the bull-*

shit!

"No, Becca, I'm not. I'm sorry about my behavior before, after I got here. I wasn't myself. Now, a lot of things have changed for me drastically." She starts to sob.

"I'm sorry this happened to you, Stace. I'm sorry he didn't pay for what he did to you." I begin to cry as well.

"And you!" she adds.

"Yeah," I agree.

"Becca, I wish I didn't remember. What is the point? He's dead, and now I'll have these visions for the rest of my life! I'll be haunted and tortured by it!" she cries. I know exactly what she means. "I'm so sorry, Becca. I know you went through this for years."

"Hey, hey now ... that was a long time ago. Don't apologize to me for venting. It's okay. You need to get mad; it's a part of the healing process. He's burning in hell, Stace—that much we know. He'll never come back to hurt either one of us." I wrap the towel around her and help her out of the shower.

"When I think of what he could've done ... what he almost did." She holds me to her.

"Hey, you are here and he got his!" I palm her face to make her look at me.

"Becca, I'm pregnant," she says, bewildered. I feel as if I'm going to faint.

"With George's ... ?" I can't even finish the sentence.

"No ... it's Ray's." She bites her lip. I'm speechless—not because I don't have anything to say or any questions to ask. I have an overwhelming fear that I will sound like Porky Pig: dat-dat-dats Ray's ka-ka-kid? *Focus, Becca!*

"Um ... da-does he know?" *Shit!*

"No. I found out at the hospital. I thought it was George's until they did an ultrasound. I'm nine weeks." She sighs. "Ray and I got shitfaced after you two left abruptly, and, well ... here I am.

Knocked up in every way possible." I grab her hands. I'm dying to tell her that she's only one week ahead of me, but Grayson would have my head on a platter.

"When are you going to tell him?"

"I'm not sure. I suppose when I see him again. When I've fully recovered, I'll go visit." She starts to get dressed. I help her when needed.

"Stacey, he's coming here today to bring Annie for a sleepover. I'm sure he'll want to see you."

The look of panic strikes her face so fast she couldn't have stopped it if she wanted to.

"Becca, I can't see him like this. I can't tell him yet. Oh, you can't let him see me!"

"Well he visited you a couple of times at the hospital, so he saw you at your worst." I'm not sure if I'm helping.

"He did?"

She's surprised. Humph.

"Yeah." I nod. I guide her back to the room. "Where's the ultrasound picture?" I ask excitedly. Her face goes blank. "You said they did an ultrasound. Didn't they give you a picture?"

"Uh. No. Maybe because the tech wasn't sure what kind of news this was for me," she says. Huh. Odd, but she could be right.

"Well, I will schedule an appointment for you with my doctor here. Are you taking prenatal vitamins?" I brush her hair, watching her expressions carefully.

"Okay. Yes I am. Or, was ... they made me sick."

"Oh. Try the ones over the counter at Walgreen's. I use them as a multivitamin still. I'll pick some up for you." I smile as I put her hair up.

"Are you and Grayson still trying?" she asks quickly.

"No. We're not trying right now, too much going on." I sigh. *Yeah, that coupled with the fact that I'm already pregnant!* She did technically ask if we were *trying*, so it's not a lie ... we're not!

"There you go. Makeup?" I offer.

"I'll do it—I'm sure you want to spend some time with Morgan. I'll be out soon." She smiles and taps my hands.

"Okay. Any special requests for breakfast?" I kiss her head.

"Nope, surprise me!"

I smile and head out of the room, but I feel my expression drop as soon as I'm out in the hall. I move slowly, trying to process the information. I know she said they were drunk, but still—Ray is a levelheaded guy. He wore protection with me, and I'm the one he wants to be with. I'm having a difficult time thinking he didn't with her. I head up the stairs. I know Grayson wanted to sleep in, but maybe he's up now.

"Hey, Gray?" I say as I walk in. He puts his hand up to tell me to wait, then signals for me to close the door.

"You're fucking shitting me?!" he barks. His face is red, and the vein near his temple is pulsating like mad. This must be bad. As angry as I've made Grayson, I have never once seen that vein move like that before. "Did you alert the authorities? Oh, oh, good. Son of a bitch! Okay, very well then. Righto." He hangs up.

"Righto? My grandfather used to say that." I smile and hug him. "What was that about?"

"The explosion. The bomb was planted by one of our guys. He checked the plane with one of the others. When they cleared it and got off, he said he left his phone and went back in. Do you know the only reason Smitty is alive? All the lights on the plane were turned off, and he saw the red glow from under the seat! He got down to the ground to check it out and saw the timer. Had he come out of the cockpit one minute later, he would've died!"

We stand in each other's arms, silent. My guess is we're both thinking about what else could've been had Tanya not received a visit from "Aunt Flo from Red Bank."

"Do they know why he did it?" I finally speak up.

"No, not yet. We'll know soon enough, though." He kisses my

forehead. "Now, what were you coming up for?"

"Gee, I don't know if you want to hear about this, what with everything you're already trying to process." I look up at him.

"Lay it on me, sweetheart, we're up to our elbows in it anyway!" He closes his eyes, puts his head back, and takes in a deep breath. I give him the play-by-play of my conversation with Stacey. At the questioning of our sex life, he says, "That's bazaar." I tell him about me flat-out asking her if she wants Grayson, and her response. ("Good for you!") I also mention the Melanie thing. ("I'm sorry, sweetheart, she's not really my type. I don't know what came over me.") Then ... the Grand Poobah. ("Holy fuck!") Then her questions about us trying, and what I said.

"Good girl, Becca!" He hugs me.

"Baby?"

"Yes?"

"Do you have people that can magically look at medical records? I'm not sure if she's telling the truth." It saddens me to feel this way.

"Becca, if she's not, then we have a problem. She and Ray must know, and if they do, there was a leak at either the doctor's office or radiology department." He's on his phone again. "Jake! It's Grayson. Yes, Mass General. Yes, all records. Thanks, mate!" He hangs up.

"God, that is fucking hot!" I bite my lip.

Gray raises his eyebrows. "How hot, sweetheart?" He frees my lip with his thumb then bites it for himself, causing a small groan to release from my throat.

"The kind of hot that would make me call you 'sir,'" I manage to say before I deepen the kiss. Grayson pulls my yoga pants down a bit and gives my bum a proper greeting with his hand. "Oh!" I gasp and relish in the sweet sting. "Again, baby ... please." I bite his earlobe as I beg.

"Please what?"

"Please, sir." And I feel the sting again. He pulls my pants back up. Huh? I open my eyes and look up at him.

"Something to think about for later, sweetheart." He bites my lip again to tease me even more before he releases me. "I have to meet with security, doll." He kisses the tops of my hands.

"It's the three month itch, isn't it?" I joke.

"Oh ... there's definitely an itch, which only you can scratch. But we'll have to scratch it later, sweetheart." He leans in for another kiss and finally lets go so he can head downstairs. I clean up our room and make our bed. Shit, I have to finish wrapping Grayson's gifts!

I head over to Melissa's room and knock. "Melissa?" I knock again. Duh, she's at the meeting. Shoot! *I could just walk in, but Country Sybecca waves an authoritative finger at me.* She's right. I shouldn't just go barging in, even if it's my place. Defeated, I head downstairs. I'll just wrap his gifts later.

"Hey, Morgy! What should we do today? Do you want to start baking now?" I put my arm around her as she walks by.

"Huh?" She pulls her earbuds out.

"I said, what would you like to do today?"

"Well, Mom, Annie's going to be here in a couple of hours, so I thought we'd wait for her. What's for breakfast?" We walk into the kitchen as I'm still trying to process this information. It's not even close to noon yet, and I already feel overwhelmed! My brain is starting to think it's the end of the day instead of the beginning. Ugh! Half day before the holiday! How did I forget that? Why are they doing that for a Friday? It's a conspiracy, I swear! *Cautionary Sybecca has her ticker board out again. It reads, "Shit ... shit ... fuckity ... shit!"* And I agree!

"Omelets or pancakes?" I ask.

"French toast!" She grabs several loaves, reminding me I have quite a few people to cook for! I pull out the eggs, milk, vanilla, cinnamon, and nutmeg. My French toast always tastes like fall. I also pull out the different egg bakes I made last night and throw them in the oven to warm up. I do love my new kitchen. And I love my fiancé; he's really wonderful and thoughtful!

"Mom, how do you know when you've put enough in? You don't measure," Morgan asks, watching me from one of the bar-stools at my new huge island. Its creamy white-and-brown granite go great with the maple cabinets.

"Oh, I measure by sight. Someday, I'll take my time and measure everything out so I can write it down for you." I love that her interest in cooking has resurfaced.

"No, Mommy, I want to learn by sight like you and Susanna." She rests her head in her closed fists as she watches.

"I miss Susanna. We should give her a call later." I stop whisking. Come to think of it, I miss California. Maybe it's because it was just us there, none of the baggage from here. Well, a little, but only in the emotional sense!

"There are my girls!" Hazel smiles as she walks in. "What do we have going on in here?" She heads over to wash her hands at the sink, then begins our old routine of getting the breakfast spread ready to go. I wish I could merge my New Hampshire and California lives into one, because I'm overwhelmed with the sense of home right now! "We'll be spending a lot of time in this kitchen for the next few days, huh, girls?" Hazel cuts biscuits out of the dough.

"Oh yes, more than usual. We're going to have a lot more people this year." I exhale a big breath. A little overwhelming, but I love it!

"Hey, Mom, I have an idea!" Morgan says excitedly, slapping the island.

"What's that?" Uh-oh. When Morgan's excitement is this high over an idea, it's usually quite the endeavor!

"Well, all of our Secret Service agents are missing Christmas with their families. Why don't we make a request box instead of a suggestion box? They can each write down one thing, a dish or cookie that will make them feel closer to home, and put it in the box, then we could make sure they have it!" And she's up and probably off to get supplies.

"Jesus! I hope half of them say turkey or ham!" Hazel rolls her eyes.

"C'mon, Hazel, it's only three days 'til Christmas!" I say sarcastically, as if that's a lot of time. Within half an hour, we are bringing everything out to the dining room.

"Becs ..."

It's Ray's voice. I turn to see if my ears are playing tricks on me.

"Becca!" Annie runs to me, giving me a huge bear hug before I set down the tray I'm holding. Guess my ears are working just fine.

"Hey, kiddo! What are you doing here so early?" I hug her and look up at Ray. It's only ten o'clock.

"The nurse sent me home. Where's Morgan?" I look at Ray again, panicked. Why is he bringing her here if she's sick? He shakes his head.

"Um, she's around somewhere, sweetie. Just not in her room. You can check room 205 upstairs." I smile and she's off. "Annie, tell her it's time to eat!" I shout after her as I walk up to Ray.

"Can we talk? It's about Annie, and it's personal." He unzips his jacket and pulls off his hat. Hmm ... he still hasn't gotten a haircut. He looks so cute when his hair grows out. It's very wavy. He looks ten years younger.

"Uh, yes, we can go into my office." I wave the way.

"Hey, it looks different in here. It's nice, babe, when did you do this?" He follows me.

"While we were in California." Well, that's when Grayson did it, but Ray doesn't need to know that.

"I can't believe you painted over all of the wood. You always loved that about this place. It's really not you. Well, not the you I used to know," he says as we walk into my office.

"Yeah, that was a misunderstanding. I didn't want to paint the wood, but I'm used to it now. It's pretty. I like it." I try to hide how I really feel.

"And you're still a terrible liar." He gives me a small smile and tucks the strand of hair that's escaped my ponytail behind my ear.

"Um, so what's going on with Annie, Ray?" I sit and offer him Claudia's chair. He pulls off his jacket and hangs it up on the coat rack before he sits. He's wearing blue jeans with the brick-red shirt and creamy-white and red flannel I bought him last year. It's become a tradition that one of his gifts from me every year is a flannel and matching shirt. I didn't even get him anything this year. I didn't think of it. I didn't get anything for Annie, either. I need to fix that right away; kids are different! Christ! What are they doing for Christmas? They always spend it with us!

"Theme song, baby?" He touches my cheek lightly.

"Huh? Uh, no, I've just got a lot on my mind. Sorry. What's going on with Annie?" I refocus and pull my head back a little.

He slaps his knees and sits back.

"Well, I got a call from the nurse's office shortly after school started. Annie was down there complaining of stomach pain. So the nurse had her lie down for a little while, then try the bathroom. Annie came out very upset because when she wiped ... uh, there was blood." His eyes go wide, a look of horror on his face.

"Ray! Oh my God! Oh ... oh my God, Ray ... already?" I can't believe it!

"I know, Bec, my little girl. Agh!" He rubs his face.

"What did the nurse say?" I swat his knee.

"She just gave her a pad to put on and told her to talk to her mother! Thank God you've already told her about having a period! Can you imagine if you hadn't, how traumatic that would've been for her, babe?" He grabs my hands.

"I can't believe Mrs. Tansen said that to her, Ray! I'm going to call her right now." I raise my voice at this news, my blood boiling!

"Baby, it wasn't Mrs. Tansen. It was a sub." He gives me a crooked smile. I pull my hands from him and turn to the phone. I call the school.

"Yes, can I speak to Mrs. Preston? This is Becca Campbell. Okay. Thanks." I pause and look over my shoulder at Ray. "They're transferring me," I say, and he sits back.

"Ms. Campbell, how are you and Morgan doing?" Mrs. Preston asks excitedly when she picks up.

"Oh, we're doing fine. Thank you! How are you? Ready for Christmas?" I smile. I've always loved Principal Preston.

"I'm great; will be even better in two hours!" She laughs.

"I can understand that." I'm sure she can sense my sympathetic nod. "Hey, listen, the reason I'm calling you is Annie McNeil."

"Oh, yes, is she all right? I saw her father picking her up earlier."

"Well, that's what I'm calling you about. I know you have a substitute nurse today. Um, you may not want to have her back." I sigh and explain what happened.

"Oh, Ms. Campbell, that's awful! Well, I'll give her a piece of my mind! Is Annie okay?" I can tell she's very upset. It was quite unprofessional!

"Yeah, she's with me now. Luckily, I taught the girls about their periods, but it could've been another girl who wasn't educated about it. It may have been very traumatic." I lean my head into my hand.

"You're right. Please tell Annie and Mr. McNeil I'm sorry. When is Morgan coming back?" she asks quickly.

"I'm not sure. We're floating between here and California. We haven't made a decision yet, but I will let you know. I'll let you get back to work, Mrs. Preston. Thank you for lending me your ear. We'll talk soon. Merry Christmas!"

"No problem at all! I'm glad you told me. It was good to hear from you, and we hope to have Morgan back here real soon! Merry

Christmas, Ms. Campbell!" We hang up.

"There! That nurse will never be back at their school!" I turn, proud of myself. My smile fades as I find Ray with tears falling down his cheeks. "Ray?" It's very rare for Ray to show emotion like this. As a matter of fact, I could count on one hand how many times I've seen him cry and have plenty of fingers left over.

"Hey, thanks, Becs." He wipes his face and gets up for his coat. "What time should I pick Annie up tomorrow?"

"Ray!" I grab his arm to turn him to me. "What is it?" He opens his mouth to say something, but stops himself. He looks up to the ceiling and grits his teeth. I give him a moment to compose himself. He makes an "O" with his lips and exhales.

"I just, um ... I miss this, baby. I miss us being a team. I miss us making decisions together. I ... um, I feel like ... like I'm in the middle of a divorce that I didn't see coming, nor want. I just don't understand, Becs. Why wasn't I enough? I have to go." He tries to leave again, but I push him against Claudia's desk.

"Ray, please don't think that. Please." I palm his face and wipe his tears away with my thumbs, then grab a tissue and start to wipe his nose.

"Christ, Bec! I can wipe my own damn nose." He chuckles a little, grabbing the tissue from me.

"Sorry, habit." I giggle. "Ray, you were always good enough for me. I just ... I wasn't ready. Do you remember last year, after the sleigh ride?" I watch as he winces at the memory.

"I haven't thought about that day in a long time. I'm still mad at myself for the way I behaved." His hands find my hips and he squeezes gently.

"I haven't either. I think I blocked it out until Morgan brought it up yesterday." At this moment, I realize how close Ray and I are, how intimate we look. I swallow hard, knowing that Grayson is getting a full report. I can't think about that. I've hurt Ray deeply; I need to do my best to help him move on. "Remember afterward, when I cried in your arms for a while?" I look up into his eyes. They are bluish-gray, absolutely beautiful. I could get lost in those eyes.

"How could I forget?" A flash of anger comes across his face.

"I, um ... I wasn't crying because of what you did. Well, maybe at first, but mostly ... " I pause to take in a deep breath. He pulls my hips to draw me closer, and my hands go to his shoulders to brace myself. Christ, this definitely does not look good! *All Sybeccas are glancing over their shoulders, except for Country Sybecca. She's twirling her pigtails around and kicking at an imaginary something on the ground. She's always been Ray's biggest fan.*

"What, baby, tell me." He squeezes my hips again.

"I was crying because I couldn't give you what you needed. I was so frustrated, so mad. Everything you said that day—you were right. I just couldn't allow myself to love you the way I wanted to, the way you wanted me to." I stop for a moment, and he takes in a sharp breath. "Ray, you're a wonderful man. You're smart, funny, loving, strong, and, well, not bad to look at, especially when your hair is this length." I smile and tug at his hair. He pulls me closer. "Raymond!" I gasp. Oh, too close! His hot breath is in my face; his lips are almost on mine. I feel a slight magnetic pull between our mouths. I try desperately to steady my erratic breathing. Christ, can I just pull it together for once?

"Baby, you know what happens when you say my full name," he says, his voice deep and musky, before he tries to kiss me. I only feel a slight brush against my lips as I manage to pull my head away quickly.

"Don't, Ray. Please. I love Grayson. I'm in love with him." I push away from him and start crying, because I'm probably losing Grayson at this very moment. Maybe I'm not meant to be with anyone.

"Don't cry, baby. I ... this is very hard for me. You've always been mine—unofficially, of course. I'm ... I don't know, Becs. I keep waiting for you to tell me you've made a huge mistake." He sighs, sounding frustrated, and runs his hand through his hair.

"Ray, I really do regret the way I've handled all of this. I'm so sorry I hurt you. You have to believe that! I wasn't thinking. I was selfish and thoughtless! I shouldn't have done what I did. I feel like all I've done is lead you on, even though it was never intentional. Please believe me. You're my best friend, Ray." Tears are streaming down my face.

"You cut me out of your life completely! You cut me out like the last five years meant nothing!" he yells.

"You were acting crazy and trying to break Grayson and me up." I have to defend myself.

"Because of what you did to me!" he says through clenched teeth.

"I know. I'm sorry, Ray. I really am."

"I should've been more aggressive. Apparently, that's what you like!" he snaps.

"Ray, you did everything right. It was really me." I try to console him.

"Ha! Well, maybe I haven't slapped you into submission like he does, but I definitely have my own methods!" His voice is steady and his face says "sit and spin." "I can't believe how guilty I've felt this whole time over what I did!" He kicks one of the chair with his right foot, and it shoots violently into Claudia's desk. "Well, not anymore! Not after what you've done to me!" He backs me up to the wall with his vicious bark.

"What are you talking about, Ray? You didn't do anything wrong." I try to calm him down. He chuckles lightly and bites his lower lip.

"Oh, baby ..." He shakes his head, then loses the smile as he grasps my face in his hands.

"We'll always have your birthday."

"When we got drunk?" *Why is that such a big deal?*

"Think about what you asked me the next morning." He speaks softly as his right thumb strums my bottom lip. I look away from him, trying to think about that morning. I gasp and look back up at him. His smile is wicked.

"Oh, baby, you came so hard for me ... three times. I made sure you felt me the next day." He slams his mouth against my open one. His tongue swirls quickly around mine once, as if it was just there to say *checkmate* before pulling away abruptly. "I'll pick Annie up at noon tomorrow." He grabs his coat and heads out of the office. I go to run after him. I see security coming, with Grayson not far behind.

Ray stops to kiss Annie.

"See you tomorrow, sweetie." He hugs her, then heads toward the door. He turns before he leaves. Staring at me, he licks his lips and shoots me an air kiss and a wink. It's his signature greeting to me. It usually makes me blush. My face is red, all right, but it has nothing to do with that.

He leaves, and I don't know if it's morning sickness finally kicking in or the information he just gave me, but I run for the bathroom. I run so fast I could possibly win gold for my time. I think I'd also win gold for my projectile vomiting. It's been a record-breaking sort of day!

I feel somebody hold my hair and rub my back as I am overcome with dry heaves. *Country Sybecca has finished "throwing" herself and is now busy tearing her posters of Ray off her wall.* I finally feel that I may be finished.

"Okay then, sweetheart?" I turn swiftly, shocked to find Grayson.

"Gray, you don't like vomit!"

"Uh, sweetheart, I don't think anybody *likes* vomit. That would just be strange. And would probably warrant some sort of psychiatric evaluation." He pats my back and looks fearfully away from the toilet as he flushes it. It's quite comical, and I can't help but laugh. It's more of a nervous laugh, though, and I immediately start crying. "Let's go upstairs and talk, sweetheart." He pulls my face up to his and wipes my tears away.

"He raped me, Gray."

"I know, sweetheart. C'mon, let's go talk." He puts his arm around my shoulders, and we head upstairs.

Chapter Eight

"Okay. I want you to tell me everything, including the sleigh ride," he says calmly as we sit on the bed with our backs against the headboard for support. He grabs my hand and laces his fingers with mine. We look as if we're going to discuss weekend plans or something else pleasant, not the atrocity that Ray McNeil has committed against me. Slowly, I tell him about the sleigh-ride incident.

"Gray, what freaks me out the most is that I completely blocked it out! I didn't remember any of it until Morgan said something, and then *boom*! I got hit with it all. I need to call Patricia." I sigh.

"Who's Patricia?" he asks.

"My therapist."

"Oh. Well, let's fast-forward to your birthday. What do you remember?" He brings my hand up to his lips to kiss it.

"Um, well, Ray took me out for my birthday like every year. We drove one town over, to a bar that has karaoke and dancing. We sang a couple of songs and drank and danced. The last thing I remember at the bar was having a glass of wine on the couches they have there. Ray was toasting me, and ... and ... he told me I was beautiful. Yes. That's the last thing I remember of that night." I think to make certain.

"The next thing?" he coaxes.

"Yeah, so, the next thing I knew, I was waking up in his bed ... fully clothed, mind you." I turn my face to his sharply for emphasis. "Ray was fully clothed as well, and I was wrapped up in his arms. I think I laid there for five minutes staring at the ceiling, trying to remember what the hell happened and how I ended up in Ray's bed. I was also wondering why I felt so sore. Even my nipples felt tender. My head was pounding. I moved to hold my head, and that's when Ray woke up." I close my eyes and transport myself into the memory as I continue.

"Good morning, birthday girl." He kissed my neck. "If I didn't know any better, I would've thought it was my birthday, getting to wake up next to you like this. You feel so good in my arms, baby." He kissed me again, his hand caressing my stomach.

"Ray?" I could barely speak. I felt so confused.

"Yeah, babe." He nibbled at my ear.

"What happened? Why am I here ... in your bed?"

"Uh, we had a little too much to drink, you more than me. I live closer. Also, because you were meant to be in my bed." I gasped as his fingers went over my nipple, confirming that it was indeed sore. He smiled at my reaction and leaned down to kiss me. I was so confused that I let him. I returned his kiss until he tugged at my nipple. It was painful. I pushed him off and I sat up quickly, only to feel the full effects of my soreness.

"Ray, did something happen last night?" I remember trying to

remain calm.

"Uh, yeah, we got drunk, Becs." He sat behind me, placing a leg on either side of me. He moved my hair away from my neck and started kissing me there. "Becca, I'd like something else to happen, baby," he whispered as his hands went under my shirt and up my back. He undid my bra and reached around to palm my breast. I leapt off the bed. He came after me, pushing me against the wall. "Baby, please, you have no idea how good we are together."

"What do you mean, how good we are?" I asked and shoved him away.

"Becca, why are you acting so weird?"

"I'm just disoriented. Ray, you promised you wouldn't pressure me." I put my hand on his chest to keep him at arm's length.

"I did, didn't I?" He gave me a wicked smile. "Okay, baby. But I am going to kiss you one last time, and then we can start pretending again." He grabbed my hands and held them against the wall on either side of my head.

"Ray, stop," I said, and turned my face from his.

"Oh, baby, if you don't turn those sweet, beautiful lips my way, I will be forced to kiss you in other places. I'm not playing, baby. I'm going to kiss you, you decide where. On the count of three. One ... two ... darn." He smiled when I turned to face him.

"You are so on my shit list, McNeil!" I snapped.

"Yeah, well, you're on my kiss list right now, so shut the fuck up, baby, and kiss me." I complied. After several minutes, he finally let me pull away. "You were so fucking hot last night, baby. You really know how to move your hips." I jerked my head back to him. "You really know how to dance, babe." He gave me another quick kiss, then released my arms. I went into his bathroom to wash my face and pull myself together. I felt him come up behind me. He started rubbing my ass.

"Jesus Christ, Raymond! Knock it off! Now!" I yelled when I stood up. He fought back a smile and grabbed his toothbrush. He

applied toothpaste to it and brushed, watching me with that goofy grin on face. "Did something happen, Ray?" I asked again, trying to keep my lip from quivering.

"No, Becca. Why do you keep asking, baby?" He put his arm around my waist and looked at me in the mirror.

"Because you have this fucking goofy grin on your face like you know something that I don't!" I snapped.

"Baby, it's common knowledge that whenever I'm around you, I always have a goofy grin on my face." He kissed my cheek. "If something happened last night, it would totally be happening again right now," he said with such veracity. He rinsed his toothbrush before offering it to me.

I snatched it from him, annoyed as hell.

"Whatever happened to ladies going first?" I snapped as I applied toothpaste to it.

"Don't worry, baby, when the time comes, I'll let you go first." He flashed me his best boyish grin. I rolled my eyes at him.

"Do you have any Advil? My head is pounding." I opened his medicine cabinet behind the mirror.

"You don't remember anything from last night, babe?" he asked. I grabbed the Advil and closed the cabinet. "Here, I'll open it," he offered. I turned to him and was met with his nicely toned bare chest. I gasped, not expecting that, of course. Cue the goofy grin. "Touch it. It's real." He put my hand on his chest.

"Shut up!" I smacked him. He laughed.

"So?" he prompted.

"Last thing I remember is sitting on the couch at the bar. You said I was beautiful." I sighed.

"You are beautiful, and I have a confession." He kissed me again.

"What?" I pulled away.

"We kissed ... a lot. And I, um ... touched you ... a lot."

"Where?" My eyes widened and my heart raced as mortifica-

tion came over me.

"Just here." He lightly tweaked my nipples.

"Stop!" I smacked his hand.

"And your butt. That's it. You passed out, and I did too. Are you mad?" He touched my chin to lift my face.

"What do you think?" I was terse.

"Hey, we were both drunk!"

"Yeah, but Jesus, Ray, I'm raw there!" I bit my lip then looked away, feeling the heat rise to my cheeks.

"I may have bitten them a little." He winced and held his hand up, almost pinching his forefinger and thumb together. I was so irritated; I just walked out of the bathroom and grabbed my shoes.

"I'll wait for you downstairs," I said. When he met me, he was more like his usual self. No more advances or sexual banter.

"Grayson?" I look over at him, my eyes filling up again.

"Hmm," is all he can manage.

"Why did I block this all out? This is making me nervous. I feel like I've gone crazy."

"Shh, love, c'mere." He pulls me to him. "Fucking bastard! He definitely slipped something into your drink," he says angrily.

"How could he do that to me? That's so unlike him."

"Becca, unfortunately, there's a lot about Ray that you don't know, love." He sighs.

"What, Grayson? Please tell me what you know. Please," I beg.

GRAYSON

"Okay, Becca. I'll tell you, but I'm nervous to do so." I'm not sure if I should do this, especially now that she's learned what he is capable of. But that's also why she needs to know.

"Why are you nervous?" She looks up at me.

"Well, I just don't want you to get caught up in the heat of the moment and blurt out the information we have."

I wait for her to get mad at me. She opens her mouth, but then closes it again, waiting to listen.

"Here goes nothing." I sigh. "Ray was a military man as well. At one time, his unit was stationed at the same place as George's. We're pretty sure he got to know George then. We're also pretty sure he found out George was alive, and then went to see him to make him an offer he couldn't refuse. Ray had moved a lot of things around and liquidated one million dollars of his assets. First, five hundred thousand about a month before your kidnapping, then the rest the same week you were kidnapped. We think he was paying George to kidnap you, but not harm you. He just wasn't planning on me or you seeing George at the inn. He wasn't planning on the security team. He didn't walk you to your truck because he knew George was there. We think his plan was to 'find' you and protect you. The end result would be you seeing the light and finally being with him. This is all theory, of course. We have no idea where the cash went. There's another person involved, but we haven't figured that out. It's not Stacey. Ray brought Stacey in when our arrangement started. We have the phone records, and records of their texts. You okay, sweetheart?" I just realized I haven't stopped talking.

"Yes, I'm okay. Keep going, please." She glances up.

"Well, we're really at a dead end. The only other info we have is that Will has slowly been depositing an extra nine to ten thousand dollars in cash a week into his accounts. It's a bit of a red flag. That's a lot of money for a mediocre dance studio in Ashland, New Hampshire. I believe Ray when he talks about Will. He truly despises him. From the info we've gotten around town, Will is not a big fan of Ray's. I guess Ray has threatened Will a time or two over your honor." I rub my face. This whole thing is crazy. It's all sitting right in front of us, and we can't seem to get all the dots connected.

"Well, that's Ray, I know he's done that. I've talked to him about it before." She says this almost as if she's forgotten—then her mouth slowly falls into a frown and her nose flares. I can see she's trying to fight back tears. "Baby," she almost whispers.

"Yes, love." I pull her face up to mine.

"Thank you for not yelling at me or breaking up with me. Thank you for being kind and understanding." She kisses me.

"Well, I was about to call the office phone and tell you I was going to spank you every time he called you *baby* or *babe*. I refrained, though, and didn't barge in, because I honestly felt my heart breaking for him. I thought to myself, *Better keep your mouth shut, Gracie, or you'll be worse off than this poor bloke!* But when I heard him basically admit what he had done, I couldn't get to you fast enough." I hold her to me tightly and kiss her head.

"You have my office bugged?" She pulls her head back.

"Oh, sweetheart, c'mon. You know my stalkerish tendencies know no bounds!" I chuckle. Just then, there is a knock on our door. "Entrée!" I shout. Morgan and Annie run in.

"Daddy, where's Mum? We want to bake!"

BECCA

Annie stops in her tracks when she sees me in Grayson's arms.

"Okay. I'm coming! We have so much to do! Annie, I'm glad you're here—we're gonna need all the help we can get!" I smile and stand up. "Hey, do you want to talk about what happened at school?" I whisper in her ear when I approach her.

"No." She looks down, her voice sad.

"Do you need something for your belly?" I ask. She nods. "Okay. Come with me and we'll get you something in the bathroom." I put my arm around her shoulders and lead her in there.

"Becca?" Her voice is so quiet.

"Yeah, sweetie?" I pull her hair back into a tie.

"Why don't you love my daddy anymore? He loves you so much. He wants to marry you. He tells me all of the time." She starts crying.

"Oh, Annie, please don't cry! I'll always love you and your daddy, but I love Grayson and I want to marry him." How am I to explain this to her?

"But you are our family. I wanted you to be my mom," she continues. My heart breaks.

"Annie, you are my family, and I will always only be a phone call away. I love you, Annie, as if you were my daughter—nothing will ever change that." I hug her and kiss her face. "Now, Miss Annie, its Christmastime and I need your help! We have so much stuff to make! Are you ready to turn that frown upside down?" I tickle her and she nods. We head out of the bathroom and collect Morgan and Gray, then head downstairs to find some of the security team bringing in fresh evergreen wreaths, garland, and branches. Grayson walks over to help. He brings some of it up to his nose and inhales deeply. He seems to get lost in a memory.

"Hey." I rub his back.

"Hi." He smiles. "I love this smell."

"Me, too. Do you want to start decorating out here, or do you want to bake with us?"

"Would you mind if I gave the decorating a go?" He holds the garland and looks around.

"Sure, baby, I'll be in the kitchen. Gray?"

"Yes, love?" He glances down at me.

"I love you and I'm so happy to have you in my life. It's going to be a wonderful Christmas." I lean up for a kiss.

"I love you, Becca," he says quietly as he leans his forehead against mine.

"Get to work, Mr. James." I tap his bottom.

"Oh ... Mrs. James." He shakes his head and bites his smile back. I pull his lip free from his teeth and give him a quick peck before I join the girls in the kitchen.

All three KitchenAid mixers are lined up and ready to go. There's about ten pounds of butter on the counter coming to room temperature. Large sacks of flour and white and brown sugars wait on the floor to be opened. Ovens are preheating and Christmas music is dancing around in the air.

"Aprons on, ladies! Let's get crackin'!" I grab mine.

"Shortbread first, Bec?" Hazel grabs the butter.

"Yes, they will take the longest. I think five batches will do ... that will give us twenty dozen. Is the butter softened?"

"Yep, we're ready for liftoff!" Hazel smiles.

I get the girls started on the brown sugar—one cup in each mixer, followed by the butter and flour. We knead the dough for a good five minutes, then roll it to half an inch in thickness. We cut it into three-inch-by-one-inch strips and place them on the baking sheets one inch apart. The girls prick them each several times with a fork. I didn't plan on having a remodeled, gourmet-restaurant kitchen, but am so glad for it now, especially with all of this extra food I have to make. This shortbread would've taken me a few hours in my old kitchen, but now I'm able to bake ten sheets all at once! It will only take me an hour. We move on to making some of our traditional cookies and breads.

Ah ... the smell of shortbread fills the kitchen. Karen Carpenter is singing, "Merry Christmas, darling ... Happy New Year, too ..." I feel tears in my eyes. There's something about Christmas—it's bittersweet! I clean the counter off and get ready to make peanut-butter balls.

The girls move in sync with each other—they're a great team. Annie looks so happy. She always is when she's here with Morgan and I and we're doing "mother/daughter things," as she likes to call them. Morgan just calls them boring and annoying. It's funny—we always yearn to do and experience the things we don't have, even something as simple as helping your mom with the dishes. Annie always begs to dry when I wash. I think she likes to pretend that I'm her mom and this is her chore. *Oh, my Annie ...*

"Annie?" I grab her hand to pull her away from the mixer.

"Yes, Mom ... er, Becca," she corrects herself. My heart twinges.

"Thank you for helping us. You're doing a great job, and I just wanted to tell you that I'm very proud of you and I love you very much, sweetie." I kiss her face and hug her. She holds me longer than a ten-year-old normally would.

"I wish you were my mom." She gives me a half smile, half frown. Her eyes begin to fill up.

"Well, Annie, I love you like I am. I will always love you and be proud of you as a daughter, no matter where I am or where you are. Do you understand me?" I wipe her tears away. She nods and hugs me again. I look over at Morgan, who is watching us. She smiles at me. I'm thankful that she's a lot like me. Any other ten-year-old may get jealous if their mother was this way with their best friend. *I love you*, I mouth to Morgan—just in case. She blows me a kiss to reassure me, I guess. God, I love that kid!

"Well, I don't think any of my recipes call for tears, so we better dry our eyes, young lady, and get back to work!"

"Okay." She smiles and heads back over to Morgan. Hazel and I start pulling the first ten trays of shortbread out of the oven and move them to the rolling rack to cool off.

"Sweetheart!" Grayson calls as he walks through the door. He stops dead in his tracks. "What's that?" He points to the Scottish shortbread and inhales the aroma.

"Scottish shortbread, baby," I say quietly, unable to read his expression.

"My mother's recipe?"

I nod, still unsure.

"Fresh evergreens ... today's the twenty-second?" he asks.

"Yes. Um, I don't have any of your ornaments from home, but I thought we could still hang the ones we have." I swallow hard. Why can't I read him?

"Auntie, please take the girls out of the kitchen for a moment." He looks at Hazel. I nervously find myself backing toward the wall near the fridge. Why does he want them out of here?

"Gracie?" Hazel looks bewildered. I don't think she can read him, either.

"Please, Auntie, now!" He's sterner.

"Come with me, girls." She extends her arms to them, but glances back at Grayson as she walks them out of the kitchen. When the door swings shut, Grayson brings his attention back to me. His nose flares and his jawline twitches like mad. Even his eyes seem to be filling up. My heart is pounding so hard I can hear it, along with "Up On the Rooftop," loudly in my ears. *Did someone turn up the radio?* Grayson strides toward me quickly, and I find myself trying to back up—unsuccessfully, as I already have my back against the wall.

My space is invaded by the intoxicating smell of Grayson James, sprinkled with a hint of shortbread. I know for a fact—they both taste delicious.

"Are you mad at me?" I stare straight ahead at his shirt and pull a little fuzz off of it. Maybe I shouldn't have done this. Maybe it's too hard for him.

"Mad?" He grasps my ponytail and pulls gently, making me look up at him. His left hand palms my cheek. "I'm mad with love for you." His lips caress mine, beckoning them to open so he can deepen the kiss. I relax and welcome the invasion, and we lose ourselves. "Becca ... God, I'm so overwhelmed by my love for you. My days are so much better with you in them." He leans his forehead against mine.

"Your days have been filled with one catastrophe after another since I've been in your life." I only tease because I'm the one who is now overwhelmed. By his words.

"Yes, sweetheart, you do know how to keep life interesting." He chuckles.

"Oh, the other girls in your life didn't come with explosions, murder mysteries, love triangles, assault and battery, or kidnappings?" I look up toward the ceiling as I ramble off the list of intriguing things I've brought to the table.

"Oh! Of course they did! Who doesn't?" He waves his hand. "You're just so much better at it, sweetheart!" There's that full-blown Grayson James smile. *Becca Campbell is weak in the knees. Why am I thinking in third person?* "Thank you, Becca." He holds my face and stares into my eyes. "For all of this ... for everything you do to show me you love me. I'm one lucky bloke, and I'd do well to remember that more often." He kisses me again, swiftly this time. "I'll tell the girls to come back now. I love you." A kiss on my forehead and he's off to get them. I decide to hold the wall up for another minute or two. Geez ... all this over his mother's shortbread cookies and evergreens. Wait until he sees what I do tomorrow!

Hazel and the girls rush back in.

"Becca, you okay?" Hazel asks as she studies my face.

"We done good, Mum!" I smile, and she breathes a sigh of relief. We spend the next three hours baking and cleaning as we go.

"Sandwiches or pizza tonight, girls?" I ask as we put the last few things away. Grayson comes in through the kitchen's swinging door.

"Sweetheart, where are your ornaments?" he asks. "Well, look at all of this! My, you girls have been busy!" Grayson stretches his arms out, taking in all we've accomplished in one day. "I'll tell you, you have this whole place smelling fantastic!" He ruffles Morgan's and Annie's hair.

"We have been working hard, Daddy!" Morgan smiles up at

him. She runs to the counter to get a shortbread cookie, then brings it to him. "Did you try Nanny's cookies? Are they as good as when she made them?" Grayson takes in a sharp breath. I follow suit.

"Let's see, Morgy." His voice shakes. He takes a bite and closes his eyes. I wait. "Nope. No, I'm sorry. It's not as good." He shakes his head, disappointed.

"I'm sorry, Daddy," Morgan says quietly and looks down, seemingly disappointed with his answer.

"Why, little sweetheart?" He takes another bite.

"That it's not good."

"Oh. I'm sorry. I thought I said it was even better. I didn't say that out loud?" he asks, acting shocked.

"No!" She playfully pushes him.

"Oh. Of course it tastes even better! It has your TLC in it! That's the main ingredient, you know." He hugs her. "Thank you, Morgy ... for being you. I love you, sweetheart, and my mother would've adored you." He holds her for another few moments before planting a kiss on top of her head.

"Hey, what do you want for dinner?" I come up behind him and rub his back.

"Why don't you make steak tonight, love?" He looks at me as he pops the rest of the cookie in his mouth.

"Uh, I can make a phone call to a restaurant to get you steak. Kitchen's closed, baby!" I pat his back.

"C'mon, Becca! Look at this amazing new kitchen I gave you! How many hours did I save you with it? I think you can cook up a few steaks, sweetheart." He pats my bum and I catch him winking at Hazel.

"As I said, where should we order from?" I open the junk drawer and pull out a ton of menus.

"Pizza!" the girls yell.

"Pizza it is." Grayson shrugs. "Auntie, can you order? I'd like Becca to show me where the ornaments are." When Hazel nods, I grab his outstretched hand and lead him into the stockroom.

"Unless everything was moved, they should be back here in this corner." I look around. "There they are!" I point up.

"Did you tell her to do that, Becca?" Grayson asks. I feel his hands at my hips.

"Who? Do what?" I try to turn to him, but he's holding me tightly. I only manage to crook my neck enough to look back at him.

"No, no. I'm enjoying the view here!" He smirks. "Did you tell Morgan to call my mother 'Nanny'?"

"No, not at all, Gray. Why would I do that? We are talking about Morgan here. She started calling you 'Daddy' right away without anyone telling her to. Gray ... oh, Gray, please stop." I close my eyes and lose focus as his hands caress my bottom and work their way up my shirt.

"What is it with this room?" he mutters against my ear. I turn my face to him and give in to his touch.

"Mom, Grammy Hazel said Aunt Stacey needs you!" Morgan yells into the stockroom. Grayson and I jump.

"Ugh!" He groans. "Go see what she wants. I'll get these down, love."

"Okay, baby." I try to regroup. I free myself and head out of the stockroom.

"Ms. Campbell!" Grayson yells before I'm out the door. I turn around. "Shag you later?" He smiles.

"As always, Mr. James." I return the expression. I've decided that we are a very cute couple!

"Hey, way to get out of baking today, you hermit!" I tease Stacey as I head into her room.

"Sorry, I've been on the phone with Ray. We need to talk." She sighs.

"You know what, Stacey? I'm not doing this! I'm having a wonderful evening with my family, and I'm not going to ruin it by discussing Ray with you! You know what you can do, though? You can sit back and think about where your fucking loyalty lies! I have been your best friend for twenty-three years! If that means nothing to you anymore and your friendship with Ray is more important, then maybe you should go and recoup at his house! I'm done trying to figure you out, Stacey! I don't know what the hell is going on with you, but I'm done!" I yell like a crazy lady and storm out of her room, slamming the door.

"Sweetheart, what the hell is going on?" Grayson grabs me in the hall.

"I can't do this anymore, Gray!" I yell at him without meaning to and start crying.

"What? Wait ... what did I do, sweetheart?" He grabs my arms and searches my eyes.

"Huh?" I look at him with complete confusion.

"What did I do?" He asks me again. *What the hell is he talking about?* "Becca, you said you couldn't do this anymore. What did I do wrong, love?"

"Oh. No, baby, not you. I'm sorry." I touch his face and kiss him. He visibly relaxes. "It's Stacey. She avoids us all day, and then the moment she shows signs of life, she wants to talk to me about Ray!" I let my emotions win.

"Go out there with the others, love. I'm going to have a chat with your friend." His words are calm, but there's all kinds of flaring and twitching going on.

"No, I'll handle this, Gray. You can't take care of everything for me." I bring his face back to mine.

"Yes I can, and I most certainly intend to, doll. So, unless you want to argue with me as well, I suggest you follow my orders." He's terse.

"Your orders?" I snap, but quietly. *Women's-Lib Sybecca is burning her bra in protest. All of the other Sybeccas sneak up behind her and hit her over the head with their rolling pins. She's rendered unconscious.*

"Yes! My *orders!*" he says again through gritted teeth. *Cautionary Sybecca stands with the red ticker board. "Go now!" runs across it.*

"Okay ... sir." I quickly grasp his lips with mine before I follow his orders. He swats my ass as I leave. It's not the playful type. It's more the painful, full-of-promise type. I should've known it was coming. Ever since he read my books, whenever I call him *sir* it's like a gateway drug for him. He's gotta push the envelope. *Hmm ... love the envelope-pushing around here!*

GRAYSON

"Stacey, it's Grayson. Are you decent?" I ask before I stroll in.

"Depends on your definition, gorgeous!" she replies. Always fucking flirting, this one!

"I'm coming in," I state.

"Oh, Grayson, I wish you would, honey."

Christ!

"Just what are you playing at, lady?" I lay right into her. She's taken aback.

"What do you mean, Grayson?"

"Becca flew three thousand miles to be by your side! She spent countless hours at the hospital and hotel, never mind the weeks she spent away from Morgan! I want to know what you are playing at. You two have been best friends more than half of your lives, but I only see one of you fulfilling that role! Now, what say you?" I could choke her for the pain she has caused Becca.

Stacey is sitting upright in her bed in her pink robe and matching turban.

"I say, I guess I haven't been a very good friend." She looks down at her hands. "Becca's always been the strong one, Gray. I've always been the flirty and fun one. That usually worked for me, until the guys I dated realized I was actually smarter than them. Then I was all wrong. No problem, I always had a backup—until Steve. Steve was the first guy who was fascinated by the whole package."

I try waiting for her to reveal her big aha moment, but I'm not known for my patience.

"Stacey! What the hell does that have to do with anything I've just said?"

"I don't know, Gray! I'm trying to figure it out myself!" she snaps back, sounding frustrated. "I guess I'm jealous. The only guy who appreciated the whole package no longer appreciates it! I come here and here's Becca—sweet, doe-eyed Becca—with two incredible guys fighting over her like she's Bridget Jones and this is her fucking diary! I just don't get it! Becca and I are very similar in every way. Well, except for our looks, and the fact that I'm flirty and she's not. But both of us are outgoing, funny, and smart. We're so much alike it's ridiculous, and yet half the fucking men around here have it bad for her! Why, because she's the *mysterious* Becca Campbell? Well, mystery solved—there is no mystery! She's just fucking oblivious, and all you fucking morons romanticize it into being *mysterious*! What a fucking joke!" she yells through her tears.

"Well, she is oblivious, I'll give you that. But, Stace, maybe you should take this time for you. You were with Steve for so long. Maybe your needs and wants are different now. I bet if you take this time to just concentrate on yourself and where you are in life, the other stuff with fall into place. From what Becca's told me—and even what you just said yourself—maybe you need to figure out who *Stacey* is without being on the arm of a gentleman. You know, the whole *mystery* of Becca is not just her being oblivious, it's that she was not looking for any of this. She just wanted to raise her daughter right. She wanted to be a positive part of the community and to be a good person. She's a challenge to men—that's why we all want her. She doesn't need us. We *want* her to need us." I'm amazed this is all coming out of my mouth, because I haven't put much thought into it. I just knew she was going to be mine.

"Everybody thought she would end up with Ray. He's been in her life pretty steadily for the past five years. So how did you win her over so quickly, Gray?" She crosses her arms, waiting.

"Chemistry ... moth to flame ... love at first sight. Whatever you want to call it, we have it. And I'm selfish and persistent. I wanted her. I gave her no chance to think about it—that's all." I shrug.

"Speaking of selfish, Ray told me what happened today. Grayson, he really is beside himself for so many different reasons. I can't believe he did what he did, but I can see why, as inexcusable as it is. He's worried about Annie." She grabs a tissue and dabs her eyes.

"Why is he worried about Annie?" I'm puzzled.

"Well, if he's arrested for what he did, it will destroy her. He's also worried that with his parents away, Annie will have to go to Child Protective Services. That's why I wanted to talk to Becca to see if she would wait at least until after Christmas. He wants Annie to have a good Christmas and his parents will be back by then." Hmm ... Becca and I haven't even talked about what she is going to do, although I'd be very surprised if she pressed charges.

"I think that is something Ray and Becca should discuss together. Speaking of Ray, why were you trying to help him break us up?" I'm not leaving here without getting some old questions finally answered.

"I wanted Ray. I've always had a crush on him. So I pushed Becca toward you. Honestly, she made it easy—it was so obvious that she's in love with you. Then I finally realized he just wanted her, so I thought I could win you over if I helped him break you guys up. How am I doing by the way—winning yet?" She smirks. I pat her knee and smile. "I'm sorry, Grayson. I do feel terrible about it all." Her chin quivers.

"Well, tomorrow's a new day! Start over. Just be her friend. She needs you. Why don't you come out and join us for carols, pizza, and ornaments?" I offer. She nods.

"Okay. I'll be out in a bit."

"All right, then, I'll see you out there." I get up and head out.

Becca, Morgan, and Annie are sitting in front of the Christmas tree I had some of the detail get.

"Hey, what do you girls think?" I ask cheerfully. I think they chose a magnificent tree! I turn to them, only to have the smile fall off my face. Becca's expression is flat. Morgan looks like she's on the verge of tears, and Annie's more interested in playing with the zipper on her sweater. "What's the matter? What's wrong with it?" I look back to the tree.

"Nothing, Gray, it's a beautiful tree." Becca sighs.

"Then what is it?" I can't help feeling annoyed.

"It's not *our* tree, Daddy. We didn't pick it out together. We always pick out our tree. It's our tradition," Morgan says through her tears.

"Oh," is all I can say. "Well, we can go tomorrow and pick out a tree. We can donate this one, or we can have two." I feel awful. I didn't even think to ask what their traditions are. I'm so focused on trying not to be depressed about my parents, mainly my mother, that I haven't even thought about what Becca may be feeling.

"Grayson, it's a lovely tree and it will be fine." Becca grabs my hand and squeezes. "Hey, Morgy, it's okay. It's a special tree because the people that are here to protect us picked it out. Maybe they do that at home, and since they can't be there for Christmas, it brought them some joy. Remember, it's not just our tree this year."

No mystery here ... she's absolutely wonderful! Morgan cheers up with a smile and hugs me.

"Sorry, Daddy. I didn't mean to make you feel bad."

"Next year will be different, little sweetheart. I promise."

"Hey! Pizza's here!" Aunt Hazel announces. Derek, Joshua, and Ryan carry in several pies each and bring them to the dining room. I grab Becca's arm before she follows everybody in.

"Becca, I am sorry." I pull her to me.

"It's okay, baby. You're doing and worrying about so much. Please don't give it another thought. Hey, how did everything go in there?" She kisses me and glances toward Stacey's room.

"She was a bit all over the place, really. But the gist of it is that she's upset with where her life is at. And she's a bit jealous of you. There is some merit there, but I don't think it's everything. Something's off." I shake my head. I just can't put my finger on it.

"I definitely agree with you there. Did you get that info from Jake?"

"Hmm, no, I haven't heard. Say, listen, sweetheart. She did mention Ray and what she wanted to talk to you about," I say. Becca rolls her eyes and takes in a deep breath. "He's worried you are going to press charges. With his parents away until Christmas, if you press charges and have him arrested, Annie will go with Child Protective Services until he posts bail. He's hoping you'll wait until after Christmas." I rub the top of Becca's arms.

"Uh, Gray, I haven't even though that much about it yet." Her eyes are wide and she has a trace of panic on her face. Panic? Why panic?

"Well, I told her that was a discussion for you and Ray to have," I add.

"You did? That's what you think?" She furrows her brow at me.

"Yes. Why, what did you think I was thinking?" I hold her at arm's length.

"I ... I don't know, Gray. I'm really not sure of how you feel about this whole thing." She looks down.

"Well, I'm pissed about what he did. Yet I feel sorry for him. I'm actually quite confused regarding how I feel. It's very strange, very unlike me. Becca, whatever you want to do, I'll support you, sweetheart." I pull her back to me.

"I just wish I could talk to him. Without him trying to touch me or kiss me." She sighs.

"Becca, how do *you* feel?" I tilt her face up to mine.

"I'm mad as hell. And hurt. I get that I've led him on terribly over the years, but I'm confused. I just want to understand why he did that to me. It was really out of character. Does this sound weird? I feel like I shouldn't be concerned with it, though. That I should just have him locked up and throw away the key." I thumb away her tears.

"But you didn't even think of pressing charges?" I ask gently. She shakes her head. "I think, sweetheart, that's because it was Ray who did it, not some random bloke. Ray has had a big and lengthy investment in you and your well-being. Becca, I know he loves you very deeply. I knew that from the moment I met him. That's why even though most arrows point to him, something's not sitting right with me." I suddenly feel as if we're being watched. I glance up. "Stacey—come to join us now?" I ask, almost too loudly.

"Uh, yes, if that's okay." She seems very fidgety. Hmm. Something is really off with her, and I don't like it.

"We'll finish up our conversation later, sweetheart," I whisper in Becca's ear.

"Okay, baby." She turns her head and kisses the corner of my mouth ... then my lips. She's not interested in stopping. I know what she's doing—and I'm always willing to play. Stacey watches us as we devour each other.

"Ugh! C'mon, you two!" Morgan yells. We laugh a little as we pull away.

"Oh, man, do I have an itch I need you to scratch," Becca says breathlessly before she quickly lays another one on me.

"Oh, I'm itching to scratch it, love!" I smack her lovely arse before we head to the dining room. "Come, Stacey." I hold my hand out to her.

"I'm okay." She smiles and limps along.

They are quiet all through dinner, allowing only a glance or two toward each other. I wish I could fix this for them, that I could figure out what is going on with Stacey.

"Becca, can I stay for the weekend?" Annie asks quietly. Becca looks to me. I nod. I'm falling for Annie—she's quite the girl.

"I'll talk to your father and ask him," she offers as she collects everyone's plates.

Stacey looks at me, her eyes wide. I give her a quizzical look. She mouths, *She's calling him?* I ignore her.

"Come, let's all go to the lounge and sing some Christmas carols." I get up and lead the parade in there while Becca brings the leftover pizza to the kitchen. "What shall we sing first?" I strum my fingers down the keys of the piano.

"How about something fun like 'Dominick the Donkey'?" Stacey suggests. Annie cheers.

"Well, I know the jingle, but not all of the words." I play around with the keys 'til I get it right. Everyone starts singing except for Morgan and Aunt Hazel. I follow Morgan's glance and see Becca. Her face distorts a bit, like she's about to cry. She shakes her head as if she's trying to push off whatever is bothering her and promptly turns to go back into the kitchen. "Scott, can you take over for a moment, please?" I ask. He's one of the guys on our team—plays pretty well.

"Becca, sweetheart, what's the matter?" I follow her into the kitchen.

"Oh, nothing. It's silly, really." She wipes her tears.

"No it's not. Tell me, please." I grab her hands.

"That song reminds me of my dad. He loved it. Loved to sing

it. He would really make an ass out of himself." She giggles, a bit lost in the memory, I think. "It's such a silly song to get sad over. I do like to hear it, though, because it makes me feel close to him. What made you play that?" she asks, and I feel my concern turn toward anger.

"Somebody requested it." I won't dare give Stacey the satisfaction.

"Oh. Well, come on, maestro. There are many other songs I'd like to hear!" She pulls me back out. "Hey, Stace." Becca grabs her hand. "Let's sing. Gray, can you play 'Merry Christmas with Love'?" She pulls out sheet music. I guess she had Melissa pick it up for her.

"Sure, baby." I put it up in front of me. Becca walks around to the other side so she and Stacey are facing each other.

"Our usual?" Becca smiles.

"Okay, Becca." Stacey seems unsure and emotional at the same time. I start playing. Becca sings the first verse, Stacey does the next. They take turns with the lines in the third verse and join together for the chorus. They sound lovely. They are having quite the moment with each other. I can see their connection again. They finish to a round of applause. After another hour or so, we're all caroled out. The girls grab me to watch *A Christmas Story*.

"I should go call Ray," Becca says with a sigh.

"Okay, love, then you'll join us?" I rub her back. She nods and leans into my chest. "Take as long as you need. He can't try to physically persuade you over the phone." I kiss her hair.

"You're right." She plants a kiss on my chest and heads off to her office.

Chapter Nine

BECCA

I take several deep breaths before I dial the familiar number I've been dialing for five years.

"Hello?" Ray answers. I can sense his guard is up.

"Um, hi." I swallow.

"Becca, is Annie okay?" His voice shakes, as if he's nervous. I guess he thinks the only reason I'd call him myself is if something was wrong with her.

"She's fine. She's having a great time. She'd like to stay the whole weekend, if that's okay with you." I'm deafened by the silence on the other end. "McNeil, stop thinking so hard ... there's smoke coming through the receiver over here." I try to break the ice. "I'm not pressing charges against you." That should do it! I hear a sigh of relief on his end.

"Not that I want you to, but why?" he asks. I can picture his furrowed brow on the other side.

"I have my reasons. I do want to know what led you to the decision to do what you did. Please tell me. That's all I ask, Ray." I'm both relieved and mad at myself for finding it so easy to talk to him about this. He didn't take my car without my permission—he took *me* without my permission! "What did you slip me?"

"Ecstasy," he breathes.

"Now, why?" I shake my tears away.

"Becca, I have to spell it out for you, baby?" I can hear him trying to control his annoyance.

"No, I know I've strung you along. Not intentionally," I add quickly.

"Yeah, babe, not intentionally. For over five years!" he almost yells.

"I'm sorry, Ray." *Wait ... why the fuck am I apologizing?*

"Well, you paid for it, didn't you?" A verbal slap.

"Ray!" I gasp, then start to cry. *Who is this person?*

"Becs ... Becs, stop crying, baby." His voice softens. He sounds like my Ray again.

"What ... what brought you to ... ugh, Ray—you know what I'm asking." I feel so defeated. I just want to understand. What was the straw?

"Yeah. I just don't get the point, baby! It's over and done with."

"Because I want to know!"

"There's nothing *to* know!" he yells back. "I slipped it into your drink, and as soon as I saw it was working, I took you home and fucked the shit out of you for hours! There's nothing else to know!"

I pull the phone away from my ear. It is vibrating with his rage—I can only imagine what it would be like if he was right in front of me. I'm glad he's not.

"That's all it was to you? That's all you wanted?" I swallow hard. I thought he loved me. I thought he wanted more.

"No, baby, I made love to you first. Oh God, you were so ... oh, I love you, Becca, I do. I'm sorry for what I did. I hope someday you will forgive me." His voice is the one shaking now.

"You haven't answered my question. Take the extra day to think about it. Pick Annie up on Sunday." I slam the phone down.

The private line rings as soon as I sit back.

"Hello?" I sigh.

"Don't hang up, baby. I'll tell you what you want to know. Becca, I just ... I love you so much. I'm hurt and upset—I may yell and get impatient. Becs, are you there?" Now he's the one who sounds defeated.

"Yes, I'm here." I'm barely audible.

"Can I come over there and talk to you? I need to see your face, baby. Please." His voice is thick with yearning.

"I don't think that's a good idea, Ray—for either of us." I sit back and close my eyes.

"Because I'll touch you ... because you'll like it ... because you'll hate that you like it? Some things never do change." I sense his smile.

"Tell me everything that happened. Start from what made you decide to get one of those pills." I decide to ignore his comment.

"Oh, there's that convenient pretending. In Becca's world, things aren't said, kisses aren't kissed, and touches aren't touched. You are the queen of denial, baby."

Butterflies erupt in the pit of my stomach.

"Ray, you called me back to tell me what I wanted to know. That is all I'm asking. If I was any other girl—you wouldn't have it this easy." I give him my best *don't fuck with me* voice.

"Easy?" he questions flippantly. I await a comment about being a whore or something. "If you were any other woman, you'd have my fucking ring on your finger and we'd be on our third kid by now! Nothing with you has been easy, Becca!"

"Please stop yelling at me. Please, Ray, just tell me. I need to be able to work through what you did ... for Annie's sake."

"What the hell does Annie have to do with this?"

"Ray, I love her. She loves me. Morgan's her best friend. I don't want to lose her, too." I can't help it—I'm crying.

"You haven't lost me, baby. I'm still yours. I'll always be yours. Becca, I love you. I'll wait for you to wake up and realize who you're supposed to be with." He's reassuring me. He's yelling at me. He's trying to seduce me. He's making me feel guilty. He's doing everything but telling me what happened.

"Ray, please, sweetie. Please tell me. I need to know. Please, Raymond." I speak as softly as I can.

"Oh, baby, you are so lucky I'm not there right now. You want to know everything, baby? I mean *everything*?" He's calm. I need to keep him this way.

"Yes, please. *Everything*," I emphasize. I hear him inhale deeply just as a text lights up my phone. Glad I put it on vibrate. I look at it.

December 22, 2012   9:15 p.m.
Gray: SWEETIE?! WTF, Becca? R U 4 real?!

"Shit! Hold on, Ray," I say quickly.

"Why?"

"I spilled my coffee on my desk," I lie. "Hold on."

"Becca, are you alone right now?" He's getting nervous, I think. Rightfully so—I am engaged to Grayson, who has brought stalking behavior to a whole other level!

"Yes, Ray, I am. Call Stacey and ask her to check if you don't believe me!" I snap.

"Okay, baby, I just know how he is." He sighs.

No ... you really don't!

"Hold on, sweetie," I say again.

"Okay, baby."

December 22, 2012   9:18 p.m.

Me: Bait! Please trust me. Bear with me, baby, and later you can slap my ass 'til it has more shades of red than inside a crayon box!

Gray: Don't call him baby! I swear to Christ, Becca, your ass will be black and blue.

Me: I would never! Black and blue, huh? Ouch! Now let me get back. I love u. U r my world.

Gray: I've got my mental purple pants on!

Me: Mmm. I'm mentally pulling them off.

Gray: Looking for something incredible? :)

Me: Already found it! :) Love you!

Gray: Oh, Becs, baby :)

Me: Shh. Stop now! Love you!

Gray: XXXXX Love u 2!

"Becca?"

"Sorry, I'm such a klutz." I sigh.

"Yeah, I know. I'm coming over. I don't want to have this conversation over the phone, baby."

"Oh, so you want to have it in front of security and Grayson instead?" I'm snarky. I can't help it.

"Well, I don't feel comfortable talking about it on the phone!"

"Ray, I already told you I'm not pressing charges."

"Yeah, Becs, you also told me that you loved me!" he sneers.

"I do love you, Ray. I love you very much." It's the honest-to-God truth, and he knows it.

"I need to see your face. I want to touch you, yes, but I need to read your face, baby." He sounds defeated again.

"We know each other well enough to know exactly what the

other is doing. For instance, when you said that, you placed your head in your hand, fisted your hair, and pulled." I take in a sharp breath, feeling overwhelmed by how well I know him—how much I've noticed.

"I'm not going to tell you who I got it from. I got it right after Christmas. I had it on me every time we went out, but I always found a reason not to use it. Mostly, I was afraid you'd either get hurt or find out and kick me to the curb."

"Kick you to the curb? Now who's stuck in the nineties?" I laugh.

"Baby, don't interrupt me, or I'll stop."

"Okay. Sorry," I say softly again, because it has always visibly stirred something in him when I do.

"The night of your birthday, you said you made sure you could sleep your hangover off if you got one. You had coverage for Morgan and the inn the next morning. You wanted to stay out late and forget your age. Forget all your worries. I cleared my schedule for the next day. I still wasn't sure if I was going to go through with it. We were having such a great time. It's funny ... you get a few drinks in you and you forget to pretend. You have to remember some of it, Becca. Don't you remember us dancing and kissing? That happened well before I slipped the pill into your drink." He waits.

"Ray, I don't know why I've been blocking stuff out. I'm putting a call into Patricia after Christmas. It's actually scaring me."

"So, you're really not pretending? You don't remember?" He sounds miffed.

"I don't remember kissing you on my birthday. No ... wait a minute. Was everybody chanting for us to kiss after we sang?"

"'Don't You Wanna Stay' by Kelly Clarkson and Jason Aldean. Yes, we gave them a lot of reason to. You remember, baby?"

"Yes." My voice shakes. This is really freaking me out.

"After that, we couldn't stop kissing. I thought, *Oh God, finally ... she's ready to be mine*. I was so happy. Then somebody said what a cute couple we were, and you said, *Oh, we're just friends*. All of a sudden it was like you put yourself on lockdown. You told me to stop kissing you, that people were getting the wrong idea. I saw red, baby." He takes in a deep breath.

"I'm sorry. I know I've done that to you a lot." I shake my head—I'm such a jerk.

"Yeah, well, after I'm done telling you all this, we're going to have a conversation about that!" he snaps. "So, I said fuck it! I got you another glass of wine and slipped it in and let it dissolve."

"Ray, I had a lot of alcohol in me at that point. There could have been very serious repercussions for adding drugs to the mix!" My voice gets shakier the harder I try to control it.

"Baby, I only gave you half. I was worried about that, too. I wanted you in my bed, not dead." He chuckles.

"You should write that in a poem to me," I say sarcastically.

"Yeah, I will. So, do you want me to continue?"

"Yes." My voice is soft.

"Um, so, typical Becca couldn't leave a drop of wine in her glass! Don't roll your eyes," he says, and I giggle. "Stop biting your lip."

"Yes, ba ... Ray." *Shit!* My phone lights up. Grayson's texted me a ton of symbols. I fan myself with a folder.

"After about fifteen minutes or so, you kept closing your eyes and biting your lip. Finally, I pulled your lip away from your teeth and you opened your eyes. I leaned in and kissed you. Your breathing was erratic and your eyes were shifting quickly back and forth. I asked you if you were ready to go home with me. You nodded. I said you were coming to my house—to my bed. You nodded again. I grabbed your hand and we left. I helped you into my truck and we kissed. I asked you if you were feeling all right. You said you were okay and just wanted to get back to my house. I said, *Becs, I want to make love to you.* You said, *I want you too, baby. I need you.* I think I floored it all the way home. I could barely concentrate on the road—you were all over me."

"I called you *baby*?" My mouth just went dry.

"Yes. You called me *baby* a lot that night. You rarely call me that. It was nice."

I look to my phone ... nothing. That's not good.

"Um, so, we got to my house. Becca, are you crying, baby?" He stops.

"Yes." Why lie?

"Do you want me to stop?"

"No, keep going." I try to catch my breath.

"I carried you upstairs."

"Why? Was I passed out?"

"No, baby. Once we got into the house, we threw our coats off and you jumped up on me, so I carried you up."

"It's disturbing that I don't remember any of this."

"Well, I don't know what to tell you, babe." He sighs.

"Why did you redress us? Why didn't you just let me think I was a willing partner in all of this?" I don't get it.

"Becs, we almost had sex several months before that and you wouldn't talk to me for six months! I was pretty sure if you woke up naked next to me after drinking, we'd pretty much be on a permanent break!" He's annoyed ... and right. I would've completely flipped. Then again, maybe not. I remember feeling sore the next day—and liking it, once I got over my initial anger. I was pretty sure Ray's fingers had ventured down there, but I didn't think he remembered or that it went further than that. I feel my face flush. I start fanning myself again. Why did I not remember all of this until today?

"Theme song, babe?" I hear him flicking through sports channels.

"No. What song could cover this mess?" I pick up my stapler and play with it.

"What mess, baby? You're not referring to your birthday, I

hope. That wasn't a mess—that was hot. You were so hot, baby. I just wish it didn't happen the way it did. It's ridiculous that I had to drug you to get you to relax enough to act on your feelings."

"Oh! Is that what you did, Ray? Helped me to *relax* enough to act on my feelings? You're an asshole!" I slam my stapler down.

"Are you abusing your office supplies, baby?" He chuckles.

"Are you fucking watching hockey, Ray, while we're having a serious conversation?" I yell.

"No." I hear the TV go off.

"Liar! That's all you are, Raymond, a fucking liar!" God, why can't I go longer than ten minutes without crying?

"Liar, huh? Look in the fucking mirror, babe!" He's getting angry, which means his eyes are turning a stormier color.

"What are you talking about?" I don't lie. I'm terrible at it!

"You've been lying to me—and yourself—for five years!" He's got his "sit and spin" expression on his face, I just know it!

"About what?"

"About your feelings for me! You love me, Becca!"

I move the phone away from my ear again.

"I said I love you. I haven't denied it." I speak softly, hoping to calm him down and save my eardrum.

"Really, babe? Really?"

"Yes, really, Ray. You know I do."

"You don't get what I mean. You love me more than a friend. You've been too afraid to act on it until recently, and that's only because loving Grayson scared you more than loving me." His voice is shaky. We sit in silence as I let his words marinate. "Are we going to fall asleep listening to each other breathe? We haven't done that in a while, baby." He's calm now. He's my Ray.

"I'm sorry, Ray. I'm sorry for both of us. I'm sorry I fought off my feelings for you. You were always more than enough. I need you to understand and know this. If I could go back in time, I'd tell myself to stop being an idiot, but I can't. And everything happens for a reason."

"Your nose is flaring, your eyes are turning emerald, and I just want to kiss you—like I always do when you're crying, or getting ready to. I'm so in love with you, Becca. The past five years have been the happiest of my life. We had it all, baby. We just didn't have it on paper, and we didn't get to go home to it. That's all. We had it everywhere else. I miss you. I miss us. I'm lost without you. My theme song ... 'Who Knew' by Pink. I've got to go, Becca. I'll pick Annie up on Sunday after lunch. I love you, baby."

I take in a shaky breath.

"I love you too, Ray."

We hang up. I sit at my desk for another fifteen minutes and have a good cry.

I wipe my face and put on my mental big-girl pants. I have to go and face Grayson now. I really don't know what to expect. It's after ten already ... geez! I'll check on the girls first.

I open the door to room 205. The TV and a small lamp are both on. There they are—Frick and Frack, asleep. They're holding hands and their heads are leaning against each other's. They're just like sisters ... who look nothing alike except for eye color. I take a picture of them. I unblock Ray and text him the picture with *Our Sleeping Beauties* under it. I turn off the lamp, plug in the night-light, and turn the TV off. My phone pings.

December 22, 2012   10:33 p.m.
Ray: 'Need You Now'—Lady Antebellum
Me: G'night. C U Sunday. BTW what does Annie want 4 Xmas?
Ray: Same thing as me.
Ray: YOU!
Me: Night
Ray: Love you, baby ... always.

I don't answer—what is there left to say? I take in a deep breath and head into our room. Grayson is sitting up in bed, wearing nothing but PJ bottoms and his glasses. His back is against the headboard. He's finishing a phone call.

"Hi." I'm nervous. I can actually feel hives forming on my upper chest. He holds his hand out. I reach for it, but he smacks my hand away.

"Phone!" he snaps. I hand it to him. He fools around with it. My guess is that he's re-blocking Ray. *It's tough being this brilliant.* "Unblock him again and you will regret it! Do I make myself clear?" He sounds extremely British—extremely authoritative.

"Yes, baby." I can't argue any more tonight. I'm physically and mentally exhausted.

"I've drawn a bath for you. Not as hot as you like it because it's not good for the baby, but I think it's warm enough to relax you." He picks up his latest financial novel. Ho ... hum ... snore!

"Is there a glass of wine with that bath?" I smile.

"Don't be ridiculous. You're pregnant. You think I'd encourage hurting my child?" He flips the page of his book with a gust of aggressive irritation.

"It was a joke, baby. Would you like to join me?" I sit down and rub his feet. He pulls them away.

"No, Becca, I don't care to join you."

I can't help my frown. I thought women were *supposed* to be difficult, trying, and exhausting.

I head into the bathroom and peel myself out of my clothes. Ugh! This is not warm enough. I turn on the jets to hide the sound of the faucet as I run it and drain some of this water. I sit back and close my eyes.

"Here are your pajamas, Becca. What are you doing?" I open my eyes to find Grayson checking the water temperature with his hand. "Becca, this is too hot! You can't have it over one-hundred degrees, sweetheart!" He turns the faucet off and sticks the tub thermometer in the water. I smile a little. He's so cute. "No, no, Becca! You've got it at a hundred and one, love. Why can't you just do as you are told?" He rubs his face.

"Come join me, Gracie." I smile up at him.

"No, I'm going to bed." He seems too calm.

"What happened to scratching my itch? Seeing you in just your pajama bottoms ... the way they hang like that ... mmm ... I feel extra itchy, baby." I bite my lip.

"Take some Benadryl. Good night, *Becs*!"

I can't help but notice his emphasis. Ugh! He leaves the bathroom. I close my eyes again. I quit.

I get out of the tub and dry off. Where the hell are the PJs he brought in? I wrap my towel around myself and head out to the bedroom. It's lit by twenty or so candles. Grayson is standing there, smiling. He holds out his hand to me as Norah Jones sings sweetly in the background. I reach for his hand, and he pulls me to him. He smells incredible, as usual. We sway slowly to the music. I let go of his hand to explore his chest with both of mine. I trail soft kisses across it. He pulls my towel off as he guides me to our bed. I climb onto it backward and tug at his bottoms, letting them fall. Grayson grabs my hands as he moves closer to the bed. I feel another pair of hands on my hips. I take in a sharp breath and turn my head to find a very naked Ray. He captures my lips sweetly. I feel Grayson softly caressing my breast, and I turn to him. He kisses me as Ray's right hand slides down on an angle.

"*Ahh* ..." I moan. I'm not sure if it's from Grayson's harsh play at my nipples or Ray's fingers diving deep inside of me. My left arm goes over Grayson's shoulder and my right arm reaches back and encircles Ray's neck. My body moves in rhythm with their touch. I pull away from Grayson's mouth to find Ray's. I feel myself slowly climbing.

"That's it, sweetheart ... pray for me," Gray says, egging me on.

"Come for me, baby." Ray bites my ear as they work me into a frenzy.

"Oh God. Oh. Oh God!" I yell.

I open my eyes.

"What ... *the hell* was that?" Grayson asks, his own eyes wide. I swallow hard, trying to adjust to my whereabouts.

"Um ... I guess that was a wet dream. Ahem—literally." I can't help but giggle a bit.

"Who was in this wet dream of yours?" Grayson asks flatly as he hits the drain.

"You, baby, and those damn PJ bottoms." I lick my lips and turn him into a steak. Why mention Ray's presence in my dream? By the way—*what the fuck, Becca*? Man, I need to get in to see Patricia!

"Let's go to bed." He holds up my towel and wraps it around me when I stand.

"I thought you'd never ask," I tease, and lean in to kiss him. He backs away.

"To sleep, Becca." He helps me out of the tub.

"Why are you avoiding me like this?" I try to kiss him again.

"Becca, please, I'm so mad. Just do as you are told ... please!" He looks down.

"Do you want to spank me?" I try to lighten his mood.

"Not when I want to beat the shit out of you. I don't think that would be a good idea," he snaps. "What I'm feeling is irrational, and I'm trying to work through it. It would help if you would just listen and go to sleep!"

As I dry off, I feel his gaze on me. I purposely turn and bend in front of him, putting my leg up on the step of the tub.

"I'm moving you and Morgan to California permanently after Christmas," he says. I think he's trying to piss me off in answer to my theatrics.

"Okay, baby." I sigh with indifference. "What day will you be taking us, sir?" *Horny Sybecca is by the campfire, pouring a can of fuel on it. She's tramped out in leather and looking to be tied.* I feel the breeze as Grayson shuts the door after himself. I'm disappointed. I was hoping to feel the sting of his slap. What the hell is going through his mind? *All Sybeccas hold up their white flags.* We're too tired to continue the charade.

I put my PJs on and head out to my bedroom cautiously, just in case. *Mental facepalm!* Like they would ever think of doing what they did in my dream. God, that was hot. I'd like to fall asleep to that instead of the cold shoulder I'm getting from Grayson.

I climb on my side and start applying my lotion. Grayson eyes me.

"Can you do my back, baby?" I try to hand him the lotion. He turns away. "Wow, really?"

"Yes. Really," he says with a sigh.

I close the cap and place it on my nightstand. I soak in the sight of him. His bare, beautiful back, all the way down to his bum. Hmm. If the roles were reversed, he would give me a good swat. Well, what's good for the goose ...

He gasps and jumps.

"What the—?"

I bite my playful smile back. My smile fades as he glares at me angrily.

"Grayson, please talk to me. It's obvious my conversation with Ray struck a nerve. We promised we would communicate better." I move closer to him and kiss his shoulder. He exhales loudly through pursed lips.

"Sweetheart, I'm trying to sort everything out in my head. I'm all over the place, and I don't want to behave irrationally. I'm mad. I don't know if I have the right to be, or what exactly I'm mad about." He plays with my fingers. I cross my legs and tap his knee, asking him to do the same. We sit face-to-face and hold hands.

"Let's sort it out together, baby. I'm having a bit of trouble myself. Maybe we can help each other."

He nods and releases my hand, then retrieves a few papers from his book.

"What's that?" I bend my head sideways to see. He looks up at the ceiling and turns the paper toward me.

"Wow—you are a master! You should teach classes, or at least let the FBI use you as a teaching tool!" I joke. It's my entire conversation with Ray, dated and time-stamped. I grab it and start giggling. "This is like a play! It even has stage directions! Well, you know what I mean. *Becca gasps ... remorseful tone ... Becca cries ... they sit in silence.*" Grayson smiles a little, no doubt in spite of himself. "Who did this? Wait! It has our texts!" I can't help it. I'm in a full fit of laughter.

"I'm glad you find this amusing, Ms. Campbell," he snaps.

"Oh, stop! C'mon, let's have a look." I hit his shoulder playfully.

"Well, give it to me. I have notes." He grabs it back.

"Ahem, would you like your glasses, professor?" I ask, then reach for them. He slaps my ass. "Hey, don't make promises you're not sure you can keep." I raise an eyebrow and place his glasses on his nose. He stares into my eyes. "What?" I almost whisper.

"You scare me."

"Well, it's been a long day. I can't always look my best." Joking is my defense in the face of overwhelming words.

"You're beautiful, sweetheart. You know what I mean. My feelings for you scare me."

A shot of electricity goes to my groin when he grasps my hips.

"What was that, sweetheart?" I open my eyes to find a delighted look on his face.

"Um, this pregnancy ... all of my senses are heightened when you touch me." I close my eyes again and place my hands on top of his.

"Did this happen when Ray grabbed your hips earlier today?"

I open my eyes again and look at him as if he has five heads. "No, not at all."

"Just me?" He squeezes.

"Just you ... only you." I palm his face.

"Let's go over this." He picks up the papers again. I nod and kiss his lips before I sit back.

"Okay. Let's see." He sighs and peers at the paper. I giggle. He looks up.

"Sorry. It's just, you look like Clark Kent. It's very cute."

He gives me a half smile, then turns his attention downward again.

"What does this mean? Pretending things haven't happened?"

"Um, I really don't know. I'm just discovering that I've blocked a lot of things out."

"You love him?" he asks without looking at me.

"Yes. I love him." I'm honest, and his nostrils flare. "I'm *in love* with you, Grayson, there's a difference." I touch his cheek.

"I think you are in love with him as well. You're just denying it to all of us, including yourself." He won't look at me.

"No, you're wrong. Next question." I'm flat.

"You called him *baby*."

"I was drunk and high and it's hearsay!" I have to defend myself.

"Why did you cry when he told you?" He glances up quickly.

"Because you didn't text me, and I was worried about what you were thinking." Rightfully so, I guess!

"You almost said it again tonight." He continues to look down.

"Grayson, I'm used to talking to you. I caught myself, didn't I?" Now I wish I just went to sleep!

"Was he right about you being scared to love me?"

"Yes."

"Why?" He pulls his glasses off.

"I've never felt this way before. It was intimidating ... you

184

were intimidating. I couldn't shut it down." I swallow hard. "I've explained this to you before. Remember my roller-coaster comparison?"

He gives me a thoughtful nod, then looks back down at his notes.

"You wish you could go back and change your behavior with him?"

"Yes. I don't think what I did was fair to either of us. You heard me say that." I throw my hands up, completely irritated with the direction this conversation has taken.

"So, hypothetically ..." He presses his fingertips together and brings them up to his chin. "You would go back in time and be with Ray if you could. Therefore, you would not be with me now. But you would change it anyway?" I roll my eyes.

"Read what I said next."

"Everything happens for a reason."

"Right! You are the reason I held Ray off for all these years. I just didn't realize it until you came. Are you almost done? I have a few questions for you."

"Just two more." He looks down. His eyelids are going mad. He's nervous. Good—I'm tired of this crap!

"Why did you stay in the office and cry for seventeen minutes after you hung up?"

"Seventeen minutes? Really? How many seconds, or did you not document that?"

"Twenty-four seconds."

"Well, good, I thought you were slipping. I shouldn't have to tell you why I cried for seventeen minutes and twenty-four seconds. It's pretty apparent!"

"I think you cried because you feel torn."

"Last question, Grayson!" I snap.

"Why did you unblock him?" He puts the papers to the side.

"I took a cute picture of our daughters and thought he would like it," I say through my teeth. "All done?" I smile.

"Yes." He takes his glasses back off.

"You need to decide what you want, Grayson!" I poke him with my finger.

"What are you talking about, sweetheart?"

"This ... this interrogation, do you know what it tells me?" I shuffle my hand between us as I gather my strength for the knock-down, drag-out I'm sure is coming.

"What, Becca? What does it tell you?" He gives me an *oh, here we go* look.

"That maybe you're not too sure about this. I think you're looking for a way out. Looking to blame me!" I yell. Grayson stares at me in disbelief.

"What on earth are you talking about?" he yells.

Ghetto Sybecca dings the bell at the boxing ring. Gloves are up ...

"I'm talking about your trust in me, or lack thereof! You keep questioning how I feel about you!" I get up on my knees to tower over him.

"I trust your feelings for *me*—it's your feelings for him I worry about! I do recall you proving me right once before!" He gets on his knees as well.

"Oh, there it is! The fucking cloud that looms over our relationship, brought to us once again by Grayson James!" I am at my sarcastic best. Grayson's hands slowly run down my arms. I catch my breath.

"Sweetheart," he whispers before he leans down to kiss me.

"No." I turn my head.

"No, sweetheart?" He runs his hands back up my arms to my neck, then palms my face and turns it up to him. "It has been established that I am a selfish and persistent man, has it not?" He grasps my lips purposefully with his.

"I hate you," I breathe as his right hand reaches into my hair.

"Oh, I beg to differ, darling. It's common knowledge that—you—are—very—much—in—love—with—me," he says between kisses. *Horny Sybecca must be working my lips, because my mouth opens and my tongue welcomes his. Damn it!* "Promise me," he whispers as he pulls my top off.

"Promise what?" I trace the lines of his abdominal muscles. He lifts my chin.

"Promise me you are mine. I'll try to let my guard down."

I giggle. "Beep, beep, beep, be-beep," I tease before I kiss each eyelid. "I am yours ... always. Good luck with the letting-your-guard-down thing." I kiss him. "I won't hold my breath, baby."

"Good. I don't think I'll be very successful." He sighs.

"Okay, Mr. James. Less talk and more action." I caress his neck with my lips while my hands slip into his bottoms and grasp his butt.

"Coming right up, Mrs. James—pun intended." He bites at my shoulder and slaps my ass hard. I attack his mouth. He lays me down, and slowly ... we begin to devour each other.

Chapter Ten

'm wide awake, and the alarm clock is blaring its green numbers at me: 3:17 a.m. I was asleep until I had one of my crazy pregnancy dreams. This time, there was a Great Dane telling me to take her home, that she was good with kids. I was amazed to hear her talking English, but apparently, I was the only one who could understand her. Then the people around me started barking instead of talking!

Grayson grumbles and turns over. I do the same, taking advantage of the last week or so I'll be able to lie on my belly. I stare at the clock and let my mind wander to my conversation with Ray. *What did he mean by my pretending about kisses, touches, and things said?* Why am I blocking some things and not others?

I try to think about the different times I've been with him. There are so many to choose from—until Grayson, Ray and I did everything together. We even had unintentional sleepovers. I did like waking up with him the next morning. I even bought him a couple of PJ bottoms for here because he'd fall asleep in his jeans, and it looked uncomfortable. Who wants to sleep in jeans? I remember when I first told him about them.

He called me to see what I was doing after Annie had gone to her grandparents' for the night.

"Just having a couple glasses of wine and watching a movie. What are you doing?" I asked.

"Nothing, babe. Want some company?"

"Sure. I'm picking the movie though, McNeil! You chose the last one!" I made myself clear. He always picks the damn movies!

"Okay. See you in a few."

Within twenty minutes he unlocked my door and waltzed in.

Wait! He had a key for the inn, but how did he have one to my room? Why didn't I wonder about that then? Hmm.

Ray kicked off his shoes and removed his jacket as I poured my third glass of wine. He put his beer down.

"What are we watching, baby?" He looked at the TV as he pulled his watch off and set it on the nightstand

"Baby Mama." I sighed.

"Oh, c'mon, babe. There's gotta be something better on." His usual complaint.

"I want something funny!"

"Becs, who are you kidding? You'll be asleep in twenty ... thirty minutes, tops. Don't subject me to this crap!" He grabbed the remote. He was right—totally my M.O.! He chose Star Trek.

"Okay. This is fine. Thanks for asking!"

"You're welcome." He kissed my forehead.

"The guy who plays Spock is hot," I said as I sipped my wine.

"Babe, hate to break it to you but ... he's gay." He laughed.

189

"No he's not!"

"Uh, yeah he is!"

"Damn it! Theme song: 'Another One Bites the Dust' by Queen." I sighed sadly. *"Hey, in the top drawer over there are the PJ bottoms I bought you."* I pointed, then took another sip. Ray just stood there, staring at me. *"What?"* I looked up at him.

"Um ... nothing. Okay." He went to the drawer and took the top one out. He smelled it, which made me laugh.

"Why are you smelling them?"

"You washed them?" He looked over at me.

"Of course I did! Why?"

He just shrugged his shoulders. I looked forward toward the TV as he pulled off his jeans and his underwear.

"Baby, don't strain your eyes. Go ahead and look at me if you want to."

I could sense his smile.

"Cocky bastard!" I snapped under my breath. I turned and fixed the pillows so we could sit with our backs against the headboard comfortably. Ray pulled the covers back, uncovering me.

"Nice PJs, babe. I especially like these."

My shorts had hiked up a little when I turned. He hooked his finger under the edge, caressing my butt cheek before pulling my shorts back into place. If I'd had panties on, I would've needed to change them. But I ignored him anyway.

"Ray, you pulled the covers back too far!" They were almost on the floor, so I leaned over the edge of the bed to retrieve them as he got situated. Once I had them, he grabbed me by my underarms like a child and pulled me back to sit between his legs. I was going to tell him I set up my pillows, but it felt nice lying back against him. Instead, I complained and rubbed my underarms. *"Ow, Ray."*

"Sorry, baby," he whispered. He touched my left cheek and turned my face to his, kissing my lips softly 'til I opened my mouth for him. I remember feeling so nervous.

"Ray ..." I pulled away, unsure.

"Shh ... the movie's starting." He nodded toward it. I laid my head back on his chest—his naked, well-sculpted chest. He smelled amazing. I tried to reach for my wine. "Would you like your wine, baby?" He smirked as he stared ahead.

"Yes, please," I said softly. He closed his eyes and inhaled deeply, then grabbed my wine.

"What number is this, babe?" He held it away from me.

"Third. I don't have to get up early tomorrow."

He shook his head and handed it to me. I took three long sips to calm my nerves.

"Thirsty?" He raised his eyebrows. I handed it back, not saying anything. Within minutes I felt more relaxed, so I leaned back against him.

"Sit up for a sec, babe." He nudged me. I did so. "Here." He unsnapped my bra. "Why are you still wearing that?"

"You were coming over." It's true. I had put it back on.

"That's ridiculous! You hate sleeping in a bra." He was right. I took it off and settled back against him. "Better?" He caressed my stomach, and I jumped a little.

"Yeah." I looked up at him. He kissed me again and again. His hands traveled up to my breasts, his fingers working at my nipples. I gasped and tried to pull away.

"Shh ... stop." He tweaked my nipples hard, and I moaned against his lips. I grasped at his knees with my hands as his touch sent electric currents to my groin. My hips moved against his, and I ground my ass into him. "Stop." He grabbed my hips to still them. "You keep doing that, baby, and I'm not going to be able to control myself." I laid my head back against his chest and closed my eyes. I felt so confused about what I wanted. So scared. I listened as he drank some of his beer. The light gulps sounded so loud.

"Wine, please."

"No. Pace yourself, baby." He squeezed me to him and kissed

my hair.

"I only have a little left. I just want to finish it." Because I didn't feel relaxed enough.

"Here. No more, though—you drink too much, babe." He handed me the glass.

"I only overindulge every once in a while. When I have the next morning off, for instance."

"Or I stay over," he said under his breath.

"What are you talking about, Ray?" I snapped. He ignored me. I took the last few sips and handed the glass back.

"All better now?" He wrapped his arms around me. I ignored him and watched the movie. I felt my eyelids start to get heavy. "Hey," he whispered, and nudged my head with his.

"Hmm?" I looked up at him. "Oh, did you want me to move?" I started to shift.

"No, c'mere." He pulled me back and held me tighter. I placed my arms on top of his and nuzzled my face into his neck, giving him several soft pecks.

"I love you, Ray." It was true, but it was definitely the wine that made me brave enough to say it. At first, I wasn't sure if he had heard me. I listened to the steady rhythm of his breathing and felt my eyelids get heavy again.

"God help me, Becca, I'm so in love with you," he said. He collected my lips with his, then laid me down on my back and climbed on top of me.

Oh God ... how could I have forgotten about this? Did this really happen? I feel like I'm going crazy!

I bring my focus back to the memory.

I caressed his back and opened my legs to give him better leverage.

"Oh God, Ray." I pulled away from his mouth and moved my

hips with his. His teeth clenched at little pieces of my skin, working his way down to my breast. I bit at his shoulder as I felt myself come undone. "Oh ... oh, Ray," I groaned, lost in the sensation.

"That's it, baby." He pulled both my shorts and his bottoms off.

"What are you doing?" My heart and stomach both fluttered in a panicky state as he lifted my leg.

"Bec, stay with me, baby. Please!" He kissed me and entered me quickly. We both gasped.

"Stop! Stop! Get off of me!" I hit his back and pushed at his shoulders. He thrust into me several times, then finally rolled off of me.

"Goddamn it, Becca!" he yelled and got up abruptly. He pulled his bottoms up, then went into the bathroom and slammed the door. Several minutes later he came out and went over to his clothes. He changed and picked up his watch from the nightstand. We stared at each other. He was so angry—his jaw was pulsating off the charts.

"Ray ..." I wanted to say something. I just didn't know what.

"Shut up, Becca! I've had enough of this! Outside of stuff with our girls, don't call me for anything until you are ready to commit to at least the shit you start!" He threw his coat on and stormed out of my room.

I remember crying myself to sleep that night.

What night was that? When? Why am I only remembering it now?

Christ, its half past four. I get up and go to the girls' room. They're still asleep. *Yeah, Becca, everybody's asleep but you!* I find Annie's emergency cell phone and call Ray.

"Annie!" He picks up after the third ring, panic in his voice.

"No, it's me," I say quietly, and duck into the girls' bathroom.

"Becca, what's the matter, baby?" I can sense him jumping out of bed.

"Ray, we need to talk. I ... I'm having flashbacks of things with you. I need to talk to you about them. I feel like I'm losing my mind." I start crying.

"Now?" he asks.

"No, tomorrow's fine. Can you meet me here at nine?" *Grayson is going to flip his shit.*

"Yes, baby, I'll be there. Becca, everything is going to be fine. I love you. I've always loved you."

"Thanks, Ray. Love you too. Good night." I hang up and put Annie's phone back into her overnight bag. As I close their door and turn to head down the hall, I walk right into Grayson getting off his phone. I look up at him. He seems concerned, which is a relief—I was expecting him to be pissed.

"Everything all right, love?" He grabs my hand.

"Yes." I squeeze and we head to our room. "I called Ray. He's coming by at nine to talk. I've been awake for two hours now, and I've been having some memories."

"Um ... should I be worried about us, sweetheart?" He sits down on the bed, looking so uncomfortable and out of his element.

"Oh, no. No, baby, we're okay. I just don't understand why this is all coming back to me now. I don't know if it's real, or what else may have happened. Ray is the only one who can answer these questions, Gray. For my sake, can I please talk to him without security? There's bound to be some embarrassing stuff." I kneel in front of him. He shakes his head.

"I'm not comfortable with that."

"I'm not asking you to be. I'm just asking for your trust and the courtesy of privacy."

"You'll be bugged." He sighs.

"No!" I plead.

"Yes, or it isn't going to happen," he says through his teeth.

"Only you can listen."

"All right, then. Let's try to get to bed now." He leans forward for a kiss and pulls me up to get into bed. Finally ... sleep finds me again.

"Up and at 'em!" Grayson says loudly as he slaps my bum.

"Ow! Babe!" I yell. I glance at the clock. Ugh—a quarter to nine! I want to go back to sleep. Oh. Oh, wait! Ray's going to be here in fifteen minutes.

"Come on, love, your boyfriend will be here any minute!" he teases.

"You're my boyfriend," I grumble, then climb out of bed.

"I am your fiancé, and we are getting married in two months and seventeen days. I can't wait!" He pulls me into his arms and gives me an *I never want to let you go* hug.

"Hi." I smile. *What has gotten into him?*

"Hi." He grins boyishly and kisses me. "Is it okay if I start baking with the girls this morning?"

"Um, aren't you going to be busy eavesdropping?" I wrap my arms around his neck as we sway.

"Nope. I've decided not to do that. I trust you. I don't trust him, but I'm sure Ghetto Sybecca will take care of it if he crosses the line." I can't contain my laughter. I recently told Grayson about some of my mental counterparts. He loved that they didn't exist until he came along.

"Did you tell security?" I raise a single brow.

"That you're crazy? No, love, they already know that."

This warrants a slap from me.

"No, about Ray and me speaking privately."

"Yes, they will keep their distance." He kisses my nose. I walk to the dresser and pull out a pair of jeans and a shirt, then head into the bathroom for all morning essentials ... pee, teeth, deodorant. If I were Stacey, I guess I'd be putting makeup on, but alas—I am basics Becca! I head out of the bathroom and realize Grayson must've headed downstairs already. I lock up and follow suit.

Ray looks up and smiles at me as I come down the stairs. God, he is so good-looking.

"Hey, leave your coat on. We're going to go to the office in the barn." I grab my coat as well. He holds out his hand for mine, and I grab it. *Old habit.*

"So, how did you manage this?" He swings my arm and looks over at me as we walk the perimeter of the inn.

"Manage what?"

"This, babe. Us ... alone. I couldn't even give you a hug at the hospital a few weeks ago without them breathing down my neck." He glances back and finds my detail slowly following us.

"Grayson knows how important it is that I talk to you right away. I'm very upset, Ray."

He opens the door to the barn and we head in.

"Oh, my guys did start in here! They weren't sure if they'd be able to before Christmas." He eyes the plastic drapes and scaffolding. I glance around as well.

"Yeah, I can't wait to see it when it's done."

"Well, come on." He points and we head in. "Oh, hey, they installed the fireplace!" Ray heads over to it. "It's all set to go, baby. Should I turn it on so you stay warm?" I nod. He turns the dial.

"It's beautiful." I pull my coat off.

"Yeah, quite the sight." He stares at me.

I throw my coat over the chair and sit sideways on the new couch. The door is closed and the blinds on its window are down. I'm glad for the privacy—but also nervous. Ray takes off his coat and sits so we're facing each other. "What's going on, baby?" He touches my face.

"Um, as I've mentioned, I didn't realize anything intimate had happened between us except for the kiss in the rain and me playing Lady Marmalade a few months ago. I just remembered the sleigh ride because Morgan brought it up, then my birthday because you brought it up. Last night I woke up and couldn't get back to sleep. I started thinking about our conversation." I take in a deep breath.

"And?"

I'm thankful that he is my usual patient Ray right now.

"Well, I was trying to figure out what you meant by me pretending things didn't happen."

"Becca, you've been doing it to me the past five years." He sighs and runs his hand through his hair.

"Well, what do you mean exactly?" I feel irritated, but not with him.

"Becca, baby, stuff happened. Kissing, touching. Sex. And the next day, it was like it never happened." He sounds equally frustrated.

"Ray, I wasn't pretending. I really truly didn't remember, sweetie. I'm really sorry. It's not your fault. This is why I have to see Patricia. It's all coming back to me now. I had no idea." I fight my tears.

"Shh ... baby, don't cry." He pulls me into his arms.

"Ray, this is scary. I'm missing important pieces of my life." I cry into his neck.

"Important?" He pulls my chin up.

"Yes, Ray, You know you're important to me. Please don't kiss me.".

"Baby, I'm so going to kiss you before we leave here—just so you know."

"I need you to tell me everything first." I turn away.

"Wait. You're going to let me kiss you?" He brings my face back.

"Ray, if I wasn't with Grayson, I'd give you a complimentary fuck for putting up with my shit for so long." *Yeah, I'd do that! I'm fearless these days!*

"Complimentary, huh?" He gives me a big Ray smile. I giggle

and nod. "What do you need to know?" He takes my hand and kisses it.

"How many times have we had sex, and when was the first time?" I swallow hard.

"Right to the good stuff, huh?" He chuckles.

"Was it good?" I bite my lip to hold back my smile.

"It was when it lasted more than two minutes ... if that." He rolls his eyes.

"Ohh ... yikes. Problems, Ray? You know, you are getting older." I'm teasing, because if my memory from last night is correct, I was the problem.

"Oh, yeah, there was a problem all right. A problem caused by one Becca Campbell." He pushes at my shoulder playfully.

"Okay, so, when was our first time?"

"Baby, do you mean the first time I got that far, or the first time you actually let me finish?"

Wow ... this is terrible.

"Um, I guess start with when things started happening in general." I feel my face flush and my stomach tighten into knots. I lean my cheek against back of the couch. I'm still facing him—I just need to stop this dizzy spell.

"Babe, you okay?" He touches my face again.

"Yeah, I'm just overwhelmed. Seems like that should be my permanent theme song. I should ask Grayson to write me a song called 'Overwhelmed,'" I blather on.

"I'm sure there's one out there. So, from the beginning?"

"Yes please." I open my eyes and look at him.

"Well, obviously I had a crush on you from the moment I met you." He starts laughing. I know exactly what about—parent-teacher night, five years ago.

We sat next to each other, listening to their kindergarten teacher, Mrs. Finley. She was talking about us all working together and how, when children act up, there's something going on, and as parents and teachers we should stop ... collaborate.

I piped up and said, "And listen." I bit my lip and shook my head. Sometimes things just can't be helped. The teacher agreed with me.

"If there's a problem ... we'll solve it," Ray added. My body started shaking and I bit my lip to the point of almost drawing blood to stifle my giggle. I dared to look at Ray, and he was doing the same. Everybody else was so serious—I assumed we were the only ones on this planet in the nineties. It felt like Ray and I were good friends in school, laughing about something but trying not to get caught. Well, we were, except we were the parents.

After the teacher's speech, which we both went into Charlie Brown *mode over, we finally introduced ourselves. We were so excited to find out who each other's kid was. Both girls had already declared themselves best friends. We ended up talking for an extra hour out in the parking lot after the conferences ended.*

"Hey, Becca, did you have dinner?" he asked.

"No, I was going to wait until after." I looked at my watch.

"Well, it's after. I haven't eaten, either. Do you want to grab a bite?"

I agreed. I felt very safe and comfortable with him right away. We went to a local pub and talked for hours. I had just bought the inn and I was looking for a contractor to build the store.

"Becca, I'm an architect. I'll stop by and look at it," he offered.

"Well, I have a budget," I said nervously. An architect sounded much more expensive than a contractor. I wasn't too sure how the whole construction process went.

"Most people do, Becs. Let me check it out. I'll give you a good deal." He reached up to push a strand of hair behind my ear. It was a very familiar gesture that caught us both off guard—we had only met that night. "Uh ... sorry ... habit. I do that with Annie's

hair," he said quickly.

"Wow, one hundred points to McNeil for quick thinking." I bit my smile back.

"Yes, Alex, I'll take awkward situations for two-hundred points," he said, then thumbed my lip away from my teeth. "What is, please stop doing that for reasons I can't discuss right now?" He took a swig of his beer. I'm pretty sure I had a stupid grin on my face.

"Ah ... so, you were subjected to the nightly 7:00 p.m. torture of Wheel *and* Jeopardy! *as well?"*

He rolled his eyes. "Still am."

"You live with your parents?" I couldn't help my laughter.

"Hey, I've got my own apartment in the basement!" He jokingly tried to defend himself. He didn't really live with his parents, of course.

"Shut the fuck up!" I hit his arm.

"Becca! I'm shocked! Such language!" He tried to sound appalled. "Where are you from? So unladylike."

"I'm from Jersey, where we only had one 'sight word' to learn." I smirked.

"What was that?" As he asked, I flipped him off.

"Oh, we are going to get along great!" He laughed. I smiled and finished my wine. "Another one, baby?" he asked, and my eyes went wide. "Oh, I'm just clearing that 'awkward' topic on the board." He gave me that boyish grin. God, I remember how handsome I thought he was then. Right from the start, there was just something about him. We were already silly stupid with each other. I felt like I'd known him forever.

He made eye contact with the waitress and pointed to our drinks.

"Oh, Ray, I shouldn't have another." I really wanted one, though, and I didn't want to go home yet.

"You're fine! Look, they're starting up karaoke. We're both in

the same boat—we rarely get a night off! My parents are with An-
nie. Oh, who's with Morgan? Can they stay?" he asked.

"My friend Stacey is. Yeah, she's visiting." I pulled out my
phone to text her. I don't remember everything she said, but she did
tell me to "get some." Of course, I didn't see that text 'til I came
back from the bathroom to a Ray who was trying to pull himself
together.

"Um ... Stacey texted you again. The screen lit up and I saw
her text ... sorry." He laughed. I didn't even have to look, because
Stacey has no filter sometimes. I slid my head into my hands, al-
ready defeated by embarrassment. I finally put on my big-girl pants
and glanced at the message. My head went back into my hands.

"We have Ray and Becca coming up now! Ray and Becca ...
you're up!"

I lifted my head and looked at the DJ, then at Ray. He stood
and held his hand out to me. Oh, Christ! I went up with him and
grabbed a mic. "Ice Ice Baby" popped up on the screen.

"Aww ... it's our song, sweetie!" I said to Ray with a hint of
playful sarcasm. The music started and Ray and I busted out the
lyrics all serious, like it was our job. Kind of became our M.O. for
karaoke.

We stayed there until they closed at one in the morning. He
followed me home in his truck just to make sure I got home all right.
We were still at the rental home then. He walked me up the steps.

"Hey, Becs, I had a lot of fun. Thanks for sitting next to me and
coming out tonight."

"Technically, you sat next to me," I said.

"Yeah, well, I guess old habits are hard to break." He smiled.

"Huh?" I gave him a look that I'm sure matched my confusion.

"I always tried to sit next to the prettiest girl in the class." He
touched my cheek softly. I rolled my eyes at his comment, then bit
my lip. He was so close to me.

"Please, Becca, you have to stop biting your lip, baby." He

pulled it away, then bit it himself. I gasped, which opened my mouth enough for his tongue to enter. The kiss was so urgent and so sweet. He took my breath away.

I open my eyes to find Ray watching me.

"Ray, did we kiss the first night we met?" I ask quietly to confirm the memory.

"Yes. That was the best first date I've ever had in my life." He frowns.

"Me, too." I grab his hand.

"So, great, you forgot." He sighs.

"What happened after?" I ignore his comment. I can only apologize so many times.

"You wigged out the next time we saw each other." He raises his hands for emphasis.

"I wigged out like *wiggy-wiggy*?" I pretend to scratch a record. "Or like *wigged out*?" I pull an imaginary wig off. He just sits there and stares at me blankly. I decide to fight against the urge to hold up a pretend microphone, tap it, and ask if it's on. "Well, why did you stick around?" I ask, feeling defensive.

"I talked to Stacey because I wasn't sure of what to do. She told me about George and the PTSD. She told me to run, and fast—unless I liked you enough to be extremely patient. She also told me I was the first guy you even gave the time of day to. I found that encouraging, but what did it for me was watching you play in the leaves with the girls and hearing all three of you laughing. I just knew at that moment that you were the one." Cue the waterworks. *Damn it!*

"I've loved having you in my life, but I wish you *had* run. I've done nothing but hurt you." I let my tears fall freely.

"Moving along ..." He sighs. I nod. "I held off on kissing you again, which was very hard. I wanted to kiss you every minute I was near you. You and your perpetual lip biting. Stop it!" He pulls my lip away from my teeth quickly.

"Sorry," I mumble.

"Do it again—see what happens." He gives me a mischievous grin.

"I can't help it." I sigh.

"Yeah, I'll use that excuse, too."

"Ray, the next time?"

"Uh, well, I went slow ... hand on your back, arm around your shoulder, holding your hand." He scratches at the inseam of his right leg, which he has bent under him on the couch.

"Well, I remember that stuff. Our familiarity with each other." I grab his hand to make him stop. He laces his fingers with mine.

"But you don't remember us kissing?" He gives me an unsure look.

"No. I may have when it first happened, but I guess I pushed it out."

"This just doesn't make sense, Becca. How can you lose all these memories with me?" He lets go.

"Do you think I want this? Do you think I like coming to you to ask about our past? I don't!" I yell in a low tone. I'm beyond frustrated.

"Okay. Okay. Stop."

Geez ... what is it with the way he says that word? *Country Sybecca is twirling her pigtails and slowly circling around a pole.*

"Tit for tat, baby."

"Huh? What?" I look up at him. He moves closer.

"You've hurt me over and over again. I understand now, sort of, what was going on." His face is so close I can smell the mint from his toothpaste. "So, how does it work? Do you remember events once they're mentioned?" He thumbs my bottom lip away from my teeth. "Baby, baby, baby ..." he whispers, then bites my lip.

I gasp, just like the first time he ever did it. He deepens the kiss, and I match his urgency. I don't know why. Well, I do, I think. Oh God, I'm so confused! Ray pulls away and grabs his phone.

"Theme song," he says, and glances up at me as he hits an app to get into his playlist. After hitting the screen a few times, he puts his phone back down and palms my face. Slowly, he leans in to kiss me again. "The Scientist" by Coldplay blasts as loud as it can on an iPhone. The words help a sob escape my throat. Ray grabs my hips to pull me down onto the couch. He hovers over me, but doesn't come any closer. "The second time we kissed like this, it was the evening of our first Easter. We fell asleep on the couch at my parents' house when we were up there for Easter vacation." He pecks my lips again.

"Yes, that was the week before I opened the inn. You convinced me to come up to your parents' and have a vacation before I forgot what one was. Boy, were you right!" I roll my eyes and shift a little, unintentionally rubbing against his erection. His breath catches.

"I'm right about most things, baby." He attacks my lips again. His hips roll skillfully, grinding my effect on him against me. My perfidious hips leap into action to support his efforts. *Hips, stop! Ray, stop! Oh God ... I can't stop either of them! Oh ... oh, sweet Jesus!* "That's it, baby. Come on." His words encourage the rise in me.

"No. No, stop!" Ah-ha! I do still have a voice and a working mouth! I feel the sweet tightening deep within and I'm blanketed with the results of my dilatory refusal. I close my eyes, unable to escape the warmth ... the guilt. Ray kisses away the one lonely tear that braves the journey out of the corner of my eye.

"Think about our first Easter, baby. We fell asleep on the couch together. Remember?" he whispers near my ear. My eyes remain closed as I nod. I can't look at him yet. I go into the memory instead.

Chapter Eleven

woke up in the middle of the night. The moon shone brightly through the window. Ray stared at me, his fingers grazing my cheek. I was in his arms on the couch. Everybody was in bed upstairs. There was a blanket covering us.

"My mother must've covered us up," he whispered when I glanced down at it. I looked back up to his beautiful eyes. His thumb traced my bottom lip, and I pursed my lips slightly to kiss it. He leaned forward and pecked my lips as I reached up to touch his cheek. He took in a sharp breath and scanned my face. I tilted my chin upward so he could kiss me again. It started out sweet ... soft ... reluctant.

We were both hesitant. He was probably afraid of rejection. I was scared of everything that had to do with the opposite sex. After a few minutes or so, we threw caution to the wind. He deepened the *kiss. I tugged at the hem of his shirt, and he pulled away so I could bring it off over his head. He followed suit with mine, then attacked my lips again with such intensity I remember almost forgetting to exhale. His mouth ran down my neck, and he yanked the cup of my bra off of my right breast to allow his mouth access. I moaned and rubbed up against him as he teased my nipple, sending electric currents down to my groin. I fisted his hair and brought his mouth back to mine. Oh God, I wanted him!*

"Becs ... I need you, baby," he said breathlessly against my mouth as his fingers ran along the band of my PJ bottoms. He hooked them and started to pull the right side down.

"Ray, no. Please stop. Stop, Ray." I wriggled under him.

"Okay. Okay, Bec, shh ... I'm stopping." He pulled my PJs back up. I fixed my bra as Ray sat up to grab my shirt. I looked up to find him holding it open so I could put my head through.

"Thanks," I whispered. God, I felt so silly and stupid. I moved to get up.

"Wait, where are you going?" he whispered, and hooked his arm around my waist.

"I was going to go upstairs to bed." I bit my lip—as I always do in every situation ever. He thumbed it away.

"Please just stay here with me. I just want to hold you, baby. I'd like to kiss you again, too, if that's okay. I won't do anything else. I promise, Becca, please." He caressed my cheek with the back of his hand.

"What if everybody wakes up before us and sees us?" I couldn't look at him. I felt so shy.

"Well, we're dressed, and my mom covered us up instead of waking us. No one will think anything other than what happened ... that we fell asleep watching a movie. Okay, baby?" He gently pushed my hair behind my right ear with his left hand. His fingers slid down, his thumb massaging my earlobe. I closed my eyes, soaking in the calming effect of his touch. "Becca ... baby, I'll nev-

er do anything you don't want me to do. I promise." His fingers slowly moved from my ear across my jawline. He grasped my chin between his thumb and forefinger and gently raised my face to his. "Can I kiss you again, baby?"

I looked into his eyes and gave him a slight nod. He cupped my face and caressed my lips with his. He made me feel so delicate, like he might break me if he added too much pressure. I placed my hands on his arms as he slowly guided me onto my back. Once there, he deepened the kiss.

We lay there like that, kissing, for—I don't know—it had to be an hour or so. The rest of the week we held hands and kissed like any other new couple starting out. It was so exciting, comforting, calming. Right.

"Are you finished with that memory yet, baby?" Ray grabs my chin and shakes my head a little, like I'm saying *no.*

"Yes." I open my eyes and smile at him.

"That's how it is when we visit my parents. You're okay with being my girl there, and anywhere else we go where people don't know us. I've always secretly felt like you are ashamed of me." He frowns.

"Oh, Ray, no! I could never be ashamed of you! I hate myself for what I've put you through." I start crying again. Ray watches me for a moment, then grabs the tissue box off of the coffee table. I take two and wipe my nose. His blue-gray eyes, ugh ... they're like a storm. He stares at me intently, and I lick my lips, biting my bottom one.

"Mmm ... there it is."

There's something about the way he says it that has me needing my, like, fifth panty change since I've been secluded in this room with him. He licks his lips before he captures mine again (not that they are running anywhere).

Donna Summer is softly singing "Toot toot, hey, beep beep"

in my head.

"Oh, shut up, Donna!" I snap. Ray chuckles and kisses my tears away. I sigh. "Next memory, please."

"Hold on a minute! Donna interrupted us. I need a little tit for my tat." He smirks as he reaches under my shirt and cops a feel.

"Raymond!" I snap, then wince.

"Tsk, tsk, baby." He says playfully and tweaks my nipple through the cloth of my bra. It ignites the direct line to my mother-board. (*What?*)

"Don't do that. Next memory, please." I lean up and kiss him.

"Ugh!" He groans. "Okay. Big memories or little memories?"

"Well, what do you mean by 'little memories'?" I ask as I pull his hand away from my chest. He runs it down my side and under my bum.

"You've lost a lot of weight, Becca." He furrows his brow at me.

"Hmm, yeah. I went down two sizes, but I've recently gained five pounds back." I half frown.

"Due to the hostage situation?" He raises a brow.

"Probably, and I'm not a hostage!" I smack his arm.

"You are choosing to be a prisoner. I wish you would just see it." He sighs.

"I am not!" I snap.

"Yes, you are!"

"I don't have a choice!" That did not come out as brilliantly as I hoped it would.

"Which is it, baby?"

"Ugh, Ray! I need the protection!" I yell.

"From who? From what? George is dead! He can't hurt you anymore, except in your mind, and you seem to finally be moving on from that!" I can almost feel his frustration escalating.

"He had a partner!" I say impulsively.

"Who?"

"We don't know yet." I lower my voice, trying to calm down.

"Probably the same person who set me up to think you were in trouble." He touches my face. "God, if anything ever happened to you, baby ... " He kisses me.

"I believe *you* happened to me, McNeil. Please answer my earlier question about little memories."

He takes in a deep breath. "Well, things like day trips, outings around town, classes we took together, movies."

I think for a moment.

"I'm pretty sure I remember everything about those times. I remember holding hands and you kissing my hair. And the big dude farting in yoga class." We both start to laugh.

"That was terrible." Ray shakes his head.

"Is there anything specific about those times that I'm not remembering?" I turn my head to him.

"No ... just that, as usual, everything was fine until we ran into somebody we knew. Then my hand would get dropped and it was over for the rest of the day. There was no bringing you back." His nostrils flare. *God, I was awful.*

"Ray, why did you put up with that for so long?" I touch his face.

"I was really patient in the beginning. I knew George had done terrible things to you. I knew you weren't playing games—you were just really scared. I tried not to take it personally. I looked at the upside." He gives my hip a squeeze. "I was the only one you gave your extra time to, whether on the phone or in person. I fell in love with you so fast, Becca. I never met a woman I could be completely myself around. Not only did you put up with me, but you were just like me. Since the first day I met you, I knew in my heart of hearts that you were *the* one—the person who was meant to be my forever. I've never experienced this type of clarity in my life. Not with Liz, not with anyone ... just you. Always you. When you're 'on'—you know, being my girl—I get an overwhelming glimpse of what it would be like to have you completely, without the shit in your head haunting you. Oh, baby, it's so worth fighting for." He rests his forehead against mine. I gasp my sob back. Ray has never fallen short on saying the most wonderful things to me. "Shh, shh , baby ... next memory?"

I nod and kiss him quickly.

"It was September, and the girls had just started the first grade. We went to my cousin Bethany's wedding,"

"I remember that, Ray."

"Really? You remember *everything*?" He again raises an eyebrow and bites his lip.

"Well, I remember we went. We had a good time. Danced a lot ... drank a lot." I frown and shrug my shoulder as if to say *that's it, no big deal*.

"That's all you remember?" he asks. I nod. "*Faaaaack.*" He slaps his head. I inch out from underneath him. "Where are you going?"

"Just getting on my side." I turn. He echoes my movement so we're facing each other.

"Here." He puts a long red throw pillow under our heads.

"Thanks. So, what am I not remembering about this wedding?" I smile.

"Close your eyes, baby ... this is a doozy! When you start to remember, squeeze my hand and I will shut up so you can work through it."

"Okay. Go ahead." I close my eyes.

"I'm going to need to do a panty check after this one, baby."

I sense his smile.

"Um, Ray, I probably should've changed my panties like five times by now." I open my eyes to find his stormy ones staring at me. I feel his fingers tug at the button of my jeans. He unzips them. "Don't, Ray." I put my hand on top of his. A slow smirk comes across his lips.

"Close your eyes." He moves his hand up to my hip. I comply. "I came to you a few days before the wedding to ask for a favor. My parents already considered you my girlfriend, and I knew that was how they would introduce you. I didn't want to tell them not to for various reasons. First being that my mother would've hounded you and you would've flipped. Second being that my family was already starting to think I was gay." He pauses when I squeeze his hand. "Wow, already?"

"I think so." I furrow my brow, deep in thought.

"Okay. Well, real quick—thirdly, you *were* my girlfriend ... to me. Now, go ahead. I'm just going to watch you and think about your wet panties."

I slap him.

"Shut up!" I laugh. He leans forward and kisses me again. "Ray, please, let me think." I pull away.

"Okay," he says. I feel his breath on my forehead. I close my eyes and think back—falling into the memory.

I was restocking the shelves in the store. Dinner was in the oven. It was Wednesday, and I expected Ray to walk through the door at any minute. I kept Annie with me on Wednesdays after Daisy Scouts, and we'd all have dinner together when Ray came home ... well, to the inn.

"Hey, baby, still at it?"

Hearing his voice, I turned.

"Just finishing." I smiled and grabbed the plastic wrapping off the floor, then I threw it in the garbage can behind the counter. He was leaning up against the counter on the customer side, and I stepped around to join him. He was in dark blue jeans and a lavender dress shirt. His wavy locks were almost at the length I find delicious. "Hey, you look beat." I went on my toes to kiss his cheek, but got the corner of his mouth as he turned his head toward me. He grabbed my hips.

"Becca, goddamn it ... could you just fucking give me a real kiss, baby?" Though he said it quietly, his impatience and frustration came through loud and clear. I stared at him, trying to figure him out. "Jesus, Becca!" His hands dove into the hair behind my neck and he pulled me forward, taking my lips for his own. "Open your fucking mouth, Becs!" he snapped with annoyance against my lips.

I think I meant to argue, but didn't get the chance. My white flag went up and I let his tongue have its way with mine. After a few minutes, he pulled away and topped it off with a soft peck.

"There ... was that so hard, baby?"

We stood forehead to forehead. I didn't say anything. I was trying to catch my breath and muster up the energy to remind him that we were just friends. "I'm going to go check on the girls. Should I send them to the kitchen?" His thumb traced my lip.

"Um ... yeah." I finally opened my eyes.

"Hi. There you are." He smiled. "I love your eyes, baby." He gave me another quick kiss and went off to find the girls. I headed to the kitchen to regroup, or something. I poured a glass of bravery and gulped it down before I could feel it come up to scratch, then poured another glass and put it by my plate. After opening a Corona for Ray and popping the lime slice in, I took the chicken bake out of the oven.

"Hazel at book club?" Ray asked. I dropped the casserole on the counter nervously. I didn't even hear him come in.

"Um, yes, 'til seven." My voice shook. I'm sure it had nothing to do with Ray's hands claiming my hips, or the feeling of him right up against my backside.

"The girls will be in in a few. They—are—finishing—up—their—homework," he said between the kisses he planted on my neck. "I love Wednesdays ... I get to come home to my favorite girls ... especially you ... a home-cooked meal ... and you ... my favorite day of the week, baby." He was speaking so softly it was almost a

whisper. I felt drugged. Of course, I had just gulped down a rather large glass of wine.

"I picked up my dress for the wedding," I announced, trying to distract myself from him distracting me.

"And we have Becca Campbell coming in from left field once again, ladies and gentlemen!" Ray the Sportscaster announced, like he always does when I do this. I giggled.

"I'll have you know, I never played left field. I always played second base."

"Hmm." He kissed my neck. "I'm more than happy to play second base with you." His hands slid up and grasped my breast. I gasped and turned to him, intending to object. Apparently, my mouth did not agree with my thoughts.

"Baby, did you already have a glass of wine?" he asked. His hands still caressed me. The girls walked in and he casually slid his hands down to my waist, then turned and greeted them. I brought the casserole over to the table and served everybody. "Looks good, baby." Ray patted my bum.

"Thanks. Hope you guys like it." I sat down.

"Mom, you're bright red. Are you okay?" Morgan asked. Normally I would be touched by her concern, but I wished she hadn't said anything.

"Yeah, baby, what's got you so flushed?" Ray gave me a mischievous grin, then puckered up and blew me an air kiss.

"It's just from cooking, Morgan," I answered, trying to ignore him.

"Yeah, I noticed it was real hot in here when I walked in. Right, babe?"

I offered him an eye roll and delayed giggle.

"Daddy, are you going to sleep with Becca tonight, too?" Annie asked, and Ray nearly choked on his food. I couldn't help but laugh—I didn't get a chance to remind him about the girls having the next day off for a teachers' workshop. I was keeping Annie that

213

night. He clearly forgot, because she didn't bring clothes.

*"Teachers' workshop tomorrow, Ray. Annie's sleeping over,"
I said.*

*"Oh." He tried to pull himself together, but let out a few more
small chuckles. It was the way she worded it, obviously.*

"Grown-ups are so weird!" Morgan sighed.

"Especially the boy ones," I added.

*"Becca, I forgot. I'll run home and get a change of clothes for
us."*

*My smile dropped. His got bigger. I took a large swig of my
wine.*

*After dessert, Ray ran home and I ran a bath. Hazel was home
and visiting with the girls, and I needed to calm my nerves. The
three glasses of wine I had weren't helping enough. I put my Sarah
Brightman CD on in my room and left the bathroom door cracked. I
sunk into the deep tub and let the jets take me away. I took a shower
earlier, so I didn't have to do anything now but relax.*

*A few minutes later, I opened my eyes to reach for my wine—
only to find Ray sitting on the bathtub step with his back against
the wall, watching me. He had his legs stretched out in front of him,
and he was already in his PJs.*

"Hi." He smiled.

"Eh ... hi."

*"Would you like me to wash your back?" he asked me very
calmly, as if this were an everyday occurrence.*

"No, I'm good. I took a shower earlier."

He cocked his head at this information.

"Then why are you taking a bath?"

*"To relax. It helps me to relax." Why did I say that twice? Ap-
parently the wine-and-bath combo was unsuccessful at its one job.*

*"I know of a few things we can do to help you relax." He gave
me a crooked smile. I swallowed hard, trying to keep the butterflies
at bay.*

"Um, I'll be out in a minute."

"Or you could stay in." He touched the water. "It's still hot. I'd love to join you. I've had a long day. It might be just the thing to relax me." He started to take off his white cotton undershirt.

"Ray ... don't," I gasped. He pulled his shirt back down.

"You really should have that tattooed to your forehead. 'Ray ... don't.'" With his finger, he drew a line across my forehead for emphasis. "Then you wouldn't have to say it so much." I remember wondering what the hell he meant by that. "Finish your wine and your bath. I'll pick out a movie for us, baby." He kissed my lips quickly.

I gulped down my wine as soon as he left, then got out of the tub and dried quickly. All I brought in was a camisole T-shirt and PJ bottoms. No bra. No panties. I didn't think he was really going to stay over. I applied my lotion thoroughly before getting dressed. I pulled my long, thick, wavy brown hair out of its tie and let it fall around my shoulders. It was still damp from my shower earlier. Grabbing my lotion, I walked out into the bedroom and, because I suddenly felt braver, asked Ray to apply it to my back.

"Yeah, baby, c'mere." He was sitting up against the pillows and headboard on the right side of the bed—my side—with his legs stretched out before him. He put one foot on the floor and patted the bed between his legs. I sat with my back to him.

I tried to steady my breath as he lifted my top. I heard him open the lotion and squirt it on his hand. The sound of his hands rubbing together to warm the lotion made my heart race—the anticipation of his touch was almost more than I could bear. I felt him leave small, soft, wet kisses on my back, and my breathing became very difficult to control. His hands were so gentle, yet so strong. It was hypnotic, the way he massaged me.

"There," he whispered in my ear. I opened my eyes as he lowered my shirt—just in time to watch him walk into the bathroom. I heard the faucet run for a minute, then he returned with my wine

glass.

I set up the pillows on the other side of the bed while he poured me another glass of wine.

"What are you doing? This is my side." Fuck the glass—give me the bottle! *I thought as he sat down behind me again.*

"Hmm ... this is my side, too. I guess we'll have to share," he said nonchalantly, then hooked his arm around my waist to pull me back against him.

"What are we watching?" I tried to remain calm and unaffected. He pushed my hair away from the right side of my neck over onto my left.

"Drink up, baby. I had a tough day. I need my Becca."

I open my eyes and hit Ray.

"Ow ... what?"

"It's a wonder you haven't turned me into an alcoholic! Do you always make me drink so much?"

"No, Becs, I only push it when I really need you to be my girl without overthinking it. I hate that I have to do that; doesn't help my ego much." He frowns.

"I really don't believe your ego is suffering." I smile.

"Shh, close your eyes and go back to the memory. Where are you?" He touches my face.

"You're sleeping over. You pulled me to you and told me to drink up."

"Oh, yeah ... that was a shit day. I really needed you. Go ahead, baby."

I close my eyes and go back.

"What happened?" I asked before taking a huge gulp.

"I lost the bid on the contract I wanted." He grabbed his beer.

"Oh no! Not the Science Museum." I remember how hard he was trying to get that. His designs were incredible.

"Yep!"

"I'm sorry, Ray. I wish there was something I could do."

"There is something you can do. Don't push me away tonight."
He took my wineglass, then leaned his head back and closed his
eyes. I just stared at him, not knowing what to say. I stood up.
"What are you doing, Becs?" He was snippy, like he was agitated.
I know it was from work. Wait ... was it?

"Let me massage your shoulders. Scoot forward." I patted the
bed where I had just sat. He stared at me, his eyes wide. *"C'mon,
McNeil, or the offer goes off the table in five ... four ... three ... "*

He pushed forward, a huge, boyish grin on his face.

"Good boy!" I quickly kissed his lips before I climbed in behind him. *"Take your shirt off and turn on the movie."*

"You don't want to watch ESPN?" He smiled, knowing the answer. He helped me pull off his shirt, then picked up the remote.

"Lotion?"

"With or without a sock?" he asked. I smacked his shoulder
and laughed. *"No. Just your hands, baby."* He closed his eyes as I
started to knead his shoulders.

"You're so tight, Ray." I dug my thumbs in.

"Funny, I always imagined me saying that to you."

I remember thinking how much I'd love that. Rubbing his
shoulders, working at his muscles ... it was turning me on. I always
thought he had beautiful shoulders.

*"Bill will be here tomorrow with the guys to fix anything you
need. So make sure you have your list ready, baby."*

Talk about left field!

"Should I pay him, or your firm?" I asked, knowing this might
lead to an argument.

"You're not paying a dime to anybody." He sighed.

*"Ray, I have money set aside for those things. You just lost the
bid; you can't keep paying these guys to do work around here and*

not accept money from me."

"It's all part of the package, baby."

He pointed to a different area on his shoulder, and I began to work at it.

"What package?"

"Being my girlfriend, baby. It's my job to take care of you. End of discussion." He reached up to grab my hands and pulled me forward to kiss my cheek.

"Ray, I'm not—"

"Becca, don't fucking say it! I swear to God, I can't put up with this shit tonight! Any other night, baby ... not tonight." He threw my arms off of him.

"Um, well, it's just ... you're always taking care of me. Why won't you let me help? I want to take care of you, too." I softly began to kiss across his shoulders.

"You do take care of me, the best you can. Baby ... c'mere." He turned to me and brought me down in one swift motion. His stormy eyes stared into mine. "I'm going to kiss you, Becs. I'm going to touch you. I need you to not flip out tonight. Can you please, please try not to push me away?"

I felt so confused. I didn't know where this was all coming from.

"I won't hurt you. I'll never hurt you, baby," he promised before his lips met mine.

I opened my mouth for him and tried not to worry about how fast my heart was racing. He ran his mouth down my neck and slipped his hands beneath my cami, which slowly began to hike up. I placed my arms over my eyes to help me cope with what he was doing.

"Ahh ..." I jolted a little as his teeth clamped down on my right nipple and he tweaked my left with his fingers. My hips betrayed me, grinding at his touch. His mouth continued its journey down my torso to my belly. His tongue dove into my navel, sending an

electric current to my sex. His hands grasped at my bottoms and pulled them down. "Um ... Ray." I tried to sit up, but he kneeled in front of me and lifted my legs, sending me onto my back. He nipped me as he ran his tongue along the apex of my groin, which made my hips betray me even more. I covered my face with my hands and clenched my legs together tightly.

"Open up, baby." He tried gently to part them. I ignored him. "Goddamn it, Becca, now!" His voice was so loud I was afraid the guests could hear him—and the thought distracted me so much that, before I knew it, my legs were open and his face was buried in between them. I grasped at the sheets as he did things to me with his tongue that no one had done in so long.

At that moment, I realized he was there, there was no fighting it. He was very skillful, and we cared deeply for each other. I raised my mental white flag once again, lost my right hand in his thick hair, and encouraged him with my hips.

"Oh, Ray. Oh, baby, please," I begged. As I came undone, his thumb worked at my clit and I felt his tongue dart deep inside me, forcing me to release the butterflies that had stacked up high into my throat. They rushed out in a song that was foreign to me. Just as I finished my last quake—and the butterflies their last verse—Ray slid two fingers inside of me and slowly massaged the front wall. My G-spot awoke from its long slumber.

"You want more, baby?" He bit softly at the skin of my most intimate area before retracing his steps with his tongue. "Ugh, Becs ... you taste so good." He groaned. "Ready, baby? Tell me you want more, baby ... tell me." God, he sounded so fucking hot. Usually, whenever a guy talked to me in bed, it made me roll my eyes because it sounded like cheesy porn banter. Always a major turn-off for me. Not Ray. He wasn't trying to be hot—he just was.

"Yes, baby, please." I was barely audible, but that changed once Ray again started giving me the solid tongue lashing he felt I deserved. It didn't take long for me to come undone again. He

quickly climbed on top of me, his mouth on mine. I could taste my-self on his tongue and lips.

He shifted and I could feel him at my entrance. "Ready, baby?" he whispered.

Ready? Ready for what? Oh, no ... no, no, no!

"No, Ray, stop! We can't. I can't. Please don't," I begged and pushed at him.

"Baby, please. Please, Becs. I need you. Don't do this, please." He kissed me between short sentences. He slid his erection slowly up and down my sex. If I wasn't flipping out, it probably would have enticed me.

"No! No, Ray, stop!" I yelled as he brought it to my entrance again and pushed a little. I could feel myself trying to open for him.

"Baby, let me just dip it in once ... please," he begged (like a teenaged boy, mind you!).

"That is not a fucking potato chip in your hand, and I'm not a container of French-onion dip! Now get the fuck off of me!" I yelled. He laid on top of me and released a sigh of defeat, then started to laugh uncontrollably. "What are you laughing about?" I asked through my teeth as I tried to control my anger.

"You say the funniest shit sometimes, baby." He looked up at me with that boyish grin and I couldn't help but laugh a little at my-self, too. "I guess I'll take that lotion with a sock now." He sighed and rolled onto his back.

"I don't have a tube sock around, but I do have a towel and my hand. If you guide me, I'll help you work things out." I gave him a half smile. He raised his head and supported himself on his elbows, looking at me.

"Okay, baby," he said softly. I put on his T-shirt before I went to the bathroom for a towel. As I settled back down on the bed near his midsection, he sat up and pushed my hair behind my left ear. "You're so beautiful, baby."

I took his hand in mine and guided them downward, finally

looking for the first time. Oh ... wow ... um. Bow-chicka-wow-wow! I must've looked nervous, because Ray caressed the top of my hand with his thumb.

"Don't worry, baby, it will fit ... when you're ready."

I bit my lip to stifle my giggle. It was sweet that he was trying to comfort me, but kind of silly, too. I mean, I did deliver a nine-pound baby only six years earlier. I was pretty aware that he would fit— that wasn't the question. I actually don't know what the question was. I just couldn't get the porn music out of my head.

"Theme-song alert!" I giggled.

"You have a theme song for this?" He thumbed my lip away from my teeth and I nodded. He turned his head sideways, intrigued.

"Bow-chicka-wow-wowwwww." My upper body danced around a bit. Ray released a laugh, then palmed my face.

"This is the shit that keeps reeling me back to you, baby," he said in a very serious tone, like he was answering a question that kept being asked.

"Come on, now," I said after he kissed me. "Show me how you like it." And so began my lesson on how to please Ray with my hands. After a few minutes, once I got it just the way he liked it, he was able to let go of my hand and fully enjoy what I was doing to him. I loved watching him and listening to him, knowing that I was the one bringing him to the edge.

"Ah ... Becs ... baby ... oh, baby, that's it." His face scrunched up and his head went back as he erupted in my hands. I quickened the pace for a moment like he had told me to, then slowed and squeezed a little for the end. I suddenly felt this insatiable urge to taste him. I don't know if it was the wine egging me on or if my white flag was suddenly replaced by my freak flag (I didn't even know I had one of those!), but I bent down and took him into my mouth.

Ray breathed sharply and fisted my hair.

"Baby," is all he could say as I sucked the last few drops out of

him. I licked the tip and gave him a sweet, quick peck there before sitting back up. I contemplated the taste. Warm, a little salty ... it was Ray, which raised the bar up to it tasting divine. Hmm ... I'd do that again, *I thought, as I meticulously wiped him* up. *I brought the clean part of the towel up to my mouth to dab the corners of it—like a proper lady would. That's when I noticed Ray's intense gaze. "Intense" may be too harsh of a word ... it was more of a full-of-wonder look.*

"What?" Suddenly, I didn't feel so brave.

"Nothing ... that was just ... unexpected." He caressed my cheek with the back of his hand.

"Um, I think everything tonight could fall under that category." I got off the bed and put the towel in the hamper, then picked his bottoms off of the floor and handed them to him. "Can I wear your shirt to bed?" I crossed my arms, rubbing my shoulders through the soft material. He stood up to pull his bottoms on.

"Of course, baby." He chucked my chin and planted a soft kiss on my lips. I wrapped my arms around his waist and hugged him tightly to me. He had just the right amount of chest hair, and it tickled my face. "Hey. Hey, baby, are you okay?" He rubbed my back.

"Yes." I smiled up at him. For the first time in a long time, I felt like I was home. "I have to brush my teeth." I leaned up and kissed him again before I let go. The credits were rolling on the TV. "So, which movie did we not watch?" I asked as I walked into the bathroom.

"Uh, Good Will Hunting,*" he said as he turned on the side lamp and shut off the TV. I brushed my teeth and washed my face. As I dried off, I glanced into the mirror to find Ray leaning against the doorframe, chewing the inside of his lip and smiling.*

"What are you doing?"

"Enjoying the view." He glanced down. It suddenly dawned on me that I had no panties on and had been bending over the sink. I rolled my eyes and shook my head. He walked up behind me and

kissed my hair as he grabbed my toothbrush. I watched him apply toothpaste and brush his teeth ... with my brush. Hmm. I guessed there was no point in mentioning the swapping of germs! "C'mon," he said as he rinsed and shook off my brush.

We walked out and both climbed onto my side of the bed. Guess we were sharing. I didn't mind, though, being wrapped so tightly in his arms. He grabbed his phone and set his alarm.

I remember waking up the next morning with a slight hangover and a folded note in front of the alarm clock. I sat up and opened it.

Good morning, baby,

I hope you have a good day with the girls. My day has already started out fantastically! It always does when I wake up next to you. I don't know how I'm going to wipe this stupid grin off my face today. I'll see you around five tonight.

Love, Ray

P.S. Loved that you called me "baby" last night!

Don't forget Bill is stopping by today.

You look so beautiful ... I hate leaving! XXX

"What are you smiling about?" His voice pulls me back to the here and now.

"Oh, the note you left me. That was lovely."

"Wait! You haven't gotten to the wedding yet?" He widens his eyes.

"No. To you, these are just memories. I feel like I'm experiencing them all for the first time," I explain.

"Christ, Becca, we'll be here for a week! Actually, I wouldn't mind that."

"I called you *baby*, huh?" I'm a little taken aback by this.

"Yes. You only do it when you are drunk or high." He frowns. *High? Oh yeah ... the ecstasy.*

"Well, what happened with the whole note thing?" I can't seem to remember. What else is new?

"Oh! The 'lovely note'?" he says. I can tell by his air quotation marks that it was not pretty. "Well, let's see. Between waking up with a hangover, in my shirt, with no panties, no recollection of the night before, and the 'lovely note'—it's safe to say you flipped out a little. Well, *a little* is an understatement." He sighs.

"What happened?"

"You called me at work. Like an idiot, I was so excited when my secretary said you were on the line. I actually thought you were as giddy and ridiculously happy as I was." He shakes his head. "I picked up the phone and was all like, 'Hey, beautiful!' Hearts flying out of my eyes ... sunshine beaming from my ass."

"Really? Sunshine was beaming out of your ass?" I giggle.

"Shh." His finger touches my lips. Giggle stifled. "'How dare you get me drunk and take advantage of me? What did you do, you selfish son of a bitch?' you yelled. I actually felt my heart breaking. I didn't say anything. I just hung up on you. I told Gwen to clear my schedule for the day, that I had to go get Annie—she was sick. I left and went right to the inn to pick her up. I walked in through the store entrance and saw you in your office. You looked up and saw me."

"I remember." I put my hand up to his mouth.

"Good. You think about it, because I really don't want to go through all that again." His jawline twitches, and I wince.

"You were very mad." I kiss him.

"Baby, you have no idea. I was so tired of you hurting me. I just wanted to smack you hard across the face and be done with you." A tear escapes the corner of his eye.

"You should've run from me, Ray." I kiss his lips over and over again. "I've never been good enough for you. You deserve better than me."

"Don't say that, baby. You are everything to me. You are the center of my universe. I've tried being without you ... several times. The pain is far worse than when I'm putting up with your bullshit. I need you, baby. You are like air to me. Without you, Becs, I can't breathe." His kiss becomes urgent. "Sorry, c'mon. Go back to the memory. I need to bring you back to me." He pulls away.

What does he mean? I wonder before I refocus.

I opened my office door. I was so upset and confused.

"What are you doing here?" I snapped.

"I'm picking Annie up. Where is she?" His tone was flat, but he was obviously irritated. He clenched and unclenched his fist, looking everywhere but at me.

"She's in the kitchen, eating her breakfast. Don't you think we should talk?" I asked angrily through my teeth.

"What the fuck is there to say, Becca? You drink, you do shit you don't remember, and then you fucking yell at me for it! Well, I'm done! I'm going to grab Annie and I'll be out of your hair—and your life!" His eyes turned into a storm and his jawline pulsated.

"Yeah, now that you got what you wanted! You like all your women incoherent?" I pushed him.

"That's what you think of me? That's who you think I am?" A look of rage passed over his face. Never in the year had I known him had I ever seen that expression. He grabbed my arm and forced me into the crop room, slamming the door behind us. He shoved me up against the wall.

"Let me tell you something, baby! If I fucked you last night, there is no question that you would be one sore little girl today!" He was all teeth and anger. "It's official, Becca! I fucking hate you! I hate you!" he screamed in my face and pounded on the wall

next to my head. The next thing I knew, his mouth was on mine. It was raw and painful. He cupped my chin harshly with his hand and pushed my head back; it slammed against the wall. He walked away and out of the crop room. I slid down and cried on the floor. A few minutes later, I heard Annie saying that she didn't want to go. Then I heard nothing but a truck's engine starting outside, and the sound of it speeding away.

"Did you really hate me?"

"Obviously not, Becs. I just ... I really needed you. I was counting on that bid. Remember, it was a multimillion-dollar one, and I thought it was in the bag. To have that pulled out from under me—it was devastating. I was worried and I needed you and just when I thought you were finally there for me ... you pulled that rug out from under me as well. Had that happened at a different time, I wouldn't have reacted the way I did." He thumbs away my tears.

This is so hard to listen to and remember. All I've ever done is hurt him. All he's ever done is try to love me and be patient. I didn't do any of it on purpose, but that certainly doesn't make me feel like any less of an asshole.

"Well, how did we end up at the wedding? That was only a few days later."

"Hmm? Oh, my mother had a hand in that. I love you, Becs." He kisses me again.

"I know you do, Ray. I love you, too. How did your mother have a hand in it?" I need him to stay focused.

"My parents came down that day because we were all going to go to Boston together on Saturday. With everything going on, I forgot they were coming. My mom could tell that I was really upset about something. She and I took a walk while my dad stayed with Annie. My mom had always known what I was dealing with when it comes to you. I needed someone to talk to, Becca, and I've always been close to her."

I think he's waiting for me to be upset about this, but I love Elise very much and I love his relationship with her. I love *my* relationship with her. I'm glad he had somebody to turn to.

"It's okay, baby, go ahead." I touch his face. He takes in a sharp breath. "What? It's okay that you talked to her. I'm glad you talked to someone."

"Um ... well, I told her what had happened with the bid, and then with you—without full detail, of course. I told her about your reaction and accusation, and then my reaction. She said, 'Son, if you love her, it will all work out. I know she loves you. I have proof. When we get back to the house, I'm a-gonna show you somethin', sweetie.' Then she said, 'Ray, I know this alls been tough on you, but that girl's been through somethin' awful. I think she has PTSD, son. She just needs a good therapist, some time, and some Ray McNeil. She'll come around, sweetheart. Now we goin' pick her up like we was plannin'. I'm a goin' give my baby girl a talkin' to today. Ain't nobody quittin' on nobody. She loves ya, son. Have faith in God's plan, baby, it'll all work out.'" Ray always does an excellent imitation of his mother's sweet Georgia accent.

"I love your mother even more for saying all of that." Suddenly, my heart breaks for what she must be thinking of me now.

"She's always loved you, baby." He smiles warmly. "Do you remember her stopping by that day?" He plays with a strand of my hair. I try to think back. *Oh, yes!* I nod. "Will you tell me as you remember it?" He kisses my nose.

"Yes. Um, let's see. I was just cleaning up from lunch, and she startled me. 'Whadju make today, darlin'?' I turned around and immediately ran into her arms. Her blue eyes were bright with tears and her hair was perfect and silver as always." I smile.

"My silver fox." Ray smiles, too, at his nickname for her.

"She said, 'You got a minute, baby girl? We need to have us a walk.' I nodded and kissed her cheek again. 'There, there now, baby, everythin' gonna be all right. Let's go get us some fresh air.'

We took a walk up toward the trails. 'Ray told me you two had an argument this mornin'. Becca, he's beside himself, honey. You know my Raymond loves you. Ever since he met you, he's been head over heels, darlin'. Now you two have been togetha for a year now, you're still figurin' each other out.'

"I said, 'Elise, Ray and I are just friends.'

"'Becca, now I'm goin' stop you right there, baby girl! What you been tellin' yo'self and what you been showin' the rest of the world are two differn' thins', honey. When ya'll come up an' visit me an' Artie, you an' Ray are kissin', playin' and touchin' like a pair a teenagers. When we take day trips with ya'll—it's the same thin'. Now I don't think it's intentional, but you been flippin' yo switch with him since the beginnin', honey, and he's just 'bout had it. I know what happened to you was very traumatic, but I think it's high time you went an' saw somebody to help you through that. You need to do it for yo'self and for Ray, honey. You can't keep stringin' him along. You can't be kissin' and lovin' one moment and pushin' him away the next. He's been nuttin' but good to you and Morgan, Becca. He takes care of you the best way he can. Now we goin' pick you up for this weddin' and you are goin' to act and be the attentive girlfriend Raymond needs and deserves. An' you goin' *stay* attentive an' not flip out an' embarrass him. I hope you know I love you, sweetheart, an' I'm not tryin' to be the bitchy mother-in-law, but I love my son, too. He needs his girl, Becca. He's goin' through a tough time an' he jus' needs you. You goin' to come and leave this baggage behind!'" I take in a deep breath.

"Mother-in-law, huh?" He smiles.

"Oh, yes. She always refers to herself that way and introduces me as her daughter-in-law." I smile because I never minded. I love her.

"So what did you say to all of that?" His eyes widen.

"What I always say to your mother when she gives me a 'what for'... *Yes, ma'am*." I laugh.

"Mmm ... you were so very, very attentive, baby. Do—you—remember?" He pecks at my lips.

Oh God, I want to be with him. The memories are sucking me in—confusing me. I need to stop. "Close your eyes and think about the wedding. Do you remember us picking you up? My dad drove ..."

I nod.

It was noon when they arrived. I was sick to my stomach with nerves. I hadn't seen or talked to Ray since Thursday morning when he declared his hatred for me.

My hair was in an updo with soft curls. It looked flowy and carefree, but it was cemented in place with product. My dress was a plum chiffon halter top that ended just above my knees. I accessorized with the one-carat, pear-shaped diamond earrings and matching necklace that Ray gave me for my birthday. I added the diamond tennis bracelet from Mother's Day and a few spritzes of the Birmane perfume he bought me—just because. I took one last look in the mirror before I headed down with my overnight bag.

"Hi, Becca!" Annie ran to me. She gasped. "You look beautiful!"

I smiled and thanked her, but all I could concentrate on was the heat from Ray's stare.

"Morgan's in her room, honey. You girls be good for Hazel, okay?" I tapped her bottom.

"We will!" she yelled and ran off. I grabbed my bag again and headed toward Ray. I could feel my face flush.

"Let me take that." He reached for it. His face was so close to mine. He stood back up, my bag in his hand, and stared at me intently. I moved closer 'til my body was pressed up against his. I licked my lips and leaned up toward him. It was a very vulnerable kiss, and I pulled away reluctantly. His gaze remained intense. I leaned up and did it again. He responded slightly. I cupped his face

with my hands and put a little more urgency into my kiss. He parted his lips and I deepened the kiss with a slip of my tongue. His tongue greeted mine, softly caressing it.

"C'mon," he whispered when he pulled away. He took my hand and led me out to the car. Artie was driving and Elise was in the front passenger seat.

"Well, hi, darlin'!" She got out of the car to greet me. "Now, don't you look beautiful, baby? Doesn't she look beautiful, son?" She held me at arm's length.

"She always does, Mama." His smile seemed reluctant. "Mama, I'm gonna sit with Daddy up front."

"No, son, you're goin' sit in the back with your girlfriend," she stated with her Southern authority.

"She's not my girlfriend, Mama. I'm not sure what she is. Maybe you could clarify that for us, Becca. What are you to me?" The words were snarky—he was still angry. I looked down and played with my fingers like a child would. "What are you, Becca?" he yelled, making me jump.

"Raymond!" Elise snapped.

"Stay out of this, Mama! What are you, Becca? Tell me!" He grabbed my arms.

"Raymond, that's enough, son!" Artie got out of the driver's seat and raised his voice. I looked up at Ray, tears slipping from the pools in my eyes.

"Tell me," he said calmly.

"I'm yours. I'm yours, Ray," I cried. He released my arms and grasped my face instead. I heard his mother tell his father to get back into the car. Both of their doors closed and I was lost in a kiss with Ray.

"C'mon now." He gave me a small peck and nodded toward the back seat. We both got in.

Our two-hour drive to Boston started out pretty silent.

"Your jewelry is pretty, baby." His mom turned and pointed.

"Oh, thank you. Every piece is from Ray. These two were for my birthday, and this one was for Mother's Day." I pointed to each piece proudly, then glanced over at Ray to catch his satisfied smile. I sat back a little closer to him. He wrapped me in his arms.

"I've missed you," he whispered in my ear.

"I missed you, too." I welcomed his lips on mine.

"I can't wait to get you to our hotel room and get inside of you." I turned my eyes sharply to meet his. He stared at me as if I was a steak and he hadn't eaten in weeks. I swallowed hard and decided to engage the McNeils in conversation the rest of the way down to Boston.

"Jesus, Ray!" I say when I open my eyes.

"Now what did I do?" He smiles, looking half asleep.

"What you said to me in the car on the way down to Boston."

"Hmm ... your cheeks went bright red. Go back. It's about to get real hot." He rubs and squeezes my bum. I close my eyes and try to forget what his touch is doing to me.

We checked in at the Harbor Hotel and headed upstairs to our room. It was nice, with a king-sized bed and a large window with a view of the harbor. The rich blues, reds, and golds in the fabric used for the bedding, drapery, and chairs added a romantic feel to the room. I had been through the lobby of this hotel a million times, but this was the first time I'd actually stepped into a room. I found it to be quite lovely.

We had another hour before we had to catch the shuttle to the wedding. Thankfully, the reception was back here at the hotel.

"I used to go whale watching from here." I pointed to the boats at the docks. Ray walked up behind me.

"Why don't we do that tomorrow?"

"Eh, I don't know. It's four and a half hours. That wouldn't be fair to Hazel." I sighed, then gasped as his hands ran up my thighs,

hiking my dress up.

"Are you mine, Becca?" He spoke softly in my ear. My breathing was erratic as he kissed my neck.

"Yes." I breathed.

"Is this mine?" His right hand caressed me between my legs. I could feel the heat rise to my cheeks as the want in me grew. My core tightened. My panties were on the verge, if they weren't already, of soaking through.

"Oh, um ... yes." I closed my eyes.

"Good. I want what's mine, baby. Now." He turned me to him and unzipped my dress.

"This unhooks here." I showed him the hook in the front, which unfastened the fabric from the halter position. I unbuttoned his shirt as he worked at my strapless bra. I ran my hands up his chest to his shoulders, pushing his shirt off of them.

"Baby, I'm not going to stop." He thumbed my lip.

"Yeah, I think I got the memo on that." I kissed his thumb. "You got the skills to get the job done without messing my hair up, McNeil?" I gave him the thug nod—one of our many inside jokes.

"Bravery without wine ... I'm impressed, baby." Half boyish grin.

"I've got my big-girl pants on," I agreed.

"Hmm." He hooked his fingers under the elastic of my panties and whipped them down. "Not anymore, babe." I thought about bringing up the fact that he basically just called my panties big, but the fact that he was biting me down near the apex of my groin was a bit distracting.

I closed my eyes and fisted his hair to brace myself. His mouth traveled up to my stomach, and he dove his tongue deep into my navel as his fingers slowly separated me and plunged inside.

"Ah!" I gasped.

"Oh, baby, you're so ready for me." He pulled his fingers out and sucked my taste off of them. He slid his hands up my body as

he came to a standing position again. He stared down into my eyes as I unbuckled his belt and worked at the button and zipper of his pants. "You okay, baby?" He touched my cheek.

"I love you, Ray. I want to be with you." I leaned my head into his touch.

"You love me?" He seemed unsure.

"I do. I can't imagine my life without you." I remember feeling the guilt rise as I said it. Why did I feel guilty?

"Becs, baby ... stay with me. Focus, honey, please. Stay with me. Don't do this, baby ... please. You promised you wouldn't flip out. Damn it!" His mouth was on mine with a sense of urgency. He brought me down to the bed.

"Ray ... Ray." I felt the panic coming on. What was I doing? Ray thrust himself inside of me. I could feel myself aching as I expanded around him.

"Becca ... oh God, baby."

I closed my eyes, soaking in the sensation of Ray making love to me. I felt myself focusing and calming down. I opened my eyes to find Ray's tormented ones.

"Let me hold you," I begged, and glanced at my arms. He had them pinned.

"Oh, Becs." He released them and found my mouth. I held on to his back as my hips met his powerful thrusts. He felt so good ... so right. I couldn't get close enough to him. I know he felt the same. He was trying to climb higher—deeper into me—and my hips were coming off the bed to meet him, help him. All of the sudden, I felt it come on. It was like a choir of angels singing out the most beautiful note.

"Oh, Ray. Oh, baby. Please. Please," I practically cried. The choir broke out the chorus section of Madonna's "Like a Prayer." He worked me through my quakes—there were so many of them!— all the while egging me on. I began to squeeze around him.

"Oh God, Becs. Oh, baby. Jesus ... agh!" He groaned and

scrunched his face. *"Baby. Baby, wait. Oh ... oh, Becca ... oh, honey."* His lips formed a perfect *"O"* shape as he came inside of me so deeply I couldn't help my added whimper of approval. The full weight of his body crashed down on top of me as he tried to catch his breath. He nudged my lips with his as he reached down and slowly pulled himself out, making me wince. *"Becs ... I'm sorry."*

"For what?" I touched his cheek.

"Um ... I, uh ... well, I wasn't prepared."

"Are you saying we just had a whoops?*"* I propped myself up on my elbows and looked down.

"Uh ... yeah." He bit the inside of his cheek.

"We should be all right. I'm on the Pill." A look of relief came over his face, but a furrowed brow quickly followed.

"Why are you on the Pill, and why didn't I know?"

"For the men I randomly sleep with at different expensive hotels. And because I didn't want you to know about them." I held my hand up to my mouth like I accidentally released secret information.

"Smartass! I'm just surprised I didn't know. I know everything about you, Becs." He laid his head back on the pillow.

"Oh, you think you do. But you don't." I rested my chin on his chest.

Chapter Twelve

"**R**ay." I nudge him.

"Huh? Oh ... hi, baby." He smiles and kisses me.

"Why are you so tired today?"

"I was up most of the night working on a special Christmas gift." He winks.

"So now, in my memories, I've made love to you without any help from wine. How long did it last? That whole attentive-girlfriend thing?" I'm confused. It should've been settled then, because both Ray and Elise called me out on my behavior.

"It was gone by Monday morning." He sighs.

"Oh, Ray, I'm sorry."

"Well, we made love a lot that weekend. It recharged my dealing-with-it batteries. You also started to see Patricia about your past. I felt hopeful that one day you would look into my eyes and say, 'I'm ready to be yours, Ray. I'm ready for us. I'm ready for our present and our future. I'm ready to be all you need now.'" I watch as his chin quivers and his eyes fill up. *Oh, why did he stay? How could he stay and wait for me like this?* My heart is aching for him—for me.

"I don't deserve you. You didn't deserve me." I wipe his tears.

"Why don't I deserve the girl of my dreams? Why am I not good enough for you? Why couldn't I ... why can't I fix your heart? What could I have done differently?" His eyes are like the ocean in the middle of a hurricane.

"It wasn't your job to fix it. I needed to be ready to face what happened to me. I was stuck between two worlds—two lives, really. Reliving these memories ... Ray, I'm realizing that I felt everything with you that I feel with Grayson. I think my mind just wasn't ready to listen to my heart. I thought I just *loved* you, but that I'm *in love* with Grayson. It turns out ... I'm in love with you, too. What am I supposed to do with that, Ray?" I stop when his lips quiet my mouth. "Honestly, how did you put up with this for so long? I know you love me, but this is a lot to deal with. I feel like I'm Lucy from *50 First Dates*," I say, and Ray starts laughing. "What?" I give a toothy smile.

"I tried to do what Henry did in that movie. Sometimes it would work a little. I also refer to us as Allie and Noah from *The Notebook*. Those movies actually help me a little. They give me inspiration. Mostly, you are Lucy. Forgetful Lucy, and *Peanuts* Lucy where I am Charlie Brown always thinking, 'This time ... I know she won't pull the football away!' Then I land on my ass and wonder ... when am I ever going to learn?" He sighs as he lays his head next to mine.

"So, when I clearly didn't remember what happened, you would just pretend with me?" *I don't think I'd be able to do that!*

"Yeah, I learned how to read you. When you have a few glasses in you or you're on painkillers for something, my chances are really high. Whenever we go to Maine to be with my parents, you're ultra-focused on me. Actually, whenever my mom is around, you are very *on* as my girlfriend. I always tell my mom she's got some sort of spell over you." He chuckles lightly.

"I love your mom. It probably stems from me not wanting to disappoint her, something psychological with me losing my mother so early. I am quite the case, huh?" I laugh, but it's really sad, actually.

"Whatever it is, I keep begging them to move here! Oh, baby, you're so good when we go to Maine." His lips are on mine again. His tongue slides across them, beckoning me to open up. I allow him to deepen the kiss, then match his urgency. He pushes me on my back and his hand dives into my pants, under my panties. *Jesus, I never did refasten from his earlier attempt!* "God, baby, is this all from me?"

"Yes," I answer. His fingers swirl around, spreading my wetness. My hips betray me again. *Country Sybecca is flying around her stripper pole, and her Daisy Dukes are MIA.* "Ahh!" I gasp as his fingers plunge deep inside of me. "Ray ... Ray, no." Panic sets in.

"Shh ... stop, baby."

Country Sybecca holds onto the pole. Running around it, she jumps into the air like a Ninja Warrior and kicks Cautionary Sybecca in the head, rendering her unconscious. Her red ticker board lies on top of her ... screen smashed ... message not received. Country Sybecca is back to working the pole. Horny Sybecca is coaching her on how to bounce that ass.

"Ray ... oh God, Ray." I clench his shirt in my fists as I rise. *One lonely beam of white light hits the stage in a perfect circle. Operatic Sybecca steps into it, Viking helmet intact. Hmm ... she's new. She opens up her mouth and lets out a beautiful, deafening sound.* Ray works me through my last quakes and muffles my cries with his mouth. He pulls away and stares at me. His hand slides out from between my legs and onto my bare hip.

"I love you, Becca," he whispers.

"I love you." I lean up and kiss him.

I feel my nose flare as I try to hold my tears back. My heart is breaking. At this moment, I realize I am deeply in love with both Ray and Grayson, and that today, I will lose them both. Grayson will walk away once he finds out what went on in here—if he doesn't already know. Ray will walk away at the end of our trip down memory lane, because I will tell him that I'm having Grayson's baby. I will be alone, just me and Morgan and now this little one. I've thrown everything away. I feel so selfish and fucked up!

"Baby, stay with me. Don't leave me, baby ... come back." Ray kisses me. "I'll never stop fighting for you. I love you. Please, Becca ... come back ... don't go." I return his kisses.

"I'm here. I'm not leaving," I reassure him.

"Next memory?" he asks, kissing my tears away.

"Okay, baby." I try to regroup. Ray's eyes light up. I just close mine and listen.

"The next time you showed me any affection was right before Christmas, when you fell off Rocco and smashed your arm. God, you really did a number on it." He grabs my arm and kisses my surgery scars. You can barely see them now, but Ray knows just where every single one is.

"You took such good care of me, Ray. You were so tired, running your business during the day and mine at night. I was so out of it from the meds. Not that I could do much with my arm like that anyway." I look at it all better now.

"Baby, I wasn't just exhausted from running both business-es. You were on painkillers around the clock, and we had sex at least three to five times a day! You were insatiable, baby ... and I loved every minute of it!" If his smile could get any bigger, I think it would swallow his face. "It was a *very merry* Christmas." He chuckles.

My mind flashes through a montage sex tape of Ray and me during that time. I feel my face flush as I watch myself riding him hard, begging him to make me sore. Us up against the shower wall, in my closet, on the round table in my room ... the floor ... the dresser. Yeah, we pretty much covered every surface. *Porn Sybecca pulls up a chair and takes out a legal pad. Apparently, my blow jobs are noteworthy.* From the look on Ray's face in the memory reel, he would agree.

"Wow! You've must've cried when I didn't need the pain pills anymore." I giggle.

"It was bittersweet. I knew it would be a while again, yet I was exhausted and welcomed the break. As I said, baby, you were insatiable." He rubs my belly gently. Reminding me.

"What's next?" I mentally shake myself away from thoughts of the baby. He takes a deep breath and blows it out aggressively through his lips, trying to think.

"Um, took you up to Maine for your birthday weekend. That was nice. I love watching you and my mother together. You genuinely love each other. It makes me feel good ... complete." He rests his head on the throw pillow again.

"I love your mom so much." I turn my head to add a smile to my comment.

"When we made love that Saturday morning, it was the most intense, beautiful thing I have ever experienced. I'm pretty sure you felt the same. We were both in tears. That's never happened to me before." He speaks softly, his forefinger playing lightly at my lips.

"You being the King of Alpha males and all," I tease. His words overwhelm me—I can't help it. He gives me a knowing smirk. I close my eyes, trying to remember that morning.

I awoke to find Ray looking out the window. The sun was slowly trying to rise. I looked at the clock. It was a quarter of seven. I was naked and felt a little sore, and then I remembered that Ray and I made love for the first time the night before.

My giggles pull me back to the here and now.

"What?" Ray raises his lips into an inquisitive smile.

"Oh, Ray." I laugh. "It seems that every time with you really *is* like the first time." I shake my head at myself.

"Yes, Lucy, it is." He makes me laugh harder.

"Okay, let me get back." I pull myself together and shut my eyes.

I gathered myself up in the quilt and walked up behind him.

"Hi." I kissed his back. He was shirtless, wearing just his PJ bottoms.

"Hi." He continued to stare out the window.

"What are you thinking about?" I asked, my stomach in knots. Did he regret what happened last night?

"Us," he said with a sigh.

"Um ... Ray, nothing has to come of last night. We got caught up in a moment ... it's okay." I patted his shoulder, then immediately felt stupid for doing so. I turned to find my PJs, trying to feel unaffected by this moment. I felt his hands on my hips.

"You think I regret last night?" He kissed my shoulder.

"Um ... yeah." I turned to him. The quilt was wrapped under my arms like an oversized towel. I couldn't seem to pull my eyes up to look into his, so I stared at the knotty pine floor instead.

"God, is there any moment of the day that you don't look beautiful?" He pushed my hair behind my ear and grazed my cheek with his knuckles. I finally found the strength to look up at him. His hands cupped my face and he stared at me like he either hadn't seen me in years, or worse, like he was never going to see me again. He looked like he was making a memory.

"Is something wrong?" I couldn't help my shaky voice.

"I'm just ... I'm so in love with you. Becca, I have never felt

this way before. It hurts." And with that, he collected my lips with his own. It was reluctant, sweet, like he was tasting me for the first time—or the last. He pulled the quilt from me as he deepened the kiss. I crawled back onto the bed. He crawled with me, our mouths never losing contact.

My neck arched, pulling my mouth away as he entered me slowly. He grasped my hip for leverage as he tried to fill me to capacity. I released a gasping moan. It was painful and wonderful all at the same time. He pulled back slowly, then plunged into me. I held onto the small of his back and his right cheek, trying to help him reach the place he was aiming for. It was slow. It was urgent. It was so many things. I was overwhelmed by what I was feeling, by what my body was feeling. My orgasm was like no other I've ever had before. It was sweet and tight, lingering little blossoms, a cere- monious eruption. I cried as he came undone as well.

Ray finished his last wave as the sun was slowly showing itself into our room. His eyes were damp like mine. He tried to blink it back, but a drop fell on my cheek. I reached up and wiped the tear with two fingers, then kissed the saltiness off without ever losing contact with his eyes. I ran my lips over his, enticing him to kiss me. His mouth made love to my mouth 'til we heard the girls laughing as they ran down the hall. Ray smiled against my lips before he pulled away. He watched me as he pulled out. I think he liked to see me wince.

The rest of the day was wonderful, although Ray seemed a bit off. I was, too. The remnants of my orgasm stayed with me all day, like an itch I couldn't scratch.

We took the girls ice-skating at a local rink after we spent time in the snow. Elise and I cooked up a feast! Thank God we're two hours apart, because her Southern cooking would push me right into a size fourteen!

It was a much-needed break for me. The inn was a lot busier than I had expected—or hoped for. I barely took any time off, but

Elise called and demanded I come up for my birthday. As usual, "Yes, ma'am" was all I could say. Ray needed the break too; he had been getting so snippy.

That night, after Ray and I went to bed, the most amazing thing happened when he entered me. I had a full-blown, bone-chilling orgasm.

"What the hell was that, baby?" He looked at me, his eyes wide. I was on top of him, and I guess he scratched my itch perfectly at this angle.

"Remnants from earlier," I said, a little embarrassed. And then it was like I poured a can of fuel on the fire—he was ignited! He threw me back and held my left leg up as he pounded into me. He moved my leg over toward my right and flipped me in one swift motion, then pulled my hips up so I was on my knees.

"Holy shit!" I gasped in shock of the acrobatics. I pushed my face into the pillow to muffle my groans and let him have at it. At the pace he was going, it didn't take him long to unravel.

"Thank ... you ... ma'am!" He said each word with each of his final thrusts, then rested on my back before he pulled out and settled down beside me. I slowly let my knees slide back so I was lying on my belly. I half expected to be in the next room over when I raised my head. He fucked me so hard, surely the bed went through the wall!

"Hi." He smiled, rubbing my bum.

"Um, hi. All better now?" I giggled.

"Hmm, yeah." He quickly slid his tongue into my mouth. "You feel so good, baby. You taste so good."

We made love again that night before falling asleep. He took me twice Sunday morning. His mood shifted greatly after we packed and headed downstairs for some of his Southern mama's breakfast. They went for an hour-long walk. When they came back, Elise was visibly upset. Ray was, too.

"Is everything all right?" I asked, unsure of what was going

on. I began to wonder if I did something wrong. Elise just hugged me and said everything was fine. When it was time to leave, she pulled me in for a fierce hug.

"I love you, baby girl. Ray loves you." She started crying.

"Elise, Mama ... what's wrong?" When I called her mama, *she just cried and hugged me harder.*

"You be good now, ya hear?" She smiled through her tears. Ray looked uncomfortable. No one was telling me anything.

"Let's go, baby," Ray said quietly, and grabbed my hand. Something told me not to pry.

We left. Our drive focused on conversations with the girls. Ray listened to sports on the radio. I read my book. Everything felt so ... different. Something wasn't right. I kept looking at him. He was deep in thought. It felt like we arrived at the inn too quickly, and yet I was looking forward to breathing in the atmosphere of normal. The girls took off running once he pulled in.

"Annie—damn it!" he yelled and hit his steering wheel.

"Ray, did I do something wrong?" I fought back my tears.

"No, baby, I'm just tired, and I have a hell of a week coming up." He sighed. I was not convinced, but got out of the truck anyhow. He followed me into the inn to get Annie.

"Can you guys stay for dinner?" Morgan asked, and Annie nodded.

"No. Sorry, Morgan. We have to go. Annie, get in the truck," he said sternly. Annie hugged Morgan and walked out with her head down. Morgan went off to find Hazel. Ray and I were left—feeling awkward. Something wasn't right between us, and it broke my heart. "Why are you crying, baby?" He sounded defeated.

"I don't know. Why don't you tell me?" I couldn't help snapping at him through my tears.

"I'll see you on Wednesday." He kissed my forehead and left.

I open my eyes.

"You hurt me. You made me feel used!"

"Terrible feeling, isn't it?" he asks defensively. I sit up and cry out, feeling that old pain. "Becca, that weekend was very difficult for me. I decided to 'break up' with you. I just couldn't do it anymore. It was killing me, baby." He rubs my back.

"I remember ... well, I remember you being very distant from me. You only talked to me about the girls. You stopped eating dinner with us on Wednesdays, then coming over altogether. I stopped asking you if you were mad at me, and no longer called you about things around the inn."

"Yeah, that pissed me off. That, and you dancing with Will—fucking asshole!" Ray has always gotten irritated at the mere mention of Will.

"You started dating ... what was her name?" I wince, trying to recall.

"Michelle." He clears his throat.

"Did you? With her?" I suddenly feel hostile over something that happened three years ago that I have no right to feel anything over. Ray looks up at the ceiling. "Did you find it?" I glance up as well, leaning toward him.

"What?"

"Your answer. Is it up there?" I elbow him playfully.

"I have needs, Becca. It wasn't like being with you. She was nothing like you in any way, shape, or form." He sighs.

"Why did you start coming around again?" I lean my head on his shoulder.

"There were several reasons." He rests his head against mine, grabs my hand, and plays with my fingers.

"Name them."

"Uh, well, first, I couldn't stand being apart from you. It was killing me. Second, Annie was pissed and she hated Michelle. My mother nagged me and cried all the time. I felt like I was cheating on you. I didn't like what Will was saying around town, and it wasn't even that bad back then. I just didn't like that he wanted you and made it known." He brings my hand up to his lips and pecks softly at it over and over again. I nudge him with it, silently asking him to continue. "I was at the pub with Michelle one night. We were dancing. I didn't realize you had walked in with Stacey. I looked up and saw your face. You looked as if someone stole the breath from your lungs." He glances over at me.

"That's exactly how I felt. I felt my heart break. I wasn't exactly sure why. Well, no, that's not true. I guess I just thought you were mine even though I didn't think you were mine. It's complicated."

"Ya think?" He laughs.

"Stacey made me stay and have a drink. I remember her badgering me. 'Don't let him think you care. You did nothing wrong! We're gonna have a good time. Just act like he's not here!' she said as she started texting. I asked who she was texting and tried to look, but she hit *send*. 'Just Steve!' she said as we sat at the bar. We ordered our drinks. Her phone pinged. She smiled wickedly, texted real quick, and put her phone away. I knew she was up to something, I just didn't know what."

"And then magically ... as if on cue ... Will shows up with his fucking touchy-feely paws!" Ray raises his hands, wiggling his fingers for emphasis. "Fucking Stacey!" he snaps.

"You know she did that?" I look at him shocked.

"Oh, she made sure I knew! She kept giving me her wicked *F.U.* smile! Then, while you two were dancing, she texted me, *Cute couple, huh?*"

I can't help but laugh a little. Stacey's always had a big pair! I think she kept them tucked away in her clutch purse.

I remember Will coming up from behind me.

"I was walking by and got distracted by the most beautiful creature I've ever seen. Have you seen her?" he asked, and looked around. It made me laugh.

Of course, I knew he was talking about me. That was always his way of flirting with me— acting uninterested in a playful, sarcastic way. Usually, he was trying to talk me out of "my crush" on him. He didn't feel right dating students.

"Oh, they are playing our song, Becca, let's go now!" He grabbed my hand and led me onto the empty floor. We started dancing to "Halo" by Beyoncé. It was a sultry, seductive piece that we had been practicing. His hands were very suggestive ... well, the whole dance was, actually. He pulled me up out of my arched back for the finish. "You did awesome, baby!" He smiled, hugging me and kissing my cheek. "Damn, you're a natural!" He slapped my hip playfully.

"Stop!" I laughed, then turned to find Ray at his table—front row to the dance floor. His nostrils were flaring and jawline pulsating. His eyes kept scanning from Will back to me. The look on his face was nasty. *His girlfriend was trying to talk to him, but he wasn't breaking from his very concentrated stare-down. I felt like a child getting caught out past curfew or something. That was so un-Ray-like. It was sorta hot!*

Will grabbed my hand and led me back to the bar. Stacey had a few guys around her. Fucking Stacey! I was on my third glass of wine, feeling on the edge of tipsy. Will seemed to become more flirtatious—more touchy-feely. I knew it was time to go. He was starting to make me feel uncomfortable.

"No, c'mon, one more dance, baby." Will cupped my face and rested his forehead against mine. That is, until Ray grabbed him by the back of his shirt and threw him off of me.

"Keep your fucking hands off of her!" he yelled. The music stopped so we could have everybody's full attention.

Will got up and pushed him back.

"She's not yours anymore, Ray! She's free to date who she wants!"

Ray went to go after him, but I jumped in the middle.

"Stop it, you two!" I yelled. The lights came on—just in case people couldn't see, I guess. So at about eleven in the evening the music was off and the lights on in the busiest, most popular bar in Ashland, New Hampshire. Guess we were a real showstopper! That and, this being a small town in New Hampshire, there's not much going on.

"Are you kidding me, Ray? You're fighting over your ex-girl-friend?" Michelle yelled from the sidelines. Ex-girlfriend?

I guess Ray read the question on my face.

"Don't ... don't you fucking dare say it, Becca," he said in an angry whisper near my ear. I could see Stacey trying to nonchalant-ly give me the slashing-across-her-neck sign—her code to not ask the question either.

Michelle took Ray's intentional tuning her out as her cue to leave the bar—and him. Smart girl. Ray stared into my eyes. I did the only thing I could think to do. My answer to everything. I bit my lip. He thumbed it free and leaned forward to kiss me. I pulled my head away from him. This only provoked him to fist my hair with one hand and palm my cheek with the other. His lips assaulted mine. I gave in. I had no choice. He had a death grip on me. Most of the people in the bar knew us. They hooted and hollered. The lights went down and the music came back on. Ray finally let me come up for air.

"Stacey, you okay to drive?" he asked her, not taking his eyes off of me.

"Yeah, why?"

"Becca's coming home with me."

Panic set in.

"No, I'm not!"

"Yes you are, baby!" he said through gritted teeth. I suddenly felt damp, and not at my brow, either. Ahem.

"Oh shit, Becca, you better go with him. He just made my panties wet!" Stacey said, staring at Ray in awe.

247

"Stacey, I'm going to buy you a goddamn filter for your birth-day!" I yelled as I pulled away from Ray to grab my keys and throw cash on the bar for our drinks.

"I got it, baby, put your money away." Ray was all candy-and-ice-cream sweet as he took the cash off the bar and gave it to me.

"Baby, baby, baby!" I snapped and gave Jimmy, the bartender, my money. I then went up to Will and kissed him, tongue and all. "Sorry, Will," I said in his ear before I turned around. "Fuck. You. Ray!" I yelled and flashed my "sight word." I made eye contact with Stacey and nodded toward the door.

"Coming!" She ran toward me, trying to escape the shitstorm that everybody felt coming. We headed outside and got into my Honda Pilot. I cried all the way home, except for the times Stacey joked about me slapping my new bronze balls across Ray's face.

"You should've seen Ray's face when you kissed Will like that. I thought he was going to go apeshit!" She laughed.

"Yeah, well, I don't know if that was too smart. I probably opened up a can of worms with Will that I wasn't even looking to take off the shelf." I rolled my eyes. Christ ... what did I do?

"Wow, a whole bar scene incident ... classic!" My tone is sarcastically playful. Ray looks at me with complete irritation. "Really? Three years later ... still bothers you?" I widen my eyes.

"Yeah, really! I hate that guy!" He shakes his head.

"So, what happened after that?" I'm trying to remember myself.

"Nothing. I stayed away for another month."

"Until?"

"Until I came home to my birthday carrot cake and a gift from you on my porch. My parents were still out with Annie. I brought it all in the house. I opened the cake box and there it was. *HAPPY BIRTHDAY, RAY!* in green icing, except for the 'A' in my name that you always replace with a carrot designed in icing. I opened your present. You made me that scrapbook of Annie and me. Some pictures had Morgan in them. They were pictures from things we had all done together, or been together for. Not one picture of just you and me ... not one single one." His voice goes quiet.

"I didn't think you'd want a picture of us. You had been avoiding me for months and you had a new girlfriend." I defend my choice.

"Well, there I sat at my table, crying like a little bitch until my mama came home and made it all better." He pokes fun at himself.

"Mama's boy!" I tease him. "What did she say?"

"Well, she saw me and immediately told my dad to take Annie outside. 'That from Becca, son?' she asked. I nodded and cried harder. 'Now, do you know why you cryin'?' I told her it was because I loved and missed you. She said, 'Well now looks to me like my baby girl's feelin' the same way 'bout you.' I said I couldn't go back to the way things were. She said, 'Seems to me that you can't go on this way either. Go to her, Ray. You want me call her to come join us fer yo birthday, baby?'"

"She did call me!" I cut him off.

"Yeah ... you came ... twice," he says with a mischievous grin.

"Mama worked her magic, huh?" I nudge him.

"Mmm ... yes, she did." He nips at my earlobe.

I smack his arm. "What's next?"

"Next? You don't want to remember that night?" He seems nervous.

"I just did. Next, please." I close my eyes.

"Becs, you did not!"

"It was very sticky and sweet, because you wanted to have your cake and eat if off of me, too!" I tap his lips with my forefinger. He bites it.

"It tasted so much better that way! Okay, let me think. Well, you got really busy at the inn. Even my mother couldn't get you to break away. We did things locally, but it wasn't the same. You were so distracted."

"Well, I had a lot of weddings that year, on top of the crop weekends. We didn't have any sleepovers?" I ask.

"No. Not until Christmas. I was actually very busy, too." He rests his head back on the couch. I snuggle up to him. "This is nice." He kisses my head and puts his arms around me. *Apparently, I like to play with fire.*

"Oh. That's when you had that hospital project in Maine." I remember us now, barely seeing each other.

"The assisted-living facility," he corrects me.

"Right. You did a beautiful job." I smile up at him.

"I hated being away from you guys so much. I was glad Annie had you to take care of her, but I felt like I was losing you. Remember your *no-wine diet*?" He chuckles.

"Oh. Um, yup! Meant *no Ray*, huh?" I wince.

"Yeah, basically. I found myself begging for hugs. I even got into a fight with you one evening. Tried the whole 'Fucking kiss me, Becca!' thing. It didn't work. We just got into a huge fight."

It was late on a school night. Annie was over so often that I kept clothes for her at the inn. I hadn't heard from Ray by eight, so I just had Annie shower and go to sleep with Morgan. I'd send her on the bus with a note in the morning. By ten o'clock, I was putting the sign out for my guests and doing the last few preparations in the kitchen for breakfast.

"Hey, baby." I felt Ray's hands at my waist. He sounded tired.

"Where have you been?" My tone showcased my irritation. Christ, he could've called!

"Oh, baby, please don't be mad ... I'm so swamped." He started kissing my neck. His hands rose to my breast. "Mmm ... I need you, baby."

"Get off of me!" I shoved his hands away and turned to him. "What are you doing?" I yelled.

"*Becca, I don't need this shit, baby! You haven't kissed me or touched me in months. I have been patient, but I need you now!*" *He pulled me to him aggressively.*

"*What are you talking about?*" *I tried to push him off.*

"*Just fucking kiss me, Becca!*" *He held my head in place and attacked my lips. I pushed him away and smacked his face. He pressed his hand to his cheek and shook his head.*

"*I don't know what's wrong with you. Maybe you're over-tired,*" *I said, still in shock over the fact that I slapped him.*

"*Becs, you have a tiny birthmark right here.*" *He went to touch me, but I backed away. He took in a deep breath.* "*I just want to show you. I'm not going to do anything else.*" *He reached again, this time kneeling in front of me.* "*Right here.*" *His finger poked at the area between my pelvis and leg.* "*I've kissed you there a million times, baby. I know every inch of you. Shall we see if I'm right?*" *He looked up at me and started to pull my pants down. I pushed him away.*

"*You've seen me in a bathing suit. You probably saw it then.*" *I backed up to the sink.*

"*Becca, it's the size of ... of a pencil dot! I wouldn't be able to see it unless my face was right there. And, like I said, it has been—many, many times!*" *He was up against me. His mouth found my neck again. I remember feeling scared. He was behaving so strangely.*

"*Ray, please stop.*" *My voice shook.*

"*No. I want to make love, baby. It's been too long.*" *His hands cupped my breasts again.*

"*Ray, you're overtired. We've never made love. Ray, please, you've got to stop.*" *I started crying.*

"*We have made love, baby! Jesus, Becca, I can't live my life like this! You're going to lose me ... you don't even remember to care.*" *He sounded so defeated.*

"*Of course I care—you're my best friend, Ray. I don't want to lose you. I don't want a relationship with you, either. I can't. I won't get hurt again." I fought to regain control over my tears.*

"I won't hurt you, Becs. We've been together for two years—I've proven myself. I won't hurt you, baby." He held my face.

"You can't promise that." I pulled away from him again.

"Where's Annie?" He let go and backed up.

"Sleeping. I'll send her off to school in the morning." I turned to close the box of sugar packets and put it away.

"Good night. Tell Annie I love her," he said, and left before I could turn around.

"What did you do when you left?" My hand covers his. He keeps rubbing my belly, and it's making me nervous.

"I called my mom. I was brokenhearted ... once again, Lucy!" He taps my belly.

"Is that your permanent nickname for me?" My fingers lace with his.

"Until you remember everything, yes." He brings my hand up to his lips for a quick peck.

"Then what happened? Wait, is that when your mom called me about Christmas at the inn?" I ask.

"Yes, it was our year to have my parents over for Christmas anyway. So, my mom suggested we all just stay with you to give you and I more time together.

"Did it work?" I ask as I try to remember for myself.

"Eh ... not really. I, uh, couldn't stop. Not proud of myself, baby." He sighs.

"Ray, I don't remember you forcing yourself on me." My brow furrows.

"I didn't. I couldn't stop eating! It was terrible." He shakes his head.

"You asshole!" I elbow him.

He laughs. "No, baby, it wasn't as *merry* as the year before, but it was definitely ... mmm ... so good." He moves my hand to feel his growing excitement. I use every ounce of willpower I can muster to push my desire away.

"We went to Maine for your birthday again, but you were completely off. I told my mother that she had lost her magic. You wouldn't even kiss me. It was weird." He sits, pondering.

"We slept in separate rooms."

"Yeah, I was pissed! You had one with Morgan—not like I could creep in. You wouldn't even watch a movie with me. I felt like it was over between us. After that trip, I backed off. Not like before, but I gave you space." He gets up and grabs a water out of the fridge.

"When did the whole *Star Trek* sleepover happen?" I take the water from him and sip it.

"Huh?"

"I had a flashback last night of you coming over. I had PJs for you, and we were going to watch *Star Trek*. I was drinking wine, so I guess that diet was over!" I laugh a little.

"Oh. That wasn't until the following February. Man, you pissed me off!" He plops back down onto the couch.

"So, nothing happened until then?" I look at him, confused.

"No. I mean, yes. The pictures of us at the carnival ... we made love the night before and that morning, then that night ... so on and so forth. Mama got her magic back." His smile becomes huge again.

I try to think back to that weekend.

Elise yelled at me over the phone. Between her and Hazel, I gave in and cleared my weekend. Ray picked up Morgan and me that Friday morning. The girls got right to giggling in the backseat. Ray took our suitcase and slid it into the back of the truck, underneath the bed cover. He looked well. He was wearing the outfit I had bought him for Father's Day. Plaid shorts in light, creamy shades of blue, gray, and white with a matching polo. He wore black flip-flops aviator sunglasses. I'm not a fan of aviators, but I had to admit—they looked great on him. His hair was shorter, but choppy—the way I like it at that length. He had a great tan going from all of the work he'd been doing outside.

Ray loves to design, but he doesn't like to just leave it at that. Whenever he can, he gets his hands dirty with the build. He's a hard worker by choice.

"What are you thinking about?" He touched my cheek.

"Oh, I was admiring your tan." I pushed his sunglasses up. "I can't see your eyes with those. Hi." I smiled.

"Hi." He took them off.

"You are putting sunblock on, right? Especially on your ears?" I reached up and grabbed his right ear gently. He winced and touched the small of my back as I leaned in closer to look. His ears were clearly burned. "Ray, come on! I've told you a million times to apply it in the morning before you leave. I bought you some and put it on your dresser! Do I have to come over in the morning and apply it myself?"

"Hi," he said again, completely ignoring my sunblock tirade. "It's nice to see you, baby. I've missed you." He nudged my lips with his. I nudged back. His right hand came up to my face to steady me so he could deepen the kiss. He groaned—a dull, aching sound.

"Shit, Ray!" I pulled away.

"No, baby, please." He brought my face back to his and kissed me again.

"Ray, I forgot the crumb bars on the counter." I stepped back and gave him a crooked smile.

"That's why you're pulling away?" he asked, unsure.

"Yes. I promised your mom. She'll have my head if I forget them. I'll be right back." I kissed him quickly and ran back into the inn.

"All set?" he asked when I handed him the dish.

"Yep. Let's go! By the way, McNeil ... your ass is looking pretty sweet in those shorts." I swatted his butt and walked around to the passenger side. We both got in and Ray started the truck.

"Hey, babe?" He looked over at me, then at the girls. He leaned over. "You still on the Pill?" he asked quietly in my ear.

"Yeah, why?"

"Oh ... you'll find out." He kissed my cheek and took my hand before he drove down the hill of the driveway.

Our two-hour journey only took ninety minutes. I kept yelling at Ray about his speed, but he just pulled me over to him and slung his arm around my shoulders. I leaned up against him, putting my feet up on the passenger seat. It was relaxing, as if we were on a sofa instead of the front seat of a truck.

On the last leg of the trip, the girls fell asleep in the backseat. I felt drowsy myself.

"They asleep?" Ray asked softly.

"Mmm-hmm," I murmured. Ray slowly slipped his hand into my tank top.

"Shh," he whispered as his fingers found my left nipple. He began to play with it, running his fingertips in circles around it, tweaking it harshly. I held on to his arm, trying not to make a sound. "Feel good, baby?" he whispered.

"Yes." I tried to catch my breath.

"Are we almost there, Ray? I have to pee," Morgan grumbled. Ray casually slid his hand up to my left shoulder.

"Almost, baby, can you hold it for ten more minutes?" he asked her as I tried to compose myself.

"Yeah, I guess." She turned the other way in the backseat. Ray's hand started to slide down again, but I smacked it lightly as I sat up against him so he wouldn't have such easy access. I put my left arm around his shoulders and my right hand on his chest.

"Wait," he said, and brought his arm down from my shoulder.

"Sorry."

"It's okay." He smiled and grabbed my hand. I rested my head on his shoulder. Ray placed my hand on the zipper of his shorts. He was as hard as a rock.

"That's going to feel so good, baby," I whispered in his ear before I nipped at his earlobe. I reached my hand under his shirt to scratch lightly above the top of his shorts.

"Jesus, Becca, if the girls weren't in this car—we'd be christening 95 North right now." He squeezed my hand, and I bit my entire bottom lip to stifle my huge smile. He gave me a half smile. "When we get home, we'll send the girls outside with the grandparents. We should go right upstairs and settle in. I've got quite the bone *to pick with you, Becca." His casual sexual banter always made me laugh.*

"Yeah, I think we have a few things we need to work out, Mc-Neil." *I played along.*

"We need to come *to an agreement, baby."*

"Well, I feel confident that we'll be able to relate *to each other, McNeil."*

"There may be a lot of pressure, considering the time we'll have." He sighed.*

"Hmm ... could be a tight *squeeze."*

"Oh ... I think we'll be able to fit it in *and* come *together as one." A smirk crossed his face.*

After a beat, I laughed "I have nothing!"

"McNeil, one!" He licked his index finger and stuck it in the air, then turned his attention to the sign coming up. "Finally!" He sighed and pulled off at the exit. We arrived within a few minutes. The truck barely stopped before the girls' seatbelts were flying off. They jumped out of the truck as soon as Ray parked.

"Nana! Pop Pop! We're here!" They yelled.

"Someday, baby ..."

"Someday what?" I glanced over before I opened my door.

"There'll be a couple of boys running around with our girls

yelling 'Nana! Pop Pop!'" He pulled me back to him.

"Oh yeah, you're in good with the Big Man? You get to pick what we have?" I meant to tease because I felt overwhelmed, but I ended up overwhelming myself more when I said this.

"Actually, I don't care what we have. All I know is that I want to have them with you, baby." He reached up into the hair at the back of my neck, holding me steady as his mouth covered mine. "Becs, I need to take you inside."

"Yes." I broke free from him and opened my door. He took my hand and we ran toward the house. The girls were already heading to the pool.

"Mama, we'll be with you in twenty to twenty-five minutes, tops!" he said as we rushed by her and ran up the stairs of the farmhouse. I couldn't stifle my giggle at the embarrassment I knew I would feel later.

Apparently, I didn't run fast enough. Ray pulled my arm and threw me over his shoulder to carry me up.

"Jesus, Ray!" I gasped. He took long strides to our room, then shut and locked the door once we were inside. He put me down and we attacked each other. Clothes flew everywhere. I almost fell trying to get my panties off. Ray caught me in the hook of his left arm and threw me down onto the bed, parting me from my tricky knickers.

"Baby, we don't have much time." He climbed on top of me. "I'll make love to you later, but, right now ... " He thrust inside of me, the force of it making me arch my neck. It was aggressive and rough, but I remember thinking about how familiar he felt to me and wondering how that could be possible. Everything seemed right. "Babe?" He stopped. Looking into his eyes, I sensed this wasn't our first time. I glanced around the room, and suddenly the morning we made love and cried flashed back to me. "Baby ... please ... don't." He commanded my attention.

"Sorry, Ray." I leaned up to kiss him and slowly moved my

hips, which encouraged him to do the same.

"Then the kiss in the rain?" I wince. I'd mention that the flash-back I had during the last memory, but I know it's pointless.

"Yes ... the infamous kiss in the rain! Why were you coming to my house again?" He takes a swig of his water.

"Annie needed her poster board for day camp. You forgot it, so I was bringing it over. Or so I thought. Seems I forgot it anyway ... I have no idea why." My playful sarcasm does not go over well with Ray.

"Six months for a kiss and a moment that you remembered. If only you knew how much more we had done ... how much more we meant to each other. Six months, baby. It killed me." He rests his head on my shoulders.

"Sorry." I kiss his forehead. "I know what happened with the sleigh ride, but I don't know when we made up."

"The week before, my parents came down. My mom sent me to the grocery store to pick up a few things. She and Annie were baking for the nursing home like they do every year. Anyway, I ran into fucking Twinkle Toes."

"Knock it off! You're terrible!" I laugh.

"Well, anyway ... there he was, looking to dig! Only, he didn't realize you were within earshot. Neither of us did. You basically came up to me like we were shopping together and asked me if I was ready to go," he says with a laugh. "Oh, the look at that ass-hole's face as we sauntered up to the register was priceless."

"Yeah I remember. You were all over me the whole time in line, all touchy-feely." I imitate him with the wiggly fingers.

"There's just something about you, babe ... makes a man want to touch and feel you." His hand travels from my knee up my inner thigh.

"Stop right there, McNeil!" I tap his hand.

"I tried to get touchy-feely with you outside as well. I really had my hopes up that night. It felt so good to kiss you again." He kisses my cheek.

"I felt bad for leading you on, but I didn't like what Will was saying to you and I didn't like how he was getting toward me." I notice how small my hands are in Ray's.

"I was just glad that you were willing to let me back into your life. Even though I had to promise not to pressure you and that we were strictly friends. I missed you—I would've walked across hot coals for you. I still would." He spins his empty water bottle around on the coffee table. I stop him.

"So, what's next?" The atmosphere has changed somewhat in the room. We're getting close to the end of all my forgotten memories. I'm pretty sure he's wondering what is going to happen once we're done here.

"We stayed at the inn for Christmas. I had my own room, but I didn't stay in it." Ray stands up and starts stretching. He lowers the heat on the fireplace. *Nervous energy.*

"Feel like a jog, Ray?" He's not a jogger, but that's what he does when he gets like this.

"Yeah, babe, I do." He smiles sheepishly. I know him. He loves that I know him. "Do you remember waking up next to me Christmas Day?" He sits back down. My eyes scan the room. Apparently, that's supposed to help me retrieve this memory. Not working! I look down at the chocolate-brown Berber office carpet. Hmm.

"No, what happened?" I glance over.

"Um, nothing, actually. You woke up and asked me what I was doing in your bed. After you unraveled yourself from my death grip, of course."

"Why were you in there?" I ask.

"The truth, or the reason I told you?" He chuckles.

"Both."

"I told you I wasn't comfortable in the other bed and after a few hours I gave up and joined you. The real reason should be obvious, babe." He taps my nose with his finger and pecks my lips.

"I guess it is. Did I flip out?"

"No." His eyes widen.

"That's weird. Was I, as you like to call it, *on*?"

I head to the bathroom in the office and pray it's set up. Ahh, yes! My bladder and I are grateful.

"I can hear you!" I shout.

"No, you weren't *on*. You were kind of like, *whatever*," he yells. I wash my hands and wipe them on my shirt. *I prayed for running water, not towels.*

"So, next?" I come out to find him sprawled on the couch again. His jeans are a faded medium blue, relaxed in the legs. They sit low on his waist. I can see his happy trail peeking out from between his shirt and waistband. His arms are beneath his head, biceps accentuated under the short-sleeve blue T-shirt he's wearing. God, he's fucking hot! I have such a strong desire to snuggle up to him (amongst other things ... ahem).

"Admiring the masterpiece?" he teases. *Ugh! You have no idea!* These hormones are driving me crazy!

"Always." I sit on the edge.

"Lay with me, baby." He stretches his arm out for me to rest on. I decide I should rest—being pregnant and all. I lay down. His hand immediately caresses my belly. Why does he keep touching me there? Does he know? Can he tell? "Theme song?"

"No." I sigh and count the number of recessed lights.

"Running out of songs, baby?" His hand slowly heads toward my breast.

"Stop." I grab his hand.

"Or what, baby? What are you going to do?" He gives me a playful smile.

"Probably enjoy it, then get pissed about it." I close my eyes in defeat and let go of his hand. He slides it back down to my stomach. "Next, please." I sigh, a bit disappointed.

Chapter Thirteen

It was New Year's Eve. I was in a pretty shitty mood. Annie and I came over for Chinese, and we went around the table and said our New Year's resolutions, as usual. Mine was to have more fun. I decided to start that night!"

"Carl called you," I interrupt.

"Yes. Go ahead, then. I'll lie here contemplating all the different ways to turn you on with my touch—aggravating the piss out of you." He smirks and walks his fingers up my side. I can't help laughing.

"Hey, babe, Carl just called me. Can you watch Annie?" he asked as I poured popcorn into a big bowl for all of us to snack on. The girls were waiting in the lounge for us to watch a movie before watching the ball drop.

"Why? What's the matter? Is he okay?" I was worried. Carl wouldn't pull Ray away from us on New Year's Eve unless something had happened.

"No. I want to meet him for drinks. Brooke is at the pub asking for me, so I kinda want to see her, too." He tilts his head and winces a bit, seemingly unsure.

"Brooke who?" Oh no! A flicker of jealousy stirred in me.

"Actually, I don't know her last name. I only met her a few weeks ago. She's home from college, visiting her parents. Will you watch Annie for me?" He put his hands in his pockets and rocked back on his heels.

"College, Ray? Aren't you a little too old for her?" I snapped, my voice more forceful than I intended.

"She's legal, she's fucking cute as hell, and I'm pretty sure I'll get some. That's all I care about right now. I have needs, Becca. Unless you want to meet them, baby, I will go somewhere else." He backed me up to the counter. "Well? Do you want to meet them? Or should I go?" We were nose to nose, and I felt my breath catch. His hands held my hips. I wanted to tell him to stay. I would meet his needs.

"Go," is what I said instead.

"What?" He seemed to have lost his breath.

"You heard me." I looked down to the black and white tiled floor.

"You want me to go and fuck somebody else?" he asked angrily.

"I don't want you to fuck me!" I was mad as hell. Mostly because I knew I was lying.

"I have fucked you—more times than I can count!" Oh, he was pissed!

"Get off of me," I hissed.

"Make me." He smirked before he grabbed my bottom lip with his teeth. I tried to push him away, but he pinned my arms. "Tell me

you want me." His request stirred something deep inside me. That, and the way he nipped and kissed down my neck and back up again. "Tell me this is still mine," he whispered in my ear as he let go of my arm and ran his hand underneath the band of my PJs—directly between my legs. He caressed me there purposefully. "Tell me it's mine," he said again. His fingers circled my opening then darted in. "Oh, baby, I think I found my answer."

I felt so many things in that moment. I couldn't quite sort them out. Betrayal. Hurt. Disgust. Confusion. Familiarity. Want. Need. I laid my head on my free hand that rested in defeat on his shoulder and cried.

"Come for me, baby," Ray commanded. "Come on." He worked harder. I wasn't even close. It felt all wrong. I felt violated.

"Please stop, please." I raised my head to look into his eyes. He leaned forward to kiss me. I pulled my head back. He stared into my eyes—stormy ocean to emerald sea. I felt my chin quivering. Slowly he pulled his fingers out and his hand away.

"I'm sorry. I'm sorry, baby." He hugged me. I just stood there. "Please forgive me." He held me at arm's length.

"They're waiting for their popcorn." I felt numb, melancholy. I wiped away my tears, pushed Ray to the side, and grabbed the bowl of popcorn. When I walked out to bring it to them, Hazel was sitting with them.

"What's wrong, Becca? Were you crying?" Hazel asked quietly near my ear. She took my arm.

"No. Don't come too close, Hazel, I just got sick." I lied because I wanted a good reason to just be able to go to bed.

"Oh no! Do you think it was the food?" she asked. I just shook my head. "Okay, sweetie. Go on, I'll take care of the girls." She rubbed my arm.

"Girls, I'm going to say good night, but I can't kiss you—I just got sick." I glanced at Ray. He diverted his eyes, looking ashamed. The girls complained a little, but then started the movie. That was

my cue to exit stage left and up the stairs.

"Becs ... baby." Ray sighed behind me. I turned around to look at him.

"I want nothing to do with you. It's over! Our friendship is over! Don't use the girls for leverage, either. Find someone else to take Annie after school. I'm done!" My voice shook and my tears fell, but I was as stern as I could be.

"Whatever—see you tomorrow, baby." He smirked, turned, and left.

"Ray, you asshole!" I elbow him.

"Well, this asshole sat outside your door for two hours listening to you cry and dying to go in to make it all better. God, I felt like a selfish pig. That was so not me. But I was mad. I couldn't even read your body language. I just wanted you to give in." He traces my jawline with his index finger.

"Did I forget? Duh ... never mind." I laugh and turn to him. He raises his head to look down into my eyes, then palms my cheek.

"I am sorry I behaved that way, baby. I don't like when I do anything that hurts you." He softly pecks my lips and nudges my nose with his. I move closer to encourage another kiss.

"I'm sorry, too. Next please." I try to steady my breath.

"Valentine's Day. You had the flu, then pneumonia."

"Ray, I remember that. You took care of me the whole time. Surely we didn't have sex then?" I turn my head to him.

"No. I hated that you were so sick, but I love the memory. It wasn't like the riding accident. There were no pain pills. There was no wine. There was just me and you, and you needed me. You gave into that need. I don't know how to describe it, but you allowed yourself to be comfortable with me. It was a glimpse of ... real. There was no flipping out over intimate moments. I slept in bed with you every night and you woke to me being there. No flipping out. Kisses didn't get a 'Ray, don't'—not that I was trying to make out with you or anything." His index finger slides gently over my lips. I kiss it.

"I remember how much better I felt with you there. You were so good to me, Ray. You didn't take any of my shit, either. You were the only one who could get me to eat. You made sure we did everything Dr. Peto said. It was cute. You were cute. You let me fall asleep against your chest every night because I couldn't get the right angle with pillows. I know your back was killing you after a few days." I turn on my side toward him, then run my left hand through his hair. I kiss his forehead, each of his eyelids, and his nose. "I wish I had loved you better ... I should have," I say softly before I collect his lips.

"Make up for it now, baby. Come back to me." He holds my chin.

"Is *Star Trek* next?" I ask.

"Yes!" he snaps, and lets go.

"Then my birthday?" He nods. "Then ... what?" I rest my head on his arm again.

"I wanted to see Patricia with you, but you didn't want me to go. We fought about it, but I couldn't get through to you without explaining what was going on. I had already tried that several times. So, um ..." He rubs his face.

"What?" I ask with a smidge of irritation. He is taking too long.

"So I made an appointment for myself."

"Why?" I give him my award-winning look of confusion ... well, it should be, anyway.

"Becca, for the most part, we've been together for five years. That's a long time to put up with what I've been putting up with."

"Yeah, but with HIPPA laws ... and those aside, you're not my husband. She couldn't discuss me with you unless I signed a release."

"Becs, I know that! And I *should* be your husband!"

I don't blame him for his irritation—I wouldn't have been this calm.

"Sorry. Go ahead." I offer a sheepish smile.

"I went through the *backdoor*. I told her all about you without telling her who you are."

"What did she say?" I'm intrigued.

"Well, we talked about PTSD and the short-term memory loss that can be associated with it. We weren't sure if it was that, or if you were pretending because of guilt, or both. She explained how to do some easy memory triggers. I asked her if I should have you journal when you were *on*, writing or a video, but she said that that could end up being a good thing or a really bad thing. It all depended on where you were mentally ... you know, what you'd be able to handle." He slides his right arm around my waist as he shifts onto his side again. I snuggle into him more. "I could lay here forever like this, Becs ... holding you. You feel like home to me." He gives my forehead a prolonged kiss. I seem to have two homes, and I love and find comfort in both of them.

"Well, did you have me journal or anything?" I ask as I inhale deeply the smell of Ray McNeil and hold it to memory.

"Yes. You know how my mother has a thing with photography?"

"Yeah, she has a great eye. She's very good at it." I smile, thinking of the girls calling her "Nanarazzi." I giggle.

"What?"

"Nanarazzi," I remind him. He chuckles.

"Well, Nanarazzi put together a whole scrapbook just about you and me. She did a beautiful job journaling on most the pages, describing our mood and where we were. I love that book!" He pauses, I think to collect himself.

"Sounds lovely. I'd like to see it."

He lets out a frustrated breath.

"Becs, you've seen it about fifty times. Christ!" He swats my ass. I inhale sharply. He studies my face and a slow smile forms. "You really do like that, don't you?" He does it again.

"Stop ... that's Grayson's." I try to steady my breath.

"Yeah, that's Grayson's thing. He loves to slap you around and hurt you." He's being snarky.

"You hurt me, too," I say quietly, hoping to prevent a full-blown Ray McNeil explosion.

"I ... have done *nothing* but love you and *be patient* with you for *five fucking years*!" he says through his teeth.

"Now, that isn't entirely true, is it?" I look him straight in the eye, matching his frustration.

His face softens and he leans his forehead against mine. "No, babe, it's not. I'm sorry. I should have never done that to you."

"I'm sorry you wasted so many years on me." I touch his cheek as he pulls his face back slightly.

"That's all going to change now—*right*, baby?" He presses his nose to mine.

"Nothing's changed, Ray. I'm sorry." I bite my lip to stifle the sob that wants to escape.

"He can't have you! *You. Are. Mine!* He can't have you any-more! You belong here with me! You love me. You're in love with me ... you said it yourself! If you think I'm going to throw away the past *five* years like it meant nothing, you are sorely mistaken, Becca Campbell! You are going to wake up one of these days and you are finally going to see me! You will see us, and you will see the family that we have built and nurtured. I am not going anywhere! I will wait for you. You are *my* forever! He can't have you! I love you, baby, and I need you!"

There is a mixture of passion and anger in his tone. My eyes stay closed, letting his words absorb. I'm sure they will haunt me from time to time in the future. His lips caress mine gently.

"I love you, Becs ... don't leave me ... don't leave us."

I kiss him back reluctantly, because I know I'm only going to hurt him more today. He caresses my hip, then grasps at my jeans as he deepens the kiss. "I need you, Becs." He quickly unfastens my pants again and starts to pull at the fabric.

"Stop it! Stop!" I smack his hand and try to get up.

"Baby, wait!" He pulls me closer. "I'll stop ... for now," he adds, with a smile full of promise. "Next was your birthday. You know about that."

Good distraction tactics, McNeil!

"I was sore for two days." Ugh ... I should learn to keep my mouth shut.

"Jesus, baby, don't tell me stuff like that." He closes his eyes tightly, like he's fighting something back. It's not sympathy. Most men wouldn't feel sympathetic toward making a woman sore like that. They are too busy patting themselves on the back and doing a mental fist pump.

"Okay ... next."

"I felt guilty about what I did, so I was on my best behavior. The only time we kissed was when you looked at the book from my mother. I'd leave it out when you'd come over. It never failed." He chuckles. "'What's this, Ray?'" He imitates me and laughs. I elbow him. "I'd tell you, 'Oh, my mom made that! You'd be proud of her!' Then you'd pick it up with a gesture that asked if you could open it. I'd say, 'Yeah. Let's sit and look at it together.' We'd get all comfy on my couch. You'd be smiling all big, like a kid on Christmas morning. You know, babe ... it really doesn't take much to bring a smile to your face. You always get so excited about the simplest things!"

"Yeah, okay, keep going." I swat his arm.

"Okay, okay. So, you'd open the book and your Christmas smile would become more of a caught-off-guard one. The first page is titled 'The Story of Us,' and it has a close-up picture of our pro-files. We're laughing. Then under it, it says:

RAY AND BECCA
Laughter and Love Since 2007

Y'all met at Annie and Morgan's first parent-teacher night on September 5th, 2007. You two were laughing with each other before you even knew one another's names. You've been laughing with each other and loving one another ever since. I've enjoyed watching you two grow as a couple and seeing how happy you make each other.

Love, Mama

You always look up at me like, *huh?* I just ignore your expression and stifle my smile 'til you focus back on the book. Sometimes I have to turn the page for you. The next page is titled 'Our Family' and it has a collage of us with the girls over the past five years. That distracts you, because you focus on how much the girls have grown. The next page's title freaks you out a little." He makes the *uh-oh* face.

"Why? What is it?"

"'We Were MAINE for Each Other.' There are several pages of us in Maine. We're holding hands in some. A lot of us sleeping in each other's arms. Swinging on the porch swing, laughing. Fishing, my arms around you helping you reel a fish in. Then I'm smiling down at you and you up at me. Me giving you a piggyback ride down the beach in the early fall. Us kissing on the beach. Your favorite page is titled 'You Are My Dream Come True.' We're both asleep on the hammock. Then I'm awake and smiling down at you. Then you're smiling up at me. Then we're kissing. It's all in black and white."

"Your mother is quite the stalker, huh?" I laugh.

"Yeah, she is." He laughs with me.

"Well, how do I handle all of this?"

"Most of the time it gets you thinking. You're so cute. You always look at me, unsure, but I can see the lightbulb is on, so I inch closer and start showing you pictures that I love. I point to us kissing and tell you I love how soft your lips are. That usually is the key to you letting me kiss you." He leans forward and captures my lips.

"So, what happens when I don't handle it well?" I pull away.

"That only happened once. You said, 'Ray, why did your mom do this?' I replied, 'Because you taught her to scrap things through her eyes and heart. This is how she sees us, baby.' Then you asked, 'Well, how do you see us, Ray?' And I said, 'I love this book, Becca. I love you.' I was honest."

"How did I reply?" I wince.

"Yeah ... not good. You're not remembering this at all?" I shake my head. "You said, 'Well, I'm sorry, Ray, but I don't love you like that. It makes me very uncomfortable, looking at this.' I snapped at you and said, 'Well, don't fucking look at it, Becca! It's not yours!' And I took it from you. You said, 'Don't you think your mom is leading you? Making you believe there is something more than there is?' I said, 'Well, I don't know, Becca ... let's see.' And I opened the book back up and found pictures of us kissing or looking very intimate. 'Nope, not my mother's tongue down my throat. She's definitely not the one leading me on!'"

"Good for you!" I interrupt, forgetting that he's actually telling me off in this story. We both laugh over this. "What did I say?"

"You went pale as a ghost and said, 'Ray, I don't remember any of these moments. Did she use Photoshop or something?' Well, needless to say, I went apeshit! I called you every name in the book and told you to get the *eff* out of my house. You were really upset. I feel bad about it, because you ended up in the middle of this shitstorm you weren't aware you started. You don't remember any of this argument, babe?" His brow furrows.

"No. Not one second of it." I shake my head again.

"Well, I'm glad, actually. It wasn't pretty." He sighs.

"Why? What happened?"

"Let's just move on. So, the next time ..."

"No, Ray! Tell me—what happened?" I raise my head.

"Becs, you have to understand ... I just ... I reached my limit. I wanted to hit you. It actually scared me. I grabbed your face and shook your head. I called you a number of things and said I wished I had never met you, then I pushed you away a little too hard. You fell on your butt. I didn't even ask you if you were all right. I just yelled at you to get out. You did. I thought that was it. We were done. I'm sorry I did that, Becs." He pulls me in for a hug and kisses my hair.

"Well what happened? How did we make up?" I yawn.

"Oh, I'm sorry, Lucy ... are you just joining in on this story now? It's about a very forgetful woman named Becca," he teases, which warrants another slap on the arm from me.

"I know but, how? When?" I ask.

"You called me the next day to see what I was up to. You had a few hours free, wanted to know if I had lunch, that you would stop by the office." He smiles and shakes his head.

"What did you say? How did you feel about me calling?" My head pops up.

"Um, I was shocked yet happy for the do-over. I told you that I was working from home and I didn't have lunch yet. You said you'd bring something. I told you I'd make it."

"Gourmet peanut butter and jelly, Ray?" I laugh because Ray's not one that should be allowed in the kitchen. He's gotten a bit better over the years with my help, but still, I don't jump at the chance to eat over there except when I know it'll be takeout.

"Close ... grilled cheese. Burnt grilled cheese, which is why I was glad that you brought a backup lunch. You were so cute with your picnic basket. I was like, 'Babe! I told you I was making lunch!' as I fanned the smoke out of the kitchen. You raised your basket and said, 'I know,' and laughed. You set it down on the counter and opened a window. You started cleaning up my mess. I loved watching you."

"You loved watching the 'little woman' clean? How chauvinistic of you." I nudge teasingly.

"No, no. It was watching how comfortable you were in my kitchen—like it was yours. You just glided around, knowing where everything was—where everything went. It was like watching my wife. It sounds silly." He waves at the air.

"It sounds sweet, but Ray, the reason why I'm so comfortable in your kitchen is because I reorganized it like four years ago. It's set up exactly the way I like it." I smile.

"Pop!" Ray pokes the air. I give him a strange look. "You, bursting my romanticized bubble." He smirks. "Do you remember this, babe?" He raises an eyebrow. I think for a moment.

"No, Ray. Hmm, it seems the closer the memory, the less I'm remembering. That's strange." I sigh, a bit frustrated. I'd rather relive each memory so it becomes mine. It's weird having him tell me about these things like I wasn't there.

"Okay, well, stop me if it does come to you." His knuckles graze my cheek. I nod in agreement. "So, after you cleaned up, you grabbed plates and handed them to me. You smiled and asked me why I was looking at you like that."

"Like a lovesick puppy?" I smile.

"Yeah, basically, baby." His lips peck my nose. "I said, 'I just appreciate you, babe, and I'm grateful for you.' I came around the counter and hugged you. 'You all right?' you asked me. 'You rarely work from home. Are you feeling okay?' You felt my forehead. I remember closing my eyes, just enjoying your touch of concern. I said I was fine, just felt like playing hooky. We set the table. I touched you every chance I could get. You know ... the whole touchy-feely effect you have on guys," he says. I slap him, but am unsuccessful at hiding my smile. "We ate your wonderful lunch, then decided to head to the living room to relax. You asked me if I wanted you to leave so I could get back to work. I said, 'I never want you to leave, babe, you know that.' You gave me one of your

half smiles ... you know, big enough for your dimple to pop out?"
He looks at me for confirmation.

"No, I don't know." I smile.

"Yeah, it's cute, baby. So, we were heading into the living
room, and you noticed my mom's book on the floor by the built-in
bookcases. You went over and picked it up. 'Here, I got that,' I said,
trying to take it from you. I didn't want a repeat of the day before.
You pulled it away from me. 'What is this?' you asked, and opened
it. 'Stop,' I said again, but you'd already saw. You studied the first
page as you walked over to the couch with it. 'C'mere,' you said,
and patted the seat next to you. 'Who did this?' you asked me. I
fought the urge to roll my eyes. I just pointed to the part that says
'Love, Mama.'

"'Oh,' you said, and started reading it. 'This is beautiful. Ray,
why was it tossed in the corner like that? It looked like it was
thrown.' I told you I did throw it, which was the truth, but I said
I was mad at something and just grabbed the closest thing. 'And
you didn't bother to pick it up later?' you asked, and looked disappointed. I said I got distracted. You just nodded. I leaned my chin
on your shoulder and looked at it with you. You pointed to your
favorite page and commented how beautiful it was. You were saying how you loved that she chose black and white for the pictures,
and you turned as you finished your comment. You licked your lips
and kissed me, then pulled away quickly and said, 'I'm sorry, Ray.
I don't know why I did that.' You were so flushed and seemed quite
mortified. It was difficult for me to keep a straight face. I brought
your face back to mine and said, 'What a coincidence ... I have no
idea why I'm going to do this.' I kissed you, then said, 'Maybe
Mama knows something we don't.' I kissed you again. I laid you
back on the couch and we had a nice full-blown make-out session."
He laughs.

"Why is that funny?" I grab his chin and shake his face lightly.

"I'm always amazed when we do something for the 'first' time.

It really does feel that way, like we're teenagers awkwardly experimenting with each other. It's sweet, but pretty funny. We did make it up to my room that day, but only got as far as getting our shirts off." He starts laughing again. "You said to me while I was biting at your nipple, 'McNeil ... I can't believe we're doing this!' Like it was our first time ... well, I guess it was for you, huh, Lucy? Then you said, 'Ray, why aren't you announcing that you're on second base?' God, you crack me up, babe!" He chuckles.

"Well you're always announcing when I come in from left field, like a sportscaster!" I laugh with him.

"I said, 'I'm waiting to announce the home run.' You said, 'Oh yeah, McNeil? You think you're gonna get a home run?' I stopped and looked up at you. I said, 'I have you in my life, baby ... I've already won the World Series.'"

I lean forward and kiss him.

"That was so sweet, Ray. Only you could make sports talk romantic."

"You said something like that that day. We got back into a groove then, as if on cue, Annie got home from school and yelled up the stairs to let me know. We were rushing around like a couple of teenagers trying not to get caught. We didn't even realize how late it had gotten. Needless to say, I was very disappointed. But Annie was so excited to find you there. She immediately started reporting her day to you—something that's like pulling teeth when it's me asking. You sat right down and took her book bag so you could see her school folder and go over her homework. It was like you were her mom and did this every day." Ray is getting a bit teary-eyed—a rare occurrence. He's much more of a "let it roll off of his back" kind of guy. I know I'm the cause of his uncharacteristic behavior ... I feel bad.

"Well, I mean, I didn't give birth to her, but she definitely feels like a second daughter to me. I have been helping you with her for the past five years. She comes over after school a lot. She's a wonderful girl, Ray. You've done a great job. You should be proud of yourself."

"*We've* done a great job," he corrects me, patting my bum. "Becca, I'm sorry I haven't been as carefree and natural with Morgan over the years. I try to take notice, but I'm usually too late. Annie notices and reminds me, which, I guess, means Morgan notices," he says, unsure.

"Oh yeah, she's noticed big time. It doesn't make her feel very good. You don't make her feel special at all. You act as if she's just Annie's friend and it's your turn for carpool." I sit up and swing my legs around to face forward. "Then you lie to me! I ask you how Morgan did, and you say *good*, but I found out that you never ask about Morgan at all! You know, Ray, you always talk about Annie not having a mother and how I've really been there for her. You would think that would push you to be more of a father figure to Morgan. She's had the opposite problem of Annie, but you never seem to be sensitive to that! I know our own child is our priority and first focus, but goddamn it, Ray! I never let Annie feel like she's not top priority with me!" I stand up and do the walking around now.

"You're right, Becs. I'm really sorry. I do love Morgan like she's mine, though. I've missed her. She's so much like you, Becca. She has your quick wit and sarcasm. She's so smart and creative. She's a wonderful friend to Annie, and a loving, genuine little girl." He walks toward me.

"No, don't touch me!" I back away from him.

"Becca, I'm sorry! At the end of the day, I'm a guy! We're programmed differently! I don't think to do the things you do." He runs his hand through his hair.

"Grayson does! Since day one he has made her feel important, loved, and special." I shrug my shoulders and smirk, knowing I've blown his theory out of the water.

"Grayson doesn't have any other children to think of!" he yells. "I'm all Annie has—she is my top priority!"

"If that's how I thought and acted, Annie and I wouldn't be so attached to each other! By the way, McNeil, you should make up your mind. Is it that Annie only has you, or is it that Annie has both of us? You sure keep flip-flopping on that!" I get in his face. Ray charges, backing me up to the wall. His left hand crooks around my neck and his right grasps my hip. We're nose to nose.

"That's a question only you can answer, baby. Does she have both of us?" He runs his lips over mine—teasing me. "Well, baby? Us?" he asks again.

"Was that our last memory?" I ignore his question.

"No ... there's one more. Answer me, Becca, please." His lips caress the corner of my mouth and move across my jawline. He massages my bum purposefully with his free hand.

"I want my last memory." I try to remain calm.

"And I want my answer!" he yells in my face.

"Forget it ... don't tell me. It's time to leave." I sigh. *I've had enough.*

"No ... it was that weekend." He sighs, defeated. "My parents took both of the girls to the Cape with them. They've done that the past few years." He looks into my eyes to see if I recollect. I nod. "I asked you to come over to hang out. I could see that your switch was not going to be flipped naturally, so ... " he pauses, taking in a deep breath. "I slipped you the other half of the pill. We made love all night. I didn't bother redressing us."

"Did I flip out?" I stare into the storm.

"That's an understatement. You woke up panicked. I pretended to still be asleep. You kept saying 'Shit, shit, shit!' under your breath and holding your head. You looked around for something to wear, but could only reach my T-shirt. You threw it on, got up, and grabbed your clothes. 'You look cute in my shirt, baby,' I said, trying to calm you down. You went all doe-eyed on me. 'Come back to bed.' I held my hand out to you. You ignored me and ran into the bathroom. I heard you start the shower, so I decided to join you. I was done with all of the pretending shit. Come on, baby." He grabs my hand and leads me back to the couch. I sit forward, not allowing him to pull me to him.

"Okay, so, I went in and walked into the shower behind you. You were crying. 'Becs, come on, baby. Why are you crying?' I rubbed your back. You jumped. 'Get out! I don't even remember what happened!' you yelled. I said, 'Baby, we made love ... like, all night. Why are you so upset?' This time, you screamed at me. 'I don't remember it and you didn't even use protection, Ray! What the hell is the matter with you?' I told you I never use it with you because you're on the Pill. You said you stopped the Pill two months earlier. Then, I guess after you thought about what I said, you went wild. Hitting me and cursing me out."

"What was I saying?"

"Well, you accused me of getting you drunk and taking advantage of you. You had no memory of any time we've ever had sex. So, of course, I laid into you ... and not in the way I like to lay into you, baby." He chuckles and taps my left arm with the back of his hand. I don't bite. I'm still pissed about our whole Morgan conversation, and the fact that he used ecstasy on me twice.

"You got out and dressed. I followed you all the way outside, naming all of the times we'd been together. You got into your truck, but it wouldn't start. We tried jumping it, but the battery was completely dead. So I drove you home. I didn't want you to go. I wanted to work everything out. You just screamed at me the whole way. It was nasty, and we didn't talk again until the day I came here and met Grayson. When his secretary called and asked me about your property, I thought it was odd. I was nervous that something was wrong, that you had to sell or that you were going to move. I don't know. I was all over the place. That's why I went rushing right to you. Then I saw that you two were together, and I don't know how I was able to keep myself from falling apart right then and there. Maybe the years of pretending with you paid off. I had to leave the office, though. I couldn't bear watching you kiss him. That's why I interrupted." He rests his elbows on his knees, his head in his hands.

"Ray ... I am truly sorry for everything I've put you through. I wish I could make it all better."

"You can, baby. Tell me it wasn't all for nothing. Tell me I didn't throw away five years of my life. You love me, Becs. We have a family. I want to grow that family with you." He grabs my hand.

"Ray, I can't be with you. I'm marrying Grayson ... if he'll still have me. I'm ... I'm having Grayson's baby," I finally spit out.

"Becca, you are having my baby. Not Grayson's." Ray sighs.

"No, Ray. It's not yours. I'm only eight weeks." I turn to him. He shakes his head in disagreement. Maybe it's just plain denial. He rubs his face and stands up. I get up as well. "I'm moving to California," I add.

"No, you are not! You are *mine*—he can't have you!" he says through his teeth.

"I'm really sorry." I try to hug him, feeling tears sting my eyes.

"You didn't know, baby. It's not your fault. But you know now. Here, I've been working on this for a while. I was up all night finishing it." He goes over to his coat and pulls out a DVD.

"What's on here?" I grab it and look at him sideways.

"You'll see, baby. I hope ... I hope you'll really see. I love you, Becca." He kisses my forehead, then grabs my coat and helps me into it. I slide the DVD into my pocket. Ray fists the two zippered sides of my coat and pulls me to him. I don't fight. I give him the best good-bye kiss I can muster.

"Theme song—'A Drop in the Ocean' by Ron Pope," Ray says quietly. He turns the fireplace off, then takes my hand and opens the door. It's chilly in the rest of the building. We walk past the scaffolding and plastic sheets. "Are you going to tell him what went on in there?" he asks as he opens the door to the outside.

"Yes, I am."

"*Everything?*"

"Yes, Ray, everything."

"He'll leave you ... then what? You'll call me? You know, Becca, I just went down memory lane too. I think five years is way more than anybody would put up with. I should be the *only* choice—not the second! You have a lot to think about, babe." I can hear in his voice that he's trying not to be angry.

It's an odd situation. I have this deep, long, loving history with Ray that, until today, I had no recollection of. The past three months I have been building this amazing, crazy, and complicated relationship with Grayson. I'm out of my mind in love with him, and obviously, I've been mentally present for the whole experience. I do have a lot to think about.

I have not been myself for three months now. For seven years, I had no concrete relationship—at least, not one I was aware of. The moment I step into one, awkward from being out of practice, insecure about my past, and faced with the whirlwind that is Grayson James, I get hit with Ray and my past, both forgotten and unforgotten. I can't help but wonder what the hell happened to me. I got swallowed up by this huge shitstorm I did not ask for. Suddenly, I've lost my identity as Ashland's "Sweetheart." Now I'm indecisive, irrational, impulsive, and an emotional mess. I want to go back into my bubble ... but that bubble, that self-protective covering, is a lot of the reason I've gone wild.

It's like going on a diet. Then, one day, there it is right in front of you—that deliciously rich, sweet, baked goodness that won't take no for an answer. You say, *Oh, I'll just cheat a little,* but you've deprived yourself for so long that you eat the whole piece plus two more, wash it down with chips and dip, and, since you've already done a number, you shrug and drink a large glass of chocolate milk or soda. *Tomorrow I will go back on my diet,* you think. But, alas, *tomorrow* doesn't arrive for another six months and thirty pounds—fifteen pounds past the fifteen pounds you lost depriving yourself in the first place. Vicious cycle! Apparently, sex is like chocolate cake ... or, to me, Tiramisu. I've gained two men, a baby, and title of town whore, at least in my mind!

The worst part is that I've been hurting these two amazing, wonderful men. No, this is not me! Maybe I'm just not meant to have my happy ending. I don't deserve the love of either of them.

Ray and I approach the door of The Mad Scrapper. I look at my phone. Lunchtime. I honestly felt like we were gone longer than three hours.

"Becs, I can't let you go. I'm in love with you. I believe in you. I know you are going to wake up and figure this all out. You'll come to me, baby. I know you will. I will wait. I'll pick Annie up tomorrow." He touches my cheek and grazes my lips lightly with his. "I love you so much, baby ... please."

A sob escapes my throat as I turn away and run into the store.

Chapter Fourteen

"There you are, sweetheart!" Grayson yells from all the way across the dining room. He and the girls are bringing out trays of sandwiches for lunch. I hang my coat up and grab the DVD before I join them.

"Smells delicious in here." I smile and walk into Grayson's outstretched arms.

"I missed you, sweetheart. You were gone forever." He hugs me tightly.

"I know. Apparently, I've been leading a double life." I rest my head on him. "Grayson, I need to tell you everything we talked about, and—"

"Shh," he cuts me off. "We have two days left, sweetheart. I don't want to hear anything except that you love me." He chucks my chin so I look up into his eyes. *Speaking of chocolatey things…*

"Two days?" I ask.

"'Til Christmas, darling. I don't want anything to spoil it! Now ... what do we have here?" Grayson kisses me and takes the DVD.

"It's my Christmas present from Ray. I don't know what's on it." I sigh.

"Well, let us grab our lunch and we'll go watch it in your office together." He releases me, but grabs my hand. We pick up plates off the buffet and fill them. I'm starving—I didn't eat any breakfast! A flicker of panic comes over me. What if this is a sex tape? Mental head slap! Ray wouldn't do that. It's not that. "Ready, love?" He throws another cookie on my very full plate and winks. "Just in case," he says. I pat my belly and smile at him. He puts his arm out for me to hold. I take it and lean my head on it as we walk.

"Hey, babe, I didn't see any security on the way back from the barn." I can't believe I'm just processing this information now. I really do have pregnancy brain!

"They were there, Becca, I can assure you." Grayson opens the French doors to my office and lets me in first. "Okay, let us see what we have here, Mr. McNeil." He opens the DVD case. "'The Story of Us'? That's a lovely title," he says with his British frown. He puts it in the computer and lets me sit in my chair, pulling Claudia's chair up next to me.

"Grayson." I look over at him. "I love you, baby." I lean over and kiss him.

"I will always love you, sweetheart." He smiles. He nods toward the monitor. I press play and notice the time of the DVD is one hour and fifteen minutes. The screen is black, then I hear "The Scientist" by Coldplay.

Becca and Ray: The Story of Us appears in white letters. Then a picture of Ray and I in profile, laughing, comes up on the screen. This must be the one from his mom's scrapbook.

2007 – 2008 (white letters)

Fall Festival – Ray kissing my cheek

Fall Festival – the girls standing in front of us

Halloween Party – Ray and I dressed like Beauty and the Beast

Halloween Party – Morgan/Snow White, Annie/Cinderella, Me/Belle, Ray/Beast

Me dumping leaves on Ray's head

Me over Ray's shoulder

Ray dumping me in a huge pile of leaves

Us laughing in the leaves

Ray holding my face

Ray holding my face, kissing me

Thanksgiving – Ray and I in Pilgrim hats

Thanksgiving – The girls dressed as Indians with us behind them

Thanksgiving – Us asleep on the couch

December – Ray hanging lights on the inn with me supervising ... probably annoyingly

December – us on Ray's porch, laughing with mugs in our hands

December – Ray leaning into me

December – Ray's index finger hooking under my chin

December – Ray kissing me

December – We're hugging, and Ray's kissing my hair

Christmas – Us sitting on the floor, with me between his legs leaning back as I open a CD

Christmas – We're laughing when it's unwrapped

Christmas – We're laughing against each other's lips

Christmas – I'm holding the CD toward the camera. It's Vanilla Ice.

I let a giggle escape, then look at Grayson nervously. He forces a gentle smile.

"It's Christmas, sweetheart. I promise to not act like a jealous bastard, all right?"

I press pause.

"Who are you and what have you done with my Grayson?" I palm his face and softly peck at his lips.

"I just ... I want to have a happy Christmas, sweetheart. I don't want to ruin it with an argument over your past, which you can barely remember. It's not fair to either one of us, love."

Whenever Grayson is thinking carefully about what he's saying, he frowns on the annunciation of a lot of the words. Very British ... very lovely.

"You sound and look extra British, baby—you know what that does to me." I bite my smile back. Grayson does the most exaggerated frown, making me laugh. God, I love him so much. He looks vulnerable right now ... not the confident, selfish, arrogant, overprotective man I'm used to. "Grayson, I don't want to watch this now. I want to spend time with you and focus on our Christmas preparations." Of course, I neglect to mention that it is quite uncomfortable to watch a memory reel of the past five years of my life, looking very much in love with the man I thought was just my best friend, with my fiancé.

"No, sweetheart. I want you to watch it now and get it over with so that I may have your full attention after. Becca, why don't I go and see what the girls are up to? You stay and watch. Now that I know what this is, I don't need to stay here and make you feel uncomfortable. I only have one question, though." He takes the last bite of his sandwich.

"What's that?" I thumb the mayo away from the corner of his mouth. He grabs my hand gently and sucks the mayo off of my thumb. "Oh, Mr. James." I shake my head.

"Something to think about, aye, Ms. Campbell?" He lets a small smile creep in ... his seductive smile.

"Indeed." I lean in for a kiss.

"Mmm. So, who took all of these pictures? It's quite stalker-ish! I may have to hire them." He laughs lightly.

"Oh, that would be, as the girls like to call her, Nanarazzi, Ray's mother, Elise. I'm sure it will get worse. That woman is dangerous with a camera in her hand! Sneaky little thing." I laugh, then feel a blanket of sadness come over me. I can't imagine what Ray's mom is thinking of me. It breaks my heart. She's such an important person in my life. The idea of losing her kills me.

"Sad, sweetheart?" He rubs my back.

"I love his mom. What she must think of me?"

"Stop, sweetheart." He thumbs away the tears from the corners of my eyes. "You did nothing intentional." I hug him. "All right then, get back to it, sweetheart. I love you." He kisses me.

"Love you, baby." I squeeze him to me. He gets up and heads out. I press play.

"Come Home" by One Republic starts playing. More pictures of that Christmas pop up.

Opening presents with the girls
Ray and I relaxing on the couch
All four of us dressed for church
Ray and I walking into church hand in hand

It's like I'm watching somebody else's life.

Horseback riding in January together
Dancing at the winter festival
Ray and I doing one of our many karaoke performances
We Were MAINE for Each Other – white letters

Our first trip to Maine for Easter starts with "Hey, Soul Sister" by Train.

We look so sweet, asleep on the couch wrapped in each other's arms

We're walking barefoot down the beach—our khakis rolled up at the bottom—and he has his arms around me as the wind whips our hair

Ray's giving me a piggyback ride down the beach

We're kissing on the beach

We're chasing the girls in the yard

Ray and I asleep on the hammock (black and white)

Ray wakes up and smiles at his mother

Ray watches me sleep

He touches my face

I open my eyes and smile up at him

We kiss

We snuggle

I wave at his mom

Easter-egg hunt with the girls

Ray has Morgan on his shoulders to get an egg off a high tree branch

Family-style portrait of us in our Easter best

The video continues on showcasing pictures like this to a great soundtrack. He has "Photographs and Memories" by Jason Reeves, "Somewhere Only We Know" by Keane, "Fall For You" by Second-hand Serenade, "When You're Gone" by Avril Lavigne, "Dreaming with a Broken Heart" by John Mayer, "The Perfect Boy" by The Cure, "On Bended Knee" by Boyz II Men, "Need You Now" by Lady Antebellum, "Warning Sign" by Coldplay, "From Where You Are" by Lifehouse, "I'm Gonna Be (500 miles)" by The Proclaimers, "Brighter than Sunshine" by Aqualung, and "Perfect Two" by Auburn.

Sometimes We Don't See Eye to Eye (white letters)

"Never Say Never" by The Fray comes on.

I'm yelling at Ray on the patch of grass right off his parents' porch, his arms stretched out wide

He's angry

I'm crying and talking through my teeth

Ray walks toward me

He grabs my face gently

I push his hands away

My face is turned

Ray looks sincere

He tries to turn my face.

He's trying to make me laugh

Ray goes on his knees, his hands clasped, begging me in an exaggerated manner

I'm finally laughing

Ray hugs my lower body to him

He looks up at me with his boyish grin

Ray stands up and looks down into my eyes

He palms my face

We kiss

We hold each other

We walk arm and arm back to the house

"What were we arguing about?" I ask out loud.

I have no idea what we were arguing about that day either! *(appears in white)*

I can't help but laugh.

"Fix You" by Coldplay finishes out our memories. The screen goes black for a moment. "Every Breath You Take" by The Police plays as a message pops up.

Becs,

As you can see, you are the love of my life. You and our girls are my life. I wouldn't trade a single one of these moments for anything. I'm begging you, baby, to acknowledge the happiness we bring to each other, how important "we" are and how much we truly love each other. This is our life in pictures ... the good and the bad. I can't promise to never make you mad or upset you, but I can promise to love you like hell, babe. You are my forever ... let me be yours.

So deeply in love with you,

Ray

One last picture appears of Ray and me. He's hugging me from behind, and we're looking at each other, laughing. I sit back and, for the second time in two days, have a good cry over one Mr. Ray McNeil.

A knock on the door grabs my attention. Melissa smiles as she lets herself in.

"Hi," I murmur as I wipe my eyes.

"Hi." She winces.

"Please make me laugh about something ... anything!" I beg her.

"I have just the thing! Claudia dropped this off earlier." She hands me an album.

"Oh my God, I almost forgot about this!" I clap my hands excitedly. This is one of Grayson's Christmas presents. I have to give it to him alone, because it's an inside joke. I open it up and go into complete hysterics, and my tears turn to ones from laughter. "Did you get the other gift for me?" I ask.

"Yes, it's in my room." She glances at the book and giggles, but her expression says she's confused.

"It's a long story." I close it and grab her arm. "Let's go. I want to wrap these."

"Where are you going, love?" Grayson asks as we head upstairs.

"To finish wrapping gifts. I'll be down in twenty minutes, babe." We run up. Melissa lets me into her room, which now kind of looks like her and Ryan's room.

"So, your first Christmas ... how are things?" I raise my eyebrows.

"Um." She blushes. "Really, really good." Her smile is huge. "Uh, so, here." She hands me the bag.

"Do you have scissors and wrapping paper?" I pull the item out of the bag and crack up.

"You guys are fucking weird! That's all I have to say." She shakes her head as she hands me the supplies. I start cutting like a madwoman. Melissa stares at me with her mouth open. "Those were a hundred and fifty dollars, Becca!"

"Yeah, too bad they cost so much. Oh well." I carry on.

"So, how were things with Ray this morning? If you don't mind me asking."

I don't mind. Melissa has been here since the get-go, and she's become a very close friend. I should talk to her about her next assignment, though. Not everyone will be as laid-back as I am. She's young and she showcases that in her unprofessionalism. If I were anyone else, she would've been fired a long time ago. Grayson, of course, tries to fire her every other week, but she's a very qualified and able person. I'm going to miss her when the time comes.

"Nope, it's okay. Um, it was difficult. Ray is a wonderful man and I've dragged him through the mud, basically, for five years. I didn't realize that my PTSD was so severe it was blocking out my memories with Ray ... well, all of the intimate ones. Ray just basically had to tell me about the past five years of my life with him." I apply the last piece of tape to the album's wrapping.

"Becca, he date-raped you! Aren't you going to press charges?"
I wince at her bluntness.

"No," I simply say.

"But he *raped* you!" she snaps.

"Melissa, if it were any other person on the planet, I would press charges. It's different, and it's complicated." I try to keep my patience. I know she's coming from a place of friendship and concern.

"It's *rape* and he should pay for it!" she yells.

"He has paid for it, Melissa! You have no idea! You don't know the entire story, so I suggest you shut your damn mouth before you get fired again ... by *me* this time!" I yell back.

"Then fire me! I can't believe I looked up to you! You're basically saying it's okay because this guy had a crush on you for a few years? What are you teaching your daughter?" Her chin quivers. I can see and understand her frustration.

"Meliss, you only know one side, babe. You don't know what I've done to him. I'm not saying what he did was okay, just that I forgive him. I understand that I had a pretty big hand in pushing him to a place that even he's not comfortable with. The only advice I've ever given you is to follow your heart and communicate your feelings. That's what I'm doing right now. If you were in this predicament, you may feel differently. I have to do what's right for me. I'm sorry if I've disappointed you, Melissa, but we are all in charge of our own destiny and the decisions that get us there. Sometimes role models teach us what not to do. If you feel that I am handling a situation incorrectly compared to how you would handle it, then that's good! It means you are your own person with your own moral compass. That will get you much further in life than following somebody else's." I finish my philosophical rant to a quiet Melissa. She's been biting at a hangnail, taking in every word ... so it seems.

"Am I still fired?" she asks softly.

"Unless you want to be ... no." I sigh and collect the wrapped gifts. "Thanks for helping me with these." I give her a half smile and turn to leave.

"Becca!" Melissa yells as I'm halfway out the door.

"Yes?" I turn and get a hug that could fall under the category of tackling.

"I'm sorry. It's just, I've grown to love you so much and I worry about you."

"I love you, too, and don't worry about me! I've got a kickass bodyguard!" I tease and hug her back just as fiercely. Ryan clears his throat out in the hallway.

"Hey, everything all right, Mrs. James?" he asks. We break from our hug.

"Yes, Ryan, everything's fine. Have you seen Mr. James?" I ask.

"Um, downstairs." He takes Melissa's hand.

"Thanks." I head to our room to put the gifts away. I can't help but wonder when my room will be done. It's bigger, and, well ... it's mine! But then again, I guess I don't have to worry about it since we're moving to California.

I'm never going to see Ray again. I choke back a sob. Why did my brain have to go there? It's best for both of us if I'm not here. I'll have to start my business all over again ... if I want to. Not something to worry about today. I hide the packages and make my way downstairs. I want to make sure all of the baking is done. I just want to cook dinner tomorrow and not worry about anything else.

I've decided to give Grayson his personal special gifts tomorrow night. I can't wait. I'm extra nervous and excited about the one gift. It's small in size, but huge in gesture. I'm pretty sure he will be most delighted with this one!

Finishing the last few stairs, I notice how quiet it is in the inn. I love closing down for the holiday and just having us here. Of course, there is an increase of twenty-five or so security people this year, compared to the usual two to four (depending on the year) McNeils. Wait! This is supposed to be our year with Ray's parents! Wow, Becca, you've just graduated to using a baseball bat for your mental head slap!

Following my nose, I find myself in the kitchen. It seems everything on Grayson's mother's list is done. Humph. I guess I'll start making my own stuff. It's going on two in the afternoon now. I wonder what the girls are up to. I grab eight packages of cream cheese and several containers of sour cream. Whipped topping comes out of the freezer, as well as blueberries.

"Becca, what are you doing, honey?" Hazel pipes up from behind me.

"Oh, I was going to make cream-cheese tarts, blueberry crumb bars, and pumpkin cake." I look for the little graham-cracker-crust shells.

"We did everything, honey." She sighs.

"Everything?" I'm a little upset.

"Yes, we had quite the team. And with this new kitchen ... " She waves around as if I hadn't seen it yet.

"Oh. Well, then I guess I'll cook supper tonight." I go to the fridge to put everything away.

"Grayson's taking us all out." She seems unsure.

"What about the staff?" I really don't want to go to a restaurant the day before Christmas Eve with, like, fifty people!

"He rented a room and we're having a buffet. Why don't you go talk to him? He's in your office." She starts putting the rest of my stuff away. I nod and head off.

I look up through the windows of the French doors before I reach the handle. Grayson is sitting at my computer, looking at the DVD. What's this about? I open the door and walk in. He doesn't even flinch. Then again, he's never been concerned with invading my privacy.

"Ahem." I clear my throat as he finishes reading Ray's message to me.

"You two looked very much in love," Grayson finally says.

"Yeah, I guess we did." I sit next to him, not quite sure where this is going to lead.

"Feelings like that don't just die away, sweetheart." He's not looking at me.

"I didn't know those memories existed until this morning, Gray." I reach for his hand.

"How did you feel? Did you remember once he told you?" He turns the chair to face me and grabs my other hand as well.

"Most of them, yes. It was weird, having my own memories told to me. Sometimes I felt like he was talking about two other people. Other times he would just start the memory and I was able to retrieve it." *I'm going to remain calm, levelheaded, and honest,* I tell myself. It's more of a chant, really.

"Did, um ... did you feel what you were feeling for him at the time?"

"Yes. I could sense what I was feeling at the time." I'm not sure what he really means.

"Did he touch you?" He glances up.

"Yes." My heart is racing.

"Did you make love to him?" His eyelids go crazy.

"No!" I say quickly.

"Did you want to?"

"I was turned on by our memories, but I had no intentions of acting on them."

"Becca, do you realize that I am unsure as to where I really stand with you?"

I can see he's trying so hard to remain calm.

"You stand as the man I'm in love with. The man I plan to spend the rest of my life with. Nothing has changed!" I try to reassure him.

"I sense that it has, sweetheart. I've sensed it ever since yesterday." He looks down. I sit on his lap.

"Grayson, it's because this all just happened. That's it. It's done. Let's concentrate on Christmas and moving back to California. I am giving up everything for you, because what I'm gaining—our family and our love—means so much more. Grayson, you are the one. I love you, baby." I lean down and collect his lips with mine.

"You know what, sweetheart? You're right! Let's focus on the here and now!" He perks up. Almost too much.

"Okay. Sounds good!" I decide not to bring any attention to the sharp shift in his tone. "So, a little birdie told me we were going out to eat tonight." Change of subject to shoo away the white elephant.

"Oh, is that the little birdie who 'pssts' instead of chirps?" He laughs a little, going back to our conversation about Hazel months ago.

"Yes. You know, I don't like that no one waited for me to do any of the baking!" I frown. I am still upset.

"Sweetheart, you were dealing with a lot today, and we just ended up zooming right through it. It wasn't intentional. We are going to The Break Room. I've rented their room there. We shall have a feast!" He kisses my nose and pats my belly.

"Hey, any word from Jake?" Speaking of bellies.

"Yes, actually. I did hear from him. Sweetheart, Stacey is pregnant, but she's sixteen weeks. It's Steve's. I don't know why she lied." He sighs.

"Geez, she doesn't look that far along. I think she lied to get me upset about Ray. Who the hell knows, Gray? She's not the same person anymore." I can't figure her out. It's completely frustrating!

"Maybe she lied because she can't get ahold of Steve. Did you ask Ray if he slept with her?" He rubs my upper arm.

"No. I'll ask him tomorrow." I exhale in an exaggerated manner. Gray hands me the phone.

"I will give Annie to him tomorrow. You are to stay away from him. Call him now." He nods toward the phone. I take it and dial Ray's number, praying he doesn't answer.

"Becca?" *Thanks, God! I see whose team you're on!*

"Yeah, hi. I need to ask you something." *Jesus, this is awkward!* I feel like I'm in high school.

"What is it, baby?"

Grayson rolls his eyes at Ray's usual endearment. I nudge him.

"You've talked to Stacey ... has she told you she's pregnant?" *Okay. Good angle, creeping in the backdoor.*

"No. She is? Oh man, George got her pregnant?" he asks, frustrated for her.

"Um, no. I know its Steve's. She's sixteen weeks along. But, Ray ... " I start.

"What, babe?"

Another eye roll from Grayson.

"She told me that she is nine weeks along, and that it's yours."

"Becs, she's fucking lying! I know you know that much, but baby, I never slept with her! I wouldn't! She's your best friend. I wouldn't do that to you—or to me, quite frankly. I know we said a bunch of shit a few months ago, but that's what it was ... a load of crap, baby. I don't want anyone but you, Becs."

"I believe you, Ray. I just wanted to double-check. I don't know what's going on with her. Do you think she's been acting strange?" I get off of Gray's lap and sit on the other chair. Grayson's nose flares and he taps his watch. I put my hand up in the air, like, *what?* To me, I'm only talking to my best friend, not the man from all of those photos.

"Well, sorta, but you know Stacey's always flirted with me and acted strange. I didn't really think anything of it. I don't even have anything specific to mention that was out of character. Well ... she did try to get me into bed that night you two were texting back and forth. But I told her I just wanted you. So she said she would help me try to break the two of you up." I can hear him opening a beer.

"A little early for a beer isn't it, Ray?"

Grayson's eyes go wide, and I can tell he's thinking, *Are you fucking kidding me?*

"Root beer, baby."

"Eck ... I hate root beer." I make a face.

"I know. Um ... Mama and Daddy are coming tonight."

"Ray, you're thirty-eight years old ... you sound ridiculous saying that." I laugh. He chuckles with me. "Give them my love. Tell your mother I'm sorry." My voice gets quiet.

"For what, baby?" I hear him shuffling things around. Probably last-minute cleaning before Elise gets there and gives him a hard time.

"For everything, Ray. Cleaning up before they get there?" I giggle a little.

"Uh, yeah. You know me too well, babe. You've probably been busy today, but have you had a chance to look at the DVD?" Dishes clank in the background.

"I did, actually. It was lovely. Your mother's stalking has gone above and beyond." I laugh.

"Oh no ... you have not seen the worst! There was something I couldn't put on there. A memory I forgot to tell you about." He turns the faucet off. I sit forward and hold my finger up to Gray.

"What memory? What was it?"

Ray chuckles nervously.

"What?" I'm giggling now. Grayson gets up and slams the chair under the desk, then leaves the office. The door crashes shut behind him.

"What was that, baby?" *The sound of me getting into trouble.*

"Oh, that was Grayson. He's a little perturbed." I sigh.

"Did you tell him, baby? Did you tell him I touched you?"

"Yes, Ray. The memory, please." I can't have him talking about today. The phone is bugged.

"My parents were visiting. We decided to double up and take them out on the horses. My dad's back was bothering him. My mother opted to walk home so she could take pictures of nature, so Dad rode back without her and we continued on. Remember when we got back to the meadow and jumped down from Rocco? You decided you couldn't wait to get back to the inn. After all the stuff you said to me ... I couldn't wait, either. Well, Rocco wasn't the only stallion you rode that afternoon." He's quiet. I am, too.

"I remember. Wham-bam ... thank you, Ray-man." I laugh.

"Damn, that was hot, baby. And, well ... ahem." He tries not to laugh.

"No she fucking didn't!" I don't know whether to laugh or cry from the embarrassment.

"No boundaries, babe," he answers. "In her defense, it was respectfully done. All you can see are our bare hips, the side of our bums and faces ... foreheads against each other, soaking in the sensation. She actually gave me a lecture afterward, telling me that I should take my time with you. 'Don't be in such a rush, son.' I was mortified, but had no idea she took those pictures. I took her camera's memory cards without her knowing."

"Oh my God, what did you say?" I'm in hysterics now, picturing his sweet Southern mama giving him advice on how he should give it to his girl.

"I said, 'Mama, Becca had an itch that needed to be scratched urgently, and what my baby wants, she gets.'" It's so good talking to him, and laughing no matter the topic.

"What did she say?"

"She just laughed and said, 'Oh, son!' and smacked my arm."

"Ray, I still can't believe she went that far to take those pictures!" I am flabbergasted.

"I know! What do you do with pictures like these?" He laughs.

"Yeah, it's not like we can show them to our grandkids one day!" *Oh my God! What did I just say?*

"Baby?" he asks, sounding hopeful.

"Bye, Ray! I have to go!" I hang up and sit back. Why the hell did I just say that? The private line rings. No, no, no! I can't answer that! I send it to voicemail. It rings again. We play this game five more times before he stops calling. I take in a deep breath and leave the office. I head to the lounge and find Grayson stretched out on the couch watching *It's a Wonderful Life*. *Oh, the irony!*

"Becca!" Annie yells, and I turn around. She hands me her phone and runs off. "It's Daddy!" she says when she's far enough away.

"Go into another room, Becca. I want to hear the movie, not my fiancée carrying on like a fucking schoolgirl!" Gray snaps at me. I head to the kitchen.

"Hey, what's up?" I ask, defeated.

"You tell me, baby!" He sounds irritated.

"What, Ray? I had to go. We were on the phone way longer then we should've been." I act as if what I said didn't happen.

"Goddamn it, Becca! Stop running from your feelings! You're making a huge mistake, and you know it!" he yells.

"Goodbye, Ray!" I hang up again. I leave the phone on the counter and go back to Grayson. He's still stretched out on the couch. I decide to lay with him. He doesn't shrug me off. That's a good sign. I nuzzle my head into his chest and inhale deeply. I love his smell. It's intoxicating. I lift my head to look down into his face, expecting to see anger, but I don't. His fingers touch my face.

"You're beautiful, sweetheart. I love you so very much." I lean down and kiss him.

"You love *him*, Becca," he says against my lips.

I lift my head to look at him. "I love you," I say again softly.

"I know you do, sweetheart. I don't doubt it. But you love him, too. I can see it ... plain as day." He palms my cheek.

"Grayson, please. I don't know what you are looking for here. What is it you want me to say, baby, that I haven't already said?" I almost wish he would scream at me or take me upstairs aggressively to give me a "what for" like he usually does. I'm not used to this Grayson—patient and understanding.

"It's time for you to truly acknowledge your feelings, Becca.

You need to face them. Stop running away from them. You won't be able to sort yourself out until you do."

"Grayson, I've just been hit with a lot of information. I think it's only natural for me to be a bit out of sorts. It's a lot to process. I've really hurt him on top of having this double life." I feel like I'm chasing my tail instead of explaining myself, because I'm not sure about what it is I'm trying to explain.

"Sweetheart, I'm not mad that you love him. I understand that he's been a huge part of your life. I see from those pictures how deep your love is for one another ... I'd be an idiot if I didn't. Honestly, Becca, if I wasn't me, I'd be rooting for Ray. I just think the sooner you accept your feelings, the easier it will be for you to move on."

I sit up. I am officially confused as hell.

"Are you breaking up with me?" I ask, placing my head in my hands.

"Certainly not, darling!" He sits next to me and rubs my back.

"Grayson, you have been saying the strangest things to me, and acting just the same! What is going on?" I truly feel as if I'm in the Twilight Zone.

"Uh. It's uh ... Christmas, sweetheart. I'm a little off. I always am this time of year. I'm sorry. You know I lost my mum right before Christmas." He runs his hand through his hair.

"No, babe, I didn't know that. I'm very sorry." I hug him.

"Well, you can ask Aunt Hazel. I'm not myself much around this time. Sorry, love." He sighs.

"What do you do in London? You don't visit with friends." I reveal Hazel's detective work.

"I, uh, go through the Christmas schedule. Then, on Christmas morning, I sit and look at the last Christmas present my mother gave me. I know it's something she made. I've never opened it. I just hold it." He rests his elbows on his knees.

"Why, baby? It's been over twenty years." I rub his back now.

"Becca, when someone you are so close to and love so very much dies ... well, you know. The years don't add up because it's always like they were here just yesterday. It's never truly real, you feel as if they could walk through the door at any moment. For me, opening that gift means cementing the truth into my heart—that she's really gone and never coming back. It's something I just haven't been able to bear the thought of. The finality of it all breaks my heart."

I pull his face to mine. His eyes are full, his nose red, and his chin quivering ... I just want to take this hurt away from him. It's achingly familiar. I hold him, and we cry together. Sometimes, there are no words left to say.

"Well now, look at the pair of us!" He slaps my leg and tries to collect himself.

"I love you, Grayson Michael James," I say as I palm his face. "I see you. Other people see this arrogant, controlling, intimidating, ass slapping," I giggle, "selfish bastard, but I see you ... you beautiful man, you." I lean in and sweep his lips with my own.

"You do, don't you, sweetheart? You've seen through the bull right from the get-go. You always have, Becca!" That rare, high-wattage, Grayson James smile flashes before my eyes.

"Yes I have, sir." I match the wattage.

"I knew I had to have you the moment you found me arrogant." He laughs.

"Then you proved yourself to be persistent and selfish as well," I tease.

"Best thing I ever did was pursue the likes of you! God, I love you, Becca!" He pulls me to him. Our short, sweet kisses turn into something much deeper and urgent.

"Ahem." Derek clears his throat nearby. "Sir?"

"Yes, Derek?" Grayson smiles against my lips.

"The team is preparing the vehicles for our reservation."

"Thanks, Derek." He looks up. Derek walks away.

"Um ... that sounded odd. Preparing horses, okay, but preparing vehicles? What the hell are they doing besides starting them up?" Sometimes, things just strike a funny chord with me and all I can do is giggle, even if I'm the only one who finds it funny. "Are they giving them a pep talk?" *Oh, I'm gone!*

"Sweetheart, if I didn't know any better, I'd think you had a few glasses of wine." He chuckles at me.

"I feel as if I have." I wipe the tears away. "Sorry." I smile.

"Love your dimple." He pokes at it then kisses it.

"Come on, baby. Let's prepare ourselves." I laugh and get up, pulling him with me.

"Speaking of, I have a dress for you to wear." He pulls me toward the stairs.

"To dinner?" I cock my head sideways.

"Well, it's a bit of a Christmas party for our employees. Impromptu—sorry." He winces.

"Yeah, thanks ... fifteen minutes before we leave. Brilliant man you are, Mr. James!" I tease, but not really. Grayson, however, is immune to my sarcasm. We head up the stairs with a bit of haste. As soon as we get to our room, I start stripping down. "Okay, whaddya got for me?" I look up as he walks out from the closet. He bites his lip. "Grayson ... clothes!" I snap, then laugh.

"Oh right, of course, sweetheart." He heads over with the dress, removing the plastic from it. "I saw this and thought you would look lovely in it." It's a metallic hunter-green dress in a soft, sheer material. It has a high neck, low back, and a sleeveless baby-doll style. Cute. He hands me a bag of undergarments.

"Yay ... peel-and-sticks!" I laugh. He smiles, remembering that night as well. I hurry and get dressed. Black nylons and metallic heels finish off the look. He hands me a bag from the town jeweler. I open the boxes and find an antique-looking black onyx bracelet and matching earrings. "Thanks, baby." I smile and hug him.

"Do you like it?" He smiles widely.

"Yes. You have very good taste, Mr. James."

"Yes, I do." He chucks my chin and kisses me. I run into the bathroom. I have five minutes to figure out what I'm going to do with my thick, wavy mane. It's actually not bad today! I pull my bangs back tightly and secure them with a clip that almost matches my jewelry. My makeup goes on easily—no redos needed!

"Okay, I'm ready!" I come out of the bathroom, walking into the perfume I sprayed in front of me. Grayson whistles. I stop quickly enough to blush at the look on his face.

"That was record-breaking time, my dear!" he says proudly.

"Well, as you know, Mr. James, I work very well under pressure." Statement followed by mischievous grin.

"Ugh, Mrs. James ... you are a very naughty girl. I may have to do something about that later." His smile is full of promise as he offers me his arm.

Chapter Fifteen

We arrive at The Break Room. Our private room is decorated with lights and evergreens. The DJ already has music pumping out of the speakers. After everyone settles in, Grayson gets up and grabs the mic.

"Can I have everyone's attention, please? Becca and I would like to thank you for everything you do for us. We'd like to especially thank our security staff. Many of you are spending Christmas far away from your own families to keep our family safe. We appreciate it greatly and hope we are making your holidays at least tolerable." He chuckles, and a lot of the detail that have been with us from the beginning join in. We've proven to be quite the interesting couple to protect. "This party is for you. We hope you have a great time and we wish you all a happy everything!" Grayson finishes and hands the mic back to the DJ.

The servers come out with soup and salad, adding clanking to the background noise of chitter chatter. The DJ serenades us with holiday favorites while we warm up our palates before the main course. I pause, like I do every Christmas, and look around at everyone's faces to take in the memory. A stop-and-smell-the-roses kind of thing.

Hazel and Charlie are laughing. He finally made it back from Connecticut today. Claudia and Joshua tease Morgan and Annie while Grayson adds to their banter. Stacey just stares at her spoon as she continuously swirls it around in her tea. *The lights are on, but nobody seems to be home.*

She looks up, catching my eyes. We stare at each other like strangers instead of best friends. I offer her a meek smile. She returns it. I wish I could figure out what's going on in that head of hers. I glance to the left again as Grayson kisses my right cheek. Annie stares at me, and I see her eyes filling up. Mine follow suit. This is our sixth Christmas together, and some other man has taken her father's place beside me. It's strange to both of us. *I love you,* I mouth to her. This just makes it worse. I see Morgan ask if she's all right, and they head toward the bathroom.

"What's the matter, sweetheart?" Grayson leans over.

"Annie's having a tough time with all of this, Gray. I don't know how to help her with it." I blot my tears.

"Maybe we shouldn't have kept her the whole weekend, sweetheart. I know this is hurting her, but I'm not going to put distance between us to spare her feelings. This is our time, our Christmas." His eyelids blink at a passionate pace.

"I know, baby. I'm not asking you to distance yourself." I lean my head on his shoulder.

"Mom?" Morgan taps my shoulder. I look up. "Annie wants to call Ray, but she said you have her phone."

Shit!

"I forgot it on the counter at home. Gray, can I call on my

cell?" I ask.

"She may call on your cell. Not you!"

Ugh! I shouldn't have to ask to call someone on my own damn phone! I pull my phone out and unblock Ray.

"Where's Annie?" I look around.

"In the bathroom." Morgan grabs my phone and heads off.

"Grayson, I should go with her." I try to get up.

"Should you now, sweetheart?" He grabs my arm. "I have had enough of Ray today ... Becca." He stares deep into my eyes.

I sit down.

"Sorry, baby." I glance over to Stacey. She has a smirk on her face. *What the hell?*

The servers start bringing out the entrées. Guess Gray decided against a buffet after all. We have the prime rib, along with half the table. The other half ordered the stuffed chicken Florentine. All sorts of delicious smells hit the air. There must have been several entrées to choose from. I wouldn't know, because I'm with Grayson ... what's a menu?

Morgan and Annie make their way back to the table. Morgan hands me my phone.

"We have to bring Annie home tonight. Ray said I can stay over to visit with Nana and Pop. Can I, Mom?" *Uh ...*

"Ask your father." *How original, Becca!* Morgan smiles and goes over to Grayson. He turns to me, and his flat expression shifts to a mischievous one. He bites back his smile as he eyes me up and down. *Ahh ... apparently brownie points are awarded when you give a control freak complete control without him demanding it!* Grayson's left brow darts up as if he's heard my thoughts on the matter. He gives me another once-over filled with naughty thoughts (it's obvious) and turns back to Morgan. She jumps up and down with excitement, and they walk over to me.

"Text Ray to make sure he has room for her security." He taps my phone, lighting up the screen. There are already messages from

Ray on there. I slide the bar to open it.

December 23, 2012   5:52 p.m.
Ray: Sorry Annie got upset. She loves you so much, just like me.
Ray: Can we have Morgan? Mama and Daddy want to say goodbye to her.
Ray: They want to say goodbye to you, too.
Me: Do you have enough room for her detail?
Ray: Yes, you know I do.
Me: Okay. After the party, we'll pick up the girls' things and swing over.
Ray: Good, you'll save Mama a trip ... she wants to whoop your ass!
Me: You always were a mama's boy!
Ray: I told her that's Grayson's job! :)
Me: Bye :|

I turn off my phone. The DJ starts playing dance music as people finish their meals. Grayson pulls me onto the floor when "Sexy Back" by Justin Timberlake starts playing. I had no idea he knew how to dance so well! I feel like, for the first time in a while, I'm having fun.

By eight-thirty in the evening, Grayson and I start going around to all of the tables to pass out holiday bonus checks. Everyone is wide-eyed and thanks us repetitively!

"Ready to head back, sweetheart?" Grayson's arms encircle my waist from behind and he hugs me tightly to him.

"Yes! My dawgs are bahkin'!" I decide to hit him hard with my double accent as I lean my head back on his chest. I've always tried to come up with a cool name for it, but the best I could ever come up with is "Bostersey." It's not exactly "Brangelina," but it works! That's what happens, though, when you spend half your life in one place and half in another. People are never quite sure where I'm from anymore ... well, except for when I'm mad. You can take the girl out of Jersey, but you can't take Jersey out of the girl!

"C'mon, then." He kisses my neck, then pats my bottom. We head over to the coat check.

"Mr. James, your card!" The manager hands the paid bill and his card back.

"Yes, of course, thank you! Have a Happy Christmas!" They shake hands. I love how he says "happy Christmas" instead of "merry"—it's cute. Grayson places my coat on my shoulders, then does the same for Morgan and Annie.

"Look, darling—snow!" Grayson says excitedly, holding his hands up when we get outside. I can't help but giggle at his child-like behavior. This takes his attention away from the weather, and he offers me a shy smile. I think he's a bit embarrassed at his excitement, especially with security around. He takes my left hand in his and places his right hand on my elbow, guiding me to the black Suburban waiting for us. "Easy, sweetheart, it's slippery here." He keeps his eyes peeled to the ground, scanning for any ice that may trip me up.

This is the Grayson I wish people would see. He's kind, caring, thoughtful, and loving. I have a very long list detailing his wonderful attributes. He doesn't show it often, but I know it bothers him that people think he treats me poorly. It bothers me, too. They're wrong.

"Step up, love." He nudges my elbow.

"Oh, sorry." I shake out of my thoughts and do so. He slides in next to me, grabbing my hand immediately. Once we're buckled, Derek puts the Suburban in gear and rolls out.

"Annie, I'm sorry you don't want to stay with us tonight. You're a lovely girl and we've really enjoyed being with you." Grayson leans over me to tap her knee. I take Annie's hand and squeeze it, but she pulls away. I feel a pang in my heart.

"Thank you, Grayson. I had a lot of fun baking with you to-day." She smiles as she leans forward to see him. When she catches my eye, she sits back and turns me away quickly. Annie's never once been upset with me. Never. I look past her to Morgan.

"What's wrong, sweetie?" I ask her.

"Nothing, Mum," she looks out the window. Nope ... she's ly-ing. I'll wait until we're alone to press the matter more.

Our entourage arrives at the inn. It's amazing how quiet it is when it snows, especially big, fluffy snow like this. You could hear a pin drop. I stop as we walk to the inn and bend my neck back. I stick my tongue out to catch snowflakes. The girls giggle and do the same.

"Okay, sweetheart, come now. You'll catch a death of a cold out here! Really, love, girls, let's go." Grayson touches my back encouraging me to move along.

"You're no fun!" I pout playfully.

"Well, I'll have to change your mind about that, won't I?" His brows shoot up and he lightly sucks in his whole bottom lip. *Hmm. I can't wait.* I let my eyes do the talking.

"Okay, girls, go get your stuff. Annie, I'll grab your phone." I head toward the kitchen.

"Anything I can do, love?" Grayson yells.

"Yes, can you run the bath?" I call out and walk over to the counter. I look at the screen of the pink phone. Ten missed calls all from Ray. I head back out to the common area. The girls come run-ning down the stairs. "Wait, that was too quick! Are you sure you have everything?" I try to grab Morgan's bag.

"Ugh! Toothbrush, PJs, underwear, outfit, and sneakers!" Mor-gan goes through the list.

"Phone?" I ask. She waves it at me as if she's saying *duh.* "Hey! Watch your eye tone with me!" I wave a finger. Of course not *the* finger—as much as I want to use that one, it would just be inappropriate. Grayson comes back down the stairs.

"We'll see you tomorrow, Morgy girl! Have fun, you two!" He gives them each a hug.

"Wait ... Mom, aren't you coming?" Morgan pulls away.

"No, Morgan, I'm tired." *Well, it is getting late.* "I want to spend time with Daddy before I go to sleep," I add.

"Well, Nana and Pop Pop wanted to say goodbye to you." Her voice goes up an octave. Oh, that's what's bothering her. Not only are we taking her away from Annie—we're taking her away from Elise and Artie, too. She'll see Hazel and Charlie because they are family, but with us leaving, we won't see Ray and his family. Elise and Artie have always treated Morgan like a grandchild.

"I'll say goodbye tomorrow, honey, when we pick you up. Give them my love." I put my arm around her shoulder and guide her toward the door. I give her and Annie each a kiss and hug. They follow Scott and Brian out to the car.

"Bath time, baby," Grayson says softly in my ear as we wave to them. He grabs my hand and we slowly walk to the stairs. I stop to pull my shoes off, wincing from the ache. Grayson picks up my shoes for me and we head up. "You are a very lovely woman, Mrs. James."

"Why thank you, Mr. James." I squeeze his hand as we reach the top step and walk to our room. "Will you join me, sir?" I play with the buttons of his shirt. He opens the door to let us in.

"Yes, but let me check on the water or the whole place will be joining us." He pats my bottom and heads toward the bathroom.

I hike up my dress to pull my pantyhose down and off. Sitting on the bed, I examine the damage to my feet. They are puffy, indented with the outline of my shoes.

"All set, darling." Grayson comes out from the bathroom. "Good Lord, sweetheart! Oh, you poor thing!" He sits next to me and pulls my feet onto his lap. "Flats from now on, aye?" he asks as he rubs them. "Becca, they're like Cabbage Patch Kids' feet." He laughs lightly. I look down as he massages and find myself giggling as well. He's right—they do! He brings my right foot up and kisses the top.

"Okay, come on, before the lukewarm bath gets cold." I sigh and smack his arm lightly.

"You'll be happy," he says as he pulls me to my feet. "I've made it a smidge warmer. The doctor said it was okay for now." He unhooks my dress while I remove my jewelry. I place the bracelet and earrings he gave me on the nightstand as Grayson helps me out of my dress. "Peel-and-sticks—my favorite." He smiles as he slowly peels them off of me. I feel the right side of my mouth curl up into a half smile as I work at the buttons on his shirt.

"You are quite handsome, Mr. James." I kiss each patch of skin I uncover.

He pulls my face up to his. "I cherish you, Becca. I have from the moment I first kissed you. I will always cherish you." He almost seems sad.

"Grayson ..." That's all I can manage to say.

"Come, Becca, let's frolic and play in the tub." He smirks playfully to lighten the mood. I pull his shirt off of his shoulders quickly. *God, he is beautiful!* Hand in hand, we head to the bathroom.

Grayson helps me into the tub. I can't help but shake my head at him and roll my eyes a bit. I'm eight weeks, not eight months. Grayson didn't lie. He made the bath close enough to the temperature I like it at. I immerse myself and inhale deeply the scent of coconut and vanilla.

"Scoot, sweetheart." Grayson's fingers tap my shoulder. I open my eyes and take in the full glorious sight of him.

"Grayson, you are very lovely to look at, baby." I scan up and down one more time before scooting forward. Even his penis is beautiful, which still amazes me. I have never thought that about another penis in my life.

"You seem deep in thought ... care to share?" He slips in and pulls me back to him.

"You have a very attractive penis." I sigh as if I'm discussing my favorite color or poem.

"Hmm, attractive and incredible—I'd say I'm one lucky bloke, but maybe you're the lucky one, aye, sweetheart?" He tickles my side as I wash my face.

"Stop!" I laugh and try to pull away.

"All right, give me your washcloth," he says. I comply. He applies bodywash to it and softly rubs my shoulders and back. He rinses, then kisses. He repeats this act on my arms and hands. I get on my knees and turn to him. He brings the facecloth across my clavicle, the top of my chest, over my breasts, and circles it around my nipples. I swallow hard, closing my eyes and allowing my erratic breathing (yeah, like I have a choice in how I breathe!). He travels down over my ribs and my belly, then dives in between my legs and rubs meticulously. I feel my tongue dampen my upper lip. He rinses me off and slowly trails his lips over my newly cleaned surfaces.

"Mmm ..." I moan lightly as his mouth makes its way to my left nipple. Gently I fist his hair and pull his head back so I can taste his mouth. His tongue greets mine purposefully.

"Bloody hell, Becca," he groans against my lips as he hits the drain with his foot.

"Every time we try to get clean, Mr. James, we just end up getting dirtier." I nip across his jawline.

"It's way more fun to get dirty, darling." He pulls me astride him. My back arches to allow him better access to my breast. My hips move rhythmically, anticipating when the water will drain to a safe level (it's like waiting for a pot to boil). Grayson brings my mouth back to his. I pull away sharply and stare into his eyes—his familiar, loving eyes.

"Forever, baby." I palm his face. "Forever." I shake his head a smidge for emphasis. Grayson thrusts deeply inside of me. I gasp and rest my forehead against his as we find our groove. Within minutes, we quicken our pace. But I feel as if we're sliding. "Gray ... baby, we're moving," I say against his lips.

"Yes we are, sweetheart." He attacks my lips again. I find myself refocus on him.

"No, Gray, we're moving ... sliding." I pull away. He slows his pace and opens his eyes.

"Oh." He chuckles. He stops and puts his hand back into the tub to slide us back. We move a little too quickly. Grayson loses his balance and lands on his back with me hanging off of him.

"Uh ... Gray." I try to stifle my giggle as I look around at the oil-slicked tub. "How much oil did you put in here?"

"Oh ... about this much." He shuffles his hand, pointing around the tub nonchalantly.

"So ... probably a tad bit more than recommended?" I bite back my smile.

"I believe your assumption would be correct, darling." He pulls my lip from my teeth. "Go ahead, sweetheart—have yourself a good laugh ... at my expense, mind you."

I do just that and top it off with a kiss on his pouty lips. I resituate on Grayson and rest my hands on his chest. Slowly, I get us back on track. Within moments we come undone together.

"Hey, can you call Scott or Brian to make sure the girls got there and settled in okay?" I ask as I finish toweling my hair dry. We would've called half an hour ago, but we needed to shower all of this oil off our skin and hair. I think I will smell of coconut and vanilla for a week without applying anything!

"Sure, love." He yawns and grabs his phone. "Scott, everyone settled? Good." He nods to me. "Morgan asleep? Oh." He pulls the phone away from his ear to look at it. "Okay. Just tell her that we love her and she should go to bed after the movie is over. Okay, yes. Full report, thank you. Night, then." He hangs up.

"Full report on what?" I look over as I apply lotion to my legs.

"Don't think you need the lotion tonight, sweetheart, after the hot oil treatment you just got." Raising his eyebrows, he takes the bottle and puts in on my dresser.

"Habit." I shrug. "What report?" I ask again.

"Just on the sleepover. If anything is said. You know me, Becca—stage direction and all." He plops next to me and turns on the TV.

"Let's not watch TV, baby. Will you read to me?" I turn the TV off.

"Read to you?" His index finger caresses my cheek.

"Yes!" I say with childlike excitement as I jump out of bed and head over to the bookcase. I retrieve *A Christmas Carol* by Charles Dickens, which I brought with me from Grayson's ... uh ... *our* house. "I'm right here." I open it and point to where I left off. "Will you read it to me? I love to listen to your voice ... except for when you're yelling at me. No, actually, that's pretty hot too! Damn you and your British accent!" I kiss him quickly and grab his Clark Kents. "Professor," I say as I place them on his nose. He smiles and pecks at my lips. We snuggle into each other comfortably.

"Okay, sweetheart, let's see." He sighs before he starts. "'It's Christmas Day!' said Scrooge to himself. 'I haven't missed it. The Spirits have done it all in one night. They can do anything they like. Of course they can. Of course they can. Hallo, my fine fellow!'" Grayson continues on with the ending, his voice so soft and beautiful. I fall asleep happy, loved, and safe in his arms. It all seems so familiar—like we've been together for years, not months.

I'm at an airfield. I don't hear the planes at all. I just hear "I Will Follow You into the Dark" by Death Cab for Cutie. I feel as if I am in an old movie—it's all grayish. My dad's waving. He steps into a Cessna plane. Morgan waves. She steps into another Cessna plane. Grayson waves. He too steps into a plane. Ray follows suit. All four planes are identical. They take turns down the runway. Eventually, they are all up in the sky. They are flying in loops around each other. It's like they are all dancing in the air. I feel a hand on my shoulder. I turn. "Mom!" I shout. I can't even hear myself—the music is so loud. She holds my hand and smiles at me—her green eyes matching mine. Her hair is short and wavy, just how I remember. I feel heat. I turn my head. "No!" I scream. "No!" I have no voice. Just music.

"No!" I scream again as I open my eyes. I sit straight up.

"Sweetheart, Becca, you're safe, baby! C'mere." Grayson pulls me to him as I sob. I explain the dream I just had while I catch my breath.

"I don't know who was in the plane that exploded!"

"Becca, it was probably your dad, sweetheart. Think about it. Cessna planes and your dad—that's a huge memory for you. The explosion might be just from recent events. Shh, sweetheart, it was just a nasty dream." He holds me tightly and kisses my hair.

"Yes ... you're probably right." I try to calm myself down. "Grayson, it felt so real." I release one last sob.

"I hate when you have bad dreams, Becca. What can I do, baby?" He holds my face in his hands.

"Just hold me, Gray. Don't let me go." He slides back down and welcomes me in his arms. "I love you, Grayson ... so very much." I kiss his chest and accept the tissue he offers me.

"There there, sweetheart, everything's going to be all right." He takes it back from me and chucks it into the wastebasket. I close my eyes again. It doesn't take me long to surrender to sleep.

"Happy Christmas Eve, darling." I hear Grayson's voice above me, sounding so cheerful. I feel my lips slowly pull into a smile before I open my eyes.

"You know, you don't need props to get me to kiss you." I eye the mistletoe he's holding above us.

"Oh, yes I do! Waking you in the morning can go either way. I need all the help I can get." He leans down to collect my lips.

"Mmm." I stretch under him.

"Aunt Hazel's already in the kitchen getting the sauce started, love." His mouth presses against my belly. "Hallo in there, little one. Happy Christmas! We love you!"

I run my hands through his hair.

"Proud Papa suits you." I sit up and kiss his head. "Thanks for reading to me last night. It was very relaxing." I pull the covers off and sit at the side of the bed, rubbing my face. It's going to be a long day.

"Anytime, sweetheart." He grasps my shoulders and massages them. I roll my neck back, enjoying the sensation of his hands touching me so lovingly. His lips find my neck and leave a wonderful trail of kisses down it.

"I wish we didn't need all of these security people. I'd love to just worry about cooking for us today. I'd like to just stay in this room with you and have a lazy day." I sigh.

"Sweetheart, you love cooking for all of these people. I thought *the more the merrier* was your motto!" He sits behind me and wraps me in a hug.

"Yes, usually ... but I just want to be with you today. I'd like to give you my full attention, Mr. James." I smile up at him.

"I'd love that, sweetheart, but alas, my powers stop short at making people disappear."

"Ha ... well, you're fired then." I tap his arms and squeeze them to me.

"Here, love, you forgot to reblock him." He hands me my

phone. There are a few texts from Ray.

December 23, 2012   11:33 p.m.

Ray: Babe, you forgot to give Annie her phone.

December 24, 2012   8:27 a.m.

Ray: We're taking the girls out for breakfast and an errand, then we'll drop Morgan off.

Ray: Becca, this is Mama. I want a word with you, baby girl!

Ray: Uh-oh, Becs!

Me: Mama's Boy! I'll have Annie's phone for her. Enjoy your breakfast!

"Can the man make it through a single paragraph without referring to you as *babe* or *baby* five times or more?" Grayson sighs with frustration.

"Well, look at it this way—you probably call me *sweetheart* just as much."

He ponders the idea and shrugs his shoulders.

"Point is, Becca—sweetheart—you are indeed *my* sweetheart and *not* his baby!"

I stand up and turn to him, lacing his fingers with mine. I balance against his hands as I lean in for a kiss.

"Well, Gray, he's been calling me that since the very first day I met him. I don't think that will ever change. Now come, let's get a move on, shall we?" I pull on his hands. He stands up. His chest is an inch from my face—he completely towers over me. I plant a kiss on his sternum and lean up on my tippy-toes to plant one on his lips.

His hands cup my face. "I love you, Becca ... I'll always love you, darling." Before I can question the ache in his declaration, his mouth is on mine. "Mmm, Becca, sweetheart." His breath is warm against my lips. "If we don't get dressed, I'm afraid your wish will come true and we will not be able to leave this room the entire day."

"You may be quite right, Mr. James, as you are standing in

front of me shirtless with those PJ bottoms hanging the way that they do ... the way I find absolutely delicious." I reach up to explore his chest as I bite gently at his neck.

"Oh, bloody hell, Becca!" His hands fist my hair. His mouth finds mine again and the bed withstands the weight of us falling dramatically to it.

"Sorry, Hazel!" I announce as I walk into the kitchen, instead of greeting her with something more pleasant like "good morning" or "merry Christmas."

Christmas has always been a two-day holiday to me, with Christmas Eve hosting most of the special traditions and memories I hold dear. It was so exciting being a kid in my family! My cousins and I would be sent to bed at our usual time. It would take forever for us to fall asleep, thanks to the anticipation. All of our friends were jealous of us though, because, unlike them, we didn't have to wait until morning to open our gifts. Nope! As soon as that fat bearded man in a red suit boarded his sleigh and took off, our parents ran down the hall screaming for us to get up.

"Wake up, kids! Craig! Ethan! Dan! Owen! Becca! Santa was here! Come and see what he's brought you!" Being the youngest and the only girl, one would think I got bulldozed over, but *hell no!* I charged through the stampede like a little woman on a mission! I always knew that under that tree lay a baby all wrapped up and looking for her mama ... I couldn't keep her waiting!

I tried to keep the tradition up with Morgan, but I guess it's not as much fun for an only child. Annie wasn't down for it, either. So, Ray and I would open our gifts to each other on Christmas Eve after we loaded the tree with the girls' stuff. If his parents were with us, they joined in as well. We made Christmas morning all about the girls. This is the first time in six years the girls won't be together on

Christmas morning. This will be the first McNeil-free Christmas. I can't help but feel a little pang in my heart. It doesn't feel right, but I just need to get over it. My life is with Grayson now. There are going to be a lot of changes. It only feels odd because Ray has been such a permanent fixture in my life for so long.

"Becca! Where is your head at? Becca!" Hazel barks at me.

"Huh? Oh, sorry. Sorry." I shake my head to regain focus.

"When should we put the lasagnas in?" she asks, looking at me warily.

"Um, one o'clock. I'm going to boil the sausages now." I go to the fridge.

"Becca, they were boiled yesterday. They're in the sauce." She seems frustrated.

"Well, how the hell would I know? Nobody waited for me to do anything!" I snap, which is quite odd for me to do ... well, at least when it comes to Hazel.

"Becca!"

"Sorry." I say it, but I don't mean it. Why was everything done without me? "What can I do?"

"Everything is done, Becca." She regards me cautiously, as if I'm behaving like a ticking time bomb.

"Of course it is!" I snap again and walk out.

"Sweetheart?" Grayson grabs my arm.

"Please, Gray, I just need a minute ... hormones and all, you know?" I don't look at him.

"All right then, love." He lets go and I head back upstairs. With every step I take, I feel as if a huge wave of emotions is smacking me in the face. I can't quite pinpoint the cause. It could be the pregnancy, or the fact that I haven't been in the driver's seat to my own life in three months. My tradition of preparing Christmas Eve dinner as well as dessert and other goodies has been taken away without permission or a thought. This has clearly become the *straw*!

After lying on our bed for probably twenty minutes, crying my eyes out, I come to no conclusion about anything. Probably because I'm avoiding what is really bothering me. I'm afraid to face it ... my feelings for Ray, the ties that bind us. It's not a simple situation of saying *Well, I choose this fellow*. Leaving Ray is not cut-and-dried. We are like a basket being unwoven. There's so much there, and other people involved—it's not just the two of us. It's not just Christmas without each other, it's every holiday, every life event. It's phone calls until two in the morning, or, like Ray said, until we fall asleep. It's Annie ... it's Elise. What will Grayson say when I absentmindedly call Ray to tell him something funny or just to ask him what he thinks? I won't be allowed to do that! This is goodbye forever. This is never hearing about Annie's first boyfriend, first dance, or graduation. What if something happens to Ray's parents? Who is he going to lean on?

But I have Grayson—I'm his family now— plus Morgan and our little one. I can't walk away from this, either. I've fallen so hard for him. I feel as if I've loved him forever. He's gone above and beyond to keep us safe. He treats Morgan as if she is his own. They have an amazing connection. So natural, like it's always been there.

"Sweetheart." Grayson rubs my back.

"Oh. Hi." I turn to him and wipe my tears away. He studies my face for a long time.

"Trying to sort things out?" he finally asks. I nod. "Well," his eyes go rapid, "what have you come up with, then?"

"Will you let me keep in touch with the McNeils after a certain amount of time has passed?" I sit up and face him boldly.

"Yes. Yes, I will. I know what Annie means to you, and you've expressed your love for his mum as well. If they want to continue a friendship with you, I will allow it." At this moment, I do feel as if I am some sort of prisoner.

"Ray?" I ask.

"You may talk to Ray via any method, except in person. I think you should wait a few months, though. You know, let wounds heal and all." He straightens a wrinkle in the sheet instead of looking at me.

"How do you feel about me asking you this?" My index finger pulls his chin up.

"Uncomfortable, to be honest. But I understand it, and I've also learned that if I squeeze too hard with you ... you will most certainly slip out of my hands."

I'm a bit taken aback by this.

"Mr. James, have I softened you a bit?" I bite back my smile.

"You may have, darling ... but I'm pretty sure you know how to fix that." He thumbs my lip away and sucks on it purposefully. His whole mouth joins mine and slowly he pushes me back down.

"No, Gray, stop. I can't." I try to pull away. He straddles me and gets onto his knees, then pulls his shirt up and off. "Grayson, please," I whisper as he grabs my hands and pins them down.

"I'm a selfish man, Becca, yes?" His words are soft as he looks into my eyes.

"Yes," I agree, almost defeated. I turn my head. "Grayson, please, not now. Not at this moment, baby."

He works at the button on my jeans. I reach down to stop him.

"Don't!" he snaps, and swats my hand away.

"Are you ... are you trying to push me toward him?" I ask, confused.

Grayson stops short and stares down at me. His nose flares. He jumps off of me, puts his shirt back on, and leaves without uttering a single word.

What the hell was that? I pull myself together mentally as best as I can before following him.

"Grayson!" I say louder than I had planned to as I reach the last step.

"Oh! Look, Becca—your boyfriend is here!" he snaps sarcastically.

"Stop it—you're my boyfriend!" I yell.

"I am your *goddamn fiancé* and *you'd do well* to remember that!" he yells as he grabs my upper arms harshly, crushing them.

"Grayson! Grayson, stop!" I cry.

"Get the fuck off of her!" Ray yells. He's there so fast I don't even see him coming, and suddenly, his fist connects with Grayson's face. Grayson releases my arms and swings back at Ray. There they are, the two great loves of my life, beating the Christmas Spirit right out of each other!

"Bound to happen, aye, Bridget?" I hear Stacey behind me, attempting her best British accent. I turn to her quickly. I want to laugh at her comment, and she knows this—it just doesn't seem appropriate! Security finally breaks them up. "Okay, Becca, tell us ... who is the champion of your heart? Who is your Cinderella Man?" Stacey asks me loudly with a full-blown Jersey accent.

"Wow, channeling your inner Renée Zellweger today or what?" I ask her. I turn my attention to Grayson and Ray. "Look at the pair of you! Feel better now that you've beaten each other to a pulp?" I yell.

"Becs. Becs, wake up, baby."

I slowly open my eyes. "Ray?"

"Yeah, babe." He smiles.

"What are you doing here? Where did your fat lip go?" I touch his face.

"I brought Morgan back ... and I didn't have a fat lip." He looks at me strangely.

"Didn't you and Grayson just get into a fight?" I sit up, confused as hell.

"No, but if that's what it will take to get you to see who you belong with, I'll jump right on it." He flashes me a small smile before he leans in and kisses me.

"Stop, Ray." I push away. His knuckles caress my left cheek softly. I swallow hard, trying to control my breathing. I feel the heat from his breath as he leans forward again.

"Baby ... please," he almost whispers as his lips graze mine. I feel paralyzed, like I'm about to be caught in a trap concocted by one Grayson James and his spying personality. "Kiss me, baby. My mom is holding him hostage." Both of his hands hold my face, bringing it closer to his. "Becs, I love you. Kiss me, baby." Reluctantly, I comply.

"Theme-song alert." I pull away.

"What?" His lips graze mine again.

"'Firestarter' by The Prodigy," I say quickly, and put all hands on deck. Ray pulls me up so I'm straddling his lap. Our kiss is deep and urgent. Panic rises in me as I slowly come to my senses. "No. No, Ray. Oh God, stop ... you have to stop!" I try to pull away. His arms are tight around me, holding me to him.

"Yes, Ray ... please do stop," Grayson says calmly.

"Baby, you belong with me. Don't fight it anymore. You love me." He holds my face to his.

"I love Grayson, too."

"Quite the pickle she's in, isn't it?" Grayson says. God ... he is behaving oddly.

"Let me up, Ray, please."

Ray quickly kisses me again, then lets me up. I stand and face Grayson. He is still near the entrance of the room.

"Forever, aye, love?" His nose is flaring, probably to help him to breathe deeply and keep the dampness of his eyes under control. I don't know how to defend myself, so I decide to go with the dramatics of a 1950s movie and sob as I run to the bathroom. *There, Becca, that's showing them! Wimp!* I lock the door and decide to live in here for the rest of my life!

"Becca ... baby girl, wake up." I hear Elise and open my eyes. I'm still on the bed.

"Did you guys just get here?" I ask, trying to map out reality vs. dream.

"Yes ... now scoot over, baby, we gonna have us a nice talk."

She pats my hip.

"Yes, ma'am." I smile. *Oh shit ... here we go.*e

Chapter Sixteen

GRAYSON

Ray and I sit in the lounge, studying each other, testosterone pumping out of every orifice of our bodies. Both of us have so much to say to each other and, at the same time, nothing at all. What would be the point?

"In the spirit of Christmas, Raymond, and because I like to wear big-boy pants—I must say, I have great respect for you. You've taken great care of Becca over the years, even though it proved to be very difficult at times. I know that you truly love and care about her. I admire your tenacity and I wish you nothing but happiness in the future." I wait patiently for his response.

"In the spirit of Christmas, and because my big-boy pants are bigger than yours, I don't give a flying fuck about what you think—

good or bad—you pompous prick!" he snaps. "Oh yeah, Happy Christmas, mate!"

I roll my eyes. I mean, really ... what does she see in this guy? He behaves like an ingenuous arsehole!

"Hey ... guys," Claudia says in an exaggerated fashion. "This is a strange sight to see." Her face clearly is asking, *what the hell?*

"My mom is talking to Becca upstairs," Ray offers. "Merry Christmas, Claud." He gets up and hugs her.

"Merry Christmas, Ray. Grayson." She turns to me and I stand up.

"Happy Christmas, Claudia." I hug her as well.

"Hey, Claudia!" Stacey comes up from behind.

"Ahh ... she lives!" I announce, because Stacey rarely joins the rest of us for anything.

"Hey, Ray!" She smiles at him, ignoring me.

"Fuck off, Stacey!" Ray snaps.

"What's the matter with you?" She sits down.

"Why the hell did you lie to Becca about us? Why don't you call your husband and tell him to take care of his responsibilities instead of wasting everybody's time with your fictional shit?" He's pretty pissed—rightfully so!

"What are you talking about, Ray?" She acts oblivious.

"Give it a rest, Stacey! If you're going to play these kinds of games, you should make sure you're smarter than your opponents, or at least have the proper resources to back up your lies!"

"Was she mad at you?" she asks.

"No! She knew how far along you are! Becca's a very smart woman, but most idiots can do the math!" He sighs with frustration. "What the hell is going on with you, Stace?"

"Yes ... we'd all like to know the answer to that one!" I say. Stacey gets up and heads back to her room without a word.

"Dude ... she is not right in the head at all! Something is off!"

I can hardly believe Ray is talking to me.

"I agree, Ray. We've been trying to figure it out." Well, we've found common ground that doesn't make us want to rip each other's heads off, at least.

"She's been weird ever since she got here a few months ago," Claudia adds. Joshua comes up behind Claudia and smacks her bum, making her jump. "Later, fellas." She waves and heads off with him.

"Looks like you've started an epidemic around here," Ray says.

"Guess so." I half smile.

"Well, I have an idea," Ray announces.

"What's that?" I tread lightly, waiting for a smartass comment.

"Instead of sitting here, staring and wanting to rip each other's heads off, why don't we talk about where you are in the investigation? Becca's safety is our top priority." Ray leans back and takes hold of his leg, placing his right ankle on top of his left knee.

"Well, funny you should say that." I smirk.

"Why?" he asks indifferently.

"You were number one on our list of suspects." There's no point in holding back. Everything will come to a head in the next day or so.

"What?! Why?" He seems shocked.

"Your unit was stationed in the same place, at the same time, as George's." I raise an eyebrow for the *aha* factor.

"We were? I had no idea." His strange expression makes me feel confident he's telling the truth.

"Why did you liquidate all of that money? Where is it now?" I sit back, crossing my legs and arms.

"Dude ... it's under my mattress!" he says—so seriously, we both laugh. I like him. I hate that I like him. He is a good chap. "I pulled out half a million to put into my firm's account. I was going to surprise Becca and start the renovations. She's wanted this for so long. But then, you happened. George happened. I held on to the money because, honestly, I didn't think you would last this long with her because of her memory issues. I wanted to keep the security on to protect her and Morgan. So the money's in a safe place." He's rubbing his face ... frustrated, I'm sure. "So does Becca think I have anything to do with this?" He looks up.

"No. Actually, neither of us thought it was you. Although, for a moment, you were acting a bit crazy. But Becca was pretty confident you would never do anything to hurt her or put her in danger. I agree."

"Oh, you both got the memo on that? That's good!" His sardonic reaction is pretty understandable, actually. I'd be the same way!

"What about Liz? Why did you lie about her?"

I watch as Ray's face goes pale.

"Honestly, I don't know. Does she know?" he asks. He seems a bit panicked.

"Yes. She's the one who had me searching ... when you were acting erratically, of course."

"What did she think? Did she think I hurt Liz?"

"Well, she wasn't sure what to think. Quite frankly, Ray, I shouldn't be speaking for her on this matter. She just doesn't know why you lied, especially for Annie's sake. That's what she was really disappointed about. You have Annie thinking her mother didn't want her, and that doesn't sit well with children," I say calmly.

"Oh, I'm sorry, are you an expert now? Because I'll just push aside what all the other professionals have told me!"

"I'm merely just telling you what bothered Becca, and my own opinion. That's all, Ray." I lean forward on my knees, trying to be a bit more personable. This is a delicate subject.

"That's all, Grayson? You've dug into my personal life and told Becca everything that would make her form a negative opinion against me, and that's all?" he yells. We sit in silence, staring at each other for several minutes. Ray exhales forcefully. "Liz was suffering from post-partum really bad. She was depressed before, but it escalated once she gave birth. She wouldn't take anything for it, because she was unhappy and didn't want any of this. She took off in her car to go stay with a girlfriend for a few days to clear her mind. She never made it. They had to use the Jaws of Life to get her free from the car, and it had been too long. They resuscitated her, but she's been in a vegetative state ever since. I pay for her room and her medical expenses. I will do that for the rest of my life, or hers. As you probably know, I divorced her soon after I met Becca." He reaches for a bowl of cashews and throws a fistful into his mouth.

"Why didn't you divorce her before you met Becca?" I ask. I find it sort of interesting—five years is a long time.

"I wasn't looking. Annie was going to be the only girl in my life. I mean, obviously, I fooled around here and there, but nothing serious. I wasn't serious until I met Becca. My whole world changed then. Grayson, she is the love of my life. I won't ever stop fighting for her." He states this very calmly—I'm guessing to make sure it sinks in.

"I commend you for the past five years, like I said earlier. I don't know if I could've done that, mate." I'm honest. I feel sorry for the poor bloke, to go through all of that for so long just to have some handsome fellow like me come and sweep her off her feet!

"Well, that's the difference between you and me." Ray smirks.

"That and a few gold coins, aye?" I chuckle.

"Becca's not like that. She doesn't care about your money. She's very proud and independent. You have any idea how many arguments we had over repairs here, and me not taking the money? She's not flashy, Gray, and doesn't care to be!

"Contrary to what you believe, Ray, I do know my own fiancée! Why do you think I do everything behind her back? She'd never let me do it otherwise!" Now I'm getting frustrated.

"Yeah, you know her so well you ruined her inn! She loved all of the dark wood! She would've never done this!" he snaps, pointing to all of the newly whitened wood.

"That was a mistake," I grumble.

"One of many!" He smirks.

"What on earth are you talking about?" I ask, and look at my watch. "It's been forty-five minutes!"

"She's with my mama, man. In other words, dude ... you're screwed! You should write a song by that title. It's catchy!" He laughs.

"Well, Ray, I've enjoyed your company long enough." I give him my best *whatever* face.

"Pleasure, as always!" His comment is rich with sarcasm as he grabs the remote and puts the sports channel on. I head off to find my auntie for solace. I am feeling a bit intimidated by Becca's long conference with Ray's mother.

BECCA

Elise climbs in next to me and cradles me in her arms as if she's my mama. She hugs me and kisses my hair as I start to sob.

"There there, baby. You go ahead and have yo'self a good cry. Then we goin' talk this whole mess through, darlin'. I love you, baby ... you go 'head and cry." She rocks me slightly. I inhale the light scent of Design, her signature perfume. Ray and I buy it for her every year.

"Oh, Mama, why aren't you kicking the stuffing out of me right now?" I look up into her beautiful, almost-violet blue eyes.

"Well, you know what I always say, darlin'." She smiles as she thumbs away a tear on my left cheek.

"You get mo' suga wit honey," I say in her accent.

"You and Ray are always teasin' me!" She swats my back gently and giggles. I rest my head back down. She mentioned me and

Ray as a unit. The talk is about to start in five ... four ... three...

"Becca, baby," she starts. Wow, I didn't even get to finish my countdown!

"Yes, Mama?"

"Oh, you butterin' me up already, arenchew?" She laughs and swats me again. She loves when I call her *mama*. I don't do it too much because, well, I guess it sort of cements things for me. I laugh a little as well.

"So now, you goin' tell me why you cryin', baby?" This is Elise's way of talking. She makes you figure out what's going on without hitting you with her opinion first. Interesting concept. I've been meaning to try that out on Morgan for the past five years.

"Elise, I'm heartbroken." It's the truth.

"Because ... ?" she says slowly.

"I'm in love with two men and I want them both." *There, I said it!*

"You can't have that, baby girl ... you can't have both of them."

If she were any other person on the planet, I would unleash my smart mouth and hit her with my sarcastic best! But, alas, she's Elise, and she will whoop my ass without ever laying a single finger on me.

"I know that. My mind knows it. My heart just won't listen." I sigh and lie on my back. "Did Ray tell you about our walk down memory lane yesterday?" I turn my head to look at her. Her skin is a beautiful milky white. She's so calm. How does she always remain so calm?

"Yes, he did. He told me how it affected you ... and him, for that matta. Becca, that boy is so in love with you." Her eyes begin to glisten. Mine follow pathetically.

"It brought up a lot of feelings I really didn't know were there." My nose flares to stop my tears.

"You know, baby, you just couldn't get yo mine to acknowledge what was in yo heart." She squeezes my hand.

"I'm in love with Grayson." Before I can finish my thought, she snorts her opinion of Grayson—probably the politest reaction she can give.

"Everybody is so quick to judge him! Nobody wants to stop and see the kind, loving, gentle, funny person he is! Everyone sees arrogance, overbearingness—"

"He treats you as a prisoner!" she yells. *Oh shit ... Mama doesn't yell.*

"It only looks that way because he's trying to keep me safe! He's very good to me. He's brought me out of my shell."

"Then he beats your shell!" she snaps.

"He does not!" I yell. "Goddamn it! You know, Elise, your son isn't exactly an angel either!" Elise sits up to look at me with shock. I have never talked to her like this before ... ever!

"My son would never do anything to hurt you! He would never do anything to you against yo' will!" She matches my anger.

"Oh yeah, you sure about that, Elise? Seems your Raymond has left out a few details!" I snap, but try to calm down. This isn't going to get us anywhere, and I don't feel right shedding an ugly light on her son.

"What are you referrin' to, darlin'?" She seems to have come to the same conclusion.

"I think he should be the one to tell you. I love you both very much, and I don't ... it's not for me to tell you. I've forgiven him." I sit up and bring my knees into my chest.

"This is a big mess, Becca."She looks down and shakes her head.

"Quite the pickle, aye?" I lay my head on my knees.

"Well, why don't we do this the old-fashioned way and write down what each man brings to the table for ya?" She gets up and looks for a paper and pen.

"Already did that. It's pretty even. They are a lot alike, believe it or not. There are only small differences in them." I lay back, defeated.

"Well, Ray's got five years on this guy. He's been takin' care of you as best as you'd let him. You two are gonna have a baby together ... surely those things raise the bar for Ray." She sits on the bed again, right knee bent so she can face me.

"Elise, I'm having Grayson's baby. I don't know why Ray keeps saying it's his! I'm only eight weeks. I wasn't even here when I got pregnant," I explain, my voice thick with concern. She just shakes her head at me. "I must be in the middle of another dream! Elise, you are a very smart, levelheaded woman. I had an ultrasound two weeks ago that said I was six weeks. I was in California eight weeks ago. There is no possible way I am having Ray's baby!"

"Well, let's agree to disagree," she says, as if we were talking politics. Maybe it's me! Maybe I'm losing my mind!

"Okay." What else can I say here?

"Morgan is very upset about moving away from Annie, Artie, and me."

"Yeah, notice she's not upset about Ray!" I add for spite.

"She was this morning, after he gave her and Annie their matching Christmas gifts." Her eyebrows shoot up. "A DVD of them growin' up togetha, and all of the things we've done. Places we have been. I think Morgan finally realized she already had a completed family." She picks the lint off of her pants.

"Yeah, except Ray never acted like her dad unless he was in front of me." I roll my eyes.

"Really? That's what you think a him?".

"Well, I know it wasn't intentional."

"Becca, I know you been real good to our Annie over the years ... better than her own motha would've eva been. But you dropped her like she was a hot potato when Grayson came along. You didn't call or nuthin'! You know what my Ray still did—still does—every month?" She's pointing her well-manicured finger at me.

"What?" My guilt, I'm sure, is all over my face.

"Depositing money in Morgan's college fund!"

"No, he hasn't. What are you talking about?" I just reviewed the statement the other day.

"Not the one you have for her! The one he opened for her fo' years ago!" she snaps.

"Ray started a college fund for Morgan?" Grayson didn't tell me this.

"Yes! He never tol' you 'bout it cuz' he knew you'd git mad!" She sighs.

"I'm sorry about Annie. I've apologized to her. You have to understand that Ray was acting pretty crazy at that time."

"Well, Becca, who the hell could blame him? You been his girl, his family, fo' five years, and then one day he comes over here to see about renovations and you're introducing him to yo' fiancé!" she yells. I just start crying.

"I didn't know about everything Ray and I had! I can assure you this wouldn't have happened!" I think back to that day when he was handing me the binder, when I apologized and he said he wasn't hurt, but destroyed. My tears begin their rain of sorrow down my face again.

"Becca, what were you just thinkin' 'bout now?" She rubs my forearm.

"That day ... he told me I destroyed him." I sob again.

"You did. I was on the phone with him fo' hours. Becca, if I didn't love you so damn much, I'd ring yo' neck for doing this to my boy!" she says through her teeth.

"Mama, don't say that to her. You know she can't help what happened," Ray says softly. I didn't even hear him come in. My heart is racing. Seeing him at this moment is more than I can bear. Elise gets up and heads toward the door.

"I'm a goin' keep a look out, son." She taps his arm.

"Thanks, Mama." He smiles at her.

There she goes—silver fox—right to the door to watch for Grayson! Christ, these two are quite the pair! Ray sits on the edge of the bed.

"C'mere, baby." He pats his knees.

"No, Ray, I can't." I shake my head, then look over at Elise. *An imaginary boomerang flies out of her eyes, smacks me in the head, and goes back to her.* I climb onto Ray's lap. He grasps my chin between his forefinger and thumb and pulls my face to his.

"Look at those beautiful emeralds staring at me," he says. I lick my lips and bite my bottom one—apparently, my only response to anything. "Mmm ... there it is," he whispers, sending my heart into my throat. His lips softly grasp mine. His tongue beckons for entrance. Mine greets his lovingly as I part my lips. I get lost in the familiarity of his kiss. His hand slowly slides down my neck to the top of my chest and finds its way to my breast. Elise clears her throat in an exaggerated tone and Ray's hand immediately goes back to my neck.

"Ray, stop now." I gently push him away. He lets me climb off of his lap. *What am I doing?* "Um ... none of this is helping me." I pace the floor of mine and Grayson's room.

"We'll go, baby." Ray gets up and walks over to me. "I'm not trying to pressure you, Becca." He chucks my chin so I find his eyes—Hurricane Ray eyes. "I just want you to be aware of your own feelings. You have a habit of pushing yourself to the side. You need to decide what's right for you. Your happiness has always been my top priority. I love you, Becca. I always will." He leans in and lays a soft kiss on my lips. "Merry Christmas, baby," he whispers as he leans his forehead against mine.

"Merry Christmas, Ray." I raise my eyes to look into his again. "I love you." I palm his cheek.

"I know you do, baby. I'm just glad you know now." Just as he leans in again, Elise clears her throat. Ray rolls his eyes, knowing it's Grayson, and pulls me into a fierce hug instead.

"All set then, Mrs. McNeil?" Grayson asks as he opens the door all the way. I lift my head off of Ray's chest to catch Grayson's eyes. He stares at us both intently, then finds my gaze. A sheepish smile forms across his lips and he offers me a curt nod. His behavior is so odd ... can it really all be his mom?

"You not gonna hurt my baby girl for sayin' bye to my son, are you?" Elise asks Grayson, and I feel my heart stop for him.

"No, Mrs. McNeil, I would never hurt Becca." Grayson tries to remain calm.

"That's not what I've heard," she states. *All Sybeccas get their s'mores ready.* That was a lot of fuel ... I feel a fire coming.

"Really? Well, Mrs. McNeil, contrary to popular belief— thanks to your son for that—I do not physically abuse my fiancée!" Forget fire ... a perfect storm is brewing! "Maybe I should bestow the same courtesy upon him and tell the whole world how he date-raped Becca! How many times did you do that, Ray? Twice?" Grayson looks over as if he's asking how many burgers he wants.

"My son would never!" she says, but then looks at me. I look down. "Raymond!"

"Shit," Ray says under his breath.

"You did that to her, son?" She walks over to us. I can see the heartbreak in her eyes. "Becca, is that what he did to you, baby?" Her chin quivers.

"Please, Elise, we already worked through it all," I start.

"Mama." Ray cuts me off. "I was wrong, and I deeply regret it. Please don't ..." He doesn't finish his sentence. I grab her hand and Ray finally releases me.

"I'm ... I'm so sorry, Becca. I didn't raise him to do things like that." Clearly, she's mortified. I feel the need to shoot Grayson a dirty look, but refrain from doing so. I haven't exactly been on my best behavior lately.

"Elise, Ray and I have talked everything out, and I do forgive him."

"Thank you, baby." He drapes his arm around the small of my back and squeezes my hip. "Mama, let's go now. We'll talk about it when we get home." He rubs her upper left arm with his free hand.

She glances at him quickly, then back at me.

"Merry Christmas, baby girl. I love you." She pulls me into a tight hug. Man, what is it with these McNeils and their bear hugs?

"I love you, too." I kiss her cheek. Ray pulls my hair back as if he's going to put it into a ponytail. He lets go, then rubs my back as his mom holds onto me. He's letting me know that he wants another hug. Elise and I finally break free and she heads out. I turn to face the door where Grayson was standing, only to find us alone in the room again. Ray turns when he sees me searching around. He turns back to me with a boyish half grin and aggressively pulls me to him by my hips.

"Ray, please." I take in a sharp breath and continue to look at the door, waiting for Grayson to return.

"Oh, I'd love to please you." Ray chuckles lightly as he kisses down my neck.

"Ray, stop!" I place my hands on his chest to hold him at arm's length. He palms my face and straightens it, forcing me to give him my full attention. His somewhat playful grin from a few moments ago is officially gone.

"I don't want you to leave, baby, but please promise me," he shakes my head a bit for emphasis, "that you won't leave without saying goodbye to me." He's searching my eyes, waiting for my promise. All I can think about is how I don't want to say goodbye. It's a miserable word that I want no part of. How can I say goodbye to him? How am I going to do it?

"I'm leaving in two days." I don't know why I just said that. He winces as if I've verbally slapped him. His hands almost crush my face.

"Why do you like to hurt me?" he asks through his teeth.

"No. No, I didn't mean to, baby, I'm sorry."

He muffles my pleading with a harsh kiss, then pushes me back and walks away.

"Two songs, Becca. 'Hold Me Now' by Thompson Twins and 'Time After Time' by Cyndi Lauper." With that, he and Elise leave—slamming the door behind them. I sit on my bed and stare at the plush gold carpeting. I'm not aware the door has opened again until Grayson is in front of me. I look up and am surprised to feel the gentle caress of his knuckles on my cheek.

"I don't know what to say, Grayson." I shake my head. Why can't I pull it together?

"Don't say anything then, sweetheart. I'm doing my best to get through the next two days. I suggest you do the same. It will get easier in two days. I promise, Becca." He kneels in front of me.

"Have you retired your purple pants?" I try to make light of the situation.

"No, darling, I'm just keeping them in check. I know your heart is in a complicated place right now. I'm trying to put myself in your shoes as best as I can. This is not exactly how I pictured our first Christmas together, but we're together and I'm hoping it stays that way." His eyelids are going at Morse-code speed.

"I don't deserve either one of you." I place my head in my hands and fall to pieces. Seems like that's the only thing I know how to do right anymore.

"Please stop, sweetheart. Let's just take a deep breath and enjoy our family for Christmas. I know it's very different for you this year, but it is for me as well. Please, I beg of you to put your worries aside just for the holiday. Just give me Christmas, Becca, please. I don't want to fight. I don't want to know that you kissed him. I just want to be a completely oblivious, happy idiot and enjoy the next two days together." He takes my hands and thumbs the tops of them, then kisses my forehead. I pull my hands away and wipe my eyes.

"Okay, baby. What would you like to do? I have a few hours

before I have to put the lasagnas in." I grab a few tissues and blow my nose.

"Well, why don't you run along to the bathroom, sweetheart, and wash your face up. Then we'll head downstairs for a surprise." He helps me up.

"A surprise?" I suddenly feel childlike excitement come over me.

"Yes, sweetheart. I'm pretty sure you will love it!" He only offers a small smile, but his eyes dance with joy and excitement.

"Do I need to change?" I ask as I head to the bathroom.

"No, darling, just freshen your face." he says.

I close the door behind me and look in the mirror. Yikes! I do look a mess! I turn on the faucet and splash cold water onto my face, and I feel my skin perk up immediately. I pat my face dry and look back at the mirror. Ray is right—my eyes turn sea green when I cry. Grayson pops his head in after a few minutes.

"Ready?" he asks.

"Yes." I smile and take his hand. He leads me out of the room and downstairs. "What is this?" I smile as we head into the lounge. There is a group of five, three men and two women, all dressed in fancy 1800s garb.

"Have a seat, sweetheart." Grayson smiles as we sit on the empty sofa. Charlie and Hazel are sitting on the other one. Morgan plops onto Gray's lap. I lean up against him, and he puts his arm around my shoulders. "There's hot chocolate there, love, if you'd like some." He points to the coffee table.

"I'm good right now, sweetie. Would you like some?" I smile up at him. He shakes his head. Morgan grabs some and gets re-situated on Gray's lap. He then nods to the performers and they begin singing "Carol of the Bells," my favorite Christmas song, in a cappella. From there, they sing "God Rest Ye Merry Gentlemen," another favorite. They entertain us for the next hour or so. What a great, great surprise. He amazes me. Grayson gets up and brings me with him to thank them.

"Lovely ... absolutely lovely." Grayson shakes the hand of the director. He's almost as tall as Grayson. His round face is covered by a short, well-cared-for beard.

"Thank you so much for coming today—you guys were amazing!" I'm still in awe.

"Oh, thank you, Mrs. James. We were happy to do it," he states cheerfully.

"Do you always perform on Christmas?"

"No, ma'am, but your husband can be very persuasive." He laughs as Grayson hands him a check. He nods and exhales aggressively, his lips forming an "O" as he looks at the check. I find myself wondering how many zeroes were involved in my *husband's* persuasiveness. We bid The Christmas Carolers, which is the actual name of their group, adieu.

"That was wonderful, Gray. Honestly, I don't know how you come up with these things. How did you know I would like something like that?" I hug him.

"I've told you a million times, sweetheart," he says with a sigh, "you are my favorite subject." He palms my face and stares into my eyes. I stand on my tippy-toes and collect his lips with mine. "Can we go upstairs, sweetheart?" he breathes against my lips.

"Abso-bloody-friggin-lutely, baby!" I smile.

"Mom?" Morgan interrupts us.

"Yeah, Morg?" I turn to her.

"Can I use your office computer to watch the DVD Ray made me?" She holds it up.

"Um, yeah, sure. Just don't go into anything else on there, okay?"

"I know, I know! Thanks!" She runs off. My smile fades as I bring my attention back to Grayson ... an irritated Grayson.

"Let's go, baby." I touch his cheek. He grabs my hand and, though I'm willing, drags me up the stairs. He pushes me forward into our room and locks the door after us.

"Undressed and in bed now!" he commands. I stand there, paralyzed by the look on his face, and swallow hard. "Now!" he yells, then adds, in a softer tone, "please." He unbuttons his shirt and walks up to me. "Becca, please do as I say, darling."

I help him out of his shirt. He pulls at my hem.

"Arms up, love," he says. I lift my arms, not taking my eyes off of him for a second. He pulls my shirt off.

"Grayson?" I reach up and touch his cheek. He closes his eyes at my touch. I lean up and graze his lips with mine.

"I'm mad, sweetheart ... I'm frustrated. I feel like the reigns are being pulled out of my hands, even though I'm grasping tightly." He keeps his eyes closed as he divulges his feelings to me.

"You have a right to be mad and frustrated. I'm sorry I'm the reason behind it." I speak as softly and calmly as I can.

"Raymond is the reason behind it, and your feelings for him, of course ... let's not forget about those creeping around," he says with a bit of sarcasm as he walks away from me. "Pants, Becca!" he snaps. I don't know whether to be frightened or a bit turned on. I'm feeling quite the mixture of both, so I pull my pants off dutifully. I walk up behind him and softly kiss across his back as I reach around to work at his belt and jeans. I guide them and his boxer briefs down to the floor.

"Come, baby." I kiss his shoulder.

"Oh, I plan on it, sweetheart!"

He's terse. I don't blame him. He turns, grabs my hand, and pulls me over to the bed. He sits on the edge and hooks his hands under each side of my panties, practically ripping them as he pulls them down. God, he looks so angry. I work at my bra and yelp loudly, grasping his shoulders to brace myself as the sting sets in from the harsh slap on my bum. Just as I recover from that, he does it again--even harder this time. A sob to escapes my throat.

"Sit astride me now, Becca." He pulls at my hips. I take in a shaky breath and climb onto his lap. He greets me harshly, making me cry out. "Quiet!"

"Grayson, please." My voice is barely a whisper. I begin to move at a pace he seems to enjoy and rest my forehead against his. "Grayson, look at me," I beg. Slowly, he opens his eyes. "I love you. Please, Grayson." I press my lips to his, and he cups my face to deepen the kiss.

He turns us around and lowers me to my back, then pulls away from my lips and stares into my eyes as he slowly makes love to me. My hips meet his urgently, then keep their position for a few seconds before he pulls out to thrust back in. This is how he's always made love to me—holding onto the connection, savoring it. It's powerful, it's urgent, it's beautiful, and it's achingly familiar. I arch my neck as I feel myself climb. "Oh, baby ... oh God ... baby, please," I practically cry as I try to encourage a faster pace with my hips.

"Oh ... no, sweetheart. I want you to bathe in ... this." He holds my hip with his left hand, slowing me down and continuing at his own pace. *A very flushed Operatic Sybecca walks into the spotlight, her Viking helmet completely uneven. She's donned in the British flag. Her mouth opens wide. "Ave Maria ... Maria ... Maria ... Maria," she belts loudly through my orgasm, finishing with a never-ending high "C" note. I swear she holds if for five minutes. A tall tenor joins her on stage, singing a note just as long. An ocean wave heavy with white seafoam hits them. It pulls back and they embrace, trying to catch their breath.* Grayson thrusts into me one last time before collapsing on top of me.

"Sweetheart?" he asks, smiling at me. "Were you singing 'Ave Maria' during your climax?" He chuckles a bit.

"Nope, that was Operatic Sybecca," I say, straight-faced. Grayson lets loose a roar of laughter, and I can't help but laugh with him. I'm delighted that he once again seems happy and in good spirits. "Feel better, baby?" I ask, and kiss his sweaty head.

"Mmm." He snuggles into my neck. "I wish we could stay like this forever, Becca. You don't know how much I wish it, sweetheart. If I could go back in time and change one moment in my life, I'd do it in a heartbeat. I would, Becca, I'd change it and everything would be the way it should be. It's terrible how one moment, one decision, alters everything without you even knowing it's a game changer. It isn't fair!" His accent becomes very thick in the midst of his passionate rant, and I'm not sure I know what the hell he's talking about.

"Grayson, what moment? What moment do you want to go back and change?" I palm his face to help me hold his gaze. He goes into Morse code. That's not good.

"Just forget it, sweetheart. I'm blathering on. It's nothing I can change now, and I just need to let it go and not fall back into my selfish ways. My purpose is your happiness. That's all I want for you, love. It's all that matters." His eyelids slow to a passionate pace, accentuating his frown.

"Grayson ... baby, you are all over the place. I'm getting a little confused." An understatement.

"I know, sweetheart. I'm sorry. It will all make sense soon, love ... I promise." He kisses me swiftly and rolls onto his back. *Um ... yeah, should I tell him that only confuses me more?*

"Can I at least ask what flipped your switch before?"

"Why, sweetheart—you managed to flip it back, didn't you?" He leans on his elbow.

"Yeah, but the point is that it got flipped. Why?" He's not slipping out of this one with his usual trick of equivocation!

"This is my time with Morgan! Why did he have to give her a DVD of his memories with her? I'd rather be beaten to a bloody fucking pulp than get a slap in the face like that! I know I said I stowed them away, sweetheart, but I'm sorry, the purple pants are coming out for this one! Those should have been *my* memories with her! She's my daughter!" he yells. I sit up and look at him. I can only imagine how my face is portraying my thoughts, because I am beyond confused at his outburst. "Well, you know what I mean, darling. I feel as if she's really mine. I wish I had all those years with her. I don't know. I'm being a bit oversensitive, I guess. Possibly a bit ridiculous." His eyelids go at warp speed. I feel as if he's backpedaling.

"Grayson, you are behaving rather strangely. Are you feeling okay?" I touch his forehead.

"Sweetheart, honestly, I do believe I have the right to be a bit all over the place!" His frustration is creeping back into his words. I sit up and reach for my shirt.

"What are you doing?" He sits up as well.

"Getting up."

"No! Lay down ... if anything, just to lay here in peace and quiet with me. Away from other people and the possible distractions they offer!"

"This is peace and quiet?" I ask, lifting my hands. He leans over to me. His lips fall to my right shoulder and slowly caress it with kisses.

"Well, I'd love another piece ... and, by all means ... no need to be quiet about it." He smiles against my skin as his hands creep up to cup my breast.

"Stop it!" I push his hands away. "I don't want to!"

"Oh, I believe you do ... you are a very obsequious wife. I appreciate that about you very much, you know." He grabs my wrists as he straddles me.

"Get off!"

"Nuh-uh," he says with a wicked grin. His beautiful naked body is such a distraction from my anger.

"I want you and your swinging meat out of my face!" I yell. This only provokes a laugh from him. I would join in, but I'm too damn mad. *Swinging meat? Really, Becca?*

"Oh, darling, as I recall, you love the look of my swinging

meat—as well as the taste. Which reminds me," he steadies my arms, "it's been a while since I've had the pleasure of experiencing one of your fantastic blow jobs. Darling, why don't you give it a go for me?" I can see he's having a difficult time stifling his amusement.

"You're a tall, flexible man ... suck your own dick!" I snap.

"If I was confident I could do it as well as you, sweetheart, it might be a thought to ponder on. But, alas, I lack the confidence in your area of expertise!" His grin becomes smugger. He leans forward, trying to grasp my lips with his, but I pull back. "Oh, Becca, you know how I love the chase." He tugs me forward and kisses my neck aggressively. "The catch." Another kiss. "The conquering." He fists my hair and presses his mouth to mine. I try to pull away again. He tightens his grip on me.

"Let go!" I yell.

"Ooh, you are really getting mad, sweetheart." He smiles, then bites his bottom lip. "Do you even know why?" He raises his eyebrows.

"Yes! Because you're being an arrogant asshole!" I say through my teeth.

"Mmm." He kisses me. "I absolutely love when you get like this, sweetheart. It makes you insatiable in bed ... love it!" He pushes me down. He seems so massive as he climbs on top of me.

"Grayson, please get off of me. You've got me so aggravated." I struggle against his arms.

"Mmm ... baby." He kisses across the top of my chest. "Have you not heard. A single. Word. I've. Said?" He brings his mouth up to mine and teases me by attempting to kiss me, then jerking away as I reach my mouth for his. *I hate when he does this ... it drives me crazy!* My breathing is erratic and I can hear my blood pumping loudly in my ears. He leans in to kiss me again, but quickly shifts his head and playfully bites at my chin. I feel him growing against me and, as usual, my perfidious hips jump into action. "Eager, Mrs.

James?" he asks seductively in my ear before he bites at my earlobe, reluctantly releasing it after a long suck.

"Grayson—goddamn it—let go of my arms!" I try to pull them free.

"Do you want me, sweetheart?" He rubs his nose across mine. "Hmm?" he hums near my ear as he grinds against me.

"Grayson ... please." I close my eyes.

"What, sweetheart? Tell me, love. Tell me you want me. Tell me you need me." He stares down into my eyes.

"You know I do," I barely whisper.

"What's that, Becca?" he asks as he teases me with another purposefully failed attempt at kissing me. *How is it possible to be so turned on and so pissed off all at the same time?*

"Damn it!" I breathe, frustrated. "I want you, baby." White flag flying at full mast. A satisfied smirk blankets Grayson's face.

"Now—in order—to give—you what—you want, darling," he says softly between kisses across my jawline and down my neck, "I have to—release—your arms. Do you—promise—to be a good—girl, sweetheart?" He brings his face back to mine and nudges my nose before he finally collects my lips. "Promise?"

"Yes." I lean up to kiss him again. This time, there's no teasing involved. He releases my left arm and I immediately fist his hair as we deepen the kiss. "Ahh!" I gasp as he plunges inside of me. His thrusts become powerful and urgent. My hips meet them with the same intensity.

"Becca, I can't get close enough." He releases my arm and dives his own beneath me, grasping my shoulder. His right hand squeezes my left hip as he pulls it harshly to him. I gasp at the fullness of it all.

"Grayson ... please." I bite at his shoulder. I'm not exactly sure what I'm begging him for. I just know how much his intensity overwhelms me. His mouth finds mine again, and I am devoured. After several minutes, I can feel myself begin to climb.

"That's it, sweetheart ... pray for me!" His command sends me over the edge as I come undone.

"Oh God, baby!" I cry as my hands grasp harshly at his back. Grayson's face scrunches up as he groans my name. His hips slow down as he spills himself inside of me. He crashes down on top me and we pant in silence for a minute or two.

Grayson lifts his head and stares into my eyes.

"Do you have any idea how truly amazing we are together? I'm not just talking sex, Becca. We're bloody amazing in every way!" He says this with such passion I can't help but smile. I close my eyes and let a slew of amazing non-sex memories hit me. We're in a bookstore. I don't remember what we were saying, but I sense the mixture of intrigue and irritation. Dancing in the aisle at the grocery store. Sitting on his lap in front of the computer, laughing. Him chasing me in the backyard at the California ranch with a can of whipped cream. Horseback riding down the beach, with him sitting behind me. I'm leaning back ... we're laughing at something. He's in front of me, down on his knee—there's foliage all around us. Where were we? When was this?

"Becca ... wake up, sweetheart." Grayson shakes me.

"I'm not asleep." I open my eyes.

"Good. Well, let us have a shower, then, before we head downstairs." He climbs off and pulls me with him.

"Gray?" I look at him. I'm a bit confused.

"Yes, darling?"

"Have I forgotten any of my memories with you at all?" I wince.

"No, sweetheart, why?" He pulls me along toward the bathroom.

"Well, I just had a flash of memories about things I don't remember us doing."

"Becca, you fell asleep. You must've dreamt it, or you're psychic and saw memories that are yet to be!" His eyes widen with amusement.

"Shut up!" I smack him playfully as we walk into the shower.

Chapter Seventeen

"Is it safe to come in?" Hazel asks as I start putting the lasagnas in the oven.

"Yes." I turn around, sighing. "I'm sorry, Hazel. I'm very hormonal lately." I walk up and hug her. "Can you forgive me?"

"Of course, Becca. I know where it's coming from, dear. Here we were, thinking we were helping you, and none of us considered that you enjoy your holiday traditions." She holds her hands out for emphasis.

"It's that, along with a few other things," I say with a sigh. "It wasn't right for me to take it out on you, though. I am really sorry."

"Well, it's all over now. Let's drop it." She pats my arm and heads over to check on the sauce.

"So, why are you guys not with Charlie's family for Christmas?" I continue, putting the other trays of lasagna in.

"Security. Grayson wanted us here." She shrugs.

"Sorry," I offer.

"Stop, it's okay." She smiles.

"Grayson's been a little funny the past couple of days—a bit off, really." I wipe my hands on a dish towel after placing the last tray in.

"Quite a bit of that going around, aye?" Her arched brow tells me I may be placing high on her shit list.

"What do you mean?" Maybe I'm overreacting.

"Your behavior with Ray. You know, you *are* engaged to my nephew." She's flat. I'm definitely not overreacting. Not only am I high on her list, but I fear my name may be highlighted as well.

"I know who I'm engaged to," I say under my breath.

"Oh ... well, maybe things have changed since my day. Used to be when you were engaged to one man, you wouldn't have your tongue down another man's throat!"

"Hazel!" I gasp.

"Don't 'Hazel' me! I have to tell you, Becca, I've about had enough of you hurting Grayson!" She slams the lid back down onto the sauce.

"I'm not trying to hurt him. I love him, Hazel."

"Could've fooled me!" she yells, then storms out of the kitchen, leaving me and my guilty conscience to myself. Yep, I should've stayed in bed today! I set the timer and head out to the lounge. I find Grayson and Morgan laughing on the couch.

"What's so funny, guys?" I smile at them.

"Oh, nothing, Becca." Grayson clears his throat.

"Daddy, c'mon. It's Becs ... baby." Morgan imitates Ray.

"Morgan!" I smack the back of the couch near their heads. "Ray put so much time and thought into your Christmas gift to show you how much he cares about you, and you're making fun of him?" I yell.

"Whoa, Becca, calm down!" Grayson raises his voice to me.

"No! She's been nothing but completely disrespectful toward him!" I have to defend my reaction. "He's only tried to help me take care of her for the past five years! He's been good to you, Morgan!" I am definitely flirting with overreaction now. I can't even stop myself. "Considering all of the shit I've put him through, he's been an awesome dad to you!"

"*That's enough!*" Grayson stands up and yells in my face. "You are overreacting, Becca!"

He's so right.

"Morgan." I look over at her. She's crying. "Excuse me," I say to Grayson so he'll move out of my way. I walk up to her and hug her. "I'm sorry, sweetie. I'm a little nutsy today."

"Mom, I was just joking with Daddy. I wasn't ... I love Ray, Mom. I know he tries. I love the gift he gave me. I know he worked hard on it."

Sometimes I feel like she is fifteen instead of almost eleven.

"I know, Morgy. I am sorry. I'm not myself today." I kiss her face and hold her against me. *I'm sorry,* I mouth to Grayson. He shakes his head and looks away, then grabs his coat and heads outside. "Excuse me, Morgan. I need to talk to Daddy." I rub her arms before I fetch my coat as well. The cold air hits my face as I walk out. It's refreshing and brisk. Snow is lightly dusting the ground.

"We're supposed to get six to eight inches tonight," Grayson says, his back turned to me. I walk up to him, wrap my arms around his waist, and hug him from behind.

"I feel as if our roles have been reversed." I lean my forehead against his back.

"What do you mean, sweetheart?" He's barely audible.

"It used to be you saying *I'm sorry* all the time. It's a terrible feeling to always be apologizing." I turn him to me. "What can I do? What can I say besides those two words that are becoming quite irritating to hear?" I play with the stubble on his chin.

"Becca, I told you what I need. I haven't gotten it yet." I can feel his frustration.

"I'm trying." I play with the buttons on his coat. He grabs my hands to stop them.

"It's simple, Becca. Full focus on me! No mention of Ray! No thoughts of Ray! I'm asking now the same thing I've been asking for two days. So far, you have failed to deliver! Do you think you can manage the rest of the day and tomorrow? I am trying so hard to be patient with you, and you are not making it very easy." His eyes are closed as if he's trying to muster the strength not to blow up at me.

"You're doing a great job," I offer, instead of apologizing.

"Becca, damn it!" He throws my hands down.

"Okay, okay! I'm not doing this on purpose!"

Grayson palms my face.

"I love you, Becca. I love you with every fiber of my being. This is killing me, sweetheart. Please! One day of just our family ... that's all I want." His lips softly caress mine. I lean up on my toes and allow him to deepen the kiss.

"Hey, let's grab Morgan and take a walk in the snow." I smile up at him.

"Now ... that ... sounds like a lovely idea." He offers me a few more pecks.

We head inside to grab Morgan and our boots. With Morgan's hands in each of ours, we take off to the left past the stables and barn.

"Hey, baby, where's the detail?" I look around. Nobody is with us.

"We're fine, love. They're watching." He smiles down at Morgan as he swings her arm with a bit of exaggeration.

"Where? I don't see them." I look around harder.

"Becca, we're safe! Stay focused." From the look on his face, I decide it's best not to push it. It's so pretty and peaceful out here.

"Look at the trees, Gray. They're like a painting." I point at the limbs, heavy with snow. It is quite the sight. My admiration of God's beauty is short-lived, though, as a snowball lightly explodes against my cheek. My jaw drops, and I hear Grayson and Morgan having a good laugh at me. "Oh ... it is so on!" I announce, and wipe off my face before I squat down to retrieve some snow. A full-blown snowball fight ensues. The three of us run around chasing each other, laughing and carrying on. I stop and have a "smell the roses" moment as we collapse to the ground. They start making snow angels. I take my phone out and snap a few pictures before I join them. Grayson reaches above Morgan's head. My hand meets his and our frozen fingers lace together.

"There's my girl." He smiles at me, a full-wattage Grayson James smile. My heart leaps as I commit his smile to memory. It's one of those moments that bring tears to your eyes. Maybe it's because you are aware of the sweet memory you are making—who knows?

"Sir." Derek clears his throat.

"Yes, Derek?" Grayson leans up on his elbows.

"Your aunt wanted me to tell Mrs. James that her timer went off."

"Shit!" I jump up. "Thanks, Derek!" I pat his arm and run toward the house.

"You're welcome, Mrs. James!"

"Becca! Careful, darling—don't fall!" Grayson calls after me. Of course, I slip at that moment, but catch myself and chuckle as Grayson yells obscenities behind me.

I go in through the store and strip off my scarf, coat, and boots. I give myself one final shake to release any snow that may have ended up in an unusual place. I run into the kitchen to find Hazel already pulling trays out. I grab serving bowls and spoons for the sauce, sausage, and meatballs.

"I already cut the bread into halves. We just need to put the garlic butter on and get them in the oven." She points to the bread. *Guess I'll do that ... since she's pointing and all!*

"Can I help with anything?" Stacey pipes up. I turn and take in the sight of her. She's looking well ... more like herself.

"Do you want to help me with the bread?" I pull out the garlic butter.

"Sure, Becs." She pulls up a stool to sit at the island, then grabs the tub of garlic butter out of my hands and pulls the plastic seal off. I offer her a butter knife.

"Thanks." She takes it, then reaches out and squeezes my hand quickly. "Merry Christmas, Becca. I'm sorry." Her eyes fill up. I cover her hand with mine.

"Merry Christmas." I squeeze her hand back. We finish up, and I have Melissa call everyone to dinner.

The dining room is buzzing with thirty-two people. From the looks of it, everyone is enjoying themselves and the meal.

"People watching, sweetheart?" Grayson asks, and nudges me. I smile up at him. He knows that I do this quite often to take everything in. I look back down at my plate and fight the urge to think about the McNeils, what they're up to, and how Ray is handling our first Christmas apart. Usually when something is bothering him, he's pretty quiet at mealtime—either rushing or barely focusing. He'll smile through small talk, but mostly he'll stare at his glass of whatever he's drinking.

"Mom!" Morgan yells, snapping me out of my thoughts.

"What? Sorry." I shake my head.

"Where were you?" she asks.

"I know exactly where she was." Grayson's nose is flaring. I place my hand on his leg to say sorry, but he grabs it and whips it off.

"I was saying we should call Susanna and Sam after dinner, Mom."

"Yes, absolutely!" I agree cheerfully.

"Becca, everything tastes incredible." Stacey sits down with her second helping.

"Thanks! I agree. It's been a while since I've had something incredible in my mouth." I say, keeping my face straight and nudging Grayson.

"Shut up!" He tries to be stern, but a smile breaks through the barrier. He finds my knee and squeezes gently. I lean my head on his shoulder.

"I can't wait to give you your gifts tonight." I pat the top of his hand.

"Yes, I can't wait either." He kisses my forehead.

Cleaning up would be more of a breeze if there weren't thirty people trying to help me!

"Less is more, people!" I announce. "I appreciate all the help, but it may go smoother if we split into two teams! Half of you help with dinner, and the other half can do dessert. That way, we're not all on top of each other," I say. Everyone makes a quick decision and half of the room retires elsewhere, while the rest of us clean up and get ready for dessert.

"Becca, it's for you." Claudia hands me the phone. It must be my aunt and uncle. Shit, I usually call them in the morning.

"Merry Christmas!" I answer.

"How was dinner, baby?" It's Ray. *Shit!*

"I ... I can't really talk right now." I look around, searching for Grayson.

"Becs, baby, please ... I can't do this. This is too hard."

I can hear the pain in his voice.

"I'll see you before I leave." I try to keep calm.

"I won't let you leave!" he snaps. Grayson pulls the phone away from me.

"Goodbye, Raymond!" he yells, and hangs up.

"Grayson, I didn't know it was him." I grab his arms.

"I know. Just ... forget it." He throws the phone onto the counter. "Come now, we're all getting cozy for a movie." He takes my hands.

"What movie?" I walk with him and ignore the ringing phone.

"*White Christmas*, I believe."

"Oh, Stacey must've picked it. That's her favorite." We head to the lounge. Stacey saved two seats next to her on the couch.

"Hey," she says, and leans over to whisper in my ear. "Ray is blowing up my phone. What do you want me to do?" At that moment, I realize my best friend is truly back.

"Tell him I said to *bugger off*!" Grayson says angrily.

"What do you have—bionic ears?" Stacey asks him.

"Yeah, something like that." He sighs and puts his arm around me. I shrug my shoulders at her and she begins to text Ray. She shows Grayson, then turns her phone off and puts it aside when he nods. I guess she's back on Team Grayson. Or, maybe she's just back on Team Becca, the only team she should be on. We all sit back and watch the movie. Of course, Stacey and I lip-synch the words to "Sisters." We haven't done that in a long time!

Before we know it, Bing Crosby is singing "White Christmas." I get up and go to the kitchen to turn the coffee on and get the cold stuff out of the fridge. Grayson walks in a few minutes later and scans the room.

"What's the matter?" I ask.

"Nothing," he murmurs, giving me a half smile. I continue to look at him curiously. "What can I help you with, love?" He stands over the desserts, waiting for my orders.

"Um, take that tray and set it out on the buffet. I'll grab this one." I load it into his arms and grab the other. We head out to the dining room and the "Dessert Crew" jump into action. I'm actually glad there are so many people here, or I would be getting ridiculous with all this dessert!

It's seven o'clock and I'm ready to go into a food coma. Ray and I usually nap between dinner and dessert. Not on purpose, but we always fall asleep on the couch. That didn't happen this year. No Ray ... no nap.

"Tired, sweetheart?" Gray wraps his arms around me from behind. I yawn and nod at the same time. "Aunt Hazel, will you make sure Morgan gets into bed? We're going to retire early."

"I'll take care of her," Stacey offers.

"Thanks, Stace." I hug her before I give Morgan a kiss. We say good night to everyone else and head toward the stairs. Grayson hooks my arm around his neck and picks me up to carry me up them. "Gray." I laugh. "Put me down."

"Nope, I intend on pampering you tonight, sweetheart." He kisses my lips and carries on.

"Well, you won't be able to do this much longer." I smirk and pat my belly.

"I know." He sighs with a hint of sadness.

"What is it, baby?" I touch his cheek.

"Nothing, Becca." He puts me down and launches into his usual grumbles over having to always unlock our bedroom door. We should be in a normal house, not living at the inn.

"Two more days, baby, and we'll be back at the ranch. You won't have to unlock our bedroom door—unless you piss me off, of course." I rub his back and pat at it as he walks in.

"Bath, darling?" He turns to me and closes the door behind us.

"Nah, not tonight." I shake my head.

"Well then, let's get comfy and open gifts, shall we?" He clasps his hands together.

"Sounds like a plan." I go to my PJ drawer.

"Uh, I'll pick it out, thank you very much." He pushes me to the side gently.

"I thought you said *comfy*." I bite my smile back.

"Yes, not *frumpy*, dear." He opens the drawer. I shrug and go to retrieve his special, just-between-us Christmas Eve gifts. When I look back, I notice he's picked a camisole and shorts for me.

"Gray, those are for summer."

"Honestly, sweetheart, within an hour ... you'll be in far less than this." He tugs at the hem of my shirt. I lay his gifts on the bed and raise my arms so he can pull my shirt up and over my head. He slides his hands down my shoulders to my upper chest, then covers my breasts before reaching around back to unhook my bra. "I think you'll be quite warm in this for now, seeing as you're already getting overheated." A slow, sexy smirk crosses his lips and I take notice of my erratic breathing. *Damn it!* He tosses my bra to the side. With his fingers, he traces the area just above the waist of my jeans. I close my eyes, intoxicated by his touch. I feel the tug of my button and hear him undoing my zipper. I open my eyes to find him kneeling in front of me. His hands hook under my jeans and panties and he slides them down. I hold onto his shoulders to brace myself as I step out of them.

"You are so very lovely, sweetheart." He sits back on his heels to admire me, then leans forward again to caress my growing belly with his lips.

"Did you just make yourself sound extra British?" I giggle.

"I'm pulling out all of the stops tonight, darling." He chuckles at himself as well. "Come now. Let's get you dressed so I can do this again in a bit." He holds out my shorts. I step in and match his smile as he pulls them up. He stands and grabs my camisole. I lift my arms, and he slides it on. "There you are, baby." He chucks my chin and plants a swift kiss on my lips.

"Your turn." I grab his shirt and pull it over his head. I run my hands up his chest as I leave a trail of kisses along his sternum. I trace the outline of his abdominal muscles with my index finger and rest my other hand on his belt buckle. "Hmm ... feeling overheated, baby?" I tease as his breathing also shifts.

"Always, sweetheart, whenever you're around me." He palms my cheek, his thumbs caressing it as he pulls my face to his. "Becca," he whispers before his lips find mine.

"Patience, Mr. James." I pull back and unhook his belt. He tries to steady his breathing. After I work at his zipper, I guide his jeans down at the same pace that he guided mine. "Hmm." I graze my knuckles over the bulging area of his boxer briefs. "I think something incredible may be happening here, Mr. James."

"Becca, sweetheart, I think I should finish here or we will never get to other things." He moves my hand away. I plop onto the bed and watch him, delighted with myself and the effect I have on him, as he walks over to his drawer and grabs PJ bottoms. "Now," he practically jumps onto the bed, "who shall go first?" He looks at the gifts eagerly. He couldn't hide his curiosity and excitement if he tried!

"Um, well, this has to be last." I hold up the small box.

"Hmm, great things come in small packages." He tries to grab it, but I'm prepared and am much quicker.

"No, no ... be patient!" I wave my finger at him and place the package behind my back.

"All right, which can I have first, then?" He holds up the two other packages.

"Open that one." I smile. He puts the wrapped album down and begins to unwrap the clothing box.

"This better not be a tie, sweetheart," he teases. He yanks the top off, digs beneath the tissue paper, and goes into hysterics. "You're bloody fucking mad!" He laughs as he pulls his torn purple pants out of the box. He stands up and holds them to himself. "Did they come like this, or did you do it?"

I roll my eyes in response.

"Who the fuck would buy those like that ... on purpose?"

"Sweetheart, who the fuck would buy purple pants on purpose at all?"

We are both in stitches. He pulls his PJs off and slips into the purple jeans.

"Oh God!" I laugh and get up to run to the bathroom—surely I would almost be pissing my pants even if I wasn't pregnant!

"How did you get these?" he yells.

"Melissa picked them up for me," I say as I come out of the bathroom. "And then proceeded to tell me we were fucking weird when I started cutting them." I finally get my giggle under control.

"Well, I don't know how you are going to top this, you clever, funny girl." He kisses my forehead aggressively.

"You keeping those on?" I ask, my stupid grin still intact.

"Yes, of course, darling! Let's see what's next!" He claps his hands and rubs them in anticipation. I can't contain my mirthful smile as I hand him the wrapped album. I sit next to him as he unwraps it. "An album," he announces, as if I didn't know. It's made from thick, professional-quality black leather. He opens it and roars again with laughter.

The first 8" x 10" is of me in a short, tightly curled, red-headed wig. I'm wearing a blue tracksuit and tan orthopedic shoes, and holding rounded glasses to the side with the chain in my mouth. Grayson is crying, he's laughing so hard.

He turns the page and "Shelley" is on a mechanical bull, making an exaggerated "O" face with one arm in the air. In the picture on the opposite side, "Shelley" is walking with her legs far apart, a look of pain on her face. Grayson's laughter has shifted to a girlish giggle. He wipes his eyes and turns the page. He leaves the book on his lap and falls back in hysterics.

"Oh, Becca, I can't take anymore!" he practically cries. He sits back up, rubbing his face with his hands. "Sweetheart, you are truly amazing." He kisses me dramatically, then looks back at the page and begins laughing again.

The new shot is of "Shelley" with a partially unzipped track jacket. She pushes her liver-spotted titties up (it's makeup, of course). She's winking and her tongue is flipped out, touching her top lip seductively. In the opposite picture, "Shelley" has her leg up on her walker with her pant leg raised enough to show off her TED stocking as she blows a kiss.

He turns the page. "Shelley" is in a muumuu, pulling the elastic neckline down and making an "oops" face. Next, she's lying on her side on a shag carpet in her housecoat. She pets the shag carpet with an eyebrow arched suggestively. He turns to the last page to find "Shelley" on her knees, her face exaggerated to look like she's climaxing and chained glasses bouncing against her liver-spotted titties. Grayson is holding his stomach.

"Christ, Becca ... you have me laughing like a little girl!" He nudges me.

"In purple pants, no less." My eyebrows dart up as I check him out.

"You are, without a doubt, fucking crazy, sweetheart!" He pulls my face to his. "Who did this with you? Where? When? How did I not know?" He pulls away.

"Claudia, the hall, a week ago, and I'm awesome." I laugh.

"You are, sweetheart, you really are," he says with wonder, and kisses me again.

"It's good to see you laugh, baby." I pat his cheek before grasping his chin and kissing him again.

"You're the only person who's ever had the ability to make me laugh like that. I never knew what true happiness was until I met you, Becca." He holds my hand and pulls it to his lips, laying kiss after kiss on my knuckles. I find myself overwhelmed by his words with no great, joking comeback. I decide instead to kiss him once ... twice ... mmm. Grayson gently pushes me onto my back. "I have something incredible to give you, sweetheart ... and the pants to back up that statement." He chuckles lightly against my lips.

"Oh, well, I think you might need the last personal gift to help you with that." I reach over to the little box and stare into his eyes, feeling anxious about his reaction, about the gift.

"Becca, I have something personal for you, too, which I worked really hard on. I'd rather give it to you the day after Christmas, though, if you don't mind." He seems unsure of how I might feel.

"Okay." I don't mind, really. I'm more focused on what I'm about to give him.

"Do you want me to open this?" He sits up, allowing me to do the same.

"Um ... yes." My voice shakes.

GRAYSON

Why is she so nervous about this gift? Christ, I feel my anxiety level rising just looking at her. I turn my focus to the small, square, jewelry-sized box. I unwrap it and pull the lid off. I can't help but take in a sharp breath.

"I asked the doctor. She said it was okay," she offers—barely audible—when I look at her, my eyes wide. I focus back on the box, not believing my eyes. I've wanted this. I've sort of nagged about it, even though I know what George did to her. I swallow hard and take the condom and K-Y Jelly out of the box.

"Becca ... sweetheart, you don't have to do this." I look at her again. She seems so shy and embarrassed all of a sudden. Her reaction to me opening this gift somehow makes her look even sweeter. "I know I've baited you on this subject, love, but I don't need you to do this."

"I want to, Grayson. I want to give you all of me." She looks up into my eyes, her face bright red. We sit in silence for a few moments before she starts giggling again.

"What?" I smile, giving her a strange look.

"Um ... of all of the times I pictured you opening this gift, your reaction, and what I would say, I never once imagined you in purple pants." She laughs. I join her. I do look pretty silly for a moment such as this.

"Becca." I get serious again. "We'll go slow. If you change your mind or want me to stop, I will. I know what he did to you. I don't want you to suffer through any flashbacks." I run my index finger up and down the arm she's leaning on.

"Okay, but I'm pretty confident it will not be the same." She moves closer to me and leans up for a kiss.

"Sweetheart, you're trembling." I squeeze her hip.

"Sorry." She takes in a deep breath.

"Becca, relax, darling. I want to make love to you first ... the usual way."

She closes her eyes and exhales. I lightly rub my lips against hers. She pulls back slightly, then rushes forward, allowing me to deepen the kiss with the slip of my tongue. I quickly tug her shirt off, then return to her mouth. I feel her work at the button of my new pants. I help her pull them off of me. Her shorts follow as well. My mouth goes on a tour of her body, savoring every inch of skin it covers.

"Gray." She gasps as I bite down on her nipple. I work my way down to her stomach and my tongue dives into her navel. I work her slowly, and her hips go into a frenzy. I still can't believe I can make her come this way! "Gray ... oh God, baby." She fists my hair as she climaxes.

"I do love the way you buck, Becca." I look at her as she finishes her last quake.

"Shut up!" She laughs and slaps my shoulder playfully, then gasps as I bite at the apex of her groin. I kiss her pencil dot of a beauty mark, and she stills. Hmm, maybe that affects her the same way it does me when she kisses the one under my eye. I kiss her there again. She sits up and pushes me to my back. Her mouth attacks mine with a sense of urgency. I grasp her hips as she climbs on top of me. Her lips travel across my jawline to my earlobe.

"Lay back and close your eyes, baby. Relax. I'm going to take my time tasting you," she says softly in my ear before she pulls my earlobe into her mouth. She takes my hands from her hips and places them on either side of my head. "Eyes closed, Grayson," she commands again. I close them and try to wipe the smirk off of my face. Her lips travel down my neck and across my chest. She pauses on her journey to pay extra attention to my nipples, kneading them between her teeth. I feel an overwhelming electric current to my groin. I can no longer control my breathing. My hands dive into her hair.

"You're not following directions." She places my arms back up by my head. "What shall I do about that?" Christ, she's driving me mad. "Be a good boy." She pecks my lips before she continues where she left off. My abs tighten as she traces them with her tongue. I fist my hair as her tongue dives into my navel. Every muscle in my body twitches with anticipation as she travels down my happy trail. She bites playfully at my V-line. Her nails lightly tickle my inner thighs as she runs them up and down, then she grasps my hips and holds them still.

"Keep your eyes closed," she warns.

"Yes, sweetheart." I breathe and feel her weight leave the bed. "Where are you going?"

"Shh." She climbs back on after a moment. "Eyes closed!" she snaps when I lift my head to look.

"Ugh." I lay my head back down. I feel her tongue circling the tip of my penis. "Ahh ..." I gasp as she blows on it. It's tingling and cool. She cups my balls and gently pulls them back away from my shaft. "Becca!" I'm panting now. She takes me into her mouth and sucks purposefully before she lets it slide out. She blows on it again. The tingling and coolness is more intense. She playfully bites down my length before she takes me in again. Her sucking becomes so intense I feel as if I'm going to lose my mind. And that tingling ... what is that from? "Becca ... please ... please, sweetheart," I beg breathlessly as she continues to tease and please me unmercifully.

"C'mon, baby ... I want to taste you." Her words, barely a whisper, are my undoing. "Mmm," she moans as I slowly spill into her mouth.

"Oh God, Becca!" I groan and feel my toes curl as my orgasm climbs powerfully up to the pit of my stomach. "Ugh!" I groan harshly one last time and pound my fist into the bed. I try to steady my breathing as Becca soothes me softly and slowly with her mouth. There's something so delicious about what she's doing. It's comforting enough to put my whole body at ease. She blows on me one more time, sending a chill throughout my whole body. I open my eyes as she climbs up to greet me.

"Hi." She bites back her sheepish smile.

"You look like an angel, but you are quite the devil, aren't you, sweetheart?" I touch her face, tracing her cheekbone. She turns into my palm, kissing then biting at the center. I pull her face to mine and attack her lips urgently. I'm aching terribly for her, so I smack her bum. She can take on some of that ache.

"Again, baby, please." Her request is barely audible. I spank her again and watch her face as she takes in the sting. God, she's so bloody fucking hot! "Grayson, you've got me in quite a state. What are you going to do about it?" she asks as she plays softly with my bottom lip. I squint, trying to figure her out. She rolls her eyes and shakes her head as she leads my hand down her body. A lightbulb shines brightly through the fog of her domineering theatrics. I no longer require her guidance.

"Jesus, sweetheart, I don't believe we'll need the K-Y." I smile against her lips.

"Uh, nope." She nudges my nose with hers. I quickly roll her onto her back and wait for her to finish giggling from my unexpected move. Finally, I have the audience of her beautiful green eyes.

"Becca." I stare into them.

"Grayson." Her smile reaches every part of her face.

"You are the greatest love of my life." Her smile fades, I imagine because my words overwhelm her. "Our love is the kind of love that is felt forever, no matter what happens. We will always be in each other's hearts. It's pure, it's unconditional, it's real, and nothing will ever take away from the memory of it or its value." Her eyes fill up and a slight look of confusion comes over her face. *Shit, Grayson—put your filter back in place!* I distract her thoughts with my lips.

"Grayson." She pulls away. "I am leaving with you. I am marrying you. I promise, baby. I'm coming with you." She grabs my face for emphasis. I offer her nothing but a mischievous grin.

"Well, let's see about that," I say before I quickly enter her.

"Gray!" She takes in a sharp breath.

"Shh ... no more talking." I'm relieved as her "we need to talk" face dissipates and her hips join mine in their familiar groove.

"You feel so good, baby," she says, the words almost a whimper as my thrusts become more powerful. I pull back and plunge into her again, holding it for a few seconds to allow her to feel my fullness. I pull her hips up to me and grind my way higher until she can't take anymore. I pull back and slowly fill her again. This is a love/hate situation for her—I know it drives her mad. And I do love to drive her mad ... sexually, of course. Her pleas ignite my fire more. Mmm ... here she goes. Her neck arches.

"Oh God, baby ... oh God." Becca praying in bed—still the best sound in the world. I'm distracted as she squeezes around me. Christ, she's a champ at Kegels! I feel the rush coming on and I quicken until the tingling pressure builds up in my shaft. I slow my pace, savoring the sensation as I erupt inside of her with such aching pleasure. I love when we come together. I rest my forehead up against hers as we both try to collect our wits and steady our breathing.

"I'm sorry, sweetheart." I take in a deep breath. My fingers trail down to her right breast and circle her nipple.

"For what?"

"You're going to be extremely exhausted tomorrow. I'm so starved for you—I don't believe I'll be able to stop tonight."

"Well, I'm good for one more, then it's lights out for me, baby. I'm so tired I could probably sleep right through it if you need to have another go after." She tosses her arm across her forehead.

"How rude!" I say, shocked. "Surely you would awaken if I took you after you fell asleep—you have before."

"Of course, don't worry your precious little ego. I'm just merely giving you an idea of how tired I am." She leans up on her elbows and studies me.

"What?" I rest my chin on her chest and look up at her.

"Nothing ... I don't know." She shakes her head.

"You must know what you are thinking, Becca. Please tell me." I lift my head up so our eyes lock.

"I'm just always trying to figure you out. Am I ever going to, or will I always be trying?"

"Sweetheart, you've had my number since the moment we met, don't underestimate yourself." I tap her nose.

"Hmm." She sighs and looks away.

"You think too much, darling." I turn her face back.

"I've been accused of worse." She smiles and plays with my hair. Immediately my heart sinks. I've called her much worse to her face, over and over again. "Gray ... ?" She pulls my chin. I see the lightbulb going on. "I meant that figuratively, not literally, baby."

"I know, but I've still been a complete arse to you at times." I sit up.

"Hey, hey." She pulls my arm, turning me to her. "I'm not exactly blame-free," she offers.

"There's no excuse for my behavior, Becca! I should've never treated you like that, or said those things to you!" I'm absolutely disgusted with myself.

"Well, you know," she quirks her mouth into a side smirk, "if the purple pants fit." She shrugs, and I can't help but laugh.

"Speaking of incredible ... " I pull her forward for a kiss.

"Ready for another shag, love? Want to have another go then?" She tries to imitate me—poorly, as usual. I just laugh at her and shake my head. "You want to sweep my chimney?"

"Oh, Becca—shut-up—for Christ's sake, sweetheart!" I laugh and attack her mouth, then pull her to sit astride me. "Just once more tonight?" I ask against her lips. She nods before she collects my lips again. I reach over and grab the condom. Becca immediately begins to tremble. "I don't have to do this," I say quickly.

"Grayson, stop talking about it, please," she says. I go to toss it away. She grabs my hand. "Stop talking ... just do it. I trust you and I love you." She opens her eyes and stares deeply into mine. I offer her the condom and she tears the packet open. Slowly, she slides it on to me. "Do you want me to turn around?"

"Yes, love. Becca?"

"Shh." She places her finger on my lips before she kisses them. Becca climbs off and turns around. "How do you want me, baby?" she asks, looking over her shoulder. Half of her thick, wavy hair has fallen out of her ponytail, but it still looks pretty. She is beautiful. I can see it ... can feel her trust in me ... her love. I run my lips across her shoulders as I reach between her legs from behind. She's drenched from our earlier tousle. I spread our natural lube around, bringing it up to her bum. Becca's breathing becomes extremely erratic. Mine matches as I slide something incredibly hard up and down her center.

I wrap my arm around her waist as I enter her in the usual place first. She physically relaxes back onto me and slowly rides me. Her hips move erotically, welcoming my hand's play at her clitoris. I grab the lube and snap the cap open with my free hand, squirting some onto my thigh. Tossing the bottle aside, I wipe the lube off with two fingers and slowly part her bum cheeks. Becca stops for a moment, but I work at her clit, my lips at her shoulders—to keep her focused.

"That's it, sweetheart," I breathe against her ear and gently insert one of my fingers. Becca whimpers softly and I almost come undone at the sound. "You're doing so good," I whisper and add the pressure of my second finger. After several minutes, Becca finally seems not only acclimated to, but enjoying the feeling of extra pressure. Her body is so relaxed now, working at thrusting herself against me and my fingers. I continue to distract her as I pull them out, then myself, bringing extra fluid with me to run up and quickly enter her bum. Maybe a bit too quickly.

"Grayson." She gasps and stills herself. I hold still as well, except for the kisses I trail up her neck to her ear.

"Tell me when you're ready," I say breathlessly. It's so tight ... so warm ... so erotic. It's taking every fiber of my being not to let loose and have at it.

"Um ... uh, okay." She catches her breath. I slowly pull almost all the way out and dive back in again. "Gray ... oh ... uh ..." She reaches back and holds my hips. I take her face and turn it as far as I can. I grasp her lips with mine and deepen the kiss as I thrust into her again. Her whimper drives me mad. She reaches her arms back, wrapping them around my neck as my hand finally brings her to climax. Her hips grind her bum toward me. This is my cue—she's relaxed enough now—so I quicken my pace and vocalize my enjoyment.

Becca grabs a pillow and throws it down in front of her. I stop as she gets herself situated. "Okay." She smiles over her shoulder, then buries her face into it. My pace is slow. But as I stare down, watching the act that I have fantasized about unfold, an insatiable fire ignites in me and I finally have at it. I grasp her hips and pull them toward me harshly over and over again. I am wild. I've lost all care and concern for Becca's well-being as I get swallowed up in my fantasy. Then it happens ... the pressure ... the tingling. I erupt inside of her like an angry volcano.

"Ugh ... God!" I grunt loudly, my last quake sending shivers through my whole body. I collapse onto Becca's back dramatically. After a moment, I get my wits about me. "Becca? Becca, darling, are you okay?" I ask with a hint of panic in my voice as I pull out. Becca takes in a deep, shaky breath and climbs out of bed. I watch as she heads to her drawers. She pulls out PJs and heads toward the bathroom. "Becca ... Becca." I chase her and grab her arm to turn her to me.

"Please, I just need a minute." She holds up a finger, but doesn't look at me. I let her go into the bathroom. After cleaning up and changing back into my PJs, I sit on the edge of the bed and wait for her. I feel nervous as hell. Did she ask me to stop? Did she say anything? I was so ultra-focused on what I was doing—I probably tuned her right out. She trusted me, and I think I may have betrayed that trust. Did she have a flashback? Oh, Christ! *Shit! Shit! Shit ... fuckity shit!* My head jerks up at the sound of the bathroom door opening.

"Becca!" I jump up.

"Bathroom's all yours," she says quietly, and pushes her hair behind her ears.

"Sweetheart, we should talk about this." I grab her hand as she walks by.

"What's there to talk about? Merry Christmas. I hope you liked your gift." She tries to pull away. I feel a sharp pang in my heart.

"I'm sorry, baby. I went into a completely selfish zone ... if you said anything to me, I didn't hear you. I didn't ignore you on purpose."

"I didn't say anything, Grayson ... what was the point?" She pulls back the covers.

"What do you mean, Becca? The point was that I would have stopped if you asked me to," I say with a bit of frustration.

"Except, you said yourself that you weren't aware if I said anything!" she snaps. "I looked back to you to say something ... but

..." She trails off.

"But what?" I sit on the bed near her.

"You had the, uh, the same expression on your face as George did. He never listened to me."

"I'm not George!" I yell, cutting her off.

"I know," she agrees quietly. "Look, it's over with. I don't want to get hung up on it. It must be something men get crazy over—the whole 'forbidden fruit' thing and all. Ray would probably behave the same way." She climbs in.

"Ray? Ray!" I yell. I stand up and begin to pace. I feel as if Becca has just handed me a first-class ticket to the crazy train, and I have no choice but to get on it! Why would she mention him? In the middle of a conversation about *our* intimate moment! Boiling over with jealousy and rage, I grab the crystal vase off the table and chuck it at the wall. The sound of the shattering glass is the opening act to me slamming the bathroom door.

My hands grasp the sides of the sink. Slowly I lift my head up and face myself in the mirror. I can't bear the truth ... my heart doesn't want to listen. I know what I have to do. I have to walk away. I need to let her go. He's the one she truly wants to be with. She needs to be with him. I see it in her face, hear it in her voice. I know she loves me. I know a part of her will always love me, but it's not enough for her. She hasn't realized this yet. I love her. God, do I love her ... enough to realize it for her. I can't be selfish any-more. My need for her to be happy is much greater than my own desires. Ray is a good man. He'll always put her first. I trust him with her life, her heart, and her mind.

I take in a deep breath and exhale aggressively. One more day. I want one more day with *my* family, then I will leave. They will be in good hands. They have been all along.

"Gray," Becca says with a knock. I rub my face quickly and splash water on it. I towel off as I open the door. Becca wraps her arms around my waist and hugs me fiercely. "I'm sorry," she breathes, and plants a kiss on my sternum.

"Me too, sweetheart." I embrace her as well. "Come ... let's get you off to bed. Would you like me to read to you?" I kiss her lips and sway her gently.

"I'd love that, Gray." Love her dimple when she smiles. I lean down and kiss it.

"What shall I read?" I ask as we head back into the bedroom arm in arm.

"I don't know—you pick." She grabs her Kindle and hands it to me. We climb into bed. Becca settles her head on my chest once my back is up against the pillows. I turn the Kindle on and start searching through her library. Before I can decide on a book, I realize Becca is fast asleep. I lay there for the next half hour or so, just holding her, breathing in her hair and skin. *I'm going to miss her terribly.*

BECCA

I'm at an airfield. Everything is gray. I hear nothing but "I Will Follow You into the Dark" by Death Cab for Cutie playing loudly. I scan the airfield and see four identical Cessna planes. My Dad, Grayson, Ray, and Morgan appear. They all wave to me and climb into their respective planes. I feel a sense of panic and put my arm out, telling them to stop. I feel a hand on my shoulder. I turn to find my mom. Her green eyes are the only color I see. I look back to find the planes in the air. My mother pulls me to her. She smiles sympathetically. I feel heat, and the ground shakes. I turn back to find one of the planes mid-explosion. "No!" I scream silently. "No!" Louder this time. "No!" I jump up.

I'm in bed.

"Sweetheart ... you're safe. Calm down." Grayson pulls me to him.

"Oh God," I cry. "I had that dream again, Grayson." I bury my face into his neck and sob.

"Did you see who it was this time?" He rubs my back.

"No. My mother wouldn't let me. The planes are identical; I didn't know who was in which one." I can't shake this sense of loss I'm feeling.

"It's probably about your dad, sweetheart. Its Christmastime ... it stirs up a lot of feelings." I'm sure he's right. I know he's going through this as well.

"Well, it's awful. I hope I don't dream it again." I grab the tissue Grayson offers.

"Let's go back to sleep, love. It's after three in the morning." Grayson takes the tissue and throws it at the wastebasket. I turn and snuggle into him—spooning with him. His hand caresses up and down the side of my body. "Sweetheart," he mutters as he cups my breast. I can feel the "pressing matter" he may want to discuss against my backside. I prepare myself for yet another British invasion. The battle is short and sweet—victory had on both sides. Grayson encircles me in his arms and I slowly drift off once more.

"Mom! Dad! Wake up!" Morgan raps at our door. My eyes shoot open and panic sets in.

"Shit ... Grayson, the gifts!" I slap his arm.

"Under the tree, sweetheart—I did it two hours ago." He yawns and rolls onto his back.

"We'll be right there, Morgan!" I shout, and slowly push myself up into a sitting position. "I feel as if I've been hit by a Mack Truck." I stretch before wrapping my arms around my knees. I rest my head on them, facing Grayson. "Good morning. Merry Christmas." I smile.

"Hmm ... it will be both in a moment." He smirks mischievously as he leans up and takes my lips for his own. He nudges me, indicating I should lie down.

"Grayson, Morgan's waiting for us, baby." I sigh, knowing it's pointless—he has that look on his face. "No" is not an option.

"She can wait, sweetheart. This can't." He climbs on top of me and pins my arms on either side of my head. "You, me, and Morgan today. I want no mention of him. No phone calls, no visits, not a glance at a picture ... nothing, Becca. I mean it!"

There seems to be a fine line between desperation and aggravation, and I'm not quite sure which way he is leaning.

"I promise." I search his eyes, hoping he believes me.

"Don't screw up today, Becca. For God's sake ... please!"

"Right back at you!" I snap. I mean, really—what the hell? Don't screw up? If that isn't a big turnoff, I don't know what is! Had I the balls, I'd yell *"Ray, Ray, Ray!"* at him just to piss him off. But, alas, my balls are MIA. *I think Cautionary Sybecca stole them, probably to hold them hostage 'til she gets a new ticker board!*

"Well, I guess I've put you in the state opposite of what I was intending." He sighs, defeated, and climbs off of me.

"Yeah, I guess so!" I get out of bed and head to the bathroom. Usual morning bathroom rituals ensue. He knocks after a few minutes.

"Sweetheart. Almost ready?"

I open the door and charge past him.

"Hey." He grabs my arm and pulls me back to him. "Becca, love ... c'mon, let's not be like this. It's Christmas. Let's kiss and make up." He leans down.

"Fuck you, Gray!" I say through my teeth.

"Then, there's always that option." He smiles slightly.

"Shut up!" I roll my eyes and pull away to hide my smile.

"Come here." He pulls me back and plants a kiss on my nose. "I love you."

"Love you." I sigh and get up on my toes to kiss him.

"Let's not keep her waiting any longer." He laces his fingers with mine and we head out of the room and down the stairs.

"Finally!" Morgan sighs, obviously exasperated.

"Sorry, Morgy girl." Grayson bends to kiss the top of her head. "Shall we see what Father Christmas has brought you, little sweetheart?" He heads over to the tree. Well, I think there's a tree there—can't really tell with all the gifts piled high in front of it. Morgan fidgets, unable to sit still, and I can tell she's overwhelmed with excitement. "First, open this." He hands her a card.

She opens it and tears fill her eyes. I peek over. Oh. It's a father-daughter card. That's so sweet. Yeah, he's officially off my shit list! I look up at him, and he mouths, *Shag list?* I can't help but giggle.

"Thank you, Daddy. I love you too!" She gets up and hugs him.

"Go ahead, open the little envelope inside." He points to it.

"Oh yeah!" She smiles and flips the paper up to pull out what's inside. "*Oh my God!*" she screeches, then does a little dance in a circle.

"What? What is it?" I try to be excited, but I'm a little miffed that he kept her gifts a secret from me.

"It's scuba-diving lessons for when we get back to California!" She shows me.

"Grayson!" I gasp as the theme from *Jaws* plays loudly in my head. "She's too young!" Yes, that's it—it has nothing to do with my horrific fear of sharks!

"No, she isn't! She's old enough to get her junior certification." He ignores my panic.

"Grayson." That's all I can say. He knows how I feel about this! We had this discussion maybe six weeks ago!

"Becca, you can't push your fears onto our daughter. It isn't right, nor is it fair!"

I mouth *shit list* to him. He shrugs and hands her the next present. She opens it and continues on with the screeching. It's a whole-system package by ScubaPro. Next come the mask, flippers, wetsuit, and whatever else one would need. "This is from Susanna and Sam, Morgy." He hands her the box. She opens it to find an

Intova Digital Sport SPK-800K underwater camera.

Morgan beams, and I feel a bit jealous. I know my gifts from "us" are not going to bring her the same kind of excitement. "One last one from just me, Morgy girl." He hands her a little box. She pulls the ribbon off, then the paper. The lid comes off, and she takes out a heart necklace that says *Daddy's Little Girl*. Her smile could swallow her face. "Turn it over." He gestures. I lean over her shoulder and watch. The inscription says *Moon and Stars Forever—Daddy*. It's something they always say. He's her moon and she's his stars. It's sweet. What a perfect gift. Grayson mouths *shag* to me and I smile. Yep, he's back on it! He helps her put the necklace on.

"You are the best daddy in the world! I will wear this forever!" She hugs him tightly.

"Thank you, sweetheart. You make it so easy for me." He sways with her. I almost swear I can see his chin quivering a bit.

"Starting without us?" Charlie pipes up as he and Hazel join us. I give Hazel a suspicious look, and she giggles and blushes several shades of red before she looks away from my stare.

"Let us all not forget that Jesus is the reason for the season," I announce out of left field, and pat Hazel's shoulder.

"Oh, Becca, really!" Hazel giggles.

"Yes, let us all thank baby Jesus, right, sweetheart?" Grayson flashes me his boyish grin. It's a vicious cycle of sexual puns, all at Jesus's expense ... and on Christmas, no less. I don't think the Big Guy approves of this banter.

"Grown-ups are so weird!" Morgan shakes her head. "Next, please!" she says. Grayson proceeds to pass her all of her gifts. I sit on the floor and lean my back up against the couch. Watching Morgan on Christmas morning never gets old. She and Annie get so excited, showing each other what they've opened. A lot of their gifts are the same, so we have the girls open them together. I notice Morgan catch herself looking for Annie a few times. We exchange small smiles.

"Do you like your new ski jacket, sweetheart?" Gray plops down next to her.

"Yes, Daddy." She looks away.

"What's the matter, Morgy?" He puts his arm around her.

"I wonder if Annie got the matching one in her favorite color." She sighs.

"I happen to know that she did indeed get this very same jacket in her favorite color." He pokes at it. I shoot him a quizzical look. "We also got Annie a round-trip ticket to visit you in California on spring break." He rubs her back.

"Really?" she asks excitedly and hugs him.

"Absolutely! Annie can come and visit anytime."

"Can I call her when I'm all done?"

I wince and watch Grayson become visibly uncomfortable—he grabs at the back of his neck and scratches (not something he normally does when he's asked a question).

"Call her tomorrow, love," he says.

"But, Dad ... " she says in a quiet, sad tone.

"No, Morgan ... not today! Damn it, Becca!" he snaps and gets up.

"Grayson!" I call after him as he walks away.

"Mom, I'm sorry." She looks to me.

"No, sweetie, it's not your fault. I'll talk to him." I get up and head toward the kitchen. "Grayson!" I say with frustration.

"I asked you not to do this today! This is our day!" he yells.

"I have no control over what she's thinking or asking! You are being fucking ridiculous!" I give it back to him.

"But you do, sweetheart. You have no idea how much control you have!" He grabs my arms.

"You're mad, Gray! What the hell is wrong with you?" I peer up at him nervously. He releases my arms and looks down.

"Go back out. I'll be there in a minute. I just need to cool off."

He walks away. I decide it's best if I just do as he asks.

"Is Daddy still mad at me?" Morgan meets me halfway.

"No, sweetie, he's upset with me. Do me a favor and just don't mention the McNeils—at least for today." I wrap my arm around her shoulders and walk side by side with her into the lounge. We sit down and watch Hazel and Charlie open their gift from Morgan. It's a framed picture of the three of them that she decorated with a pretty ribbon. It's beautiful.

"Here, Morgy." Grayson comes behind us and hands her his phone. "It's for you."

She grabs it.

"Hello? Annie!" She smiles up at Grayson. He smiles back and nudges me. I scoot forward on the floor, allowing him room to sit behind me. I rest back against his chest, letting him wrap his arms around me.

"I'm sorry, sweetheart. I'm acting like a bloody idiot," he whispers in my ear, then softly kisses down my neck.

"That was nice of you, baby ... to call. She really is like a sister to Morgan." I turn my head to him.

"I know. You can say Merry Christmas to her, too. But please don't talk to him—not today, baby." He lays a kiss on my face before he presses his cheek to mine for a hug.

"I promise." I pat his arm. We watch as Morgan rambles on about her stuff and listens to Annie. She starts laughing and excitedly planning Annie's visit out to California.

"Yeah, sure," she says into the phone, then holds her hand over the receiver. "Mom, can you talk?"

"If it's Annie, yes." I raise my brows. She hands me the phone. "Merry Christmas, Annie!" I greet her cheerfully.

"Merry Christmas, Becca! Thank you for my plane ticket and ski jacket! Have you opened all of your gifts yet?" she asks.

"No, I haven't. Why?" It's good to hear her voice.

"Well, you have to open the gift from Morgan. Tell her to give it to you!" she demands.

"Morgan, Annie said you have something I have to open." As I'm speaking, she jumps up—to collect it, I guess. She hands me a small jewelry box. "Hold on, baby," I say to Annie, and begin to open it. It's a half of a silver heart on a thin chain. It says *Annie* on the front. On the back, it says *Never Apart*. A note from Morgan says, *Wear this close to your heart and you two will never be apart. Love, Morgan.* "Morgan, this is so beautiful and so thoughtful." I look up at her. Damn, my kid is amazing!

"I have the other half with your name on it," Annie says. "I'm wearing it right now!"

"I'm putting mine on right now." I smile as Grayson helps me with it. "Can you do me a favor, Annie?"

"Sure, Becca."

"Every night at eight o'clock when you go to bed, give your part of your heart a kiss. I will do that every day at five in California. This way, we give each other a kiss good night every night." I play with the heart on the chain, running it back and forth across my neck.

"That's a great idea, Mom—er, Becca. I'll do that every night. I promise!" She's trying to sound happy, but I can hear the hint of sadness in her voice.

"Me too ... I love you, Annie."

"I love you, too. Tell Morgan I'll call her tomorrow."

"Okay, sweetie, have a good day today." I wish I could hug her.

"You, too. Bye." She hangs up and I give Gray the phone.

"Thanks, baby."

"Welcome. Now, shall we get to your gifts?" He stands up and goes to the tree. He grabs a Christmas bag and brings it over to me. "Dive in, sweetheart." He sits behind me again.

I get on my knees and reach my hand in. "Any specific order?" I look back to catch him staring at my bum. "Earth to Grayson," I say with a giggle.

"Hmm? Oh no, no order," he says, glancing up at me. I mentally shrug and select my first gift. It's a long, rectangular box. I unwrap and open it to find a PANDORA bracelet. I look closer at each charm. A double-decker bus with the British flag, an airplane, a sleigh, a plain circle with a bible dangling from it, a teacup, a Christmas tree, a baby carriage, a dangling music note, a dangling pearl, an envelope that says *To My Love*. They are divided here and there by glass beads in my favorite colors, purple and lime green. "Do you like it?" He seems unsure.

"Of course I do! Very symbolic." I smile and kiss him. "Thank you."

"Becca ... that's it?"

"Why? What's the matter?" I furrow my brow, trying to figure him out.

"I just ... I thought I would get a better reaction. I'm a bit disappointed." He grabs the bracelet and tosses it into the box.

"Sorry, Gray, I love it. I don't know what else you want me to say." I gaze into his eyes.

"Just go on." He waves his hand. I grab the next gift and open it to find the newest Janet Evanovich *Stephanie Plum* novel.

"Oh wow! I didn't even realize another came out!" I love these books!

"Really, Becca?" he snaps. "I spent countless hours choosing each charm, and you show more excitement and appreciation over a fucking book?" His voice is one octave below yelling. Everybody is quiet, trying not to stare at us. I feel so embarrassed.

"Excuse me," I say, and get up. I head into the kitchen to start breakfast. *The big fucking English breakfast I planned for that asshole!* "Fucking jerk!" I snap under my breath as I pull out several dozen eggs, sausage, bacon, beans, and potatoes.

The swinging door slams open.

"Becca! What the bloody hell are you doing? We're opening gifts!"

"What does it look like I'm doing?" I yell.

"Becca, you're being rude!"

"*I'm* being rude? You're kidding, right? Grayson, you are acting very strange today." I shake my head as I throw the bacon into the pan.

"Please, darling, please come and open the rest of your gifts," he asks calmly, placing his hands on my hips. A surge of butterflies swoops around in my belly.

"Later." I close my eyes to try to settle myself. Grayson lets out a frustrated sigh and lets go, then grabs a stool and sits at the island.

"I wish we could start this day over, Becca," he grumbles.

"Me too, baby ... me too." I grab the sausages and get them going as well. Within no time, the kitchen smells yummy and my belly is grumbling instead of fighting off the effects of Grayson's touch. "Gray?" I glance over my shoulder at my defeated-looking fiancé.

"What?"

"Don't sulk; it's not very becoming on you, first of all. Second of all, I wish you gave me the bracelet last night. I love it, and I think I would've been more expressive if we were alone. Half of those charms have very significant, personal meanings to us. That's why I didn't really carry on about it." I lower the gas on the stove before I walk over to him and lean on the island.

"You know, sweetheart," he says, and grabs my hips again to pull me to him. "I didn't even think of that. You're right. I'm sorry for the way I behaved. It's no excuse, but I do have a lot on my mind and am a bit off my game." He rests his forehead against mine.

"Things will be better once we're back in California." I squeeze his shoulders, massaging them a bit.

"Will you open the rest of your gifts after breakfast?"

"Yes. I have some for you, as well."

"You have more for me?" He lights up like a child.

"Of course, baby." I give him a swift kiss before I get back to breakfast.

Chapter Eighteen

I sit back and put my feet up with another cup of coffee—decaf this time—and watch everybody else clean up from breakfast. I don't feel an ounce of guilt running through my body, nor the ridiculous need to help. I think I deserve to relax for once, and damn it, that's what I'm going to do! I take another sip and look up to find Grayson holding the Christmas gift bag open by the handles and tilting it back and forth, an unspoken question on his face.

"Sure." I smile and put my coffee down.

"Okay." He kneels in front of me and pulls out a thick envelope. "This is last." He puts it to the side, then hands me three other boxes. "Remember, I have another personal gift I want to give you tomorrow."

I nod at his reminder and slowly open the first box. It's a new Cricut cartridge! I pull a Morgan reaction and hurry to the next box.

Another one! I look up at Gray.

"I haven't seen these before!"

"Nope. Not released yet, sweetheart." He smiles, proud of himself.

"Who's awesome now?" I kiss him. "Now, what do we have here?" I open the last box and gasp. It's a Doris Panos blue quartz and diamond bangle bracelet in sterling silver and platinum. I know this not because I have an eye for fine jewelry, but simply because I can read. That's what the card in the box says. "Grayson, it's beautiful! I love it!" I put it on immediately.

"Do you, sweetheart?" He takes my hand and looks at my wrist.

"Yes ... really, I do!" I lean in for a kiss. "Okay, I'm dying to know. What's in that envelope?" With ADD, one's focus always gets redirected rather quickly!

"Oh ... that? That's nothing." He waves his hand like he's shooing it away. "Let's not worry about that. Actually, it just may be rubbish that fell in here." He grabs it. "I'll just throw it away, sweetheart." He starts to get up.

"Give me that! Right now, Grayson Michael James, if you know what's good for you!" I pout, placing my hands on my hips for emphasis.

"Oh ... all right, darling, but I don't think you'll like it at all." He sits beside me and places the manila envelope in my lap. I turn it over, undo the metal brackets, and flip the flap up. I reach in to find a few papers with a narrow, catalog-like book. I pull them all out and start looking through them. I feel Grayson pushing my jaw closed, and I glance up at him.

"Grayson?" I can barely breathe.

"You love to fly, sweetheart. I've seen it on your face. It was your dream. I understand why it got pushed aside, but it doesn't need to be anymore. I want you to get your pilot's license. It's an honor for me to make one of your dreams come true, darling." Finally, he stops talking. My mouth attacks his with such urgency, I take my own breath away. "Shag list then, love?" He chuckles.

"Abso-bloody-friggin-lutely!" I gaze back down at the paperwork.

"Your happiness has and will always be my main focus and concern. I love you, Becca ... more than my heart and my mind can stand, really." His overwhelming words leave me with no witty comeback. I'm losing my edge ... or, maybe, my wall of preservation. Instead, I rest my head on his shoulder. Closing my eyes, I inhale deeply the intoxicating smell that is Grayson James.

"Ready for your gift now?"

"Yes! Quite excited for it! You haven't disappointed me yet!" He nudges my head up. I bite my lip and let my smile hit my eyes instead. I get up and head over to the tree.

"Here you go," I say as I sit next to him. He takes the envelope and opens it.

"Three horses, sweetheart?" he asks, looking surprised.

"No, those are the three available that you can pick from. Now you'll have your own horse here. I thought you might go for this one." I point to the black one.

"I won't be here, though."

"Well, we'll transport him out with us. You have a stable you're not using. Morgan and I will want our horses out in California." I'm feeling a bit perturbed. I don't think he likes his gift. "That way, we can all ride together."

"It's lovely, sweetheart." Half smile.

"Um, well ... that was the grand finale." I sigh, feeling disappointed.

"Well, thank you, Becca." He pats my knee and gets up. "Let's go and get dressed, shall we?"

"Yeah ... sure." I rise and follow him up the stairs. Ray and I always snuggled on the couch in our PJs for at least a couple of hours after breakfast. Sometimes the girls would have to wake me to start dinner or check on it, depending on if we were having turkey or ham. Every year he would say, *This is my favorite part of Christmas ... snuggling with you on this couch, baby.* It was my favorite, too. I miss him. I wish we were in Calabasas or London for Christmas instead. It might've been easier. There's too much Ray history here. Holidays make it worse.

I follow Grayson into our room and jump when he slams the door.

"What's the matter?" I ask.

"You can't last even a few hours without thinking about him!" he yells. How the hell does he know I was thinking about Ray? "Christ, Becca ... it's all over your face." He sighs. "I just wanted one day. You can't do it. Can you, sweetheart?" He plops onto our bed and rests his head in his hands.

"I don't know what to say, Grayson." It's the truth—I'm speechless. I plop down next to him.

"What were you thinking about?"

"Just that he and I used to snuggle on the couch after breakfast. We were never in a rush to get dressed. That's all." I leave out the latter part of my previous thought.

"We have an inn full of security, here to keep you safe. If it was just us, we'd stay in our PJs all day! We don't have to get dressed. We can snuggle in our bed and put the telly on up here," he offers. I decide not to mention that the absence of the Christmas tree and the smell of dinner cooking kind of takes away the ambiance of snuggling on Christmas Day. "I'll go ask Morgy if she wants to join us." He heads to the door and yells out for her when he opens it. I climb into bed now, wondering what Ray is doing. What the hell is the matter with me? It'll be better ... *I'll* be better once we leave.

"Is she coming?"

"She said maybe later." He closes the door and climbs in next to me. "What shall we watch, my little snuggle bunny?" He tries to lighten our moods. I feel like such an ass! "He's fine, Becca. He's with his family. You are with yours. You can see him tomorrow." He clicks the TV on. My favorite version of *A Christmas Carol*, with Reginald Owen as Scrooge, is on. Strange—they rarely ever play this version. "This okay, Becca?"

"Yes. It's my favorite one." I squeeze his arm and snuggle into him. I close my eyes to the feeling of Grayson softly kissing my cheek and my ear before he settles into watching the movie.

I open my eyes, and I'm in my bed in my room. I turn my head and find Ray sleeping peacefully. The sun is trying its hardest to peek through the room-darkening shades with a bit of success. The Christmas tree Ray surprised me with is lit and comforting. As much as I try to fight off my feelings for Ray because he's my best friend, I do love waking up in his arms. I know he cares about me. I know he wants more than a friendship. I'm just so afraid. I don't want to lose him. I'm so tormented by my past. I'm still haunted by our kiss this past June. Sometimes I wish I would've just thrown caution to the wind and made love to him.

"Morning, baby. Merry Christmas." Ray gently turns my face to his with his fingertips.

"Merry Christmas," I say, and welcome his lips on mine. My tongue is first to attempt an invasion. It's greeted urgently by Ray's, and he even adds a groan. Fuck off, caution! I'm making love to him right here, right now! I fist his hair and turn my body more into him. He climbs on top of me and pulls his mouth away. My breathing is erratic—I don't even bother to try to steady it.

"Becs?" He stares into my eyes. I look deeply into the storm brewing within them.

"Yes, Ray ... yes." I pull at the hem of his shirt. He helps me take it off of him. My shirt follows, along with both of our bottoms. He turns his speed from devouring to savoring. I match his tempo without skipping a beat. I run my lips across his shoulder and up

his neck, my tongue darting out to taste him. Back up at his jaw, I nip his chin before I capture his lips again. I nudge him with my knee. He pulls back.

"Right to it, baby? No foreplay?"

"Ah, oh ... um, Ray." I fidget as his fingers tweak and knead my right nipple in a painfully good manner.

"Feel good?"

"Yes, baby," I say softly. I know how this affects him. "Ray ... please, baby. I need you," I continue, and watch him close his eyes to soak in the sound of my voice. His eyes open—full-blown storm. He shifts his body a bit and in one swift motion, he's inside of me. Within a matter of seconds, our hips are in sync with each other. He feels so right. This feels so right ... so good. I feel as if I'm home. A good amount of time passes before Ray and I slowly begin our climb together. It's been so long since my body has gone through this motion, and I feel like flopping around like a fish out of water. Ray holds me tightly to him to help me steady myself through the waves. I squeeze around him every time he pulls back.

"Becs ... oh, baby ... that's it ... that feels so good," he says against my ear. Damn, he's hot in bed! Come to think of it, he's pretty hot outside of bed, too. He muffles my cries with his mouth as we come undone together.

"I love you, Ray. I'm so ... in love ... with you," I say in between pants as he rests his sweaty forehead against mine.

"I love you, baby. I love you," he breathes, and attacks my lips again.

I open my eyes to find Grayson staring down at me. His nose is flaring and his eyes are damp. I sit up quickly, still feeling a bit disoriented from my dream—which I think was actually a memory.

"What's the matter?"

"Nothing. We have to get dressed now. You have to cook the ham." He gets out of bed. *Shit! Did I talk in my sleep?*

"Grayson, something's wrong. You are upset."

He throws on his jeans, saying nothing. I get up and walk over to him, then grab his shirt out of his hands and toss it onto the chair. I lace my fingers with his and slowly walk backward to the bed, bringing him along. When I bump into the mattress with the backs of my thighs, I bring his hands to my hips. He reaches up around my neck and pulls my long brown hair away and onto my other shoulder, allowing him full access to my skin. His lips caress me like the tickle of a close whisper. He pulls away and stares down into my eyes. I sense a strange recognition there, like a memory I've forgotten about. It feels powerful. Grayson leans in and rubs his lips lightly against mine. Not a single word is uttered between us as we climb onto the bed and slowly make love.

Grayson and I walk hand in hand downstairs. We haven't said a word to each other in an hour. It's been a good silence, though—much needed.

"The hams are in. Stacey and I took care of it," Hazel says with a sigh.

"Thanks. Sorry I've been slacking off lately." I hug her, more so she'll know I'm not going to flip out.

"We put the Christmas crackers out as well." She looks past my shoulder, watching Grayson join Morgan in the lounge. "What's going on with my nephew? Is he all right?" Her powder-blue eyes focus back on me.

"Ugh, Hazel, he's all over the place, between his mom and Christmas and Ray. He's itching to get back home to the ranch, and I sort of feel the same way."

"Really? You're ready to leave everything you've worked hard for ... and Ray?"

"I love Grayson, Hazel, although ..." I trail off.

"Although what?" she asks flippantly.

"Nothing. I just feel like he's taking ten steps back after taking five forward. I think it's from being here, though. Then again, I don't know, because he's always been up and down about us. I feel very confused." I'm honest and open, like I've always been. She walks away from me without a word. *Um ... okay. Good talk!* I remind myself that he is her nephew. She's entitled to be a bit sensitive on this matter, I guess.

I head into the lounge, where Morgan is teaching Grayson how to play her latest PlayStation game. I grab my new book and try not to think of He Who Should Not Be Mentioned or Thought Of. After about ten minutes, Stacey plops down and elbows me. I look over at her, and she shows me her phone.

December 25, 2012   1:30 p.m.

Ray: Stacey, its Elise. Ray is destroying the house. He's drunk and out of control. We can't get him to calm down! Becca needs to help us. Please!

Grayson comes up to us and grabs Stacey's phone. *"Enough!"* he screams and throws it against the wall, where it smashes into a million pieces.

"Hey!" Stacey yells.

"Daddy?" Morgan says nervously. Her eyes are wide and her brow furrowed, like she's scared. Grayson turns his head to her sharply, then glances back at me with a look of panic.

"Becca." His tone is sharp, almost as if he's blaming me for his actions.

"Daddy, why are you so angry?" Morgan asks, and touches his arm.

"Becca ... please," he pleads. What does he want me to do?

"Uh ... Morgan, everything's okay," I offer. What the hell else can I say?

"It's your turn, Daddy." Morgan hands him his paddle. He looks down at it, then back up at me. He follows her over to the TV.

"Becca, what the fuck?" Stacey asks.

"Please, Stace, no more Ray today," I whisper, looking back down at my book. Every once in a while I glance up to find Grayson staring at me. He is so off today. It's making me nervous.

By the time I hit chapter five, dinner is ready. Grayson holds his hands out in an offer to help me up. When I take them, he pulls me to him aggressively. His fingers lace with mine as he crisscrosses my arms behind my back and holds me tightly against him. He nudges my nose with his before he collects my lips. I give in to his advances and welcome the intrusion of his tongue. He pulls away rather quick, releasing my arms as well. I feel a bit lightheaded as we walk toward the dining room, his arm draped around my shoulder.

Hazel hits her glass with her fork once everyone is settled at the tables.

"If you all look in front of you, you'll see a large foil package, a candy-wrapper-looking item. This is called a Christmas cracker, for those who aren't familiar with it. You need the help of the person next to you to pull it open. Inside, you should find some treats as well as a crown—which you must wear—and a piece of paper that has a motto, joke, or riddle on it. Have fun!" She smiles. Everyone starts pulling. Within minutes we hear chuckling around the room. More and more crowns. I turn to Grayson with my cracker. He pulls with me and I search through my treasure after I place my paper crown on my head. I open the piece of paper.

"You are the author of your life. Only you can control the drama, mystery, suspense, love, patience, tolerance, and characters you allow in your story to complement you," I read aloud, losing my smile slightly as I really take in the message and its meaning.

"Pretty relevant, isn't it, darling?" Grayson whispers in my ear. I just stare at him and swallow hard.

"What did you get?" I finally ask.

"Knock-knock joke." He shrugs. I decide to dive into my ham, wishing it was turkey instead. Too much work, though, for so many people.

Within half an hour or so, dinner is done and everyone is clearing up. It's only four in the evening. This day is lasting forever, though I think I'd feel differently if there weren't so many people here. I feel so on edge. Who wouldn't, with so much security around? Who could relax? Well, Charlie can—apparently. I study him, amazed at the octave he can reach with his snoring. He's in the armchair, glasses down to the tip of his nose, the magazine he was reading almost falling out of his hand. His mouth hangs open crookedly—to allow the awkwardly loud sounds, of course.

"Should we videotape this, sweetheart, for blackmail or proof?" Grayson asks with a chuckle from behind me. Just then, Hazel walks in to find us studying her man.

"Oh, Hazel, you must've had him praying really hard last night." I giggle.

"Stop, sweetheart! That's my aunt, for Christ's sake!" Grayson says, wiggling off an obvious, uncomfortable chill. Hazel walks away, shaking her head as her face turns a deep red.

"Speaking of praying hard, love, it's time for bible study." He kisses my ear and grabs my hand to lead me upstairs.

"We have to be back downstairs at six o'clock, sweetie."

"Yes, of course, love—Christmas tea." He smiles as he hangs his arm around my lower waist. I do the same and slide my hand into his back pocket as we down the hall to our room. "It really means a lot to me that you followed all of my Christmas traditions growing up. I know I haven't been easy to be around these past few days, and yet, you've kept right on schedule. Thank you, sweetheart." He stops at our door and pulls me to him.

"Grayson, things will get a lot easier for both of us once we leave tomorrow. Maybe not at first, for me at least, but they will." I'm not sure who I'm trying to convince more, Grayson or myself.

"Come, love, let me remind you what a magnificent creature you are marrying." He opens the door and pulls me through, unable to wipe the boyish grin off of his face.

As Grayson and I wrap ourselves up in post-coital bliss, I can't help thinking about how amazing we are together.

"Mmm," I sigh.

"Sleepy, sweetheart?" He nuzzles my neck from behind.

"Yeah, ridiculously ... why am I so tired?"

Grayson softly caresses my stomach to remind me.

"Oh, yeah." I smile.

"Go ahead, darling, take a nap. I think I'll join you." He pulls me closer.

"Mmm, okay," I say around a yawn, and give into the soporific spell I'm under.

I'm at the ranch in Calabasas, California. As I walk slowly down the hall, I notice an eerie silence throughout the house—except for the TV, which is blaring loudly from the family room. I head in to find no one there. I smile and sit on the couch when I realize mine and Grayson's wedding video is playing. Oh, it looks like we get married at the house here, outside. I love the gown! I am quite surprised that I'm not showing yet in the video. Huh ... odd. Grayson and I are beaming at each other. I start to say my vows but I can't hear myself, because "My Immortal" by Evanescence is playing loudly instead of the TV. I watch Grayson laugh. I do the same

when he says his. We kiss and run happily through a crowd of people.

The TV picture fades, then comes back to show me lying up against Grayson's chest on the beach. He's rubbing my growing belly and we're laughing. The TV fades again. Now we're in the delivery room and I'm giving birth. It's a girl! The doctor holds her up. She looks just like Morgan did when she was born. Grayson kisses us both a million times. I wipe the tears from my eyes. He's going to be a great dad.

The TV goes through its routine again. Grayson and I are walking with the baby around the yard, swinging her up every so often to make her laugh. The TV fades and comes back again. We're at Disneyland. The baby looks about two, maybe almost three. We're taking a picture with Mickey Mouse. God, she looks exactly like Morgan! A rise of panic and grief come over me all at once. I feel as if I may be sick.

The music stops playing and the TV goes dark. It returns to a newscaster on Channel Seven.

"We have breaking news. Grayson James, young bestselling author, has died in a plane crash. He was thirty-one years old and leaves his wife, Becca, twenty-eight, and their daughter, Morgan, three, behind." I change the channel quickly, only to hear another reporter.

"Rich ... sources say he was scheduled on a later flight today, but booked the private jet to get home to his family in time for Christmas. There has been no statement from his wife yet. What a tragedy for this very young family," Sharon Nevins reports. I stand up, trying to turn the TV off. I glance up at the large portrait of Grayson and me with Morgan when she was two.

"No ... No ... No!" I scream and jerk awake in bed. Grayson is there, sitting up and staring at me. I grasp him to me and plant kisses all over his face.

"Becca ... sweetheart." He holds me at arm's length.

"I'm so glad it's not real!" I cry.

"It is, sweetheart ... it is real." He's stern. "I've been gone for seven years." I close my eyes and take in a deep breath. "Becca?" He asks after a few moments.

"What?" I ask calmly.

"What are you doing?"

"I'm patiently waiting to wake up from this crazy dream." I sigh.

"Becca ... Christ, it's not a dream! Well, slightly, I suppose. Search your memories, sweetheart. We met at Barnes & Noble when I had a book signing. I'm not a songwriter, I'm an author." The more he talks, the more I don't want to listen.

"How is this possible, then? We've been together for three months." I open my eyes.

"Yes, but Becca ... you're not really dreaming. You're in a coma." He grabs my hands.

"What? How?"

"The morning Ray drove you, you two were arguing. You got into a terrible accident."

I put my hand up, remembering the spinning of Ray's truck.

"Grayson ... this is ... I ... what ..." My hyperventilating gets in the way of my words.

"Deep breaths, sweetheart, deep breaths. That's it." He rubs my arms as I take his advice. I lie back on the pillows. Grayson lies next to me. I look over at him and it really, truly, finally hits me. I throw my arms around him and bury my face into his neck.

"I've missed you. I love you, Grayson—I love you, baby!" I kiss him all over his face again. "I didn't get to say goodbye. You were just ripped from us ... no warning." I rest my forehead against his. "I could barely function that first year. How could you leave us? How could you leave me? You impossible, impatient bastard!" I half yell at him, half sob. If only he had kept his regular flight—he would've been home safe.

"If I could go back and change anything, darling, I would change that decision. I wanted to be home with you and Morgy so badly. I thought I would surprise you. That plan backfired, aye?" He tries to make light of it.

"So, how's this possible? Are you here to bring me with you? Oh no, Gray ... I can't leave Morgan!" I widen my eyes in panic and grab at my chest.

"No, sweetheart. I came to help you figure things out." His knuckles graze my cheek.

"Don't get mad, please ... but ... is Ray ..." I can't even finish my sentence.

"Ray is fine, as far as repercussions from the accident. I'm not going to get mad. He's the reason I'm here, in more ways than one," he says. I laugh lightly at him. "What?"

"You're doing one of your frowny smiles ... not sure which to go with, so you do both. I miss that, and your Morse-code eyelids. I miss everything." I lean forward and kiss his beauty mark, then his lips.

"Even my arrogance?"

"Everything." I kiss him again.

"Ready to talk about it? I'm sure you have a million questions." His index finger strums along my bottom lip.

"How much time do we have?" I ask.

"We have until tomorrow morning, love."

"That's it?" *Why couldn't he tell me all of this sooner?*

"I didn't tell you sooner because you weren't ready, sweetheart. I'm telling you earlier than I planned—you were starting to get memories about us, and you were becoming increasingly aware of your feelings for Ray. I didn't want our last day to be like this." He sighs.

"Can you hear my thoughts?"

"Yes, most of them."

"Well, that explains it!" I laugh. He joins me.

"You can hear most of mine, too."

I stop and think about that. Oh my God, he's right! Why didn't I realize that?

"So, would you like me to start from the beginning?" He turns on his side, toward me, and I follow suit.

"From the beginning, baby, like every good story starts." I kiss him again.

"Okay. Well the first thing I need to tell you is that while seven years have gone by for you, it's only felt like several weeks for me. Time moves a lot quicker on the other side. So, needless to say, it's been quite difficult for me to watch you fall in love with another man. So some of my 'purple pants' moments have definitely been my own." He closes his eyes and exhales forcefully.

"I'm sorry, Grayson. I didn't mean for it to happen. You have to know, it would've never happened if you were still here." I am overwhelmed by my guilt.

"No ... no, sweetheart, please. I want you to be with Ray. I'm not telling you all of this to make you feel guilty. I'm just explaining what I've been going through." He shakes my hip a bit.

"You ... you want me to be with Ray?" I ask, confused.

"Yes, sweetheart, that's why I'm here. If you quiet that lovely mouth of yours, I will tell you everything." He taps my lips with his fingers.

"Yes, sir." I smile, then gasp when Grayson swats my ass.

"Oh, I will have that again before the night is through." He rubs it and squeezes.

"So, wait, you have felt everything we've done?" I'm actually surprised by this.

"Oh yes! Haven't you?" He smiles, then furrows his brow.

"Well, yes I have," I say, a bit impressed.

"I thought so, because you're driving your doctors crazy." He chuckles. "Every time we have sex, your heart rate goes through the roof. They can't figure it out."

"Well, you've always made my heart race." I touch his face. God ... he is still so beautiful. "*People*'s 'Sexiest Man Alive,' huh?" I giggle.

"You nominated me every year. I thought it was a good touch." He laughs. "C'mon now, love, we're getting sidetracked." He plants a big dramatic one on my lips. I clear my throat and give him my best "listening" face. "So, naturally when I realized what had happened to me, I went immediately to the Research Department to watch you and Morgan. It hurt to see you cry so much. You've struggled terribly, darling, and while that speaks volumes about your love for me, it just smashed my heart into a million pieces. I watched you slowly put your life back into some semblance of order. I was pleasantly surprised when you bought the inn and started up your business. Proud, actually. I was glad to see Mum come out and stay with you and Morgy."

"Hazel's your mum!" I say excitedly, like I've just uncovered a mystery we were both pining over.

"You don't say?" he teases, earning him a smack on the arm.

"Stop! I'm trying to separate fiction from non here!" I pout.

"Sorry, love, you're right. I've rewired your memory a lot the past three months. But I do have to say, you've given me a run for my money! Sometimes I could barely keep up with you and all the twist and turns you were throwing out there!" He palms my cheek.

"Okay, before we get sidetracked again with questions about that comment, please carry on." I hold his palm to my face, relishing in his touch more now than ever.

"Yes. So, I watched when you met Ray. He was the first guy I truly liked. I wasn't lying when I said he felt like an old mate from university. I wish I could go have a pint with him! I noticed that you both had the same sorts of feelings. I felt relief along with a smidge of jealousy. For you, I had been gone almost two years, but for me, it had just happened. Then I saw what your grief was doing to you. You had such intense guilt over being with Ray that you just blocked out everything that made you feel ashamed."

"Does Ray know my PTSD was caused by the traumatic way I lost you?"

"Of course, Becca." He looks at me strangely.

"Who's George?" I ask, confused.

"Um ... George's character was spot on ... from your favorite book of mine, although you definitely added stuff and tweaked others." He chuckles a bit. "You're mind's a bit scary at times, Becca. I mean, almost dying from an anal stabbing, just to avoid anal sex! Christ, I had a hard time keeping a straight face!"

"That didn't happen in the book?" I bite my smile back.

"Uh ... no!" He shakes his head.

"Okay. So you saw what was happening to me." I get him back on track.

"Yes, I felt terrible for you—and for Ray. I know I've said this to you several times, but I don't know if I would've been able to hang in there like he has. I love you, sweetheart, and I would do it if I were here because we've had years of a solid relationship under our belt. But, Becca, he hasn't had that with you, aside from your long friendship. Honestly, any other guy would've thrown in the towel!"

"So, the memories 'he' went over with me are real memories that I've forgotten?" I ask, my guilt rising. Poor Ray. I've put him through so much.

"Sweetheart, those were only half of them. And yes, to answer your question. I'll get back to that later, okay?"

"Okay."

"Let me just add that Ray and I definitely agree about Will ... he's an arsehole!" he snaps with a hint of disgusted anger. I know it's not toward me. "Also, Morgy does love him very much, and he loves her tremendously. You are right to be a bit upset about him not showing equal attention. He's not as good at it by himself, but he is trying to improve. Especially with you being in the hospital ... he's, uh, he's really burning the candles at both ends, Becca." The sympathy for Ray is evident in Grayson's expression.

"What do you mean?" I prop myself up on one elbow.

"Well, he's running both businesses, trying to take care of the girls, and spending probably twenty out of the twenty-four hours a day at the hospital with you. With the exception of the medical equipment and your medicine, he does all of your personal care. He won't let anyone touch you and he won't leave you alone at all."

My eyes fill with tears. That is so Ray.

"Where are his parents and your mum?"

"Oh, they're helping out and taking care of the girls. He made Claudia manager. I visited him in a dream—as you, of course—and told him to. It's the only way I can help him. I knew he was toying with the idea but didn't want to step on your toes."

"Thanks, baby." I kiss him. "Who's helping him the four hours he's not with me?"

"Derek, Stacey, Melissa, Claudia, and, of course, Mum and Ray's parents. He'd have even more people, but you're in Boston."

"Mass General?"

"Yes." He half smiles, knowing why I know that.

"Gray, I have a slew of questions, so you'd better get back on track before I get you way off." I close my eyes, shaking my head as I try to sort through all of this information and remember who some of these people are in my real life. I feel like my ADD is on crack.

"Sweetheart, as always, feel free to 'get me off' anytime the urge strikes you!"

I open my eyes and slap him again, unable to hide my smile. He laughs.

"All right, all right! So, after the accident, I found out how long you would be in a coma for, and I asked if it was possible to be with you throughout. I wanted to help guide you for when you wake up. Because I had already done my research, and because of my passion for and sincerity about helping you and Ray, they let me do it! They did warn me, though, that everything I was going to experience would be very real to me, and not to forget that it wasn't permanent. I had to stay focused and not get lost in any delusions. It was not real and I could not come back. I agreed, but Becca, I have to tell you, sweetheart, it's been a struggle. I walked in already in love with you, and somehow I've fallen in love with you all over again. Becca ... you're an amazing woman. You're still the same girl you've always been, but wow ... you've grown so much, sweetheart. I find you more attractive than I ever have before." He leans in and caresses my lips with his.

"Hey, speaking of aging well—which is what you were really saying, Mr. James—I can't believe you made yourself younger than me!" I laugh. "You have to know that I'm not liking this aging business!"

"Overwhelming words, huh?" He raises an eyebrow. *Yeah, he still has my number!* "Just getting you back for all the years you called me your 'old man.' Also, I'll have you know that you are technically older than me now, as I forever will be thirty-one!" Full-wattage Grayson James smile.

"You want to brag about that ... really?"

His smile fades.

"Right, guess not," he says after a moment of reflection. "Well, I thought I'd come in and win you over with my usual arrogant way. I betted on your subconscious helping to push you along quickly. Of course, I sort of forgot who I was dealing with. It was like an exaggerated version of when I was first trying to court you." He rolls his eyes, thinking back to the constant chasing he was doing when we met.

"Ugh! I knew there was something weird about how quickly this relationship started up!" I slump back down on the pillows.

"Yes, I know ... believe me, I know! I had to find ways to convince you it was okay!" He shakes his head and rubs his face.

"The talks with Morgan and your mum?

"Yes. Ugh—you are so frustrating!" he says with a hint of exasperation.

"Now wait, what was the point of trying to get me pregnant?" I sit up, confused.

"Uh ... well, sweetheart ... " he starts.

"I am pregnant. It is Ray's! Wait, he said *babies*. Twins?"

Grayson nods.

"I wanted you to get used to the idea of being pregnant so you wouldn't freak out when you woke up. Christ, Becca, you even fought me on that!"

"Wait, so I'm further along?" I touch my belly.

"You just turned sixteen weeks a few days ago."

"How are the babies? Are they okay?" I rub my belly, which has now expanded a bit.

"They are fine. That's quite the magic trick, love." His eyes twinkle.

"You like that? Wait until you see my next act!" I match his delight. "Gray, how are you doing with this?" I grab his hand.

"Bittersweet, darling. I thought we'd have many more. I barely got to enjoy the one we had." His eyes fill up and his chin quivers a bit. "Incidentally, sweetheart, you have done an outstanding job raising our daughter. You're a wonderful mum. Thank you, Becca, for everything you've done, and for always keeping my presence strong in her heart and mind. I've enjoyed this time with her ... well, the essence of her. You know what I mean. She really is the most wonderful, beautiful, intelligent, and creative child on the planet. I know ... I've checked," he adds. All I can do in this moment is mourn his loss. She really is an amazing kid, which makes my job so easy! I feel tears sting my eyes. "Don't cry, baby," he says, and holds me close.

"It's just not fair! This whole situation hasn't been fair to anyone involved."

"I know, love, I agree, but that's why I'm here with you. Fair or not, we cannot change the past. The future, though, is another story. There's no reason this should continue to affect you, Morgan, Ray, or Annie for the rest of your lives." He palms my face, his thumbs softly caressing my cheeks. "I'm getting off track again. Sorry." He kisses me sweetly.

"It's okay." I lean forward for another kiss ... then another one. "Again," I whisper, and he attacks my lips with such urgency and passion.

"Bec ... Becca." He tries to pull away.

"Shut up, Grayson." I cover his mouth with my hands. "Please," I add. "This is a lot for me. I just need a break. I need a moment to just focus on you and me. Please." I uncover his mouth and caress his lips with my own. He pulls my shirt off of me. "Adagio" by Secret Garden plays softly in the background as his mouth travels down my neck and across my shoulder. "Nice magic trick." I smile as I fist his hair and pull his mouth back to mine.

"You like that, huh?"

"Mmhmm." I tug my bottoms off and straddle him.

"Ready to drive the doctors crazy?" He pulls away from my lips and stares deeply into my eyes. I nod breathlessly and shift a bit to help him. I close my eyes, savoring the familiar sensation of him entering me. He guides my hips down and rises to meet me at the same time.

"Ugh!" I gasp at the aching fullness of it. He holds me there for a minute, then releases me to rise. As we meet again, he hooks his right arm around the small of my back to hold me there. His left arm steadies his balance, his palm to the mattress as he grinds into me. I whip my head back, allowing him access to my neck as I try to help him reach the place he's attempting to go. He releases the weight of his hold. I rise and slide down again with Grayson's help. For the first time in three months, I acknowledge that I'm making love to my husband. It's been seven years, and we're still incredible together. A rush of emotion sweeps over me and I find him trying to silence the sound of my sobs. Grayson quickens the pace and soon our sweet torture erupts into an intense explosion deep inside me somewhere—maybe the place he was trying to reach. We ride the last few waves out forehead to forehead, soaking in the sensation.

"Christ, Becca ... you're so lovely."

"Lovely?" I give him a sideways look.

"Yes, on every level ... in every way." His eyes are still closed.

"Grayson?"

"Yes."

"Bit of a left-field question, but I have to ask," I start. He opens his eyes. "Do you ... will you get in trouble for the language you've used?" I feel a smidge of panic rising.

"No, sweetheart." He laughs. "All of that, bad words and stuff, it's just society's way of teaching people to be nice to each other. 'Up There,' they are just words. You're not taking anybody's name in vain. Christ, hell would be packed if that were the case!" He shakes his head. "People are wound so tightly about Heaven. It's very laid back. There are no more earthly pressures, you know, the little things that sidetrack you from what your real concerns should be." He lies back as he explains, bringing me with him.

"What does everybody do?" I raise my head and support it on my hand.

"Whatever they like, really! Visit with other relatives or friends that have stayed on. Take classes at the university. Watch loved ones down here. Some even come back—reincarnation. You can get a job. It's basically a much more pleasant version of here. You don't worry about money ... there are no bills to pay, no sickness, and no stress."

"Do people make love and have homes?"

"One-track mind you've got there, love." He pats my bum. My face flushes. "I suppose. I haven't asked anyone. Like I said, I went straight into catching up on you and Morgan. I know there are no rules saying you can't. So, we'll be good to go." He smiles wide.

"You'll wait for me?"

"Of course, Becca. I have no desire to head back ... not without you." He kisses my lips tenderly.

"I'll have quite the dilemma on my hands once again!" I roll my eyes.

"What? Oh, you mean Raymond. Yes, bizarre love triangle part two." He laughs.

"How does that work?" I am miffed.

"I don't know. Perhaps we'll have to set up another shag schedule." He laughs. "Honestly, Becca, you've become a very naughty, naughty girl!" His voice is playful, teasing.

"That was your idea!"

"Uh ... dead or not, I wouldn't share you in a million years, sweetheart! Pretty sure Raymond would match my sentiments. That, my dear, was all you! Naughty girl!" *Oh God ... I am a whore!* Grayson shakes his head. "No ... it was brilliant. It helped with my plan—pushing you away from me and to him. Of course, you had to fight me on that as well! You even had him jumping through hoops in your head. Poor bloke doesn't get a break!"

I can't help but agree with him. I don't understand why Ray loves me like he does.

"Oh, you didn't get the memo, darling? You're awesome!" He tickles my sides.

"Stop doing that!" I smack his chest.

"I can't help it." He shrugs.

"Okay. But then, you were so happy I chose you. What happened?" I try to get back on track.

"That morning, when we were talking and having that fun conversation about being drugged with love ... " He waits for me to acknowledge the memory. I smile. "I got caught up in the delusion. I allowed myself to be selfish for two months. I felt cheated, and I wanted you and Morgan for myself." He seems a bit ashamed.

"Urgent trip to California?" I raise a brow.

"I had to ... well, the selfish man had to. Everything was great, and then out of nowhere, you brought Ray back.

"The whole Stacey and Ray date-and-texts thing?"

"Yes, I was angry with you." He rubs my back.

"So that was really how you were feeling ... when you called me a ..." I swallow hard.

"Please try to understand the internal battle I was going through. I don't really feel that way about you. You have to know that, sweetheart. I was just feeding off of your emotions. It was wrong, and I deeply regret it." Morse code activated. I nod and give him a quick, reassuring peck. "California was nice—being there with you."

"I fought you a lot there too, huh?" I wince.

"Here and there, twists and turns ... not too, too bad. Loved submissive-Becca time. Although, you were right about that."

"Aha!" I laugh.

"You were a very good submissive. I especially loved when you were mad about it." He bites my shoulder playfully. "I love fucking you when you're mad."

"I know you do." I roll my eyes at him.

"Mmm ... it's so hot. You're insatiable." His eyes go wild at the thought.

"You've gotten more aggressive then I remember." I play with the hair at the base of his neck.

"Just following your lead, sweetheart. You've always been a fan of rough and intense, but it's definitely heightened. I think it's to make you feel something other than the pain in your heart." His tone gets serious. "I'm sorry about what I did the morning you went off with Ray. I would never really slap you like that. It was hard for me."

"Yeah, I think I can recall the 'hard' time you had with it." I try to lighten the mood and earn a half smile from him.

"One thing hasn't changed, though." He rubs my bum.

"Hmm?"

"We still can't keep our bloody hands off of each other." He squeezes, then gives me a good smack. I relish in the sting and bite at his chest. My tongue travels down slowly and dives into his navel. I bite at his V-line. "Now ... this is a taste of Heaven, baby. Incidentally, speaking of taste, you can make it taste like anything you want, sweetheart." I take him into my mouth. "I can come chocolate peanut butter ice cream if you'd like!" he says with exaggerated excitement, and I can't help but go into a laughing fit.

"Grayson! Honestly!"

"It's true ... just saying ... double our pleasure." He chuckles at himself as well. "Shit, I've gone and ruined a very serious moment that involved one of your fantastic blow jobs!" He stops laughing and smacks his head with regret.

"Um ... I'd prefer the taste of Grayson James. It's a bit nuttier!" I giggle.

"That it is, sweetheart." He grins with his arm draped over his eyes. "Christ, Becca." He gasps and lifts his head to watch me as I give another go at his "thirty-one" flavors.

After ten minutes or so, I swirl my tongue around his tip, slowly catching the last taste of him. I leave a soft kiss and climb back up to a panting Grayson.

"How was dessert, love?"

"Mmm ... Grayson James ... nuttier than all the rest." I lick my lips.

"Honestly, Becca, I know I've said this before, but you really do know how to drain a fellow!" He brings both of his hands up and places them behind his head.

"Should I put that on my résumé?"

"No." He does a frown-wince. "You know ... expected follow-through and all," he adds.

"Mmm." I agree. "Do you know why I involved my favorite book in our storyline here?" I snuggle into his arms as I change the direction of our conversation.

"Because you helped me with its characters?" he asks.

"No, because I fall asleep to it every night. It's the only book of yours where you recorded the audio version. I listen to it so I can hear your voice every night." I feel myself getting choked up again.

"You always loved when I read to you. Oh, sweetheart." He hugs me tightly and kisses my hair. "I didn't see that. I was trying to focus on everything else. I didn't stop to watch you go to sleep at night." He rubs my back.

"Hey, shall we get back on track?" I wipe my tears away.

"Yes, of course, love." He gives me another squeeze. "So, California. You were trying to keep the suspenseful momentum up. Love the whole investment-fraud angle you used. Quite clever, sweetheart."

"I came up with that?"

"Yes, you came up with a lot of the conspiracies that weren't in the book."

"Who came up with Stacey being attacked?" I watch our fingers playing together.

"I did. You were making me break up with you, and I had to think fast."

"I was making you?" I ask with a bit of confusion ... once again!

"Yes, and I didn't have Ray set in place for you to run to, so ... it was like a huge reality check and I made my phone ring." He sighs.

"Wow! We are two very talented people, with our writing, acting, and directing." I smile up at him.

"Yes, we are."

"Are Stacey and Steve still together?"

"No, but Stacey and Max are." He laughs. I smack my head.

We've been calling Max "Steve" as a joke for years because of the mustache he tried to grow once. It made him look like a seventies porn star.

"So, Stacey and Max are okay? Pregnant?" I ask. He nods, knowing I'll be happy. "Wow, she was a crazy bitch here, huh?" I laugh.

"Yeah, you had her riding along the lines of Lavina in *Winter's Baby*." He laughs, knowing how much that character irritated Stacey.

"I can't wait to tell her that!"

"Speaking of books, you have been reading a lot of interesting ones—several times over. I've had a lot of fun teasing you about it. I was half nervous and half excited, waiting for you to have me tie you up and perform all of those things on you."

"No, no ... fun to read, but ass-slapping is as far as I'll go with painful pleasure." I laugh, then look at him quizzically. "You said half excited?"

"Well, you know, I wouldn't have said no." Frowny expression.

"Well, I would be open to some of it, but not all."

"Ugh! Now she tells me!" He slaps the bed, coaxing a laugh from me.

"C'mon, we're getting off track."

"Yes. So, I brought you back to New Hampshire. By the way, you were so hot on the plane! Ray is one lucky mate! Ugh, no! He's going to get to do all of that kinky fuckery with you! Damn it!" He sighs with frustration.

"Grayson, you've had all of my firsts ... let him have the kinky fuckery," I say, as if we're compromising over a normal topic like who does the dishes which night.

"Yes I have, haven't I? Hold on while I swallow my face with my smile. Love that metaphor, darling." He grins ridiculously wide, making me laugh again. I stare at him ... my husband ... my true, real husband, not a crazy version of a part he's playing. "Becca, if I wasn't already naked, I'd accuse you of undressing me with your eyes." He taps my nose with his index finger.

"Wouldn't be the first time you accused me of that. C'mon now. Carry on."

"Okay. So, we came back, and I noticed that, slowly, you were bringing Ray around more and more. I almost had nothing to do with a lot of this, except for my purple-pants moments, of course. I had to come to terms with the fact that, in the end—I'm not a choice."

"The plane explosion?" I try to distract him.

"Um ... you. A little combo of what happened with me and your fear of losing Morgan."

"Liz?"

"He hasn't lied. She left, not wanting the family thing. She's in Texas. Honestly, the best thing she ever did was leave them. They are better off."

"How does Ray feel about me being pregnant? I'm sorry if this is uncomfortable for you. It's pretty strange for me." I rest my head on his shoulder.

Grayson inhales deeply.

"Becca, you have to know that, for the most part, he's thrilled. You know now that he's often thought about having children with you. He just hoped he would have the chance to marry you first. He's very nervous, though, about the babies' health, and how you will react when you come out of this. He's afraid he's going to lose you permanently."

"He did drug me?" I look down, feeling that same disappointment again.

"Yes, Becca. What he did was not right, but ..." He trails off, trying to find the right words.

"I know, Grayson. I have forgiven him. I just wish it never had to come to that."

"It didn't have to come to that, Becca. He shouldn't have done it, but in his defense, he gives in to your needs all the time. In studying him, I realized Liz did a number on him as well. She up and leaves him with an infant. Rejection. He meets you and you two have a five-year relationship that you don't even remember. He's started to feel like there's something wrong with him, that he's not worthy of love. He knows you have PTSD and it stems from that, but he still feels like you're embarrassed to be with him. Before you say anything," he holds up his hand to stop me, "you never display embarrassment. You are very proud of him, and proud to be with him, whether it's as 'just a friend' or his girlfriend. This is his internal battle as he tries to deal with your trauma."

"More like my *drama*," I snap at myself.

"Becca, every night that man prays for you to stop hurting, to realize what you have with him. When you fall asleep in his arms, he prays to you ... the same prayer every time."

"What does he say?" I lift my head.

"*Please still love me when you wake up.*"

I sit up and pull my knees to my chest, then give in to the need to cry for Ray. Grayson's hands glide up and down my back.

"I'm sorry. I'm sorry, baby." I turn to him.

"Stop, Becca! No more guilt! Does this hurt me? Yes, on some level, but I know you're not doing it to spite me, sweetheart. It hurts because I can no longer be with you. I can't come back, Becca! This is our last night. That's it, until you join me one day! You have to push this guilt away. It's destroying you. I want you to be happy. I want you to be happy with Ray! I give you my blessing, sweetheart! That's why I'm here. I wanted to give you the chance to take a second look at your life and love with him!" He sounds so passionate; one would never believe he's trying to convince his wife to be with another man.

"Thank you. I can't imagine how hard this is for you." I touch his face. He kisses my palm. "Grayson, will I remember now?"

"Yes."

"How do you know?"

I watch as he looks down and plays with a loose thread on the duvet.

"Because the tables have turned. You are always thinking about him now, wondering if he's okay. You're feeling guilty that you're not with him and Annie, especially since you went through all of those memories with him. The wall's gone, Becca. I've succeeded ... yay me!" He half-heartedly cheers for himself.

"Silver lining?" I try to boost his mood.

"Sure."

"I won't fight you on a single thing tonight ... and I don't have to go to sleep." I smirk

"I—am—so—going—to—hold—you—to—that," he says between kisses.

"Can I ask more questions?"

He nods.

"What if I wake up and remember everything, and I'm his full-blown girlfriend? He's so used to chasing me. Will he get bored? Will I not be a challenge for him anymore? You know the whole 'be careful what you wish for' saying." I bite my lip nervously.

"Sweetheart, I was with you for over six years myself. Speaking from experience, I can honestly say that I don't foresee you ever not being a challenge." He laughs. I hit him. "Seriously though, Becca, that will never be an issue. He just wants to come home from work and be able to kiss you, for Christ's sake! He tired of chasing you. He's been done with it for a long time. He just loves you too much to walk away. I understand that. Nobody understands it better than me." He runs his hands through his hair.

"Okay. So I just want to straighten out who's who."

"All right."

"Melissa?" I tap my first finger.

"Ray's younger sister. Elise and Artie's *whoops*."

"Of course! She's in the military and I tease her about being my bodyguard." I smack my head.

"And she does look up to you very much. She's always asking you for advice," he adds.

"Ryan?"

"Her boyfriend. You think he's good for her. He's not the usual type she goes for."

"Okay. Derek is your best friend."

"Yes—from university!" He smiles.

"Tanya?" I wince.

"Morgan and Annie's favorite teacher. Incidentally, they are struggling, so anything you and Ray can come up with would be great."

"Oh. Okay ... yeah, I'm sure we'll think of something. What about all of the financial stuff and the renovations?" I lift his chin so he's looking into my eyes.

"Uh, Ray fixed your finances." He starts cracking up.

"What?"

"Remember me sorting out your 'war zone'?"

"Yes."

"That was actually Ray. He cursed you out the entire time. I'm pretty sure he won't be letting you handle that anymore. Honestly, Becca, you are so disorganized! Why are you pretending that I didn't leave you anything? You should've been all set, sweetheart." He suddenly looks concerned.

"I ... I don't know. I guess it made it too real for me. I mean, I obviously had to use some of it to start my business up. I just ... I don't know. I wanted to leave it for Morgan." I shrug.

"Or for when I came back?" He arches a brow.

"And here you are." I laugh.

"I want you to go and buy the things you want. All of the stuff I bought you the past three months. I mean it, Becca! I want you to stop the weddings and do the renovations. You tell Ray I said I am paying for it. He is to take the money or I will haunt him for the rest of his life!" He taps his finger for emphasis.

"Grayson, I don't know. I want to make sure Morgan is all set. She's your daughter—it should all go to her." I sigh.

"And you are my *wife*!" he yells. "I made sure to set things in motion to provide for you both if something like this should happen! Instead, you decide to struggle for no reason and use up precious time that you could be spending with *our daughter*!" Oh … he sounds extra British.

"Gray, calm down, baby." I move to touch him, but he pushes my hand away.

"Do what you are told—for once, goddamn it! It's absolutely silly, and it's an embarrassment to me!"

"Embarrassment?"

"Yes, Becca! Everybody thinks I left you with nothing! Even Ray thought that! He knows differently now."

"I'm sorry. I really wasn't thinking about that." I look down.

"Becca, as your husband and Morgan's father, it's my responsibility to take care of the both of you. You haven't allowed me to do that. It's upsetting." He's completely calm now.

"I am really sorry. I am, Gray. I promise, when I get back, I will do everything you ask." I bring his face to mine.

"Will you please open the Christmas present I sent you?" He pulls away. A sob escapes my throat.

"When you talked about holding your mother's gift, but not opening it …"

"Yes, I was talking about you." He thumbs away my tears.

"You just … you never really made me anything before. And you … you said not to open it 'til you got back." I feel tears welling in my eyes.

"Oh, sweetheart, I am so sorry. I wish … God, do I wish I could go back and change my mind." We hug each other desperately and allow ourselves a good cry, mourning the loss of us—all of our dreams, all of our hopes, everything we were to each other and everything we were going to be.

Slowly we pull away and wipe away each other's tears.

"Do you have any other questions, sweetheart?"

"Who was working with George?" Total left-field action.

"I have no idea, Becca! You were driving me crazy with that. I was getting into it, trying to come up with ideas, and then poof— you'd throw another twist in! And all of these people, random people playing our security detail. I think one guy was our doorman at my old apartment in L.A." He laughs. "By the way, going back to our finances, we're very comfortable, darling, but not enough for me to have a private plane and be able to justify it. I do not have ten cars, but those are all the cars I wanted. If you remember correctly, I wasn't so free with my spending, except when it came to you."

"Yeah, but I never asked for anything." I shrug.

"Which is why you were so perfect for a tightwad like me! Actually, I need to correct you, because you would ask me if we could help other people or tell me what others want, and I'd say 'Sweetheart, what do you want?' You'd just ask me to help so-and-so or get this for so-and-so. You're still the same way. You're a kind and wonderful soul, Becca. I love you." He plants a big kiss on my lips.

"What about my fanbase in Ashland? That had to be an exaggeration on your part." I push his shoulder lightly.

"No, you are oblivious! The only real serious ones, though, are Ray and Will. The others have little crushes, but it's not like they think about you endlessly. That Will ... ugh! I was so happy when Ray decked him! Knocked his front tooth right out." Gray swings his fist through the air like a boxer.

"What? When did that happen?" I palm his fist down in shock.

"It was a couple of months before the accident. You were doing an event with him to that song I liked. It was the dance you did here. Well, just like here, that arsehole got the wrong message. He had his paws all over you in the dressing room. He pinned you up against the wall. You were yelling at him to get off of you, but of course he wouldn't listen. Ray came backstage looking for you. You were too busy trying to fight Will off to see Ray come to your aid. He grabbed him by his silky shirt collar and laid one right into him. It knocked him on his arse across the floor. 'Keep your fucking hands off of my wife!' he yelled."

"Wife?"

"Yes. Will called him on it, and he said, 'As far as you are concerned, she is my wife and you will keep your fucking hands and eyes off of her or I'll finish what I've started!' He turned to you and grabbed you, asking you if you were okay. You said, 'Wife, Ray?' in a whisper as you took his hand. 'Yes, wife! You are never dancing with that asshole again! Do you understand me, wife?' Oh, Becca, as usual, you picked the wrong time to mention certain things. I sided with his anger there." He shakes his head, chuckling.

"You seem to be siding with him a lot," I tease.

"Well, you are quite the handful, sweetheart ... in more ways than one." He smirks and pulls the sheets away from my chest to sneak a peek.

"Stop!" I slap his hand. "So, what happened?"

"You redirected his anger with your charm. 'Ray, this is really bad, baby, you need stitches.'" He imitates me.

"Oh ... I called him *baby*." I wince.

"It's all right, Becca. He is family and, well, he deserves that title." He sighs.

"Well?"

"He said he wasn't going to the hospital for two stitches, he had butterfly ones at home. So you both went back to his house. You fixed him up in more ways than one." He rubs his face.

"I wish I could remember the newer memories." I sigh.

"I wish I could forget ... them all!" He holds his hands out in exasperation.

"Sorry. Okay, that's enough of all of that. This is our special time. What would you like to talk about, or do?" I grab his hands.

"You don't have any other questions?" He cocks his head to the side.

"Well, one for right now." I hate to keep bringing Ray up. "How does your mom feel about Ray and me?"

"She loves Ray. She knows I would've liked him. She encourages you. She supports him. She and Elise have become quite close. They are some scheming team!" He chuckles. "Incidentally, sweetheart, please tell my mother that my father and I give her our blessing to be with Charlie," he adds.

"Oh, I'm definitely doing that!" I widen my eyes for emphasis. I can't count how many times I've encouraged her over the years. "So, what would you like to do?" I play with the hem of the sheet.

"No fighting?" he asks. I shake my head. "Well, first, I'd like to take you to church ... through the backdoor. Then, I'd like for us to go downstairs and spend time with Morgan. We'll see from there." He holds up a fisted hand with just his index finger out and spins it around. I swallow hard and turn.

Chapter Nineteen

"Are you okay, darling?" Grayson brings my hand up to his lips as we walk down the hall.

"Yes, baby." I smile.

"Much better this time?"

"Yes," I agree as we head down the stairs. It's very quiet. "Where is everybody?"

"Well, since nobody's really out to hurt you, I didn't think we needed to keep up the charades." He laughs at me, just a little.

"Sorry, kinda got used to it." I laugh at myself as well.

Grayson glances over toward the dining room.

"Morgy girl!" He picks her up and swings her around. "What would you like to do?"

"How about we go for a drive to see Christmas lights?" Morgan asks, sounding excited.

"Becca?"

"I'll make the hot cocoa to go!" I throw my hand into the air as if this were the most important volunteer job around. I head into the kitchen and grab the milk out of the fridge.

"Oh look, sweetheart," Grayson announces as he walks into the kitchen.

"What?" I turn around.

"Hot chocolates, all ready to go! In special throw-away containers, no less!"

"Smartass!" I laugh.

"Really, darling, I don't believe it's *my* ass that's smarting right now." He grabs my hips and pulls me to him.

"Grayson!" I smack his chest.

"Look, this one here is for you. It's chocolate peanut butter hot cocoa, to give you warm thoughts all night," he teases.

"Oh, I don't think I'll have trouble keeping my thoughts warm all night." I lean up for a kiss.

"C'mon!" Morgan complains.

"All right, little sweetheart." He smiles against my lip, then grabs both the hot cocoa and my hand.

"I'll drive. Why don't you and Daddy snuggle together in the backseat?" I offer.

"Becca, I'd love that. How 'bout it, Morgy? It'd be like a date with your ole dad!" He puts his arm out for her to hook hers through.

"Sure, Daddy. I'd love it, mate!" She does his English accent. We get into the Range Rover.

"Becca, if you like this better than the X5, get it!" Grayson squeezes my shoulder from the backseat.

"Stop. Let's enjoy the lights." I tap his hand before I back up and head down the hill. I drive down some popular streets where people compete with each other fiercely. I look back at Morgan and Grayson snuggling and drinking from their cups. I can't help but get teary-eyed. They look so happy and content, like I always knew they would be. She's always been blunt and to the point. Always wise beyond her years. She has his eyes and sometimes his frown when she talks. Grayson thinks she looks like me, but I think she's a combo. I used to wonder, if we eventually had a son, whether he would look just like Grayson.

Grayson's head shoots up quickly to look at me. He offers me a frowning smile. He heard my thoughts.

After about two hours, Morgan has fallen asleep on her daddy.

"Let's go back now, sweetheart."

"Okay." I was going that way anyhow. Two turns and we're on our street. I head up the long driveway to the inn. I hold the car door for Grayson and close it after he pulls Morgan out. He carries her up to the door. I quickly open it for him. We both have a little giggle that I locked it in the first place.

"Can never be too cautious, dear ... someone might jump into your brain and steal all of your ideas!"

"Stop making fun of me!" I pout.

"I'm sorry, sweetheart." He half smiles and continues to bring Morgan to her room.

"Do you want to wake her up and spend more time together?" I rub his back.

"No, sweetheart. I've had a wonderful time with her, but honestly, it's becoming more and more painful. I just want to spend the rest of the time with you now. I want to hear about raising her. I didn't see every moment. I will, but I'd like to hear it from you." He kisses her forehead after he lays her on her bed, then pulls her covers up. "Good night, little sweetheart. I love you. I'll be your moon and you'll be my stars. I'm sorry I haven't been there. I'm sorry I won't get to walk you down ... the ... aisle." His voice starts to shake. "Oh, Becca, I'm missing so much. I mean, I'll see it all, but it's not the same." He tries to shake off his sadness and leans over to kiss her forehead again. He inhales deeply, I think to memorize her scent. I kiss her good night as well and hold my hand out to him. He takes it.

"How many hours?" I look up at him as we walk away from her bedroom.

"I'm not exactly sure. I know you wake up today, but I don't know when. As soon as I sense we're running out of time, I'll let you know." We climb the stairs together one last time, and then he stops me at the top. "I can't hear your thoughts, but I can clearly tell there's something going on in there."

"Oh, I was just thinking ... you had all of my firsts. I thought you'd have all of my lasts, too." I frown.

"No, but you have all of mine, so I think we're even." He palms my face. "Sweetheart, I love you." His lips devour mine. Our kiss follows us into our bedroom, our clothes left in a trail behind us. Suddenly, I feel smaller. I look down, then back up, panicked. "Everything's fine. They are okay. I did that. I'm being selfish, but I want just you and me. All right, love?" His finger holds my chin up as he searches my eyes with his. I nod and feel his mouth crash back down onto mine. I pull away and lightly jerk my head back when he tries to recapture my lips. I trace his face with my fingers, studying every line that has started to appear, his long lashes, straight nose, perfect jawline, his beauty mark. My fingers slide down his long neck and back up around into his thick brown hair. It's short in the back, longer on top. His breath is steady as he waits patiently for me to finish making my memory. I nudge his nose with mine before I grasp his bottom lip, sucking on it purposefully. His hands cup my bottom and he hoists me up. I wrap my legs around him as he carries me to our bed.

The coolness of the sheets hitting my back sends a shiver down my spine.

"You okay?" He stares down at me.

"Yeah." I lean up to him again, but he teases me, pulling away just before our lips touch. Instead, his mouth runs across my jaw and down my neck. He pins my arms up by my head and proceeds to travel down my chest. He fills his hands with me, circles my right nipple with his tongue, and then bites down, tugging at it, kneading it with his teeth. "Ugh. Ow! Ah ... Gray!"

"SPP ... remember, baby?" he asks as he heads over to my left side to do the same.

"Surprise, pain, and pleasure." I smile, remembering, then fist my hair as he does it again. Closing my eyes, I feel his tongue dart out every so often as his mouth travels down my body. I bathe in the familiarity of his touch more than ever. Tears escape the corners of my eyes as my hips rise to greet his darting tongue. His fingers slide inside of me, helping with the cause selflessly. *Operatic Sybecca enters center stage, quickly adjusting her Viking helmet and her best bustier before the spotlight shines down on her. She clasps her hands under her rib cage, opens her mouth, and belts out a high "C" proudly. As Grayson holds my hips down, Operatic Sybecca begins to sway. The other Sybeccas catch her as she passes out. Submissive Sybecca places a pole in the ground—the British flag flies proudly.*

I open my eyes at the sound of Grayson laughing with his face in my naughty bits.

"Sweetheart, you are hysterical!" He raises his head. "Every time one of your Sybeccas comes out, I can hear your narration and see her like a movie in my mind!" He crawls up my body.

"You can?" I have no control over it. He nods.

"Becca?" he asks.

"Yes?"

"Why haven't you published our book? We worked so hard on it, love." He leans up on his elbow when he climbs to the side of me.

"I, um, I don't know. I guess because we did it together. I didn't want to share it."

"Share it, sweetheart. Most of your heart and soul went into it. I wish you would pursue writing." He kisses my temple.

"Maybe someday I'll publish that book, but I'm just putting your name on it. No one will believe I had anything to do with it." I sigh.

"That's a load if I ever heard one! I always stated in my books and in interviews that you were not only my wife, but my creative partner as well. You did most of the work, Becca—don't be silly." He taps my nose.

"Okay. Can I ask you a question?"

"Shoot."

"Why were you looking at homes for us? Was that me?" I wince, trying to figure it out.

"No, love, that was me. I wanted you to get used to the idea of not living at the inn anymore. You were pretty receptive to it. I was actually surprised," he says. I turn my head to him and touch his cheek. "You know, the only reason Ray bought the house he bought was because you loved it. He always intended to raise a family with you in that house."

"No. Ray loved that house. I mean, I do too, but that was all him."

"Of course it was, Becca. A five-bedroom Colonial farmhouse for two people. Yep!" The air is thick with his sarcasm. "Who decorated the house and found everything its place?" He raises an eyebrow.

"Well, me, but because he didn't trust himself to make it look nice." I sigh.

"Becca, he loved how much thought you put into each room. He especially loved when you said sentences that started out like 'We should' or 'We'd like.' How many times did he say, 'You're doing a great job making this into a nice home for us, babe'?"

"He meant for himself and Annie," I say.

"Yeah ... so tell Ray I said good luck, mate!" He shakes his head.

"Stop."

"Becca, knowing what you know now?" He tries again.

"Oh, okay. He meant us!" I give in. I know he's right.

"What are you thinking?" He squints, trying to figure me out as he releases my bottom lip from my teeth.

"No, I don't want to use up any more of our time talking about Ray." I smile and palm his left cheek.

"Becca, if you have questions or concerns, you need to ask me, sweetheart! I understand and respect and appreciate that you are trying to focus on me, but the whole point of me being here is to help you to let go and be with Ray. So please, sweetheart, ask." His finger holds my chin up so I have to keep eye contact.

"Okay." I sigh. "What if, when I wake up, I pour my heart out and tell him I'm his, no more chasing. What if ... " I stop and inhale deeply, feeling disturbed by this thought.

"Go on, love," he encourages.

"What if he doesn't believe me? I mean, he has plenty of reason not to. What if he decides that these three months gave him enough time to get over me? I'm scared, Gray. What if I've lost him and he's not even aware of it? What if I wake up and he just realizes he's done?" I'm losing my ability to keep my panic at bay.

"Becca, I know for a fact that is not going to happen. He's crazy in love with you—for good reason, I might add." He smiles.

"I don't know, Gray. He's dealt with a lot, and to go back to what I said earlier, what if he doesn't know what to do if he's not chasing? I just—I'm scared." I close my eyes and fist my own hair.

"Damn it, Becca! Listen to yourself! You're using excuses to push him away again!"

"I am not!"

"You are too!" he yells. "This is it, sweetheart! Shit or get off the bloody pot! I can't come back again to help you with this! I'm dead! I'm not coming back! Ray loves you! You love him—stop being such a silly, stupid woman!"

"Grayson!" I gasp in disbelief and hurt.

"Honestly, Becca, you have got to stop. Ray is a good man. You are lucky to have him. Sure, he loses his temper sometimes. Yes, he's been aggressive, and he's done a few other things that were not okay. He's still a great guy and I don't blame him for most of those behaviors. I can't say I would've done any better. He loves you—stop questioning it!"

"I know, Grayson."

"If you know, why must you always fight it?" He turns onto his back, frustrated.

"This must bring quite the flashback for you." I grab his chin and rock his face back and forth to lighten the mood.

"Yes, it does! You are the most impossible woman to try to court!" I see the smile hit his eyes instead of his mouth.

"Possibly," I add, then giggle as I think about how much I made him chase me as well. Of course, he had it much easier than Ray. Slowly, I climb on top of him. "Wasn't I worth the chase, baby?" I speak very softly—usually my weapon of choice on Ray.

Grayson stares at me expressionless for a moment.

"Yes, Becs, baby," he says flippantly.

"Sorry," I mutter.

"Well, it worked on me in the beginning, too." He smirks.

"You know, it's very odd being in such a precarious position." I look down at our naked bodies. "Asking my husband for relationship advice about the man I'm supposed to spend the rest of my life with. On top of that, making love to you as well."

"That is odd, sweetheart, given the very normal situation we find ourselves in." He rolls his eyes.

"You, sir, have been rudely poking fun at me all night!" I jab his chest with my finger for emphasis.

"Oh, come now, Becca. Not all of my poking tonight has been rude ... well, maybe the time before we left." He chuckles as he sits up so we are nose to nose. The laugher fades along with his smile. We stare deeply into each other's eyes.

"I hate this, Grayson." My nose flares to hold back my tears. "I hate that I'm not going to see you again, touch you again, for many years. Do you even know when I'll be joining you?" I lift my head.

"No, no. I didn't look. I will when I get back. I have to say, though—I sort of have it easier on my end. Even if you're here another fifty years or so, for me, it will only be a little over a year, maybe." He shrugs.

"Well, one thing's for sure—I won't be afraid when it's time to go, thanks to you." I smile and lean forward for a kiss. Grayson kisses me again and soft piano music comes out of the iPod.

"What's this?" He turns his head.

"'Gracie's Theme' by Paul Cardall," I almost whisper. He turns back to me and attacks my lips, then rolls me onto my back and enters me quickly as the melody seduces us. His lovemaking is raw, powerful, and, well—just Grayson. "Only Time" by Enya carries us through, breaking us down emotionally and physically. As our bodies still, we concentrate on the taste of each other's mouths. Andrea Bocelli's "Un Dulce Melodrama" inspires our tempo. I feel very much in a drugged state of mind. Drugged with love.

"Sweetheart." He pulls away.

"Yes?"

"We don't have much longer." He sighs and looks at the clock. It's three in the morning.

"How do you know?" I ask, feeling panic start to rise.

"Your emotions are carrying more and more over to the other side. I mean, in the hospital. Your tears are flowing there. You're mouthing your words. I'm not sure exactly how much time, we have but my guess is just a few hours." He sighs. "I love you, Becca. I'm trying so hard to fight off my selfish anger."

"Grayson, what kinds of stories do you want to hear about Morgan?" I use my old method of distraction.

"Anything, sweetheart, anything and everything you can think of." He closes his eyes and swallows back his grief.

"Um ... okay. Well, you know how she used to say 'Good night, Daddy' up to the moon outside her window whenever you were away on a book tour or doing interviews?"

"Yes."

"She's done it every night since. She never misses a night, but now she also thanks you for being her moon."

A small sob escapes his throat.

"Becca ... Becca, please buy her that necklace for me. With the engraving. Please tell her it is actually from me. Tell her I'm so proud of her, so proud to be her dad. Tell her how much I love her. Tell her I'll always be there by her side," he pleads through his tears. I reach over and grab tissues from the nightstand. He rolls off of me and sits up, trying to pull himself together. He blows his nose.

"When she was five, she said she didn't like boys with round glasses. She wouldn't marry any boy wearing them because she wasn't that kind of woman."

Grayson bursts into a fit of laughter.

"Sweetheart, remember when we played tickle monster with her? She always tried to tickle our eyes. We'd laugh because we thought it was the oddest thing! She was so cute. Always giving hugs. Always laughing." He closes his eyes, reminiscing.

"When she was six, she actually trained Butterscotch to lie down for bedtime. It took her several months. She was thrilled." I giggle, shaking my head.

"Why did she do that?" He smiles.

"Because she's Butterscotch's mom and she needed to tuck her in," I say with a hint of *duh*—teasingly, of course. "Even had a big ole blanket to cover her up with."

"She's funny, aye?"

"Oh yeah. And stubborn and adamant and sarcastic. Shall I continue down the list?" I wrap his arm around me as I snuggle up to him.

"Certainly none of these traits are from *my* genes." He kisses my head.

"Oh no, of course not." I roll my eyes.

"She's beautiful, like her mother." He hugs me to him.

"Oh, I don't know. I see a lot of you in her. She certainly gives me a lot of the same looks you always gave me. She's a good mix of both of us."

"I'll give you that, sweetheart. What kind of a student is she?" His fingers run up and down my left arm.

"Very good. A/B. All of her teachers have loved her. I'm very lucky. She's really an easy kid, very creative and outspoken. I think she's cool, but I am biased." I cross my right foot over my left and note how much further down the bed Grayson's feet end up, and how much bigger they are than mine. "The doctor's predicting she'll be 5'10", give or take." I smile up at him.

"Well, that will narrow the dating pool down for her." He laughs a bit. "Becca, please bring her out to our home. She loved it there. Sam and Susanna miss you both terribly." He plays with my hand.

"I will. It's been difficult for me. But I do miss our house. And them, of course."

"Take Morgan to Disney World. You're not being fair." He nudges me.

"I know. I can't do Disneyland, but I will go to Disney World with her for her birthday." I smile at him calling me out on my silliness.

"And I don't have to remind you to make that a family vacation, right?"

"No, you don't." I play with his hair. "Grayson, do you have messages for anyone?" I ask.

"Um, well, just tell my mother that Dad and I are okay. Thank her for being there for you and Morgan. Tell her I love that she makes those blankets for Project Linus. Oh, and please tell Derek

I said thank you for being there for you both as well. He's still my best mate!"

"You know, when he and Danielle christened Jasper, they didn't give him a godfather. They gave him two godmothers instead. I am one of them." I look up.

"Why?" he asks.

"Because you were supposed to be the godfather of his first-born." I frown-smile.

"Jasper. Jasper what?"

"Jasper Grayson Davis."

"After me? Really? Christ, Becca, please tell him thank you and that I will look after him. I swear!" He chokes back his tears.

"Ow!" I feel a sharp pain and grasp my right arm.

"What's the matter?" He grabs my elbow.

"I don't know. Ow!" I pull it away from him. Grayson closes his eyes to concentrate. "Grayson ... I hear Ray."

"Yes. He's yelling at the nurse. She's trying another spot for an IV. Your other one blew. But she's doing a half-arse job."

"Ow! Shit, that hurts!" I rub the inside of my arm.

"Is that better now?" he asks.

"Yes ... why?" I look back up.

"Ray just kicked her out and requested a different nurse."

"Grayson, is he kissing my face?" I touch my cheek.

"Yes, sweetheart. Shit, we're really running out of time." He runs his hands through his hair. "Becca, I want to make love one last time before you go, but there is something else I need you to promise me." He opens his eyes.

"What's that?"

"Get your pilot's license."

"Oh no! I don't think I can ... not after ... no ... no way!" I shake my head.

"It's something you've always wanted! You've just forgotten! Becca, what happened to me is so rare, please! And for God's sake ... let Morgan learn how to scuba dive! Do not let your fears hold her back from the things she wants to experience!" Passionate Grayson is articulating every word carefully. I kiss at his jaw.

"I will try. Is that all, love?" I attempt my English accent once again.

"Have you really learned four languages, sweetheart?" He cups my face.

"Two," I say after some thought. "Claudia and I are working on Russian now."

"That's amazing, sweetheart, and hot as hell! I was absolutely floored when you started speaking French and German!"

I climb on top of him again. "*Oh bébé Dieu* or *Ach Gott-kind*. Which do you prefer?" I bite my lip after licking it.

"The infamous prayer?" he asks. I nod. "Definitely French." He smiles, leaning forward to rescue my lip from my teeth, then grasps my hips and squeezes.

"*Please wake up.*" I hear Ray. I shake my head and look at Grayson.

"What?"

"I hear him loud and clear now." I sigh.

"Shit, Becca ... stay with me just a bit longer ... please!" Grayson begs and shifts me a bit to enter me.

"You, sir, have a one-track mind," I say after my initial gasp. Slowly, we make love again, nose to nose, basking in the sensation of each other. "To Where You Are" by Josh Groban plays softly in the background. We are completely lost in each other. There is no one else in the world to me. Just him. My husband. The first great love of my life. My lips claim his over and over again, remembering the taste and the feel of them on mine. I hold on to his shoulders to steady myself as I slowly rise—probably for the last time ever with him. "*Oh bébé Dieu ... oh bébé Dieu!*" I cry. Grayson's mouth muffles my sounds as he comes undone as well. "What are you chuckling about, Mr. James?" I ask when I catch my breath.

"Ray is looking at you like you have five heads. You just prayed out loud, in French, at the hospital."

"Well, that outta be a good ego boost for you!" I laugh.

"Yeah, a bit."

I feel a strange feeling coming over me.

"Grayson." I can hear the fear and panic in my own voice.

"We only have a few moments, Becca. Maybe five." He grasps my face.

"Come ... I want a last dance with you." I jump out of bed, pulling him with me. Grayson and I would dance all the time, with or without music. One of my most favorite memories. He pulls me into his arms and slowly we begin to move to "I Wish You Love" by Nat King Cole. We stare into each other's eyes, absorbing the words into our hearts. I feel as if I'm fading in and out.

"Becca, I love you, sweetheart. Have a good life, and remember—I *will* wait for you." He kisses me.

"I love you, Grayson. I will always love you. Thank you for loving me, for our daughter, for helping me to find my way." I cry and kiss him over and over.

"I will see you soon, sweetheart. Thank you for loving an arrogant bastard like me."

"My beautiful British bastard." I smile against his lips.

"Ugh, I was so close!" He laughs. I fade out and back. "Goodbye, Becca. I love you. I love you, sweetheart." He tries to hold onto me.

"I love you. I will see you later. I love you ... I love you, Gray." One last kiss—it's intense, and softens slowly.

I open my eyes to Ray's stormy ones.

GOODBYE UNCERTAINTY

BECCA Campbell was lost for seven years, until an unexpected person from her past came back into her life and unveiled the truth.

This truth has set her free.

If only it were that easy.

Knowing what she now knows, Becca must come to grips with reality. She has to fight for the man she loves. The man she is meant to be with.

Becca, very sure of her path, needs to get him to say goodbye to uncertainty.

What happens, though, when uncertainty with her is all he's ever known?

Acknowledgements

I'd like to thank my family, especially my three beautifully amazing children. You are the best chapters in my story.

Thank you to the ladies at Bare Naked Words Author Services, who have been my rock through my journey thus far. Extra hugs and crazy dances to Wendy Shatwell, Claire Allmendinger, and Nicola Spears. You have become such very dear friends to me.

Jennifer Bedet, the count is in! I would like to thank you 37 times for all of your love and support. My life has been richer and a hell of a lot more fun with you in it.

Becky Carnahan, thank you for cheering me on and grabbing the next ridiculously large binder with the next book and always wanting more! I am blessed to call you my friend.

To all of my friends that have supported me—thank you!

So much love to my newly formed Street Team, The G-Team! I'm looking forward to getting to know all of you and working with you! Thank you for loving my characters so much and wanting to get the word out!

All of the bloggers who have championed *Goodbye Caution*, words can't describe how grateful I am to all of you! Thank you!

And finally, the people who helped me put together this rather large book for you!

My editor—Jess Huckins, you are stuck with me, lady! I've said this before and I'll say it again: I may write the words, but you make them shine! I adore you and the laughter you bring me with your editorial comments!

My cover designer—Robin Harper, also stuck with me! I'm so looking forward to future beautiful creations by you!

My formatter—Stacey Blake, you're in the same boat as the last two! I adore you even though you laugh at me when I'm getting hit with snowstorms while you're enjoying your lovely Florida weather! :)

Want to see what I'm up to? You can stalk me here at these spots!

www.authorjacquelynayres.com

Twitter: @JacquelynAyres

Facebook: https://www.facebook.com/JacquelynAyresAuthor

Pinterest: http://www.pinterest.com/jacquelynayres/

Spotify: Goodbye Secrets

About the Author

I am a domestic engineer (born and raised in New Jersey) whose sole responsibility is guiding three young, impressionable kids into becoming phenomenal adults. This challenging yet rewarding work requires a lot of love (coffee), patience (wine), and determination (periodic exorcisms). I work all of this magic from the beautiful state of New Hampshire.

Before becoming a domestic goddess (not really), I spent over a decade working in the medical field, where I wore more hats than the queen.

I have loved the written word and the great escape it provides since I was a little girl. When I wasn't reading about people and the places they lived, I created my own characters and adventures. Finally, I started putting a pen to paper and allowing my characters to come to life. When I don't have a pen in hand, you can often find me laughing at the conversations my characters are having in my head.